To Dearest Miley

Always remember – If you believe in faeries they will come and find you.

Fondest wishes,

Uncle David
xx
x

Legacy of Bones

Legacy of Bones

Part 1 of the *Under the Eyes of God* tetralogy

David Greely

Eloquent Books
New York, New York

This is a work of fiction. Names, characters, places, and incidents either are a product of the author's imagination or are used fictitiously, and any resemblance to actual persons, living or dead, business establishments, events, or locales is entirely coincidental

Copyright © 2009 David Greely. All rights reserved. No part of this book may be reproduced or transmitted in any form or by any means, graphic, electronic, or mechanical, including photocopying, recording, typing, or by any information storage retrieval system, without the permission in writing from the publisher.

Eloquent Books
An imprint of AEG Publishing Group
845 Third Avenue, 6th Floor—6016
New York, NY 10022
http://www.eloquentbooks.com

ISBN: 978-1-60693-867-6, 1-60693-867-3

Book Designer: Bruce Salender

Printed in the United States of America

Foreword

Beyond the dense forbidding mists of Avalon a mystical world flourishes. A realm forged by the gods that created the elements: wind, fire, matter, and water. Of all such lands created, Aeria is its jewel and heralded the paradise of the Good Lord the Heavenly Father. It was formed to become the most bountiful kingdom, prospering on rewarding harvest for countless generations by its tireless and dedicated folk. A dominion steeped in fortune and purpose unsurpassed, the envy of all others with its embracing valleys, impenetrable forests and brimming lakes in which no man knows of want or creature any bounds.

Imagine then if you will, a castle within this land; I state castle because this is the nearest representation best describing such a notable formulation. A citadel, sternly built of blue-grey stone quarried from beyond the northern mountains set upon immovable granite solid as Mother Earth herself and originally intended to form as protection for the kingdom from any seaward invasion, therefore strategically positioned on the north-

David Greely

west extremities of the realm. Four high walls cling to the early morning mist angling outward to thwart any such potential assault. In the western wall, a portcullis situated off-centre presents intricate figures of heraldry and legend, carved by the skilled hands of masons past, and balancing precariously over the inner arch a fire-spitting dragon overlooks the welcomed traveller on the approach road into this hospitable place. Like an enormous oaken tongue, a drawbridge spans the deep moat fringed with overgrown reeds surrounding part of the keep, the dense outer walls fed by the cool waters that meander unremittingly from the distant mountains.

My beloved Wendatch stands proud upon a tor bordered by lush valleys to the south and east, and to the north an expanse of wilderness with thick forests and huge deep lakes fringed by the ragged often snow-capped mountains and beyond still, the forbidden mists where the gods reside, legends born and dreams aspire. To the west, the realm's craggy brink abruptly strikes the vast ocean where one can view the tireless motion of the heaving waves lapping in conflict with the land's intrusion. Often I sit here whiling away hapless hours perched upon the very rocks that make the capricious tract of land between sea and castle, sometimes daring to venture into the deep tidal hollows, defying my own trepidation of the place to culminate all I have learnt though more often than not merely appeased contemplating the world beyond Aeria.

The surrounding land is abundant in wildlife making hunting simple and the fertile soil yielding generous harvests until one particular season brought a dramatic change heralding the coming of a dark age; a contemptible duration that lingered far longer than I dare recall – but I am jumping ahead of myself. Wendatch houses a small community that farms and hunts in the nearby fields and woods, excepting those who have mastered commerce, building or smithery. Most of the regular abodes are of mud and wattle, sturdy enough when one considers the protection of the castle's outer walls. Contained too are the storehouse, stable and forge limited for the lord's services, an alehouse which is my second home, a wish tower and the apothecary where I reside with my master Treggedon. The storehouse is unique: built upon wooden stilts to the height of three men, boasting a slate roof and oak doors set at the top of the steep steps next to the gantry used for hoisting heavy stock. The reason for its elevation primarily is to prevent dampness rising from the ground ruining the food stock, suppress invading rats, or as it now transpires, thwarting dishonest hands from pilfering the contents.

Although never counted, I suppose there must be several hundred inhabitants at the tor with perhaps another thirty inside the keep but what with so many strangers wandering through Wendatch, it proves difficult to acknowledge the permanent residents.

The keep is very impressive, towering high above the south wall and equalling the elevation of the wish tower, with its apex disappearing into the constant dawning clouds. All interior walls are whitewashed and most adorned with woven tapestries hanging languidly from iron pins. The place is light and airy and as one would expect, comfortable in the summer season but bitterly cold in the dead of winter with icy blasts whistling through the long hallway into adjoining chambers, nevertheless, in the dining hall the magnificent hearth with its roaring fire cheers the coldest soul on a raw night.

Many lords, though few ladies, have sampled the good fortune of being a part of Wendatch in years past and now the lord Talteth has taken residence having previously reigned over a small group of isles in the south. He proved his worthiness and gained commission here by gracious order of his father, king Arbereth. Rumours were rife about a battle in which the islands were under threat from Laddian ships earlier in the year and Talteth, apparently, eradicated the marauding force without trace however, ambiguity surrounds his actions and I learnt he fled upon the enemies approach back to his father at Collington begging for a quieter province and thus granted Wendatch.

Arbereth is a fine and proud king, astutely overseeing his placed lords and all the provinces within Aeria. Upholding peace amongst them can never be the easiest of tasks but he

David Greely

admirably deals with the slightest upset or disruption and no such would-be pretender to his crown dare attempt to overthrow him. His prime age bears no reflection of his incredible strength or capability and often exercises his might and ability at contests. He keeps a stronghold of the best fighting men at the ready and every spring replenishes his legion by selecting his own personal guards from such tournaments held throughout the realm.

Oh, how it saddens me when reminiscing years past and ponder upon them with the sting of tears welling in my eyes, reflecting how tragically the kingdom has since altered but I shall not surrender my intent, so distressing as it is, proffer this moment to reflect upon my tale.

Chapter One

It was late one sun-baked afternoon when a contingent of guards arrived at Wendatch, and though I cannot recall the king's first visitation six years prior in the early autumn of my seventeenth year, I recall my excitement at the prospect of his coming. The harvest was as always, generous with herds fully stocked and peace prevailed. I was residing with my master at his abode, an apothecary cluttered with what was useful and equally what was useless in the many dark and dusty corners, upon shelves too high for my reach where phials and drums of every conceivable size and shape contained unknown and unused concoctions blended by Treggedon. If one word could describe the captivating feel of the place then enchantment fits that reckoning, for enchanting it was. Though small and at times somewhat stifling, particularly on hot summer evenings, I always felt in wonder. I possessed my own bedding chamber, as did my master though he seemed to spend very little time sleeping and favouring to remain slouched in his winged chair

David Greely

by the hearth. My room faced west overlooking the perimeter wall, where I regularly sat upon the sill by the large window sampling countless sunsets that would have been the envy of any artist or bard. It was basic with ample shelving to accommodate my many books and trinkets I had come to hoard, and all neatly set in an order that made my master quite envious. Not that he sneaked at my possessions, for he insisted that I needed my own space and respected my demand for such privacy.

'Helps one to think and discover' he would advocate. 'One must never encroach on a man's solitude.'

My bed was comfortable by comparison to most I have slept upon and for that, I was very grateful. I liked my bed and if no chores were pressing, preferred to stay in that opulence if only to dream and speculate. As fore-mentioned, my master favoured to sleep by the hearthside and be it summer or winter, drowse and conjure thoughts and dreams or plan the unnecessary, though more often than not his next set of demands upon me. Not that he was an idle individual, far from it, but I suppose with the gentle ebbing tide of age and my young set of legs at his disposal to do the fetching and carrying, who else would not seize such an advantage?

The living area was by far the cosiest and fire apart, contained his chair studded with brass buttons that glistened like gold where my master continually sat. A woven mat long since seen better days and spread lifelessly over the wooden floor made a feeble attempt to quell the icy drafts of winter blowing through the gaping cracks in the floor. My three-legged stool was set adjacent to Treggedon's chair and though adequately padded offered nothing in the way of comfort. Inconsequential light filtered into the room and during daylight no matter how bright the sun shone outside, it was always dingy. A cool haven however, on hot sultry days.

There were several fittings around the walls where cups, bottles of wine, books and spent tapers lay strewn and apart from his ledgers and rowan staff, my master had nothing in the way of personal possessions hence the reflection of bareness within the room. The two candles on the mantle and another set on the small table were the futile means of light, but in the still of night, the flickering wicks added their ambience by casting shimmering shadows that danced upon the walls and ceiling above our heads in harmony with the fire's flames. On such nights, Treggedon would create silhouetted beasts and birds, contorting his gnarled hands and whenever the wine mellowed his restraint, produce images of the dragon –the dragon of Avalon. Then he would tell of the romance and bravery such as those of Merlin the Druid and the young king Arthur in the triumphant days that proclaimed the demise of the dark ways. Oh, how envious I was then, desperately wanting to ride by the side of Arthur to do battle and learn too, the spells of the Merlin. Eat with them and listen to the infamous annals of their glory, however, it was a dream then and a dream that would never come to fruition.

It proves difficult to give a fitting description of my master, for no matter how dexterous I may select my words, they will render imprecise. How can a boy best illustrate a man exulting an age beyond seventy? Yes, he possessed wrinkles with furrows across his brow deeper than a freshly ploughed wheat field yet there were occasions when in a tranquil state of mind his brow became as smooth as a piglet's back. His nose was long and hooked with a ridge close to the top and continuously dripped in winter. His moods were apt to vary like the weather but I learnt when to take leave of my company to avoid one of his many tantrums. The only thing consistent about Treggedon was his long and wiry frame, for he always looked frail. His hands were almost fleshless and his face gaunt but he possessed an inner strength far greater than his physique delineated. More often than not, he had a smile for me and his mouth had a line either side that only dissipated when he displayed anger or seriousness. He presented himself well in cleanliness and though his dress sense at times was shabby, his clothes were regularly laundered. He had long wispy white hair that fused into his equally long white beard, an attribute seemingly indigenous to the average wizard I would suppose. Other than that, well, in my eyes he was the perfect old man.

Having swept the floor of my master's house, I turned my attention to cleaning the pots and leather bottles as part of my daily duty. It may seem mundane but doing this particular chore was the ideal opportunity for me to daydream and consider all my potions and spells that one day I felt sure I would perfect. In addition, it was a chance to salvage any remnant morsels laying discarded in the empty confines of the receptacles my master overlooked. Alas, he was very mean and with the exception of the odd granule of hellebore or digitalis, I had to resort to pilfering the much-needed ingredients for my own little experiments.

When the horn blew, I immediately ceased my task and sped downstairs to the outer door. Soon enough Treggedon joined me, bustling past as if I did not exist. I managed to wrench my head between his elbow and the doorframe in my desperation at seeing what whipped up the deafening commotion. The horn repeated its deep timbre and within moments of its resounding, a dust cloud rose up through the arch of the portcullis created by the hooves of the approaching horses. Five mounted guards rode through, each holding a banner bearing the Almighty's emblem of the black eagle. The embroidered detail lay on a backcloth of the deepest crimson with gold braid discoloured by the dust from the men's journeying. These fine men were clad in blackened leather with chain mail hanging heavily from their shoulders and distinct crimson plumed helmets hiding their faces.

My master called to me.

"Come Rabbit we must witness this."

My name is Arton of course, however, my master always called me Rabbit, not because of the size of my ears but he said my nose twitched whenever I concentrated. I doubted then as I do now for if it were so, surely someone else would have given mention to my inclination.

"Who are these men?" I asked excitedly squinting at the sudden brightness.

"They, my little buck, are the king's very own guards and doubtlessly bring word of the almighty. Come!" he commanded.

In the time it took us to dash into the square, a jostling crowd already gathered to greet them and their eager hands were grasping at the horse's harnesses. Others frantically gripped the soldiers' tunics and their spirited jeers and shouts overpowered the heavy snorts of the exhausted horses. One sentinel rose from his saddle, gripped the pommel and spoke.

"Behold loyal subjects of Wendatch," he shouted, spitting out the dust from his mouth, "make ready your welcome for I proclaim to receive the almighty, your king. Embellish your paths with fresh hay and prepare your vessels in readiness for his gracious lord."

A great furore echoed around the castle walls as his pronouncement fell silent.

"Take us to our host," demanded another guard struggling to remove his helmet.

"Pray sire, I will lead you." My master responded before all others, bowing his head dutifully.

Momentarily, I thought he was bowing in respect to the guards, something he had no need of doing – after all, he was Talteth's advisor and far higher in the pecking order than any guard, however, I realised it was in respect of the king's colours. As we led the horses toward the keep, all heads stooped in acknowledgement as we passed and it felt as if they were bowing to me.

'One day!' I remember repeating to myself inwardly. 'One day!'

After the brisk walk across the uneven cobbled courtyard we arrived at the foot of the steps leading up to the keep and a sudden hush crept over Wendatch after the guards began dismounting. Only the persistent caws of the abhorrent crows hovering high above the tower showed ill consideration of the event. The huge weathered doors of the keep opened slowly inward and out stepped lord Talteth. Releasing the tethers, Treggedon sped urgently to him.

David Greely

"Sire, messengers from the king are here," gasped my master excitedly.

"I can see that you old fool! I do possess eyes!" Talteth rebuffed discourteously.

"With your pardon sire…"

"…Yes! Yes! Be off with you," the lord hissed derisively.

Talteth brushed my master aside with the wave of his right arm even though Treggedon's head remained bowed to him in respect. The guards laughed in ridicule and I was surely offended.

"Greetings lord Talteth," said one of the guards.

"Wendatch welcomes you. Please, enter my house and drink my wine," the lord insisted.

I studied Talteth's surly manner and watched his tightening lips contort into a wry grin directly after he had spoken.

"Most gracious sire and with pleasure we accept," said another guard twisting uneasily in his saddle endeavouring to dismount.

"Good, then follow me if you please …and someone see to their horses!"

Talteth spun on the heels of his weighty tanned boots and sped back up the steps with his long grey cloak rippling behind him. As quick as he had emerged, Talteth disappeared into the keep leaving the doors wide open. The five guards and my master eagerly followed the lord into the keep. The last guard inched the doors to a thudding close instigating the gathered crowd to disperse and unhurriedly men, women and children filtered off into small bands continuing to mutter their expectation of the king's imminent arrival to one and other. This left me alone staring at the closed doors with my hands unwittingly clutching the horses' leathers and burdened with the animals. While I considered what possible gossip the soldiers brought into Wendatch, I hitched the weary animals in line and tugged them across the yard into the narrow passage leading directly to the stable. The smithy oblivious to the commotion worked at his anvil hammering a shoe into shape and between his hefty strikes, I ordered he feed and water the horses by command of Talteth.

Perhaps at this juncture I should briefly clarify that being an advisor's boy does hold several advantages and any of the common folk at the castle who offered their services at my demands was deemed as being 'co-operative.' Not that I really ever upheld my status in the social order for I was after all born no more than a commoner myself and deep down that was all I felt I ever was.

Having seen to the animals needs, I dashed back to the apothecary eagerly awaiting my master's return with the accounts of the kingdom, however it turned into a long wait, some several hours in fact and already the autumn sun clipped the western wall casting an orange glow into my room. I lit a taper in anticipation of the approaching darkness and placed it over the hearth before walking across to the window overlooking the courtyard. I pondered over the almighty's visit for soon it was going to be a rare opportunity for me to be among the elite throng of aides and have an opportunity to speak to his grace. What words as a boy could I proffer?

'A speech, I must prepare a speech. No, I must resort to etiquette and speak only to him should he ask anything of me. What if he asks me nothing?' I dithered in stupefaction. 'Perhaps I could compose a verse or even recite the aged words of Tibbet the bard but in my own manner…'

My impasse became severed by the approaching voices from a gang of men and cautiously recoiled from the widow daring not to peek for fear of being caught eavesdropping.

"…And remember the consequence you face should you fail the king!"

That is all I overheard and failed to recognise who said it or to whom it was aimed. Within moments, the main door creaked open and then slammed shut as if in the same movement. It was then I witnessed dread upon my master's face as he trudged the stairs and entered the room.

"Master," I uttered softly dashing toward him, "you look so pallid. Are you unwell?"

At first, he did not seem to hear or see me and called to him again to break his vacant stare.

"Master?"

"I am fine Arton," he eventually replied softly.

"Here, sit in your chair." I motioned with my arm and guided him slowly to his seat.

Though I felt helpless, I pursued my efforts to comfort him.

"I will light the fire so as you will be warm."

"Please Arton, there is no need I am fine now."

"Would you like some water? Perhaps mead or wine?"

He deliberated briefly.

"Yes that will be in order, wine I think."

I turned to the shelf opposite, grasped the leather bottle and having noticed my master staring into the cold hearth gently poured the wine. His hands gripped the chair arms turning his knuckles white.

"Here master," I offered holding out his cup. "Drink this you will soon feel better."

He seized the wine fervently sipped it with reluctance at first before greedily draining the final drop.

"Another?" I asked.

His head slowly affirmed my question and on my second return called my name.

Obviously, he was deeply troubled for he only called my name in anger or seriousness.

"Pull your stool closer Arton there is a matter in which I am in the need to tell," he whispered with his voice trembling equally as my heart.

I complied by positioning myself at his feet, facing him and remained respectfully silent and motionless even though I felt tense by the many questions that could have flowed from my lips. My eyes fixed upon his empty stare and the prevailing silence provoked me to question his sudden disheartenment but his disclosure shattered my concern.

"Something very grave has come to fruition."

"Master?" I quizzed readily.

"I have been witness to talk of treason and something very sinister is unfolding Arton."

"Treason against whom?" I asked shuffling uneasily on my seat.

"When treason threatens it can only be against one and that is our good king."

"Arbereth!" I exclaimed rather than question.

"Indeed it is so," he resigned.

"Then this talk must be silenced master we must tell Talteth immediately."

Before I could motion to stand, Treggedon abruptly quelled my contempt by placing his wiry hand on my shoulder.

"Remain seated lad. If it were that simple do you not suppose I would have done so already?"

"I am at a loss."

I sat bewildered trying desperately to assemble what on reflection was incredibly obvious.

"The problem is," he continued, "neither you nor I can turn to Talteth for justice for it is he the lord himself that utters the very words of treason. His aim is to have his father murdered and take the realm for himself."

"With respect master perhaps you may have misheard."

"I wish it was so Rabbit, but alas…"

"…I do not understand. Surely, lord Talteth will rule the kingdom soon anyway. I mean the almighty is old and he will abdicate readily enough."

"The king is a sly old fox and is in the finest of health it will be several years yet before he relinquishes his crown. No, I am afraid Talteth's patience runs thin and his lust for power surpasses all reasoning."

"Then what are we to do?"

"It is more a matter of you rather than 'we.' Unless I conform to his treachery, my life is worthless. He and others will be watching my every move and there is nothing I can do to thwart them succeeding, however, the task I have in mind is not beyond your capabilities."

A grip of fear encapsulated me and I knew whatever my master had in mind I was not going to relish hearing it.

"In the morning after breaking fast you will leave Wendatch and warn the almighty of his own son's plot to slay him."

"But what of you master?"

"I will remain here and pray for you and guide your steps along the way."

His token words of comfort did nothing to quell the fretfulness gnawing inside my stomach because I had never ventured beyond ten leagues from the walls of Wendatch, now suddenly I was being cast out into a world I knew very little of and dreading too, my dismal naivety may burden my prospect of success.

The accounts my master often spoke of on our idle nights came flooding to mind: the evil harbouring in the dense forests, the trolls frequenting the mountains and the wild creatures stalking throughout the kingdom all conjured dread within me. I shook my head to disentangle my anxiety returning to the solemnity of the moment.

"How does Talteth propose to rid his father?" I asked.

"For that lad, I have no answer. I can only surmise that Talteth will order one of his underlings to comply with his wish and be astute enough to create himself a tangible alibi. The king is expected within two days from the morrow so you have until that time to warn him."

"The road is easy enough master if our lord travels from the south…"

"…The road as you state, is 'easy' but be aware of the many hidden dangers for what may appear is not always as it seems. You are now an enemy to the pretender and if he learns of your intent he will have you killed."

It was at this moment I feared what my master designed.

"I have also learnt," he added, "that two of the king's outriders are thick in the plot and no doubt there are others too. You would be wise to trust nobody and speak only with the king himself over the matter."

"But that in itself is impossible!" I contended sharply leaning backward on my stool in resignation. "His guards will have me cut and quartered in an instant and without any question."

I was beginning to shudder.

"Have you not heeded any of my teachings Arton?"

"Of course master," I readily confirmed.

"Then this is the moment to heed them. It is time to remember all I have taught and put your knowledge into practice. You are wiser than most even at your age so follow your instincts and learn from your mistakes. God always gives a man a second chance and you must take it when granted. I am confident you will succeed, though heaven help the kingdom and us if that devil's plot succeeds.

Now you must rest, it will be morning soon enough. Say your prayers and wishes tonight lad, there will be little time for such solace in the morrow."

I retired to my room as Treggedon requested and for the first time in my life experienced dread. What should have been a night of celebration in expectation of the king turned rapidly dire at the prospect of the uncertainty of my daunting errand my master had set. I was angry with him too, for thrusting such a burden upon my inexperienced shoulders. The night seemed endless and though my eyes lay heavy, barely slept and a night among others to transpire when I yearned for my mother's embrace.

The spent candle finally died with a concluding flicker simultaneously proclaiming the arrival of dawn and the chorus of chattering songbirds chirped excitedly as if they too seemed aware of the king's coming, ominously though, the crows with their mournful squawks implied they celebrated my impending quest which drew distressingly closer and I felt downcast. Any other day's waking would witness me avidly watching and feeding the birds that always perched nearby my window counting, naming and recognising them all; but not this morn, I lay quietly for some time with a strong reluctance until finally peeling back my blanket to dress. On opening the quarter drape, the sun struck out its brilliance, reflecting into my room from the water trough across the way highlighting the countless dust motes that floated in the air by my sudden action. Already the bustle of the courtyard commenced and I wandered to the window to peer. The usual trading had indeed begun doubtlessly fuelled by the eagerness in preparations for the almighty and everywhere people carried bundles of fresh straw to line their pathways. Some of Talteth's guards gathered at the storehouse shouting their commands to the lesser folk, ordering them to carry sacks of grain, vegetables and salted mutton carcasses, and children too commandeered for the lesser chores like sweeping and laying the straw.

"Rabbit?"

My master's call broke my wistful observations.

"Come boy you have little time to dally."

Treggedon ushered me to the table where bread and milk had been prepared. My appetite was dull as the loaf afore me, and I could barely manage a mouthful. I deliberately ate slowly to delay the inevitable but my master was no fool and his face beamed in awareness of my trepidation.

"Come lad do not fret, you have a frown on your brow that boasts a man of my age."

"Master I have to admit I am terrified," I said idly poking the bread with my fingers.

"Do not confuse yourself with what you think of as fear, it may prove to be excitement. Remember the prospect of freedom and the glory the king will surely reward is yours for the taking."

He misunderstood what I meant. It was for my master I held apprehension for along with the unpleasant sense that once I leave Wendatch might never ever see him again.

"What if…"

"…Hush now Rabbit you fret unnecessarily," he interrupted as if sensing my feelings perhaps he did, for he was capable considering he was a wizard.

"All you have to do is seek the almighty, tell him what transpires here and I will do all I can to prevent such a scheme from developing further. If we are successful the king will rid himself of his unfaithful son and heir."

Treggedon lowered himself into his chair and produced a tightly wrapped bundle from the side of the hearth.

"Here Rabbit," he said gesticulating for me to approach, "I have prepared some food and a goat-bag. One cannot carry out a special errand on an empty stomach."

He handed me the red clothed pack, which I tucked immediately inside my tunic.

"Now if you remember what I said and treat everyone as if they are your enemy you are sure to succeed. Be certain to come back now, we still have much ground to cover. If ever you need me just pray and I will be there to guide you," his voice lessened to a thoughtful whisper.

"Remember this too, that in every colour shines a light, in every stone sleeps a crystal, with every night lays a dream and with every step there is hope. Never forget when all seems lost God and opportunity will always be there for you. If you believe and cast away doubt, there will be a pervasive justice, for all what you do will be done under the eyes of God. He will be watching over you Arton and the Lord Almighty as my witness, I shall be watching over you too."

He slowly lowered his skinny frame cupping my face in his icy hands and kissed me on the forehead, something he had never done before. Though he was full of love for me, he never demonstrated that type of affection before. I fully remember our parting and the moment I stepped out of the apothecary and shut the door, the tears flowed readily like a waterfall over my cheeks. Having taken several minutes to compose myself I inhaled deeply and apprehensively ventured out into the courtyard. Much as I desired to turn back and insist Treggedon should resort to using his magic to resolve the matter, I could not let myself be seen sobbing and did my best, offering a lethargic wave without turning around.

Chapter Two

    Immediately the hubbub of the arrangements for the good king engulfed me and unlike any other time, nobody cared to pass the courtesy of the day. People engaging with their menial responsibilities never even gave a cursory glance, which suited me and had they have done so by asking me of my duty at this precise moment I would have cringed and reddened with guilt. I just wanted to slip through the main gate unnoticed to warn the almighty of the impending doom awaiting him and swiftly return to my master.
    Despite the consternation and the feeling of loneliness, my air of confidence grew when setting about my undertaking and began deliberately meandering around the courtyard, aiming if not directly, toward the portcullis. Firstly, I went to the alehouse; my favourite haunt since early boyhood and though I drank little, my master insisted dilution of the mead with three parts water. My only purpose for going there was to avoid arousing any suspicion, for I do not recall any day passing

without affording a little time there and needed to make this day no exception. I dallied there a short while seated at my usual bench against the far wall, saturated in the stale and oppressive air of drifting odours of bodily smells that welcomed me as they had done a dozen times over. Forlorn bodies lay strewn where they slumped in a drunken stupor from the previous nights' revelry; men, perhaps in fear of waking to the realities of a new day, unwilling to face the turbulent tongues of their womenfolk.

To me, my bench was the optimum seat in the place for surveying all the patrons something I just relished doing and this habit became a diversion of mine at the time, where I would just sit and witness the comings and goings of the house. In time, I knew most of the imbibers and would sometimes perform small tricks for a drop of mead. Nothing much incredible you understand, just a simple deception would be to turn inanimate objects into birds or insects, say a smoking pipe into a titmouse. Such spells I learnt from Treggedon and provided I kept within the confines of little furry creatures, he gave consent.

In fact, I well remember the time he first demonstrated the art to me. A visitor from Belscotia –a township far beyond the mountains in the northern territory came into the alehouse late one afternoon. I had supped my drink and bidding my farewell when this giant man blocked the doorway, brightly clad in a golden yellow cloak hitched with a thick leather belt housing a long menacing sword. His breaches were an uncommon sight in these parts of Aeria as was his brown, strapless boots. His hair parted to one side in a plait, hanging lank with bone tassel attached. He had a full, weathered round face and thick neck possessing a deep, commanding voice that reverberated out at me.

"Sit with me lad and keep me company," he boomed loudly stretching his huge frame across the doorway.

"Sir, much as it would do me an honour my master awaits my return and insists I am not to be late."

"Are you refusing me boy, me the great Elberdor?"

He leant forward looking directly at me with his piercing and suspecting eyes.

"Pray sir," I pleaded mildly, "I mean no disrespect but my master…"

"…Is this master of yours more powerful than I?"

I declined answering what was in my heart.

"Well boy?" he pressed, inching his roughened face even closer.

"I… I mean. Well that is…er, yes!"

I tried cowering to the floor in protection of his obvious rage, which reflected in his ruddy complexion but his massive hands grasped my head before spinning me round to face back into the room.

"If your master is of greater worth then no doubt he will be paying us a visit eh? In the meantime boy you are my serf so fetch me wine and food."

The stranger succeeded in scaring me rigid, I bowed my head in nervous compliance and all but ran to the serving bar to satisfy his demand. I returned shortly and as requested sat down at his acquired table daring not to spill his drink, shake a crumb from his bread nor utter a word or doing anything out of place. The cheery idleness of fellow imbibers culminated into petrified silence anticipating another angry outburst from the stranger and I was immensely peeved no one offered to rescue me from him but in their defence supposed his size was very daunting. He greedily swigged at the wine and tore into the bread like a barbarian stuffing in mouthful after mouthful followed by further great gulps of wine that simultaneously churned in his noisy, slobbering gullet. So full was his mouth, lumps of wine-sodden dough escaped splattering upon the table. After several moments of repulsive ingest and one long belch he flopped back in the chair and demanded I fetch him more wine. As I rose for my second trip to the serving bar, my master entered. His first glance aimed directly at the empty bench that was my usual place and upon realisation of my missing, continued searching around the room with a deepening scowl that pierced the quiet like the point of a fired arrow.

"Come on boy - hurry!" The grotesque stranger roared at me for his wine.

"Ah, there you are Rabbit!" exclaimed Treggedon stepping closer toward me.

"I was coming home master but…"

The big man interrupted my soft apology.

"…So," he claimed sarcastically, "this is your master, eh lad?"

"It is, and he is advisor to the lord of Wendatch!" I said defiantly.

"Is that so? Well ain't he the one!" roared Elberdor with raucous mirth. "Come on old man join me in a drink," he invited, suddenly refraining from his impetuous laughter. "The wine is how one would say, undeniably favourable upon the palate," he laughed again sending blood rushing to his face.

"I thank you sir," replied my master impartially, "but I have much work to do and so does my young apprentice. Come Rabbit we must be off."

"The lad is indisposed at this moment. Now boy, fetch me the wine!" Elberdor's laughter swiftly transformed into rage and he slammed his open palms squarely on the tabletop with shuddering might.

"With respect sir," continued Treggedon calmly, "I believe you may have misunderstood my point. The lad is under my employ and is remaining so."

The big man lurched forward across the table gazing his deep sunken eyes directly into the stare of my master, I took this opportunity to slip away to join Treggedon, wrapping willowy arms around his waist.

"Come Arton we have work which demands our attention," my master said hanging a reassuring arm across my shoulders and ushering me toward the door.

Impulsively he turned his head as quick as lightening and pushing me aside, fully rotated to catch the flying knife in his left hand. I have never witnessed such swift reaction nor too, such anger upon my master's face. All his age lines malformed to a dull blue, disfiguring his face almost beyond recognition and he stood motionless briefly before raising his hand containing the stranger's blade. His knuckles turned white as his grip began crushing the hardened steel and within the seconds that lapsed powder began trickling through his opening fingers.

"Sir," he said, "I demand your apology."

"Demand?" Elberdor shouted in fury. "No one demands anything from me and if you continue to do so old man I will cut you down with my blade!"

The stranger's threat spurred me to make a futile gesture to pull Treggedon away from the confrontation but he brushed me aside like a leaf and without deliberation moved toward the big man neither blinking nor averting his ice-cold gaze off him. With a restraining calmness he spoke.

"I demand your apology!"

Elberdor inhaled sharply which expanded his chest and making him seem even taller. Such action forced his chair to topple and grasping the hilt of his intimidating sword drew it from its scabbard.

"You are as good as dead!" raged the man.

"That will be quite useless," insisted my master staying his ground.

"Say that when the cold steel pierces your heart!" Elberdor contested.

"Master!" I shouted in fear of his life.

"Silence boy and stay there!" Treggedon ordered without glancing to me.

Elberdor suddenly lunged with his blade and I closed my eyes biting my lip to block the scream forcing its way from the pit of my stomach. On opening my eyes, I fully expected my master to be slouched in a pool of blood with the sneering northerner towering over him and wiping his blade of the life that lay at his feet, yet incredibly, I was witnessing my master being a wizard and using his magic.

The stranger's sword turned into a hissing serpent with deep emerald eyes that epitomised death and a lashing tongue dripping with the bane of the devil. The hilt transformed to become its tail constricting around Elberdor's wrist and frantically he tore at the creature throwing it to the floor, which on impact distorted back into his cold-edged blade.

"What is this trickery?" he wailed incontestably perplexed.

Indeed, my same question for I never knew Treggedon harboured such spells and everyone in the alehouse stood silently gawping with equal astonishment.

My master called to me and with an aspect of reluctance, I walked to his side though prepared to dash if Elberdor attempted to make a grab at me.

"Arton take off your shoes and place them on the table."

Treggedon's command expressed severity and his eyes retained their frosty stare upon the big man.

"Master?" I queried doubting his peculiar motive.

"Do as I ask!" he upheld sternly.

Reluctantly I complied and reached down to untie them before setting them upon the table.

"Well stranger, I still await your apology."

The man looked, snorting with increasing agitation.

"No! Never!" he shouted.

"Then," responded Treggedon, "let this be so!"

My master flicked his right hand firing a brilliant blue flash directly at one of my shoes and repeated the same action to the other transforming them into huge black rats the size one can only imagine in a nightmare, with bulbous orange eyes and long yellow-tainted incisors encrusted with disease. They leapt from the tabletop and sunk their teeth into Elberdor's throat. He bolted to the door screaming, hurling off the creatures as he ran and after fumbling with the latch, sped out of Wendatch with my shoes in hot pursuit.

I had witnessed many of my master's tricks since that particular day but none was ever that amusing. Thus, it was from that moment on when Treggedon began teaching me all of his little tricks and enchantments and slowly but surely, I began to absorb and challenge everything in my efforts to understand the art of magic. For incalculable days and nights I practised until I could master every spell he set and thus turning those tests into practicality at the alehouse.

David Greely

I spent long enough at the alehouse to convince any prying eye it was just a normal day for me and on my eventual leaving, turned eastward slinking into the melee of the crowd. Much as I wanted to hasten my tread, I remained slow-footed withholding the pretence of lethargy to the extreme of actually stopping to aid a blind man lay down straw at his doorway. I pondered then as to why I had not noticed him before, thinking I knew everyone at Wendatch but supposed it had become a busy place of late, particularly with the imminence of the king's visit and new faces were bound to be commonplace.

Again, I continued my intent and soon enough the shadow of the portcullis towered over me. It was only a matter of a few more paces before I would pass through its hollow and out into the sunny open meadows. Beyond the drawbridge, I observed several commoners filtering down from the small rise to the south, laden with heavy bales over their shoulders.

"Hey lad, stop!" roared a thunderous voice made deeper by the confines of the surrounding walls.

At first, I cared not to stop, hoping his instruction be aimed at another.

"Laddie – stop!"

His repeated directive halted me in my tracks. My heart pounded fiercely fuelling my throat to suddenly dry and after a long nervous swallow turned to face the scowling guard blocking my exit.

"What is your business here?" he asked outstretching his long pike.

"I am on an errand for my master."

"Your master eh, and he would be?"

"Treggedon, advisor to lord Talteth," I replied softly realising as soon as mentioning his name I had said the wrong thing.

"Well if that be so what is the nature of your errand?" he continued while adjusting his stance.

"I am to fetch herbs from the fields and seeds from the wayside."

"Well not this day…"

"…But my master…" I objected feebly.

"...Take the day off boy!" the guard insisted.

"He will be furious if I do not carry out what he has asked of me," I implored.

"That is your lookout lad, there'll be no flower picking this day or any other now be off with you!" he ranted. "Scram before I pike you!"

"With respect sir," I pleaded, "do you realise who I am? I have the authority here."

"I admire your spunk little man but your authority is of no consequence now," the guard mocked.

I was uncertain as to what he meant. Was he just saying it in a bid to frustrate my ego or because of the king's coming? He would be right on the second count for a mere boy such as I, despite my master's standing, would have no such opportunity to be among the great nobility –why even Treggedon himself would be more than fortunate just to be present on the same dining table as the king.

"Then," I said sharply in return, "I will do as you say and take the day off. I will trap hogs instead."

The point of the guard's pike came level to my throat.

"Are you finding it hard to grasp my meaning? No one has permission to leave here today or the morrow or for however long it may take the king to arrive. Now be off before I slice off your ears!"

The threatening pike head was enough to send me scampering back into the swelling crowd.

I eventually stopped at a water trough and slumped over the side in a bid to gather my breath. I reached down to have a drink but the green sludge and dead floating flies quenched my thirst for me. I needed time to reappraise my predicament, thus turning my attention back to the alehouse seeing it was the only place offering me salvation. I did briefly consider the wish tower but it was sure to be milling with people saying morning grace. The streets were crammed with commotion and if I dare linger be forced into aiding with the preparations, something I would have relished rather than struggle with my fruitless mission that up until now may result in no reason for celebration at all. I also considered returning to the apothecary but knew my master would be angry with me. I was feeling peeved at the responsibility he had thrust upon me, for the love of God himself I was not yet a man so what was he expecting of me?

As the morning wore on, I sat silently in the alehouse with my diluted mead trying to seek a solution but no scheme came to mind, though in truth had already resigned to escape under the cloak of darkness. I took some consolation at the prospect that the longer I took in reaching the king the nearer he would be to Wendatch. Eventually I concluded to make a dash through the gate knowing unless habits abandoned for one night, dinner would be served in the keep at dusk and sure to preside for several hours. The townsfolk would be frequenting the alehouse undoubtedly wallowing in merriment and very few people alert on the forthcoming night.

It was barely midday and I had nowhere to go until darkness fell. It would have raised further suspicion if I remained any longer at the inn so returned my spent cup and walked to the door. On stepping out into the strong daylight, I somehow bundled straight into the blind man.

"Begging your pardon sir," I apologised. "My fault entirely."

"Ah! Young man, is that you?" he asked steadying himself against his stick. "Are you the lad that helped me earlier?" he persisted, gripping the doorframe for additional support.

"Yes sir," I responded coyly, "but it was nothing and a job easily undertaken for anyone blessed with the good fortune of sight."

"Then surely I am perplexed," he said finally steadying himself.

"In regard?" I quizzed.

"If you are blessed with sight then why is it that you did not see me?"

His head cocked to one side and he bent his frame lower.

I studied the eyes of the blind man while affording him no answer.

"Perhaps," he said sensing my stupor, "you possess certain visions that you see and not the ones of reality - being a wizard's companion and all."

"Pray forgiveness sir but I know nothing to what you refer. I am merely a humble apprentice to my master."

The blind man rested his hand on my shoulder.

"Come lad," he said softening his tone almost to a whisper, "guide me if you will and perhaps we may talk further."

"Where to?" I asked nervously.

"Wherever you wish," he replied keenly. "A partially sighted man such as I, am in no need of hurry or wanting to dwell on the delights of spectacles that cannot be witnessed. All that I see are just hazy shadows, colourless and impure. Now let us just walk."

I chose the roadway that followed inside the perimeter walls calculating I could initiate a dash through the portcullis should the opportunity lend itself. Most of the prolonged amble kept us in shade from the hot sun and not until we trailed along the south facing wall, did the blind man finally care to speak again and on doing so suddenly stopped.

"Boy," he asked leaning on his stick, "would you not agree we both endure some special gift?"

"I have nothing special," I returned, "and know nothing of your trait."

"Give it some consideration then perhaps it will spring to mind."

I did think briefly but could only offer him my blessing of eyesight.

"My sight," I said somewhat excitedly, "is that the special gift you speak of?"

The man laughed aloud rolling back his head.

"Sight is indeed a gift and to a blind man such as me, would indeed be very special but to one that can see, it is nothing other than to be willingly expected."

"Then I am at a loss sir."

"Suppose," he whispered, "I was to say magic, would you consider that to be a special gift?"

David Greely

"Indeed so," I agreed.

"Then you possess a special gift do you not?"

I laughed inwardly at the man's foolishness.

"I have no such powers. My master perhaps has a limited insight but I…"

"…Oh, come, my boy I have heard of your tricks. You must surely be in possession of the knowledge."

I was beginning to feel uncomfortable unknowing his intent and backed away from him uneasily.

"Please, I really have to take my leave."

"Why go?" he posed sensing my recoil. "You have no place to hide now and besides you have little reason to fear me."

He gripped my arm firmly and continued his banal drivel.

"How do you know if you possess something or not?"

"By having it I suppose," I sighed impatiently.

"Or testing it perhaps," he continued. "Let me explain. Unless you sample something, you do not know what it is like. I must have been about your age when struck by my incapacity. My eyes look perfect do they not?"

He crouched and put his unshaven face closer to mine offering me to examine them.

"I can blink, shed tears and move them about perfectly," he persevered rolling his eyes around their sockets, "yet I have no vision. It is the fault of no man that I am what I am but merely an act of God and yet with this sacrifice he has given me something in return, the gift of vision through the mind."

"Are you a wizard?" I posed unconcernedly.

"In some respect yes, I suppose I am but to be a proper sorcerer I need to have my true sight restored."

"Sir I am but a master's boy," I implored reminding him so.

I knew this pathetic man was about to ask of me the impossible.

"Call yourself anything you wish young man but you have the gift because I can sense it. I hear what people say of your remarkable conjuring tricks at the alehouse."

"They are as you state, just tricks.

Please, what is it you want of me?" I appealed.

"Your help and..." he added hastily, "...I will help you in return. You see I am aware of your plight in wanting to get out away from Wendatch and can assist your escape."

"And in return?" I asked wondering.

"In return just a simple spell. A spell that will give me back my sight."

"I do not hold such power," I said emphatically, "you are seeking a miracle and I am incapable of performing that."

"Have you tried?" he persisted.

"No of course not," I said.

"Then how do you know you cannot do it? That is my whole point and as I said unless you try something you will never determine your potential."

I did not know what to say or even how to react. I wanted to run off and God knew it was in my heart to do so, yet something restrained me whether it was God's own power or that of the blind man I failed to establish, nevertheless, I remained having unwittingly warmed to him.

"As I am able to get you away from Wendatch you will help me first, yes?"

The blind man's voice became soft and amiable.

Did I have a choice? Despite the futile cure he wanted from me, my primary concern was his awareness in my necessity to leave Wendatch and doubtlessly my reason why. If for some uncanny reason he knew of my plight then surely he must embrace the gift of insight he admitted to. Other than Treggedon, no other could have known of the plan.

"Very well," I reluctantly conceded.

"Good!" he beamed. "Now we must hurry. Come, follow me."

This time the blind man led the way back along the wall and although he gripped his stick, cared not to use it. He seemed quite familiar with the contours of the walls and we ended back at his abode no slower than if I had led the way myself. He insisted I entered first and bade me to sit upon the straw just inside the doorway.

David Greely

"Now then lad," he said excitedly, "this is the plan of action. After your spell I shall arrange all the necessary preparations to seal your freedom."

I could not break my stare from him as he paused briefly to take a sharp breath.

"A cart will enter the courtyard and I shall arrange for it to topple and create a diversion for you, the moment this happens, run out through the gate and head north. Remain close to the wall mind; it will help keep you hidden. When dusk falls continue northward and stay within the lengthening shadow of the keep, it should give you enough cover until you make your escape toward the forest. From there you are on your own. Now is that clear?"

"Yes I think so," I replied, retracing his scheme in my mind.

"Know so boy because this is your one chance," he emphasised.

"Yes I know so," I responded sharply.

"Very well then," he approved, returning his tone to a mild softness. "Now in return I expect no less than the sight you promised me."

I promised him no such thing! If God were my witness, he would have put a halt to this situation at this very instant.

"But sire?" I pleaded ineffectively.

"Well?" he prompted, "I await your work young wizard."

I took a long hard swallow to supplement my dry throat and slowly closed my eyes.

"If I am to perform such a miracle it has to done elsewhere," I insisted.

Of course, it sounded feeble but it was all that came to mind at that moment in an effort to delay my hopeless task but inevitably, he saw directly through my ruse.

"We have not a moment to lose. Now is the time," he urged.

His voice became stern and I kept my eyes tightly closed fearing the look of anger that surely must have been on his face. I could sense my body beginning to tremble and tried desperately to withhold the tears welling inside my closed eyelids. I sat there petrified and wished, wished in the entire kingdom I be whisked away from this unwanted confrontation. My aspiration proved useless and went unanswered.

"Well?" he pressed again.

"I am concentrating and it may help matters if you did the same."

I felt brave saying it but it kept him silent. Now I was ready to scurry through the door into the courtyard but his hand gripped my arm firmly, perceptively aware of my predetermined intent.

"My patience wears thin boy and unless you comply with my need your quest will never succeed."

I exhaled deeply and opened my eyes conceding I had to enact his bizarre yearning.

"Good!" he gasped in readiness.

In my heart, I knew the task was unachievable but nevertheless, had to undertake the gesture. Distraughtly I struggled to rekindle my master's spells for healing but alas, curing blindness was one I never witnessed or indeed, to my knowledge, did he perform.

"Culim imprendus malikus!"

I muttered an indistinct passage that meant absolutely nothing to the blind man or me but that was to my advantage and for all he knew I was summoning the incantation. A rush of blood suddenly overwhelmed me, shooting my eyes involuntarily up into my head. I tried not to succumb to its power but it was much too strong and I remembered nothing further until roused by cold water being dabbed on my forehead by the blind man.

"Some spell boy! Absolute miracle I'd call it."

I shook my head, gathering my beleaguered senses and stared directly into his eyes. Nothing seemed different and they rolled and twitched in their sockets as they had done previously.

"Well done!" he commended. "I can see! It's a miracle! Saints be praised this day and all others. I can see!"

David Greely

He shook my shoulders vigorously in his exaltation. He was indeed a very happy man.

I questioned myself as to whether I was capable of casting such an intense spell. My incantation was complete nonsense and yet this man before me suddenly had his burden lifted. I did not physically do anything!

Again, the man seemed to sense my scepticism and before I could test him, he spoke.

"Your tunic has a tear about the shoulder."

I twisted my arm to feel the hole he noticed.

"My, how this place needs a whitewash," he observed, looking around his abode and savouring everything he could now see.

Still numbed by the event, I sat quiet and motionless for several minutes until he spoke again.

"You have performed your task most admirably lad and it is my turn to proffer a favour. Wait here whilst I go and arrange for your escape. I may be gone for some time but be patient, you shall receive your just recompense."

The door closed leaving me alone in the stranger's home. Though still deliberating my unconvincing success as a spellbinder something else gnawed at me yet I knew not what. I was convinced the man was how I perceived him to be and by that, I mean no hidden pretence. Yes, I trusted him though in retrospect it was the first naive mistake in my early life as a prospering enchanter. My master warned me of such people and yet on my very first escapade, fell head first into an obvious trap.

It was to be several hours before the man returned and all the while, I sat patiently staring at the bland walls recalling the outcome of my absurd enchantment. In the boredom, I delved into my cloth package to eat some of the bread my master prepared, though sure enough it was there but so too were five tiny fleshless bones. Treggedon gave them no mention yet he must have included them for a reason. 'Perhaps' I thought, 'an oversight at one of his teachings,' I was certainly guilty at my lack of concentration and often but nonetheless, certain he never showed them nor gave them any such mention. I sat transfixed at the bones lying on the open red cloth upon my lap fingering aside the crusty bread to allow a clearer view in which to scrutinise them. I had no conception as to what they were, besides fleshless bones, or indeed their significance and knowing little of anatomy surmised they once belonged to a chicken or goose, perhaps parts of a wing. They were all much the same length, the smallest perhaps three quarters the size of my forefinger though one considerably thicker than the rest. They were smooth and rounded, reminding me of pure white ivory and appeared to have been polished or at least, well used. I dared to touch one, prodding it warily and then all of them in turn, mixing them around gently between my fingertips, listening to their soft tinkling against one another like faint wind chimes.

The approaching footsteps on the crisp straw outside interrupted my diversion and I hastily crammed a piece of dry bread into my mouth while fumbling to gather the bones. I stood stuffing the cloth inside my tunic awaiting the man's arrival.

"All is fixed," he said on entry.

He placed his strong arm around my shoulder and without resistance turned me back toward the door.

"All is ready, be there a slight change of strategy. Stick to the perimeter wall until you reach the barrel-loaded cart then carefully climb inside one and then wait. Remain as quiet as a lizard mind and dare not to peek outside, soon enough you will be on your way. Now off you go and look lively the cart will not wait"

I did as instructed and set off immediately through the doorway. I turned back to the man who smiled and waved half-heartedly before shutting the door.

My want in getting away from Wendatch was fervent and instantly made my way to the boundary wall, consciously having to quell my pace toward the main gate by daring not to run in my eagerness. The activity of the town was immense and many carts loaded with straw, lined the main roadway blocking all inward arrivals. Eventually, I sighted the cart laden with barrels thirty paces ahead of me and stopped to watch the cooper and his underling roll out another. On setting it down, the

David Greely

pair returned into the small building briefly then reappeared with another, rolling it onto the organised stack. I took check of their lapse of time, judged my sprint to the cart accordingly and dashed to the stockpile. Slowly I eased back a wooden cap and leapt into the empty keg, replacing the cover carefully. My eyes took some while adjusting to the sudden darkness and blinked furiously inside the dank pungent hollow. Light became apparent through tiny cracks near the top and these were my lifeline for both air and frugal daylight.

Throughout the late afternoon, periodic rolls of advancing barrels came thundering close, some landing on top of mine pinning me to the base of the increasing stack. By now daylight faded and it must have been well past dusk before any suggestion of departure. The sudden jolt raised my spirits as the cart began trundling off. 'At last,' I recall saying to myself, unable to hide my inward elation and my pulse raced faster than the wheels as I began relishing the prospect of my escape, but as quick as it had moved the cart slowed to a dispirited halt. Several voices bellowed out in the calm of the evening and with a confused mixture of puffs and sighs, the barrels began moving. I took a sharp inhale of breath envisaging discovery and my trembling heart sent faint echoes within the dark confine when hearing approaching footsteps. They trudged even closer and without regard, my barrel became tilted onto its side. The movement continuously bludgeoned my head and limbs against the roughened wood, rendering me unconscious.

I never heard the animal's hooves on the cobbles, the clinking and cracking of harness, nor the familiar echo through the portcullis or any words of banter from the guards. I did not know what time had elapsed in my blackout and can only recollect awakening to the sound of drunken fervour and a dim light breaking the pitch of my incarceration. My legs ached with cramp and my head pounded furiously.

'Away from Wendatch at last,' I thought, 'safe in an alehouse that would welcome any stranger.' I had in mind to loosen the cover, spring out and introduce myself, perhaps even perform a couple of innocuous tricks and melt away to set about my task of locating the king, but I chose to remain still and wait until quietness gained a sensible hold and drift off undetected. Alas, the choosing was not mine and unexpectedly, the top was prised and fully removed from the barrel.

"Here my lord!" blurted a voice. "Here's the weasel!"

A hand grabbed my ear tightly, forcing me to stand on my numbed feet. Immediately I recognised my surroundings and put name to the gripping hand inflicting further pain to my aching head. The blind man I had aided was presenting me like some callous murderer to lord Talteth and he dragged me from the tun into the great hall slumping me at the feet of the lord sitting bold and proud in a large winged chair. His huge hands trailed languidly off the ends of his seat displaying an array of rings that furnished his every finger and at his side, guards whom like their monarch portrayed an air of dislikeable decadence that endorsed an instantaneous loathing within me.

"So boy," said Talteth, "what is your say in this matter eh?"

"Lord?" I questioned dozily, overcoming the pain.

"Come now lad do you think me stupid for not being aware of the conspiracy you were set?"

"Sir, I know not of what..." The not-so blind man quelled my tongue with a swift backhand striking sharply at my head and God, how it hurt.

"...Silence boy!" he demanded. "Until the lord commands you will remain silent."

I felt wretched with limbs aching, stale breathed and body battered.

"What was to be your errand lad?" the lord asked in a somewhat uncharacteristic gentle manner.

"Sire," I implored weakly, "I know of no plot."

"I admire your pluck boy but it is quite useless to pretend now," the lord conceded.

"Answer the lord or I will cut out your tongue then no further words of falseness will you pronounce!" said my captor, laughing.

"Well?" urged Talteth.

David Greely

I said nothing and could only dwell on the act of perfidy the blind man had set. Apart from learning the aspect of patience this day in waiting so long trapped inside the barrel, I gained the misgivings of trust and cringed at the impending obviousness facing me. The man was not sightless and from the outset of our first meeting, created the pretence to ensnare me. His deception succeeded with my puerile consent and I had fallen into his trap as eagerly as a hungry mouse to cheese.

"Bring the old man to me!"

My despondent thoughts shattered with the lord's instruction and in the prolonged silence the man I hated most seized my hair, restraining my head with his strong uncompromising grip and for several agonising minutes I suffered continual pain until a sentry entered the hall tugging at my shackled master. Treggedon shuffled across the floor, his ordeal made worse by carrying the cumbersome chains wrapped around his limbs. His tattered robe stained with his own blood illustrated the lashings he had undergone. His wrists bled from the tight metal bands that bound them together and his long thinning hair matted with sweat and congealed blood hung over his soiled sweating face. I openly wept at his pitiful sight.

"Lord," I sobbed, "please show mercy and spare him. I will tell all that needs to be told."

"How very sensible," Talteth grinned.

My poor master slumped to the floor with exhaustion and his spent body sank heavily with the weight of the clattering irons.

"Rabbit," he gasped softly, "Rabbit…"

Treggedon spoke his final words and his lifeless body toppled over to one side.

"Master!" I yelled fretfully.

Despite my detention from the blind man's grip, I dashed toward my master feeling the excruciating pain of my hair tearing from my scalp, but how great was this agony in comparison to sight of the death of my master? They could no longer hold Treggedon as ransom for my knowledge and it seemed pointless now to withhold the truth further. Giving Talteth the information he sought may at least spare my life though with my master now dead his scheme to murder his father would now succeed.

The man pulled me away from Treggedon.

"I think," he said, "the boy is ready to speak."

Indeed I was, in fact I was more than ready to say exactly how I felt. My obsessive contempt for the man equalled the hatred for Talteth in having my master slain but to obtain retribution, had to manage my own regard, something I could not achieve if dead.

"So be it," I said cuffing away the flowing tears from my blooded and aching face, "I will tell all that is required."

"Good sense prevails in you boy. Now then," prompted Talteth in a softer manner, "say your piece."

"I was under instruction to get word to the king. Treggedon never mentioned whom nor why but said there was a plot against Arbereth to kill him and I was sent to locate and warn him of the unfolding misdeed. I set out this morning on my quest but as you see, failed by meeting the man that holds me now."

Talteth knowingly smirked at the trickster while I continued revealing my mishap.

"He pretended to be blind and had me do a spell to cure him in exchange for getting me past the main gate and out of Wendatch."

"Indeed so lad and for your treachery against me I must give sentence," Talteth pronounced.

"Mercy sire," I implored feebly. "I was under instruction and had no choice in the matter."

"That is in your favour and I Talteth am a fair and just man, but as to how merciful…," he deliberately pondered to witness my reaction.

My captive then spoke.

"…My lord of Wendatch and all kingdoms may I be as so bold in your moment of compassion, implore you for my just reward?"

"Name your asking Beladon," urged Talteth.

"The boy sire. I would like the boy," requested Beladon tightening his grip on my hair.

Talteth thought for a while and consulted the guards standing either side of him.

"It is granted, but heed my words Beladon, the wretch is your responsibility and should you lose control over him you will be answerable to me!"

"Gracious king I will honour your words."

Beladon turned and glanced down at me smiling and if his grip were not so tight, I would have spat phlegm directly into his spiteful eyes.

"Now take him away!" ordered Talteth. "I am sick of his dismal face…

…And," he added pointing indolently at Treggedon," remove that dead carcass from my hall!"

A guard responded smartly, dashing from the far side of the hall, clutched the loose chains and dragged my master's frail body without regard like a trussed mutton. I cursed the guard under my breath; nay I cursed them all for my master's demise and swore vengeance will be mine.

My fortune was ill-favourable hoping I be ordered to work in the kitchen instead of becoming servant to Beladon and it gave me the disposition of dejection, suffice to say I would have preferred to be escorted to the dungeon and locked in the keep's putrid depth for all eternity. Under sufferance, two guards led me from the keep across into the courtyard as I faced the humiliating confrontation of staring onlookers who ceased their activities as I was forced unwillingly back to my acquired master's house.

I sat chained, dispirited and alone listening to the escalating merriment outside. Not only did the lord and his entourage enjoy a hearty feast in the great hall that evening but the commoners too, for I had witnessed on my return to Beladon's abode, the slaughtering of at least a score of hog and mutton and countless sacks of root crops being taken to the kitchen. The celebration was at its climax and while everyone ate and drank, I sat dejected and full of contempt, facing the prospect of stale bread, water and the five fleshless bones on my open cloth.

I cry now as I did then for my dead master for it was he, having discovered me wandering the foothills of the mountains took me in and from that moment taught me everything. He always assured me in moments of uncertainty or dejection and cheered me in times of sadness but most importantly, expressed his love for me. Were such feelings set to dissipate now he was dead? I had never felt deep sorrow before and could not control the burning tears in my eyes or heaviness of heart. How was I to face my wretched future without my beloved master?

My fatigued and battered body was desperate for a rest but my mind won the battle and repeatedly projected images of my master remained with me throughout the night. In hope, I expected him to walk through the door and rescue me but alas, remained cold and very much isolated drifting in and out of slumber, waking to vivid spectres of him lying on the cold stone floor of the hall and Talteth with his conclave of murderous henchmen laughing at his demise and at me too.

Finally, dawn broke bringing heavy rain and I remember sniggering aloud.

'Repayment,' I proffered, 'for my exclusion in the previous evening's festivities and all the lengthy preparations washed out by the will of the Good Lord the Almighty,' though small justice however for the untimely slaying of my master. This was the precise moment I decided to pursue the similar path of Treggedon to become the wizard he always advocated I be capable of being, therefore that very morning I, Arton of Wendatch, began my struggle to become a sorcerer if not least of all to avenge my master's death.

Eventually, much later that morning my new master Beladon returned home. On his arrival, I scurried back into the corner, stuffed the cloth-wrapped bones into my tattered tunic and closed my eyes in pretence of sleep. Accompanying him was two of the guards I recognised from the king's advance party, confirming to me their collusion with Talteth. I made a deliberate stir upon their entry.

"Ah boy, there you are!" said Beladon sarcastically proffering a frosty and insensitive smile.

"Sire," I said making to stand but his hefty boot pushed hard against my chest forcing me back onto the floor.

He approached and adjusted my chain, checking every link with his scrupulous eyes.

"The king arrives shortly and I want you to make this place tidy and lay fresh straw the moment this confounded rain stops."

"Sire," I acknowledged feebly.

"You may consider attempting to flee but spare the worthless effort, my two friends here will remain constantly and once you've cleaned this place for your pity, I'll fetch new garments, after all, we cannot have the king witness such an ill-dressed and bloodied waif. He would be most upset and we wouldn't want that on his special day now, would we?"

Satisfied my chains were secure Beladon gave them a mighty tug before moving away. The three men laughed haughtily and dispersed into my Beladon's quarters leaving me with the mountainous chore of cleaning.

I worked continuously under my constraint for the best part of two hours until a fanfare broke the monotonous silence. I peered through the open door into the courtyard relishing the rain hitting my face with cold refreshment.

"Hey boy," yelled Beladon, "what are you doing there? You are supposed to be working!"

"It is the king, he is approaching!" I said enthusiastically.

"I wouldn't get too carried away lad, he will not be king for much longer!" remarked one of the guards breaking out into a chortle.

"I must be off now," said Beladon turning to the other guard. "Mind the boy well."

"Leave him to us," said the other.

"And here," said Beladon tossing some fresh clothes at me, "get into these."

He left promptly, slamming the door sharply behind him.

"Don't just stand there gaping boy, do as ordered and freshen up, and get into the clothes. Come on look lively about it!" the first guard snapped.

"With respect sir," I said rattling the manacles, "I need to be unchained to do so."

Both men looked at each other for agreement, which they reluctantly affirmed and while one unhooked my chain the other stood resolutely at the door. I moved toward Beladon's quarters to change but called to return instantly.

"Change here boy where we can keep an eye on you."

"Perhaps he is a little shy," said the second guard with his habitual laughter.

"Yeah," confirmed the other, "or maybe he has a little something to hide."

"That's it," continued the first guard sniggering, "he's got something to hide. What have you lad, eh?"

"Maybe he's not a boy but perhaps a budding girl," his companion teased.

Them seeing what I possessed as my manhood was the least of my concern; I did not want them discovering the bones. Treggedon packed them for a specific reason so they must have been vital to me even though I had no perception of their significance or power if indeed they possessed any regardless I had to keep them hidden. I raised my tattered tunic over my head whilst carefully removing my cloth parcel with it. I flushed red and turned to face them dropping my discarded robe to the floor.

"Well, he is a boy!" observed the first guard. "Now dress lively lad soon the almighty will be here."

Having quickly dressed the second guard confined me back into my shackles and collected my frayed tunic. Out from it fell my red clothed parcel.

"What have we here?" he questioned revelling in his curiosity.

"It is nothing sir just a little food," I replied hoping he would disregard it.

"Food eh? Good I'm hungry!"

"But sir…" I contested in earnest.

"…Silence," he hissed, "or I'll slice off your tongue!"

The guard snatched eagerly at the cloth to reveal the bread, the goat-bag and the fleshless bones, grunting disdainfully at the pathetic horde.

"Not enough here to feed a rat. Bah!"

He threw the disinteresting bundle at me with force and contempt, bursting the goat-bag open when it struck me. The bread broke into several fragments and the bones…

…Well, what transpired became most peculiar. The two guards never took notice for surely they would have reacted but true as this is my testament, all five bones landed in the palm of my hand. 'Nothing magical about that,' I hear you utter but consider this; my hand, in fact both hands were already tightly clenched and I never made any motion to catch them, it happened far too quickly. It was then I felt an element of magic contained within them. Immediately I felt light-headed and dizzy, and sensed my hand burning. I wanted to release the bones there and then but feared the guards would swipe them and trample them to dust. The nauseating wave of drowsiness remained firmly with me.

The first guard vacated that instant leaving his partner leaning against the doorframe idly peering through the torrential downpour out into the courtyard. I wished in the entire kingdom he would just drop down dead and leave me. Although it was an unholy act to consider I truly feared for my life and fretted working under the rules of Beladon, and if there was any glimmer of opportunity to escape, I would seize it readily at any cost.

'Oh master, I need you now more than at any other moment.'

My innermost prayer seemed pathetic but I was desperate. Treggedon promised he would be watching over me and yet I was alone, shackled and unable to deliver my warning to the king almighty.

The guard's cough broke my reflection. He did so again a few moments later and again and then again. I looked on silently only to watch my hands slowly wrap around his throat. He began gasping for air as my hands constricted around his neck. The gripping asphyxiation forced his eyes to bulge and face drain of blood into a dull and deathly grey. Slowly, with my hands unremitting their grip, he slid down the doorframe yet oddly and in the same moment, I was sitting against the wall merely as an observer and trying to reach him but the fetters restrained me and I could only watch helplessly until his body toppled motionless. I sat open-mouthed in disbelief.

'Do not look so shocked, it is after all what you wanted.'

A voice spoke and so distinct I turned around fully expecting to see another person within the room but there was no other and rapidly concluded it be my own thoughts. My grip on the bones induced a sudden cramp in my clenched hand signalling the realisation of what power they bestow and blew upon the sting of my burning palm.

"God in heaven," I whispered, "what have I done?"

I sat and sobbed aloud into my cupped hands though not through remorse at the death of the guard but out of trepidation for myself. I fail to recall how long I sat in the room crying but it seemed hours and would have seemed even longer had the other guard not returned. He was horrified discovering his deceased partner and his eyes met mine in a collision of mistrust. I remained seated and merely shrugged my shoulders in equal bewilderment.

"What say you lad and tell me what has happened here?" he demanded angrily while searching his companion as if for some evidence of his death.

"It was a while ago not shortly after you left. He caught his breath and choked but I was unable to help him," I grinned rattling my chains to prove my innocence in the calamity.

The guard shook the lifeless body of his comrade as if needing further confirmation he was very much dead. He had no choice other than to believe me and though true, he would never establish I was the instigator of such an act. He approached warily and wrenched at my bindings inspecting they were secure, scowling long and hard at me as if in doubt.

"Who are you boy?" he asked in an exaggerated whisper.

I shrugged my shoulders retaining a tight grip on the bones still within in my burning palm. His face leered closer to mine stooping barely inches away and I dared not to blink goading him to stare me out.

"If you hide anything from me I will thrust my blade into your worthless heart!"

"I am telling you the truth, he died choking."

The guard moved away giving me the chance to breathe fresh air again. His breath was by far worse than the back end of a hog.

After short contemplation, he disappeared and swiftly I secreted the bones under my tunic. It was a matter of minutes before he returned accompanied by two more guards. They removed the dead man by dragging his spent body by the arms and transferring him to a cart, well at least I assume so, I did not actually see it but heard the crack of a whip and heavy wheels pull away.

The guard sat wordlessly by the doorway amid a pool of rainwater trickling from his clothing until the arrival of Beladon.

"Do I hear right?" he asked with a deep-set scowl.

"Yes," responded the guard simultaneously and rising to his feet. "I have quizzed the boy who said he died from choking. There is no other explanation sire. I have checked his chains and they remain secure. The boy is innocent of any ill deed."

Beladon leered at me and his intent look gave no reflection of what he must have been thinking. He turned facing the guard.

"The king has arrived and the rear division are entering the gate."

"Good," the guard scoffed, "then soon you will be lord."

"Indeed so my faithful friend and not too soon enough," Beladon grinned.

Did this conspiracy have no bounds? Therefore, with Talteth as king, Beladon was to become lord of Wendatch.

"Come," said Beladon, "it is time to greet the king. Boy make ready, for tonight you will serve the new king and me, and remember, falter just once and you will join your dead master …in hell!"

I surely winced at his threat knowing well enough this tyrant was all too capable of honouring his words.

"Sir," I responded indifferently, "I shall not fail."

"Then let it be so," he said concluding his caution.

I was unbound and trusted to remain close to my new master's side, this I did readily though not without inward protest. It seemed pointless to slip off now the king had arrived in Wendatch and infiltrating the keep as aid to Beladon was my finest opportunity to warn him of the impending threat.

We walked to the steps of the keep, sodden from the relentless rain and joined Talteth and his associates seated under the heavy canvas. To his right Beladon stood with two of the king's sentries and immediately to his left his faithful black lurcher laid sprawled beside another two guards. Under instruction, I remained two steps further down and at the very edge of the awning, suffering the continual trickle of rainwater funnelling along the canvas ribbing and down the back of my shoulders. The wind blew periodically, whipping more rain into my face and making me feel even colder.

I stood motionless with my empty gaze upon the square and imagined sitting in my master's apothecary by the hearth with its warm radiance blushing my face and there next to me, Treggedon slumped in his chair soaking his feet in hot water I would have prepared, containing all the essences he wished to ease his aching. Cloves, mint and wild parsley all soothing his flesh in a timeless fortitude satisfied too of a full belly having previously dined on mutton and turnips. Then to sit in the depth of silence ruptured only by the crackling flames from the fire, musing perhaps on my achievements that particular day and indeed, looking forward to another morrow before my master appeals for his last goblet of wine signalling my time to retire for the night.

David Greely

The clonking hooves through the courtyard broke my contemplation, gesturing commencement of the procession and the streets and alleyways rapidly choked with people eager to greet the king irrespective of the weather. The straw painstakingly laid throughout the last few days lay torpid and sodden. Horses filed through in pairs with riders donned in the familiar deep crimson of the almighty's colour and banners heralding the black eagle high above the gathering horde, appearing richer in tone brought by the wetness. Guards seemingly undeterred with their plumes hanging lank and matted over their faces, weaved through the yard, assembling neatly to await their king. The whole procession took at least one hour to conclude before the king rode in dressed in the same garb as his retinue save for his white plumed headdress. The wish tower bell pealed, startling the roosting crows to flight and horns blew, verifying his arrival with deafening blasts. Talteth rose from his chair deliberately kicking his napping dog.

"People of Wendatch," he declared turning his head slowly to incorporate the assembling mass, "hail your lord the almighty. Hail king Arbereth, king of the realm! Bless this day and all days."

The king approached and controlled his steed to a gradual halt.

"Greetings," the king smiled with noticeable delight.

"Wendatch and its people welcome you sire," beamed Talteth descending the steps.

"Citizens and followers of the faith I bid you my greetings and I am honoured by your presence," hailed the king rising off his saddle.

"Pray father," insisted the lord, "rest your limbs and retreat from this inclemency. I have prepared good food and a fine stock of wine is at your disposal."

Talteth then bowed slightly and waved his arm toward the double doors of the keep.

"The honour is mine," responded the king.

A guard from the retinue sped to the king's horse and grasped the reins allowing the almighty to hook his leg over the saddle and dismount with relative ease. Talteth walked toward the king, hugged him and his father patted his shoulder with equal affection.

"How fares it son?" enquired the king.

"All is well," Talteth replied.

"Excellent!" remarked the king. "Now, about this wine…"

"…Excuse my manners father, come," Talteth gesticulated with his arm, "I will lead the way."

Talteth and Arbereth walked with shoulders embraced up the steps and the guards, Beladon and I bowed as they passed.

My mind challenged a plan of warning all the while the eyes of the treacherous pretenders watched me. Up until this moment, my only contemplation had been the murder of my master and indeed the demise of the guard that knowingly had I somehow caused.

"Come boy it is time to perform your duties and remember my expectancy," Beladon reiterated gripping my arm fiercely.

He proceeded the way for me to follow repressed between three guards, amid the great commotion when the almighty turned to wave prior to entering the keep.

Inside the great hall, the king and Talteth sat beside the long dining table with the throng of guards as ever, close by and I stood patiently behind them daring not to eavesdrop. Soon the wine flowed freely and the torrent of segregated chatter filled the hall. The king spoke above the great din.

"Before we dine I must change. The weather has won its day over me."

"Forgive me. Serf!" Talteth called to one of the servants insisting he show the king to his quarters.

"The ride has sapped my strength," added the king. "I will rest awhile but tonight I shall be ready for merriment."

"As you wish father," submitted Talteth, "I will have you called for the feast."

"It is good to see you again. A year for a father not seeing his son is far too long an age," said Arbereth.

"The same sentiment father," said the lord.

"God bless you," said the king finally rising and followed the servant out of the hall.

The sickly grin on Talteth's face confirmed to me the treachery Treggedon had first mentioned.

"Take your lad Beladon, his ears must be away from my words," he said.

"Sire," replied my new master complying with his order and led me directly to the kitchen.

"Dry yourself boy," he demanded. "You'll be of little use to me with the lurgy. And do not dare wander off!"

I nodded to him in good faith as he departed. It pleased me to be away from him again and this was an opportunity to think without any interruption of a plan to foil Talteth. I sat near the fire sampling the generous heat that made my garments steam like a boiling pot and gradually the dampness left me for the warmth I much sought. I remained watching the cooks and servants busying themselves oblivious of my presence. The kitchen aroma was rich with roasting meats and an open spit had sucklings speared to its bar. On one side of the hearth laid a heap of bread warming and opposite, a cauldron of potato and swede simmered gently. Large salvers lay on benches laden with cold cooked geese, salted mutton, various fruits and countless pitchers of ale stacked by the doorway, awaiting transportation to the hall. It promised to be a grand feast.

Darkness arrived early brought about by the dullness of the day and influencing the early commencement to the proceedings. Eventually, I was called to the great hall where ordered to serve only Beladon and his immediate company. Benches fully laden with the prepared food set around the entire hall perimeter and his majesty's table positioned nearest to the blazing hearth festooned with all manner of meats and vegetables. Talteth sat to the right of the king at one end and my master with his guard positioned at the other. It was here I was to remain for Beladon's contentment. Gradually the hall filled with the nobility of Wendatch followed by the king's own guards and the place began shuddering with the active idioms of the numerous guests. Talteth gave toast to his father and the mass responded by raising their vessels in tribute and pledging fealty. The king reciprocated by hoisting his own chalice with a simple gesture of endorsement.

Folk were like pigs at a trough the whole damned contingent, with their gluttonous want and ravishing, grasping hands tearing the flesh from carcasses and ripping the bread apart like aged parchment. Mouths gaped with incurable and insatiable lust filling their cheeks to the point of bursting. Wine and ale followed the food making them barely able to swallow and some one way or another managed to converse despite drooling and dribbling particles of food over their mouths matting those who sported beards with regurgitated sodden morsels. Little etiquette was evident while the ravenous multitude greedily ate and slurps, belches, coughs and extraneous gases resonated within, why even Talteth's dog possessed better manners than most! I stood tolerantly behind my master awaiting the chance of any food being availed but none came.

After a lengthy discourse, serfs cleared the spent carcasses amid a riotous chorus of belching and songs that billowed in a dull off-key commotion. Talteth clapped his hands and immediately silence prevailed. Momentarily, a troupe of jugglers and a brace of musicians filled the central area and performed their diverse acts. Minstrels too mingled about the guests, strumming their wasted melodies above the drone of imprudent mannerisms. I surveyed Talteth intently waiting for the slightest sign from him that would ignite the fuse of his treachery. Still I had not devised a plan to warn the king but I had to soon, for time was surely running thin and I feared for his life. A turn of event followed giving me the ideal opportunity.

Beladon insisted I fetch him water for his cleansing thus sending me back to the kitchen by way of crossing the hall to the door. I felt embarrassed having to stride directly across the line of performers, so opted to make my way around the perimeter.

"Where are you off to boy?" Talteth's blunt tone stopped me instantly some eight feet from him.

"I am to fetch water for my master," I said in earnest.

"Then hurry along and be smart about your business," he advised stridently.

"Sir," I bowed courteously.

"Impetuous young lad Talteth, who is he?" the king asked.

"Arton, boy to Beladon," the lord replied.

"Arton you say?" quizzed the king scratching his brow.

Arbereth appeared seemingly bemused at the sight of me exhibiting a strange expression as if I deemed some recollection to him. Never before had I come this close to the almighty nonetheless, something seemed to awaken his memory and was not going to let this opportunity slip now.

"I was apprenticed to Treggedon," I said insolently.

"Mind your manners boy and be off!" Talteth warned sharply.

I did as instructed but dallied in my pace.

"He is a handful that lad," joked Talteth.

"What of Treggedon?" I heard the king question. "Why is he not in attendance?"

Talteth wasted no time in responding.

"Regrettably he is dead. He died yesterday. Age I am sorry to say caught up with him. He was a dear and trusted friend to me and the realm."

"Indeed," agreed Arbereth. "He and I go back a very long time."

The king's mild tone suddenly changed to a suggestion of irritation.

"Why was I not informed of his death when I first arrived?" he asked.

"Father I did not see the need to tell you earlier because you were tired. His burial will be two days hence."

"Nevertheless," insisted the almighty, "I should have been informed. Surely he must have been ill prior?"

"It happened so suddenly one moment we were drinking wine together and later that day he was lifeless. It was both sudden and untimely. He really was looking forward to your coming."

Talteth was beginning to redden with guilt.

"Yet despite him being a good and trusted friend I only find out now? Did you not see the sense in informing me beforehand? Was I not just a few leagues from Wendatch?"

I could perceive the king was irritated.

"I apologise father. My intention of informing you of the ill news temporarily escaped my attention what with all the preparation of your coming –I mean what with the feast and all…" the king interrupted Talteth's pathetic response.

"…Yes, a fine feast."

I cursed Talteth and his devious words for he successfully turned the matter of asking onto a completely different vein.

"And the performers, they are excellent don't you agree? All from the kingdom and later we have a dancer from Laddia…"

I refused to listen to any more, so sickened was my feeling of Talteth's artfulness and the chance of speaking to the king eluded me. Did I have any option but to resort to shouting aloud my warning?

I made my way to the kitchen, filled a pitcher with fresh water from the well, grabbed a dry cloth from the table and went to turn back toward the door but my attention stirred when glancing back toward the table. I initiated fresh inspiration when looking at the spent carcasses lay piled and thought of my secreted bones. Quickly I set the jug down, fondled inside my tunic for the cloth and tentatively clutched the tiny bones before making my wish.

"What you doing there laddie?" enquired a guard appearing from nowhere.

The surprise caused my hesitancy.

"I…I am fetching water for my master."

His glance caught sight of the bones in my hand.

"And dining at the same time eh?" he interrogated sarcastically.

"I was hungry sir, please, I meant no wrong," I defended pathetically.

"Go on be off with you!" he fumed.

David Greely

   I bowed respectfully, picked up the ewer and sped out of the kitchen through the doorway clutching tightly the tiny bones within my burning palm.

Chapter Three

The great hall choked with combined pungencies of wine, food and body odours; not that a gathering on this scale would create anything less but when one walks into a stinking room having previously sampled fresh air it does have a tendency to make one wretch. Dancers and other such various performers had since diminished leaving a lone minstrel piping his drab levity upon his wooden flute. The assembly now consisted of smaller clusters of realmsfolk laughing and shouting in a drunken revel and at the head table, which remained my prime interest seemed equally indulgent in nothingness. Beladon and three guards teased one another with points; a painful game particularly for the novice, performed as a piteous display of courage in which one grasps a dagger and stabs its point rapidly between the opponents spanned hand spread flatly upon a table in the hope of missing his fingers. The king and his son indulged in their own private conversation and I could sense Talteth's evil plan unfolding.

David Greely

Throughout their lengthy dialogue, Talteth kept filling his father's goblet in a calculative bid to render him useless and though Arbereth appeared intoxicated, it was not enough for his sons' wishing. I had to act before the conspiracy developed further and having placed the cloth and pitcher at the side of Beladon took leave whilst he remained engrossed in the childish practice and walked slowly toward Talteth.

"Please forgive my intrusion my lord but may I have the honour of performing my act for you?" I asked apprehensively.

"Go away boy! I am bored with dancers and jugglers," he disapproved flaying his arms wildly.

"Pray lord it is nothing of such nature as yet seen and is something very unique," I persisted keeping my gaze upon the king.

"Are you deaf? I said be off with you!" Talteth shouted halting conversations in the near vicinity.

"Wait," intruded the almighty, restricting Talteth's thrashing arm, "this may prove entertaining."

The king leant forward onto his elbows proffering an affable smile.

"And this act of yours…." he continued with interest.

"…Sire," I interrupted excitedly, "I will not mar my performance by telling, just cast your eyes and marvel at the forthcoming spectacle."

"Hear me everyone," shouted Talteth loud enough to awaken the souls of every dead man that lay under the soil, "the boy here is going to perform his act…"

He stopped briefly, rubbed his chin and broke into a crooked grin forcing me to avert my gaze from him.

"…and what if we are not satisfied with his act?" the lord continued.

"Hang him!" bellowed a suggestion from a far table behind me.

"Then quarter him!" yelled another amidst escalating laughter.

"Let him join that old fool Treggedon," condemned Beladon before others roared their calls for my reparation.

Beladon's comment cut deep and stung like an arrow piercing my heart. Yes, I would have loved to join my master but under God's terms and not his and 'as far as fool, we will soon establish who is to be the fool Beladon!' I threatened under my breath.

My mind contested for inspiration to avenge Treggedon's death but the continual shouts of impatience from the throng broke such contemplation and I stood isolated in the centre of the hall besieged by the eyes of the watchers with their piercing stares and only those men too intoxicated to raise their heads spared additional consternation. I shivered, palpitating in fear should my act falter.

"Come lad get on with it!" yelled a guard from the king's table.

I responded to his prompt.

"My lords...," words stuck in my throat forcing me to cough and recommence. "...My lords I wish to perform for you in honour of my master Treggedon."

"I'm your master now!" shouted Beladon assertively.

"With respect sir I shall rephrase," I said. "My late master..."

"...That's better," approved Beladon wryly reseating himself and allowing me to continue.

"Most of you are aware of Treggedon's trait and I being his apprentice such skills have been bestowed onto me thus to prove this gift I call upon a volunteer."

No one responded and I gave it a short while before repeating my request.

"I cannot perform without a volunteer."

"Go on Beladon he's your lad, you are his master so you do it," the king promoted.

Beladon sat in reluctance despite the increase of goading. Consequently, all the spectators demanded for him to stand with me as volunteer and with eventual disinclination, rose staggering drunkenly toward to me.

"May I have a cloth?" I asked.

David Greely

Talteth responded first, throwing the cover from the back of his chair, which I accepted with a bow and continued.

"I shall now blindfold my master."

I displayed the open cloth for examination, twisting it one way then the other before fastening it firmly around my subject's eyes assuring myself of his sightlessness. I took hold of his cuff and paraded him slowly around the hall leaving him facing the king's table amidst a hail of whoops and profanities developing from the interested throng. I waited for the din to subside before continuing and aimed my asking directly at the king.

"Sire, please hold something toward my master."

Readily he grasped his chalice and held it aloft.

I must add at this juncture, what was about to occur I had never performed before. Treggedon never taught me nor had he demonstrated it and yet somehow I felt compelled to do the act even though I was uncertain of subsequent action. Nothing premeditated you understand, just an unknown force coercing me.

"Master," I turned facing him, "what is it that the almighty holds afore you?"

"A vessel," he declared immediately.

"Anyone could have guessed that," shouted a rebuke from one of the assembled.

"True enough," I retorted turning my attention back to the king.

"Sire, might I suggest you try something a little more adventurous."

The king sat a trifle perplexed and his frowning brow concealed a mind striving through an intoxicated haze to bring something else to bear. At last, he presented a fine bracelet and waved it above his head for all to see.

"Excellent!" I remarked.

"Now master," I asked Beladon, "what does the king present?"

As soon as asked, he swiftly replied.

"I believe it to be a bracelet adorned with a stag's head."

It was very uncanny for even I was not close enough to notice the carving upon it.

Most of the assembly were pleased with my act despite intermittent grunts of impatient uncertainty.

"Sir," I called to one doubter, "perhaps you possess something that can be put to the test?"

The stranger stood and before he had time to produce his object, Beladon identified it.

"A studded dagger," he confirmed smiling.

The contingent sat in muted astonishment as they witnessed the man producing his dagger with a white bone handle studded in bronze and silver. The almighty broke the quiet with a generous applause prompting others to follow, adding their whistles, hoots and howls of enjoyment. Then it happened.

My acquired master untied the cloth from his head and emitted a terrifying shriek.

"What is happening, I cannot see? Why can I not see? This is trickery! Help me someone!"

Beladon's guard dashed to his aid as he spun helplessly around rubbing his eyes in alarm.

'Dear God in heaven what have I done for I fail to understand?'

Initially I did not but all the while Beladon flapped around it began making sense. I sought revenge for his trickery by pretending to be blind and now with my reprisal rewarded he became the victim of his own callous action. Inwardly I was now content, satisfied I may have conquered the merit of my beloved master although quickly reconsidered that it was Treggedon's desire, but either way settled willingly upon the circumstance conceding through me, Treggedon somehow cast his own spell because I alone was incapable of such a power. How pathetic of me to believe or aspire I held such divine power, surely, another lesson learnt.

The guard set upon me grabbing my arm constricting the blood from my veins and the almighty looked sternly at me when our eyes met in the confusion. What transpired lost all favour with him and judging his anger my fate was about to be sealed. If the king was to show any hint of mercy then life in shackles was the least I could expect though death more probable.

"Sire let me slit his throat," suggested the guard that held me, "least of all spike his worthless body!"

"Burn him!" insisted another. "He is not righteous and is the devil's own child - a witch, and he must be burned!"

A tumult demanding my execution reverberated around the hall accentuated by stamping feet and clenched fists and vessels banging on tabletops.

"Burn him! Burn him!" The crowd wailed in unison.

I looked on helplessly knowing my pitiful life was about to be curtailed.

"Sire," I shouted my plea, "I had no idea of this outcome."

"Silence!" the king decreed. "Your tongue has done enough damage thus I command that in the morrow at noon it will be severed from your mouth before you die by flame."

"Let me amend the trouble I have caused," I begged.

"Boy you will say and do nothing more. Take him away!"

"But sire you don't understand. Your life is in peril and I did it for you. Your own son plots against your life this very night. Heed me I implore you."

"Silence your tongue!" he upheld, failing to absorb my warning.

The guard's hand clouted my ear with incredible force and blood trickled down my jawbone.

"Take him away, lock him in irons and gag his foul mouth!" Talteth commanded.

Chapter Four

The guard held my scruff tightly, forcing me down the steep well of spiralling steps and the flickering torch mounted on the damp wall revealed the sickly bowels of the keep below, sending a chilling reminder of the prospect ahead me. I managed to shake off the gag around my mouth and emitted a lengthy scream for mercy.

"There is little point screaming," he smirked, "no-one will hear your cries down here -not even the dead."

The guard's discouraging words accompanied by another slap to my head curtailed any further intent from me, my feeble resistance had me thrown indiscriminately and locked into a chamber. I leant against the corroding bars replete in self-pity and fear of my imminent death barely twelve hours away, hanging over me like a leaden shroud. In my heart, I wanted to be close to the king to repeat my warning to him but that chance had vanished and I sat alone listening to the dissipating track of the guard ascending the steps, taking no comfort in the fact that I still possessed the tiny bones.

God it stank. The rusting iron grill high upon the wall oozed decay and the damp stone floor harboured all manner of despicable creatures seemingly content in wallowing in this putrid domain. Dried excrement lay in one corner like a peculiar stalagmite crusted and fetid; proof well enough others had been here before me. What of them now, had they taken their turn on the secret gallows and who were they? Hapless victims and undoubtedly innocent for there were not nor had there ever been transgressors in Wendatch to my knowledge. Admittedly, there were petty crimes such as pilfering or swindling but nothing warranting this perdition. Above the intermittent dripping of seepage through the wall, faint groans echoed and though attempting to search the direction of their source I failed to conclude whence they came.

Realisation struck of the feasible atrocities Talteth was answerable to in his short term at Wendatch attesting he is not the kind-hearted lord the people believed but an odious and callous deviant of the devil. Did nobody else see it and unveil the thin mantle Talteth wore? 'God in heaven,' I pleaded silently, 'I beseech you to give me the wisdom if good is ever to prevail again.'

My aching limbs bore testimony to a long arduous day and despite my effort it led to nothing but the sealing of my death, perhaps if I had been more resourceful I could have succeeded in my task. Was it then fate or indeed my own destiny to be locked away in the deathly, stinking pit of the castle or perchance to await a new direction from the Good Lord?

In the hopelessness, I considered taking my own life so forlorn was I, not wanting to give the enemy the satisfaction of killing me yet my pathetic attempt at self-strangulation merely left me spluttering and gasping for breath.

I sat dejected for countless hours daring not to sleep for fear of waking to the dawn, the daylight that was to bring my ending. I stared at the high slit on the opposite wall portraying itself as a window barely a stone in width and way beyond reach. It might as well have been solid wall for what worth it was to me. In an effort to remain awake and keep warm, I paced around the cell perimeter. Unwittingly I tightened my grip on the bones in my palm and with the burning came a voice gentle as the warmest summer's breeze whispering in the damp stagnant air.

"Rabbit," the calming voice called to me.

"Master?" I questioned with self-doubt. 'This cannot be. Master? No, you are dead!'

"Rabbit, hear me."

"I do master but..." I looked around in the dimness unable to distinguish any shape other than the grill bars and walls imprisoning me. "...I cannot see you. Where are you?"

In the long silence that followed, I continued to search in the gloom but still saw nothing. Again, I called out to him.

"Where are you?"

"I am here boy, right here."

The sudden draught touching my face sent bumps all over my flesh and so cold it felt like the touch of death itself.

"I still cannot see you master," I sobbed desperately searching for him.

"Arton," his whisper came again, "have you learnt?"

"Learnt?" I questioned despondently.

Of course, I had 'learnt!' I knew all too much that day; deceit, despair, mistrust, treachery, pain and even magic but supposed my master referred to none of these.

"Belief, Rabbit. Belief."

"Master I am trying."

"Then try harder," he pressed.

Surely, I believed good enough. I believed in the miscarriage of unfairness and deemed that in the morrow I will be dead.

"Understand this boy," his voice continued, "believe in what you need and you shall have. Wanting and desiring are very much different."

Still I searched for him though without reward.

"Please, will you not show yourself to me?"

"I am where you want me to be. In your head, in your heart or in your soul…"

"…I want you here, here with me right now."

"But I am, can you not hear me?"

"Yes but…"

"…I know, you cannot see."

I nodded my head in dejected confirmation.

"Then believe you can see and thus you shall."

I sought hard in the nefariousness of my imprisonment looking for him if only to glimpse his kindly face once more and to rid the grey contorted image instilled at the sight of his demise. The gentle tap upon my shoulder made me leap out of my skin and I shrieked in wonder.

"Master!" I sighed with eyes welling with renewed tears.

Treggedon stood afore me scarcely at arms distance and as true as life. I dared not to throw scepticism at his vision for fear of him disappearing, knowing I had to believe. Slowly I reached out to him slumping to his feet but despite my touch I could not feel flesh and he was no more than an apparition.

"Master what is happening? I am trying to understand but…"

"…Arton there was much more I wanted to say and teach but alas my time with you was curtailed all too abruptly, nonetheless I have been granted divinity for this brief moment on this earth…"

"…I have failed you master."

"Hush Rabbit there is no time for recompense, just listen to my words. You have determined the wishbones have power and that is in your favour but do remember improper use of them could render you useless and may even prove your downfall, thus you must respect and use them wisely and only at a moment when all else fails.

Now back to the task in hand. The king still lives, although come daybreak I suspect that will change therefore you still have the chance to warn him."

"I did try master but my failing led me here."

"Your application in warning the king was shall I say, a little unconstructive and whilst I understood your action against Beladon you deviated from your task by allowing revenge to overpower your wisdom. Always let your head rule your actions Arton and not your heart; this is a lesson you must learn for the future if you or the kingdom is to survive. You accept embracing the magic so use it wisely and cautiously. Remember your heart is for feelings, not for actions and consider looking no deeper than the obvious for your answers. By studying everything around you, the solution you seek will always be there…

…perhaps I should demonstrate."

My master exuded a brilliance that lit the cell, highlighting what I imagined as being a dead and rotting rodent. The walls where layered with a sopping vivid green slime and the floor covered in a moving carpet of repugnant insects.

"What do you see Arton?" he asked.

"Only death and decay, and the creatures beneath my feet, no wait there is more - a rat, or at least I think it is, but now has disappeared through that hole," I verified, pointing to a crack between the stones where the creature went.

"That is good, now reflect upon it. The hole in which the rat scampered through, take note of the aspect. Now, remember the size of our friend, was the creature not at least three times bigger than its escape hatch?"

"Yes but…," before I could question my master's logic he continued.

"…There you are lad, the rat believed it could get through and it succeeded effortlessly."

I stared at the cavity trying to grasp Treggedon's lesson but the dimming light impaired my study and I turned to realise the image of my master had faded.

"By all means follow your heart Arton but decide with your head."

"Master!" my call for his return resonated in vain.

His brief visitation left me cold and wanting, staring blindly into the pitch hoping he had only temporarily vanished, but I

David Greely

was wrong. After some time I regained my wits thinking of my immediate future and took my lesson from the rat. Tightening my hold on the bones again, I approached the grill bars, concentrating on the rusting iron encapsulating me. With a deep exhale, I squeezed between the rails and once through returned the bones inside my tunic. I was uncertain of my achievement but sensed the gap widened and I got smaller. I cannot even begin to explain; it just happened that way, but then such is the power of pure magic that I chose not question but merely accept it readily.

I returned my concentration to the matter in hand, focusing on my escape, for I would surely die but not without first getting to the almighty. Reaching the king would now prove relatively simple considering I was already within the walls of the keep but convincing him I feared would be far more challenging.

The flickering tapers hitched to the walls gave me guidance through my torment and repeatedly I peered through narrow grills and portholes of craggy doors seeking the source of the constant moan that returned to defy the stillness of the dungeon. Every cell contained age-old rusting chains threaded through iron rings inset into thick stone suspending from the walls and one in particular clamped the fleshless arm bone of its victim. Tattered corpses best described as half- naked, littered many walls and although dim, trusted what I saw with my own eyes and it petrified me. A man was in severe pain and such were the victim's groans I felt compelled to find him but despite my hurried search, unable to locate him. I could ill-afford to waste further time and needed to reach the king, though promising myself however to return once I secured the almighty's safety.

Carefully and quietly, I trudged up the sapping steps back toward the great hall stopping on many occasions to catch my breath and avoid noisy gasps in my breathlessness. Already I noticed my fatigue since using the bones; they spent my energy at an alarming rate. Nearing the top of the steps the air filled with the pungency of exhausted poppy oil causing me to rasp even heavier and feared my rapid breaths would attract unwanted attention. I slipped through the break in the heavy drapes hanging across the access leading to the hall, sneaking by the sleeping guard snorting and smacking his lips. The keep remained silent save for the flickering tapers spitting random crackles and the thumping of my anxious heart. Drunken bodies littered the hall, some slumped over tables and benches and others propped discourteously against walls. I crept within the confines of the dense shadows meticulously searching for the king among the strewn, but fortunately, he had since departed, avoiding me the daunting prospect of explaining the fate awaiting him. He would take some convincing and our voices would surely stir someone.

With renewed relief, I ventured into the passage along the far end of the hall. The awaiting ascent wound equally steep as those from the dungeon and clambered up the long gruelling steps until finally reaching the corridor leading to the bedding chambers. At the top, an open doorway led into a long passageway with ten doors. One of these housed the king for sure as did those quartering Talteth and his evil conspirators. I hoped I was not too late to save the almighty. The doors seemed shut firm, giving me no clue as to which room the king resided and my new dilemma left me floundering in uncertainty. I was rapidly running out of time and already the haze of daylight must be breaking the darkness of the passing night. Soon, very soon, life would overwhelm the quiet and with no place for me to hide, I had little option but to chance my luck. I skulked slowly along the stone passageway looking and listening intently at every door in turn, waiting for my gut feeling to indicate the room his grace occupied but it was hopeless, so I resorted upon the wishbones. As I tucked my hand inside my garment, footsteps echoed from the far stairwell superseded by a deep shadowed figure of a house guard.

"Halt!"

His shout was long and loud.

Quickly I pulled my hand away from my tunic and darted along the passage with the guard in pursuit, intending to make him follow me away from the chambers to avoid stirring those in their slumber. I continued to run back through the drape and pressed directly against the wall, holding my breath long enough to avoid detection until the guard passed and ran further along to a linking passageway. I backtracked into the corridor, again stopping at the first chamber on my left and slowly twisting the iron ring, pushed the door open and entered. My eyes took some while adjusting to the darkness and at first unable to see any shapes but with inner calmness the feeble silhouettes within the room gradually emerged. I renewed my original intention by grasping the bones ready to use them at an instant should I have chosen wrongly. I approached the bed listening avidly to the snoring heap slumbering under the mound of furs but it was impossible to tell whom and I dare not stir him until certain it was the king himself. I sat on the ledge of the window clutching the bones, ready to leap off and drown in the moat below if necessary. I settled and waited for the approaching day eager, now for the sunrise to give me better light. God in heaven help me if I faced not that of the almighty.

The passing minutes eased the dimness until dawn finally arrived heralded by the incessant cawing of the crows hoisting themselves high into the air above the tower. I had not seen the land from this height before, the vista far more rewarding than from the hills that looked flatly beyond. I observed the developing mist created by the sunrise, remaining upon the sill until the wish tower became engulfed before returning my attention to the bed to face my moment of reckoning. The body lay motionless under the gathered pelts.

"Sire!" I called to the sleeping man in a nervous and exaggerated whisper.

I repeated my call again a little louder. His stir, followed by a groan fuelled my anxiety but thankfully, fate was kind to me for it was Arbereth true enough. It occurred to me either the bones or my master's influence led me to this particular room but as God as witness, I was truly grateful. His weathered hands peeled back the furs revealing his full craggy face, heavy-eyed and dishevelled. He sat upright fingering back his age-bleached hair away from his face.

"Sire I am in need to speak with you urgently," I said dropping from the sill and hastening toward him.

"God in heaven boy you are supposed to be in irons!" he gasped with surprise.

"Sire your life is threatened."

"Guard!" he yelled.

"Please listen to me I beg you."

"You are not worthy! Who are you or more precisely, what are you boy?"

"Your grace please just hear me," I continued, rapidly ready to plunge straight out of the window should anyone enter the room.

"My master insisted I warn you. You must trust me."

"Why should I?" he questioned.

"Your life is threatened. There is a plot to overthrow you. Even as we speak, they come for you. They are going to kill you this very morning."

"Foolish! Why would anyone want to kill me? I have no enemies nor quarrel with any man of the realm."

"My lord..." I hesitated.

If I were to disclose his own son as the instigator of his death, he would certainly disbelieve me more so.

"...Beladon," I continued, "and his cohorts have plotted against you. That is why I did what I did last evening to delay him and give myself time to reach you."

"How many have you killed to get to me?"

"None sire I escaped simply enough."

"If what you say is true then I will summon Talteth, he will deal with him and his murderous dogs!"

"Sire," I sighed with reluctance, "it is your own son that is the cause, he wants to rule the realm."

"Boy if I had my sword I would kill you this instant!" he declared clenching his fists.

David Greely

"That would be futile my lord, it will not stop him or the others, besides, I have the possession of magic and could turn your blade into …well, anything!"

That in itself was true and he knew now what I was capable of doing having witnessed my spell on Beladon.

"Lord, all I ask is that you come with me and afford me time to prove my words."

"If you possess such magic then surely you can thwart such intention."

"I know not how and cannot avert a plot that has yet to be put into action."

"Hold back there boy, you are confusing me with your words."

"Please accompany me and if I am wrong then you have the right to slay me. I will not hold any magic against your judgment.

People of the realm honour your wisdom and fairness so prove them right and allow me this opportunity my lord."

He got off his bed smoothing down his rumpled garment.

"Very well lad but God help you if…"

"…Your majesty please we must hurry, this way."

I motioned with my arm toward the door and grabbed his wrist pulling him with me.

"But I am not dressed," he protested.

"We will get suitable clothes in a while. Come, this way!"

I opened the door slowly, peering through the gap, examining the stillness of the dim passage and led the king directly to the stairwell. I had quite overlooked the king's age and his wheezing reminded me thus and slowed my pace to allow him to gain his breath.

"I do not know why I am trusting you boy," the king panted.

"Shh …quietly now, we are approaching the hall."

My objective was to run to the kitchen and out of the side door but the appearance of another guard averted our course back toward the dungeon.

"In God's name where are we going?"

"We have no choice but to the dungeon."

Just as we sneaked through the archway, Talteth, with his company of guards entered the great hall.

"My son how could he?" the king mumbled shaking his head side to side in dismay.

I ushered him down the winding steps conscious of the stirring above us for surely it would only be a few more moments before the alarm rang out for the missing king and have them scurrying to check on me in my cell.

The continual lament of the victim I heard earlier resounded again on our approach to the depths of the keep and regardless of the king's safety, his dulcet tones prompted me yet again to liberate him.

We reached the firmly bolted door of my old cell.

"I know not what you have in mind boy but there is no escape from down here."

"Sire I shall get you freedom by magic," I said confidently pointing to the narrow window at the back of the cell.

"What, through there," he gasped, "that is impossible!"

"Not with my magic your grace," I smiled.

I gripped the bones and...

...well just began believing.

I concentrated on the grill with deepening breaths, watching Arbereth rise from the floor amid whimpering claims of consternation and drift toward the narrow slits. His body then contorted into the same elongated shape and slowly disappeared through the gap. As the king, I inched through the grill into the cell in the same manner.

"Now sire," I continued, motioning him to one corner, "wait here a short while and I will secure our passage out of Wendatch."

I wished on the bones again and within moments was through the window and up to my neck in reeking stagnant water. The window was an ell's length above the moat's level and in full view of the road. I savoured a little instant to accustom my eyes to the bright daylight and without hesitation drifted

David Greely

slowly across the moat's staleness daring not to cause a ripple along the keep's perimeter water.

The groans from the victim inside the wall grew louder and when approaching another slit to peer through I could not see the wretched man. I scrambled through the gap replacing the bones into my sodden tunic.

In God's name, what I saw made me choke in repugnance. It was little wonder I failed to see him when searching previously, for a man hung naked from the ceiling tethered by his wrists and bound to him bunches of nettles which with the slightest movement, sent agonising stings against his bare flesh.

"Damn Talteth!" I cursed aloud.

In my fervour to release the prisoner, I wrenched the torturous plants within reach with my bare hands. My desperate plight impelled the use of the bones again and cast an exhausting spell of shredding the rope that held him, his spent body fell to the floor allowing me to disengage the devil's plants, doing my utmost to comfort him while tearing at them.

I look now at my palms and even to this day, the lumps the nettles administered upon me are still very evident.

I dragged the man over to the cell wall and with the magic managed to get us both through the slit. The water, despite its foulness, eased the stinging from my hands pacifying them enough to tolerate grabbing the prisoner and haul him across to the opposite bank. I lodged him deep in the rushes and returned to the king.

"Sire," I called to him through the window.

"Where have you been?" he asked moving directly below the slit.

"All is well. We must take leave now."

The bones had their usage this day well enough and for the third time they granted Arbereth passage through the stone.

We swam silently across the moat and lay to rest beside the lifeless prisoner in the tall sedge. I watched the sun's glow strike the castle wall while resting though discerned the peace would not prevail long enough to dally and alarm imminent.

With all energy sapped, I needed respite and even if able to summon the strength to move, the king and the prisoner were not, so without preference, lingered for some while.

Chapter Five

Treggedon proved correct about the usage of the bones, they drained my energy and I slept long, dreaming deeply although the incredulous events of the previous few days never came consciously to mind. My reverie of the lush kingdom from early childhood overwhelmed anything else that would dare surface and though grateful for the tranquillity, knew it was only ever going to be a transitory substitute to my situation.

I recollected my studious flair for flowers, in particular experimenting with harmless potions only I would have the courage to try. Even Treggedon found them to be quite useless although unbeknown to him I did manage to slip him a few concoctions by deception, however, while most failed I can boast of a few my master enjoyed. His favourite was meadowsweet I introduced as an accompaniment to mead though he also enjoyed boiled sorrel and pignuts making for a welcome change from the coarseness of turnip. You may consider I digress, but in truth nature is a significant ingredient in understanding magic because many such potions include God's flora and it is something I had to discover. God did not create flowers and roots in this kingdom just to display their pretty blooms or compelling tastes, they all serve a purpose and when no meat or fish avails, flowers become a saviour.

It was not until my thoughts disentangled, stirred by the rumbling of cartwheels did I realise best part of the day had dissipated. My sudden flinch instigated alarm and though it took several minutes to quell, I was relieved to see the king still slumbering at my side. My attention drawn to the prisoner who still lay groaning seemed to surpass my welfare and I questioned my discretion about freeing him, knowing his hindrance would unquestionably jeopardise the king's escape into exile, yet I would never have forgiven myself if choosing to ignore his plight.

The disconcerted shouts echoing from the high walls of the keep verified the urgency of locating the king and me, and I supposed the missing prisoner, although I possessed little concept of the gravity of his crime or for what other possible reason he be held captive. Nevertheless, guards wailed and scurried about the perimeter walls like headless chickens perceptibly disgruntled with their assignment at seeking us out. We remained low and well hidden within the brown and tanned rushes on the moat bank. Horses periodically thundered out from the portcullis in urgency and galloped noisily over the wooden drawbridge before fanning out in different directions across the open fields.

I was uncertain neither of the length waited nor for what duration Talteth and his men searched for us but their hunt now extended beyond the castle's interior. The sun was but a shallow orb with the mist returning to greater density than it had done in the morning, but be sure God was kind to me again for it was a fog thick enough to hide the devil himself.

An open-sided cart rumbled nearby, pulled by a single ox labouring in the sodden earthen tracks caused by the previous day's deluge and though anxious of our discovery, I dare not risk moving now we were so close to freedom. I was content to bide my time and wait for an opportunity soon as dusk fell. Cold and wet apart, I felt inwardly refreshed after my involuntary rest and heaven-blessed by comparison to that of the fetid dungeon.

A command sounded out through the fog bank.

"Search the moat," was his order. "I want them dead!" screeched the now recognisable voice of Talteth.

His tone was cold as frost and heartless as decayed sheep dung, and his chilling demand set terror in me. I nudged the king immediately.

"Lord it is time we moved on," I whispered.

"Don't spare their wretched lives. The king and the boy – I want them both dead!" Talteth iterated.

The king stared open-mouthed into the greyness, finally acknowledging confirmation of his own son's treachery and I witnessed his dread, his tears of renunciation and the utter disbelief conquer him. It was from this moment I had no further anxiety convincing Arbereth I was his only salvation.

"Come my lord, this way," I instructed quietly.

I slipped back into the stagnant water grabbing hold best I could the wretched prisoner still naked, cold and slippery. The king sank down into the moat and helped push the unconscious body while I dragged from behind, not that we could go very far for the moat merely encircled this part of the keep and its tributary to the outer walls far too shallow to swim through. I felt coerced to keep moving and dragging the poor man through the stinking water was much easier than scrambling across land and seemed sensible to aim for the drawbridge. Apart from hiding away from the open, its shadow would prove a temporary haven.

The mutterings of excitement increased as we gradually approached the bridge and commotions of varying degrees bellowed in the still air, activated by the sentry demanding to inspect everyone entering Wendatch and creating a backlog of carts, barrows and confused commoners with their hefty bundles littering the sodden roadside.

"Line up there," instructed the sentinel abrasively, perched high above the portcullis.

"Come on…" confirmed the sentry encouraged by his lieutenant's command, "…you heard him, get in line and wait your turn."

Moans of disdain and gripes of frustration added to the ensuing confusion as merchants and travellers jostled for space in efforts to remain firm. The foot guard pushed two men loitering obstinately despite his order and both plunged from the drawbridge headlong into the water, breaking the slimy blanket weed and setting off a rejuvenated pungency by their disturbance. My heart pounded in fear of discovery by the falling men and contemplated swimming off to save my own skin.

I recall my confusion and the sudden indecision at the priority to save the almighty yet something bothered me and gnawed like an uncontrollable disease spurring me to rescue the near-dead prisoner by putting his life before the king.

The floating body of one of the commoners pushed from the bridge broke my dilemma. I turned his body away from me revealing a gaping wound running from his mouth to his left eye, whether this was done prior to him entering the water by hitting the drawbridge or administered by the angry guard was and is irrelevant, the fact remained he was very much dead. The splashes and strident grunts made by the other man scrambling up the bank confirmed we went undiscovered and calm quickly resumed until the following silence broke when the grinding chains of the drawbridge tensed and slowly hauled the heavy wooden flap of the portcullis.

Although we were by no means safe from danger, I was relieved to think most of the would-be assassins remained within the castle walls and bar the few bands of guards combing the nearby fields gave rise in confidence we would be able to evade them. Sporadic shouts from the men and malcontent snorts from their breathless horses continued to resound in the chilling air until eventually the eagerness of their duties muted to fatigue replacing their enthusiasm and I felt incontestably safer.

David Greely

Progressively, stranded folk unable to access Wendatch began lighting fires along the wayside and small flickering beacons pronounced the contours and staggers of the roadway. The mist condensed into a solid fog perfect for our escape and now darkness finally draped over the land. I hauled myself up the bank keeping my belly to the ground. I dragged the stranger by gripping him under his arms whilst the king pushed at his feet but for the miserable groan sounding from the prisoner, one would have thought him dead. I still cursed at the hindrance I brought upon myself by aiding him but defy any mortal not to have done what I felt compelled to do in saving him. Once the stranger and the king were safely on the bank, I returned to the floating corpse and struggled to free his garments. Though useless sodden, once dry, they would provide adequate warmth for my naked companion and rather than carry the clothes I struggled to fit them on the prisoner.

God knows how I survived the extreme bitterness, my fingers and feet were numb from the biting iciness of the water and the added dampness of the fog chilled me through to the marrow. Doubt reclaimed my mind again and I wondered if I did the right thing by releasing the enslaved man from the clutches of Talteth and then only to subject him further misery by dragging his nigh-dead body through such hopeless purgatory.

Already I decided, once further away from Wendatch we would seek shelter beside a hearty fire and despite the necessity to eat, food was merely secondary in my desperate plight to rid the cold. I was tempted to sidle up to the first welcoming fire among the many littering the wayside from the gate but apart from unfriendly rebuff, did not want to draw any attention to the king or the stranger.

I continued crawling on my belly leaving my two companions on the bank and inched my way to a tumbrel cart hitched to an oak tree some distance off. A haggard mule stood beside it hardly without flesh covering its aged bones with ribs protruding like distorted fingers against toughened skin. I remained crouched in the shadows watching and listening intently, looking for the fire's missing owner. I rolled under the cart where a generous open fire crackled its generating and inviting warmth and but for my two companions would have contentedly sat and sojourned as close as I dare. A thick hand seized my shoulder, breaking my contemplation with piercing fingers of such force it made me wince.

"What is your business here?" the gruff voice demanded.

"Nothing other than your fire," I replied. "It looked inviting and I am in the need of warmth …that is all I swear."

"You look and smell disgusting lad. Why are you so wet, eh?"

The lean man stooped over me bending his unshaven face close to mine.

"Well?" he insisted tightening his lips.

"I was pushed into the moat by a guard."

His brow distorted in a disagreeable manor.

"Those motherless swine!" he cursed loudly, exhaling a trail of vapour into the fog.

"Indeed," I affirmed impotently.

"And why my fire?" he asked retaining his piercing grasp upon my shoulder.

"Yours looked the heartiest," I replied.

"Be that as it may I do not take a liking to strangers in my company and trust no one least of all a boy!"

His tone was abrupt and for a brief moment, thought he was going to swipe at me.

"There is something perplexing about you boy, something deeply disturbing me."

"I only…"

"…Quiet!" he retorted releasing his grip.

He turned full circle slowly and deliberately scratching his dirty roughened face as if scheming.

"Tell me lad," he spoke eventually, "what of this place?"

"Wendatch?" I questioned.

"Yes Wendatch," he gestured with his arm fully stretched pointing toward the darkened silhouette of the castle barely visible in the fog.

David Greely

"What is it that you wish to know?" I urged timidly grimacing at the pain in my shoulder.

He stood upright again exhaling further steaming vapour into the air like a boiling pot.

"I have heard conflicting tales of this place," he declared, softening his attitude to an amiable level.

"It is," I said, "or rather was a good place but since the arrival of Talteth things have worsened. He killed my master and I know he wants to kill the king too."

"Preposterous boy!" he laughed aloud cocking his head skyward. "The king is his father for the Lord's sake and his very own flesh and blood."

He continued to laugh at my proclamation and I could not refrain from showing my anger nor stop the tears falling over my cheeks.

"Come boy," he said pushing me closer to the fire, "warm yourself and we will talk more of this ill."

The blaze felt good and cheering, and even better when the man handed me a bowl of steaming broth. I took it eagerly and cupped it into my freezing hands.

"Now," he continued sympathetically standing directly over me, "what of Wendatch and these un-saintly deeds, eh? Tell me all there is to know but firstly, why am I denied entry through its gate?"

"No one is allowed out and those wishing to be granted entry need the lord's approval. Talteth seeks out his father and wants him dead so he may reign over the kingdom."

"And the almighty, what of he?" he asked urgently.

"He is over…" I stopped instantly as the man bent closer and choosing not to continue raised the bowl to my lips to hide my face.

"…Speak up boy you are mumbling."

"He is over the Mendoran Mountains at the small hamlet of Polran on the northwest coast."

I could think of little else to say other than my place of birth. The man would not have known of it or indeed any other place I could have mentioned laying north of the mountains because he was a deep southerner and his accent was sure enough confirmation.

"How would you know of this?" he quizzed. "No one goes north of the mountains any more."

"Except those in exile my lord," I added smartly.

"But the king, it is supposed, resides here at Wendatch," he disputed.

"Perhaps then it is a guise," I offered.

"How is it you know so much of this awesome affair? Come to it perhaps I should consider you arrive here under the cloak of darkness to seek reward with your knowledge of the king's whereabouts."

How witless of him to even suggest such a thing! I was the king's only ally at this precise moment and wanted to tell him so, nevertheless, had to be cautious and consider the man could also be siding with the enemy. Yet I had doubt of that for if involved in the scheme then surely he would have readily acquired access into Wendatch. I concluded him to be trustworthy although a warning ran through my head deterring me from his companionship but I was in no position to question him or his allegiance. All I wanted was to rescue the king, the prisoner and myself.

I felt increasing apprehension for my escapees and an urgent need to scurry back with aid and had to take a risk else neither of them would survive the night. My inadvertent charade began.

"Sire?" I solicited, supping the residue of broth.

He looked sternly into my face with deep unblinking eyes.

"Boy?" he scowled.

"To assume that I seek reward…"

"…There," he interrupted laughing crouching with his thick hands gripping above his knees, "I knew I was right. Nobody can fool me."

"But it is not what you think. I am not here to obtain any reward for the knowledge of the king's hideout -if only it were that simple. You see, I am on the run from Wendatch, that is, me and my two friends."

"You have friends eh? These two lads, are they here lurking in the shadows with you?"

He glanced around dispassionately.

"They are men and not boys," I emphasised.

"Then why is it not them that do the work of a man instead of sending out a boy to…"

He stopped mid-sentence pondering before asking.

"…What is it that you seek? What do you want of me?"

"Nothing other than your aid and ask only that you help my friends and me by sheltering us on this contemptible night for a short while, just long enough to warm ourselves and dry our clothes then we shall take our leave before daybreak. Oh, yes and perhaps a little food," I speculated with a nervous grin.

"And if I were to agree what do I gain out of it?"

"Recompense," I offered.

"You are confusing me boy for I see nothing with you worthy of any gain to me."

"Sire it is simple. I will give you something and then your hospitality will act as payment."

"You possess nothing that I can see, look at you!" he remarked looking me up and down contemptuously. "You are but a sodden wretch scaled in mud and slime…" he turned away, "…and you are beginning to stink too!"

I took a long hard swallow fearing my loss of words.

"Whatever you wish then so you shall have, providing of course you shelter us from this foul night."

The man laughed mockingly, slapping his thighs as he rocked back and forth on his haunches.

"You are in no position to bargain with me, besides I want for nothing. Wishes, indeed!" he continued sniggering.

"Sire!" I exclaimed, daring to shout above his disparaging laughter, "I can perform magic."

"Magic?" he doubted, hastily curtailing his laughter.

"Yes, magic!" I insisted.

"And what is a boy doing with magic, eh?"

"I inherited it from my late master, Treggedon."

"Treggedon? That cantankerous old fool…"

"...Sire!" I challenged, rising swiftly to my feet, "Treggedon was a good man."

"Was?" he queried, sceptically.

"He is dead, murdered but yesterday."

"Murdered?" he unexpectedly ranted. "By whom? I Elcris, will rip the offender apart with my bare hands."

I did not recall Treggedon ever referring to Elcris and he having just called my master an old fool would not have expected such a reaction, so his sudden display of anger perplexed me.

"You knew of him then?" I asked softly fearing his indignation.

"Yes," he confirmed bluntly, crouching by the roaring fire. "We were good friends ...nay, very good friends. Sure, we had differences but it never etched into our bond. Now what is this magic you talk of?"

I cleared my throat from the tenseness and began my bartering.

"Give me and my two friends, food and warmth and I will truly grant your desire."

"I want for nothing," he retorted, "and why do I suddenly find myself negotiating with a boy I have had the misfortune of meeting?"

"Did you not wish to gain entry into Wendatch this night, perhaps to avenge my master?"

"True enough," Elcris conceded, "but that can wait till the morrow."

"Wish it and you shall have entry now, this very instant," I posed.

"I will not succumb to the guiles of witchcraft and even less so from a boy."

"Sire," I said softly, "I assure you it is the purest of magic and quite harmless."

He became agitated and sweat began smothering his brow. Was it the thought of magic that scared him or was it me?

David Greely

"Come lord," I pursued pointing to the main gate obliterated by the fog, "tonight I can get you into the very walls of Wendatch."

Although appearing confident, my heart and head pounded furiously in anticipation of my pursuit and everything forthcoming were purely acts of unpremeditated spontaneity as if it was not me but some other superior force willing it to happen, uttering words that were not my own. Whatever it was, I had no control. The only logic I recall in my innate state was the feeling of urgency in completing the immediate task and returning to the almighty and the prisoner in the hope they were still alive.

"Very well," he reluctantly conceded, "get me inside Wendatch and you may sample my hospitality.

Come," he instructed rising to his feet.

Elcris moved away from the fire heading off eagerly into the mist and when catching up with him flung his arm around my shoulders and steered me onto the rough shale of the road.

"These friends of yours, what is their business in your affair?"

His question set me into dread and I did not know what to say in reply. I grasped the bones through my tunic and wished, yearning I could be far away from Wendatch and even further away from the stranger.

"Just friends who fear Talteth equally as me," I replied eventually.

Fortunately, there was no time for further probing and we arrived close to the base of the castle. Everything was silent and no person lingered. With my wish unfulfilled, I began speaking without calculation.

"Do you see that large stone tainted with oil?" I pointed hurriedly toward the keystone high above the moat and left of the portcullis.

He scowled in the misty dimness affirming recognition.

"That sire," I said, "will be your entry by way of magic."

"Not without a ladder," he quipped.

Undeterred, I delicately removed the bones from my tunic, gripped them tightly and shut my eyes fleetingly, and with a deep breath summoned my wish. As the burning commenced Elcris immediately shrieked, noticing his body beginning to shrink. Simultaneously he rose from the ground, floating like a spirit toward the stone and while drifting upward, his body continued to contract. His ineffective pleas became high-pitched almost to a shrill as if made by a creature of the night, the closer he got to the stone the smaller he shrank until I lost sight of him when consumed within the confines of the crack in the wall. I turned, swiftly retracing my way back to his campsite although my sudden breathlessness hindered the aspiration of rapid progress. The spell drained me worse than previously, forcing me to stop countless times and the overwhelming faintness affected my balance too sending me toppling headlong to the sodden ground. Slowly I rose only to stagger forward and fall again. I lost concept of time and though still dark, the duration of leaving the king and prisoner must have lapsed beyond an hour and began conceiving my desertion in their pitiful state would bring about their deaths. Apart from losing sense of time, I lost equilibrium and continually slumped to the ground.

The meagre flames of Elcris' fire eventually welcomed me and for a long moment sat shivering beside it until warm, then tending it in readiness for my return by adding tinder from the small stockpile. With strength restored, I hitched the mule to the cart ignoring its braying disapproval, cracking the leathers against its flanks until the animal indolently pulled me back toward the road. Apart from a few leering glances from travellers along the roadside, I steered the cart to the moat drawing very little attention though some must have thought I was hopping position to gain access into the castle but so miserable was the night no-one would have given a goat's ear.

Arriving at the moat, I impatiently leapt from the cart and scurried down the bank fearing my companions had perished in my absence. I crouched beside the stranger appeased his shallow breath verified he lived but reminded myself my prime duty was for the king almighty and shook his shoulders compelling him to awaken.

"Come sire refuge is at hand."

Arbereth possessed no energy to respond and his eyes barely opened when attempting to revive him. Without dally I dragged them from the bank, in turn propping both men against the cart's wheel and after a much needed rest continued to load them aboard the wagon somewhat surprised by my capability at managing to do so. A last furtive survey of the castle confirmed no eyes bore witness to my action and I coaxed the mule forward.

In brief recollection, I pondered over the fate of Elcris, retracting my gaze from the grey wall, satisfied my enchantment served my purpose whilst fulfilling his desire to enter and infiltrate Wendatch and now with great fortune able to enkindle my companions.

The mule trundled laboriously along the road and onto the muddied furrows, still snorting its contempt of me putting it to use.

"Wouldn't let you in, eh?" yelled a voice from out of the murkiness. "Serve your own justice trying to push to the front!"

I did not respond to the unjust shout and kept my tired eyes transfixed on the beast until the unattended fire came into view. I jumped off the cart to guide the animal to a halt and once hitched, tended the flame by adding more tinder roaring it to a sizable blaze. I disrespectfully dragged both men from the cart and lay them close to the fire. Fortunately, nobody pilfered the broth and suspending it upon a makeshift tripod returned it directly into the heart of the flame. I searched inside the cart for fresh clothing but only succeeded in finding two stinking empty sacks and a length of tattered canvas. This meagre discovery raised my suspicion of Elcris yet again, for surely, if he was a traveller covering so many leagues, would he not have boasted greater provision?

God in heaven, I was exhausted and fretful too, knowing if anyone were to stumble into the campsite, the king would be recognised and forced back into the keep where death would await us all.

The two men lay motionless but for the flickering shadows from the crackling fire projecting animated dances upon their sullen faces. Alternately, I fed broth forcibly down their throats. The almighty muttered a few incoherent words whereas the prisoner merely groaned, nevertheless, I felt gratified they were alive. For the few passing hours, I tended the flames and nursed both men best as able by turning them over like suckling pigs on a spit in an attempt to warm them thoroughly.

Unwittingly, I drifted into deep slumber yet for how long I was uncertain. Daylight had yet to arrive so it could not have been that lengthy. The fire all but dwindled and the two men lay by the dying embers expelling a dismal plume of thin smoke. The night remained damp, cold and ominously quiet as if expectant.

This was my first night out in the wilderness alone; not that the wayside from the main gate of Wendatch was particularly wild but I did at least expect the hoot of an owl or perhaps the distant howl of a wolf from the northern forest. Yet there was nothing, nothing except the irregular snorts from the mule daring to break the night's deathly foreboding.

My thoughts revisited Elcris the traveller, bestowing the feeling of uneasiness and it dwelled heavily upon me. I tried reason but for the life of me could not pinpoint my concern or scepticism of him. He appeared relatively benevolent, certainly kinder than most considering few strangers would offer warmth and food to a boy, mind I did present my magic as part of the bargaining. His reaction to the knowledge of my master's death was somewhat perplexing. Elcris' name suddenly struck me and I rose to my feet cursing his name aloud.

"Elcris the Druid! The man is full of evil—the devil's own son."

Now I recall my master mentioning him and of his brother Ulcris too, both strong advocates in Druidism.

David Greely

Druids are not particularly disliked or indeed uncommon in certain territories of Aeria, sacred monoliths still stand as reminder of their curious following. Why, folklore even depicts one huge stone circle lost in the forbidden mist, an ancient denomination of the Celts and these two men were both officers of Gorsedds, though they reputedly delved in the black arts of Satanism, which is not the true order, or belief of the original concept. This doctrine and all of its associated words meant little to me then, I could scarcely cope with my own powers of sorcery let alone trying to understand magic of other forms of power. Yet Treggedon warned me of the Druids though I knew not why, but my senses confirmed my master's caution.

I continued with my scepticism of Elcris' deceit for surely any God-loving individual such as he would have displayed some pity and concern at the persecution of the almighty. Apart from his interest in the king's whereabouts Elcris demonstrated little sign of emotion toward him let alone his lack of surprise for Talteth's action against his father. Yet more perplexing is why did he show anger toward the death of my master? The man in my estimation was the epitome of deception and was no more upset for Treggedon as I was for blinding Beladon. In addition, if Elcris was a black Druid or any other type of Druid for that matter then surely he possessed the power to enter Wendatch unaided? This unresolved question doubted my judgment.

I broke from these abhorrent feelings and fussed over my companions again. Though relatively dry, they were still cold but there was little time to reawaken the deadening fire with the new day approaching, any further delay would prove unwise. The oncoming day already clipped the hills in the east and the heavy mist persisted draping its heavy mantle over the land. With the king and stranger back on the cart, smothered in the sacks and canvas, I checked the harness and scrambled aboard, motioning the mule forward. After continual clicks with my tongue and varying snaps of the leashes, the beast eventually submitted and began moving. Though the road would have proved easier and faster the noise of the wheels would have exaggerated ten-fold, consequently, I chose the way of the fields and slowly, nay, very slowly, we rolled away from Wendatch. I continually turned my head around endorsing our safe escape yet cursing the sluggishness of the mule and wishing four stallions were pulling instead; unconvinced escaping should prove this easy.

The thought of my master suddenly overwhelmed me and with it came the realisation and prospect that leaving Wendatch will sever us forever, fearing it would be my last chance ever to feel his spirit again. I wondered of his burial or if indeed, he will even get one. Prayers would be missing without my presence and I loathed imagining he be tossed unceremoniously into a hole scarcely deep enough to cover him. He deserved more and I promised on this day to see to it, should I return and when doing so, shall sing out his acclaim and instigate prayer to the Good Lord. Oh, how I cried and if I were to be honest, it was all over my self-pity. I tried hopelessly to recall our more cheerful moments but my dolefulness thwarted such luscious memories.

Seemingly and all too slowly, we gradually crossed over the land until the shadow of Wendatch, behind, decreased and daylight though nothing but a murky grey, forced the night westward out to sea. With the dawn came an eerie crimson glow and if it were a setting sun, a traveller would have been heartened, but in this morn it gave a cold aurora that penetrated and chilled my soul. The few remaining fires along the roadside aided my steering across the fields and I took cheer when reaching the crossroads. The sun penetrated the grey of early morning but still a thick mist clung to the ground impairing my vision and thus dulling my sense of direction. I continued to follow the last fire beacons that shone in the distant haze and since their finally dissipation began to doubt my ability as navigator. Had I steered too far south off the road and missed the crossing or had my eagerness rewarded me with an error in judgment?

The mule arduously trod across furrows and ridges dragging us through the mist oblivious of the danger and urgency in our departure. Steam from its back funnelled into the cool air and the stench from its toil filled my nostrils. Groans from both passengers heartened me, acknowledging they were surviving the bone-shaking traverse. I had yet to decide where to steer, either north toward Desseldor and trundle into relative safety of the mountains and beyond or quest south back to Collington where the almighty could regain his rightful throne and govern this forlorn kingdom. I even contemplated venturing westward to the sea and acquire a vessel, and navigate to some friendly distant shore.

A loud shout broke my time of indecisiveness, and I turned my head sharply in every bearing, seeking the owner of the unwelcome and menacing call.

"Who travels this foul morn?" shouted the demand.

I drew the beast to a slow halt.

"Answer or you will face my sword!"

I had no sighting of the man and deceived myself into thinking perhaps he challenged another travelling the road at this time.

"Take warning," yelled the voice again, "I mean my words!"

I chose to remain silent though my heart pulsated franticly, when spying out of the mist a horse and its rider clad in heavy chain mail with a long white robe dragging over the horse's flanks. Without premeditation, I commanded the mule to move and steered the cart away from the approaching horseman. In spite of my urgent attempts to get the beast to quicken, it continued to amble across the sodden earth with little haste. I reached inside my tunic and gripped the bones.

"Master help me!" I yelled. "I need you."

The mocking laughter from the rider drifted into the cold stillness.

"He can't help you now that he is dead," he shouted.

"Master?" I appealed clutching the bones in desperation.

I glanced behind hoping the pursuer lost my track in the mist but with every revolution of the cart's wheels, his lean seated frame gradually neared and menacingly his silhouette approached. Not galloping nor trotting but walking his horse in unison, at the same rate as the cart. His cape and helmet covered his identity and I cursed at the failure to capture his features. His dappled steed snorted in the quiet as if in competition with the tiring mule.

"Stop!" he commanded.

"Never!" I responded feebly. "Master!" I called again.

The rider laughed at my futile beckoning.

A faint breeze soft as gossamer suddenly brushed my face.

"I am here Rabbit."

My master's words blended with the gentle wind harbouring the slightest essence of woodsuckle.

"Rabbit," Treggedon whispered.

At first, I thought it my imagination but his repeating of my name quelled such a notion and aspiration filled my heart.

"Help me master!" I yelled.

The rider came to a halt and in the brief stand off, his horse flicked its tail in agitation and scraped a hoof on the ground as if preparing for confrontation. Within my hand, the bones warmed my palm like fired pebbles, I could barely manage to hold them and as I battled to withstand the burning, a sudden gust of wind whipped up fallen leaves sending them skyward in a gathering column before spiralling into a tumult. My sight blurred as the turbulence forced me to shield my eyes with one arm raised and within the confusion Treggedon materialised swathed in white costume. The damp leaves fluttered in an addle of unwillingness equally stubborn to move, like the mule yet now stirring about my face like spitfires.

"Hold tight boy!"

My master's voice though authoritative remained calm and affable and in compliance, gripped the reins tightly with my free hand daring not to release the bones clenched in the other. The horseman cursed aloud, declaring profanities I wish not to repeat and unexpectedly the air became lighter, lifting the weightiness of the autumn mist to present gentility and purity. The cart along with the beast, my travellers and me began rising off the ground, at first with an element of difficulty but gradually with ease and the squelching of the sodden earth submitted to intermittent spatters as the caked wheels freed from the mire. We raised a short height from the ground and in a nauseating rocking motion sped off at a startling rate. My pursuant gave chase shouting further vulgarities and in his ultimate act of desperation hurled his sword high into the air. Quickly I turned my head and stooped, keeping my attention in the direction we were flying. Oh yes, we were flying well enough and whistled past trees dodging their overhanging boughs. How we never met with disaster at one of the mighty oaks is still a wonder. I soon realised I had no control over the steering and leaves, branches and acorns rained upon me as we sped deeper into the thick forest. I tried restoring calm within me and return the bones inside my garment but could barely manage to stay aboard the cart and needed both hands to steady myself. Our flight did not lapse for long and we came to a gentle stop landing in a birch copse and my dishevelled and weakened body all but fell from the cart. It took some while to recover my senses from the uncanny ordeal and my whole body smothered in uncountable scratches ached with pain. The mule stood uneasily snorting and looking equally bewildered. I scrambled to the rear of the tumbrel and peeled back the tattered sacking from the men.

"In the name of the good Lord!" I wailed bursting into a deluge of tears.

The almighty laid motionless, blood-soaked and eyes staring blankly skyward. With renewed potency, I gripped the sword's pommel slowly withdrawing the deadly blade of the horseman from his chest. I fell upon him in disbelief, cradling his mud-splattered head in my arms, brushing aside the hair from his face. I rocked back and forth consoling him and myself for an age, clutching the bones and wishing on them a thousand-fold for all in heaven to restore his life but it was not to be. Eventually, I moved the prisoner, questioning myself why he be spared and not the king.

"It is destined," said the gentle voice of Treggedon.

"Why this?" I implored but there was no reply.

I swore on this day to avenge Arbereth and sever the arms of his slayer.

Chapter Six

My uninvited sleep had been long and deep and I did not dream, or if I did, fail to recall. I felt weary, vulnerable and now very much alone. Though I had the prisoner as company, he was far from able to communicate. I knew not where I was, nor if the threat of danger had surpassed. It was time to give thought to my current quandary and more importantly the future of the kingdom. With the almighty now dead, who will reign over the land? Well damned if I was going to allow Talteth and his henchmen have their way!

I prepared a small fire and sat close to it with my knees bent tightly against my chest. Opposite, the prisoner laid restless and in obvious pain but I had nothing to offer him nor could I seek anything in the way of a remedy; the dampening autumn would have killed off anything worthy other than hips or nuts. The only plant abundant was nightshade and this I would not give to my worst enemy, except perhaps to Talteth, Beladon and the horseman.

Legacy of Bones

After much deliberation, I ultimately decided upon a plan of action to travel with haste north beyond Polran by way of the forest and mountains. The mountains of Mendoran are indeed arduous enough in the finer months of summer and if I were to cross them, had to beat the first snow of the winter. Even at this time, it may have already been too late but once over the mountains I could seek assistance at Greddick and muster up force to overthrow the pretender to the thrown. My primary intention was to take the king's body with me but after the first day's trek, changed my heart. Travelling with the cart was both slow and difficult although the beast was capable of pulling the weight, there was going to be a time when I would have to abandon it. Already, I had the prisoner to contend with and it would be impossible to continue with the king as well. I felt dubious when the eventual moment arrived of telling the fact of the almighty's murder, after all who was going to believe me? Hence my original decision in taking him with me as proof of his demise. Loose tongues travel faster than any man in the realm does and if word preceded my arrival, they would doubtlessly become distorted.

The new day brought a welcoming freshness and the infernal mist at last dispersed, allowing the sun to dance between the high clouds. I gathered a meagre hoard of nuts and berries before setting off on the tiresome trudge toward the mountains. I feared many things this day but the death of the king instilled prominently on my mind and I felt I had failed him and my master. Surely, Treggedon would have been extremely angry at my lack of success and in retrospect, if I had not wasted time in rescuing the prisoner perhaps the king would still be alive. Our escape from Wendatch certainly would have been speedier and fast enough, at least to avoid the cursed horseman.

I stopped many times, mostly to tend and feed the prisoner and although feeling dejected at the king's death, took courage in my saving the stranger from his torture. Progress was minimal and cumbersome within the constraints of the forest and the progressive coldness forced me to make a fire. I chose an ideal site for the night; a steep bank on two sides with a thick

David Greely

barrier of gorse and birch. I unleashed the animal and tied the rein loosely over a hanging bough where the mule grazed idly on the sweet grass of the forest floor. Having laid the prisoner by the warming fire, I set about gathering rocks and branches for the king's interment though hardly apt for a man of his prominence but at least my compulsion to bury him would, in the least, be some epitaph for him. I scraped at the ground for hours, making a shallow dip adequately deep to house him. My back ached and my hands bled but undeterred, I dragged the king from the cart and lay him to rest. I noticed a small leather pouch tied about his neck and removed it with a sense of guilt before finally placing the branches and rocks over him. I gave a lengthy prayer for his soul asking the Good Lord for guidance, selfish perhaps but felt inadequate without his aid, I cried too, whether out of remorse or self-pity I am unable to clarify. I walked away peering into the king's pouch, perplexed there was nothing within and devoid of forethought transferred the bones from the soiled cloth and tied it around my neck. I as good as fell down next to the fire, exhausted with body spent. I fed the prisoner who offered nothing but an occasional groan as gratitude and I ate a little, though felt no hunger and kept vigil throughout the night drifting in and out of slumber.

When the grey dawn ultimately broke, I said another prayer for the king and aided the prisoner onto the cart. There was at last, signs of his recovery but I anticipated it would still be some while before he would be fully mobile. All my imaginings from the previous night diminished; there were no wolves, no bears nor wild boar and more decisively no enemy. My night games conjured up all these fears and more beside, and to say I was relieved at not sighting my foes is an understatement. Not that I really knew whom my adversaries were any more, if I could not trust the king's own son, then who? I contemplated briefly of Elcris and his insistence of entering Wendatch, still pondering over his allegiance and already beginning to think meeting up with him could prove to be a regrettable error.

The terrain became almost impassable with the cart and if it were not for the prisoner would have willingly abandoned it, but slowly we ambled on, taking many opportunities to stop and rest. Birch conceded to oak and the ground became a confusion of matted roots ribbing across our path. Coldness penetrated my body, egging me to make fire at every halt and the day passed wearily though without event. The prisoner remained under the old sacking throughout the journey with me not having the strength to lift him off and on the cart. Ironically, I concocted a nettle broth that we supped greedily and soon hoped such warming nutrition would have him speak. I felt anxious to establish the reason for his captivity though more especially needed his company. I had notions that perhaps he is a murderer or thief, but either way, locked in the dungeon gave me assurance at least he is an enemy of Talteth thus making me his confederate.

The moonless night came rapidly and my sole consolation was the denseness of the trees keeping the hoarfrost at bay. I did not suppose we trekked much beyond two leagues this day, the mountains appeared to be no closer and at best another eight days off. Although mobile and in a conscious state, the prisoner seemed oblivious of our current predicament and me. I decided to discard the cart and unharnessed the mule hitching it to near by sapling.

Again, in a grim moment of solitude I reflected upon Treggedon. 'How far now are the luxuries of my master's abode?' I missed his conversation, his stories and him.

I still felt weak and my body smothered in cuts and bruises continued to pain me. My hands throbbed too, stinging from the confounded nettles I pulled from my dumb companion.

After devouring the broth, I bedded down for the night, wrapping ourselves in the sacking. I prayed for the good Lord to watch over me and drifted into restless slumber, inundated with the troubles of the kingdom and its future, and my misgivings too for envisaging myself at being a mighty wizard, when I could not even comprehend the strange happenings I failed to understand. The bones now secure in my acquired pouch around my neck seemed to hold such power, if only I knew how to direct their energy and overcome the fatigue they bring upon me because surely then, if I was an enchanter, did I really have use for them? Treggedon never used them; he could summon a spell at will, yet why did he give them to me? 'Perhaps' I thought, 'I needed to discover their secret for myself.'

"Elcris!"

The calling of the Druid's name woke me with a start, I thought I was dreaming it but upon repeat, confirmed it came from the prisoner's lips and I rolled over to look at him.

"The king almighty!" he suddenly shouted.

I waited several minutes studying his face in the gloom, watching his involuntary twitches and facial contortions but apart from a few inaudible mumblings, the prisoner slumped back into silence. Beads of sweat gathered on his furrowed brow as he lay in torment and his sudden restlessness unnerved me. The night sounds of the forest rattled me even further and conspired with my thoughts. I knew all too well what creatures dwelled within this grim place; the keenness of the wolves sniffing me out and if not them, black bears the size of Elberdor seizing and ravaging me to death with their rapacious claws. Fruition of my imagination suddenly became very much a reality.

Out from the darkness skulked a huge boar, the size one would wish at the grandest of regal banquets and it grunted to the extreme, beyond any feasibility. The beast, as if with vacillation stalked around us in a circle waiting for the opportune moment to pounce and strike at me. I stoked the fire without taking my eyes off it. Then it lunged with jaws agape, baring curved molars dripping with congealed saliva. As it charged, I rolled on my side to dodge it, burning my leg on the flames as I fell across the fire. The sacking ignited and when the boar bound at me again I threw the burning hessian, covering its head and blinding it. The raptorial beast squealed in wild fury like a banshee and sped headlong into the cart. Instantly it collapsed to the ground and I grabbed a thick branch from the fire, striking the motionless creature across the head with all my might. It screeched aloud once more before delivering my second blow, followed by another. Despite an effort to raise its own great hulk, it buckled back to the ground with a final submissive grunt. My heart pounded with fear, fear it may rise up and charge at me again but my last blow had sealed its fate. I smiled readily at my conquest amid gasps of exhaustion and satisfied of my dexterity in overwhelming the creature. I tried dragging it toward the fire but it was far heavier than any man. Anxious at the prospect of eating meat I moved the cart and kindled a fresh fire beside the hefty carcass, eventually eating heartily until my belly was full.

I woke the following morn with renewed spirit, praising the Lord for his deliverance and enough fresh meat to last for days. The sun was full and the sky a pastel blue. The air however quelled its deception with a chill, hinting the imminence of winter's advance. I suppressed the fire and packed the mule with my limited resources and lumps of cooked boar before rousing the stranger.

"Come," I said shaking him rigorously, "it is time for us to move on my friend."

I hoped he would respond and speak his first words to me but a feeble groan is best I could savour. Keeping my morale from dampening I whistled while pulling the mule with the man hunched upon its back. Progress proved speedier without the encumbrance of the cart as I steered the animal through thicket and muddied dips without ever faltering, and this was to be the case for the following days. The landscape hardly altered, only the sparseness of leaves and level of the forest's dankness became increasingly apparent. Eager to reach the mountains, I travelled during night, stopping only whenever hunger tore at my belly or checking the welfare of my silent companion. The fourth day in the forest transpired to be an eventful one. I spent most part of the morning in slumber, wavering in and out of dreams, conjuring ways to avenge the death of Treggedon and the king. A deafening shout peeled through my head, waking me with a sudden jolt. I sat upright, nervously studying the approaching man, rubbing the sleep away from my gritty eyes. He stopped casting his shadow over me so I took this brief opportunity to study him; an unkempt, lean individual with thick black scruffy hair curling around his neck and brandishing a menacing club in his right hand with the remnants of my roast boar in the other. His jaws engaged, tearing voraciously at the succulent flesh. His smaller, stocky counterpart shuffled alongside him, though appearing milder in manner and certainly less threatening than the rogue set afore me.

"What do you want?" I asked uncertainly.

"That depends on what you have to offer," replied the tall man flippantly.

"I have nothing of worth. You are eating my only possession," I responded.

He moved his eyes downward to the meat without tilting his head.

"Mighty tasty it is too lad. Is there more of this?" he asked.

"No, that is all."

"Why do you travel these parts?" he enquired mildly. "Are you not aware of the dangers lurking in this God-forsaken place?"

"I am travelling north. And yes, I am fully conversant of what creatures roam," I returned to him boldly.

"I refer not to wild beasts," he scoffed, "but of thieves and molesters or perhaps even murderers!"

"Like yourselves?" I proffered intrepidly.

"Spunky kid wouldn't yer say Owell?"

"Yeah," his partner agreed. "Too damned spunky if you ask me."

"Now then," continued the lean man, approaching even closer, "let us establish a few facts here. You're travelin' …north you say?"

"Indeed so sire," I offered.

"Oh, ain't 'e polite?" remarked his partner.

"Quite so…"

Owell's mannerism was as pitiful as his body portrayed; burdened to the point of hideousness and his disfigured left hand was minor in judgment. The large hunch on his left shoulder pushed his head to one side, forcing him to walk slightly sideways. He depicted an air of sadness for which I felt certain empathy.

"...And you say you have nothing of value?" continued asking the tall man.

"Nothing," I confirmed.

"You say 'nothing' but you have a fine mule."

"It is tired and old," I said protectively.

To lose the beast now would surely hinder my advance. And the prisoner...

'...My God, the prisoner!' I sat rigid glancing over to the tethered mule, aware the stranger had disappeared and cursed inwardly at his sudden escape. I thought perhaps he rolled off the cart but my quick exploration along the ground revealed nothing. 'The swine had taken flight,' I cursed under my breath.

"What is it boy?" the tall man asked sensing my uneasiness.

"Nothing," I said smartly, far more concerned for the whereabouts of my companion than the question bestowed upon me.

Both men shadowed over me with their eyes piercing like acid.

"The mule," said Owell, "we'll take the mule."

"Patience my friend, this lad intrigues me and I wish to know a little more. My senses tell me all is not as it would seem."

"Awe, come on," urged Owell, "let's find the king. Time is pressin' and a healthy purse awaits us."

"I said we will wait awhile and find out more of this boy here."

"You seek the king?" I quizzed.

They both laughed.

"Oh indeed we do," confirmed Owell. "Do you know of where he is? Have you seen him?"

"No," I replied in a pathetic whimper.

"Me thinks you are holding back from us," continued the tall man in a sarcastic tone.

David Greely

"I speak only the truth and have no need for lies. Last I saw of the almighty was at Wendatch."

The tall man gripped my arm.

"I was there five days past celebrating his coming," I added hastily.

"Let 'im be Whelp, he knows nothing," said Owell.

"How can you be sure?" his associate questioned.

"He's just a boy and don't know nothin' about any of this business," insisted Owell.

"Well, do yer lad?" pressed Whelp.

"Business sir? No, nothing." I was cowering with fear as he strengthened his grip on me.

"Come on Whelp, let's get on!"

"Wait awhile my friend, this boy has yet to satisfy my curiosity. Tell me, why do you travel north? And why alone?"

Whelp's face drew close to mine and I could smell the boar on his breath.

"I travel north because I live north. But I do not travel alone."

"Where's yer company, I see no-one else?" Whelp released his grip and looked about, sparing his energy by only moving his eyeballs.

"I travel with the Good Father. God is my companion."

"I knew it!" remarked Owell. "The boy's a bloody Christian! Come on, let's be going."

The hunchback went to the mule, untied it and coiled the leash around his good hand.

"I for one am going to seek the almighty," he said, "and get the reward myself. Huh, almighty he was but 'e ain't so almighty now!"

"Where is his God now?" Whelp laughed. "And where is your God lad? Maybe you and the king share the same one. The one which deserted him," he continued laughing.

"For that I cannot answer, but to me there is only one God —our heavenly Father," I said emphatically.

"Do you worship?" Whelp questioned in the same manner.

"Yes," I replied adamantly.

I felt guilty for saying it because I did not know how to. I was never taught the meaning, although I prayed surely enough and believed in the Holy Father, so was this then being a worshipper?

"Come on Whelp," Owell insisted, "this is quite pointless. Unless you come now I will take leave and seek the king alone. Just think," he mumbled as if uttering to himself, "the sizeable purse I will earn for myself."

I was bewildered at the disappearance of the prisoner. He showed little sign of consciousness prior to sleep and my concern for him deepened even more so than my own worth. With the bones overseeing my welfare, it was transpiring into an uncertain moment for the future of my comrade, and if they were to discover him now...

"...We shall travel together Owell. You are right, the boy holds us here for no reason..."

I sighed, feeling assured of his words, this was until Whelp persisted.

"...But what disturbs me," he continued, "is why a boy should be travelling this forest alone?"

He examined me fervently with a deepening frown. Whelp was astute and looked full of knowing, somehow I raised his suspicions.

"I was set an errand to trade goods in return for the mule."

"By whom?" he asked listening intently.

"My master. He is a farmer in need of a beast to tend the land."

"Looks like yer goin' to fail him," laughed the cripple from the distance.

"It would appear so," I agreed.

"And what will you tell him?" urged Whelp.

"Nothing," I said.

"Nothing?" he doubted.

"No sir. I cannot possibly return if you intend stealing the animal."

"Steal? Oh no, you have it quite wrong. We are not stealing it. Borrowing perhaps, but stealing…?" Whelp grinned at length.

"…Sir, if you take the beast I will be flogged for sure, if ever my master gets to me."

"Such is the cruelty of life," he continued grinning.

"Can you not take me along with you?" I asked.

"Impossible!" hissed Whelp. "How absurd! Think yourself lucky we will leave you alive and in one piece."

"But…" I urged.

"…Quiet or I'll garrotte you! Why, I've a good mind to do it anyway."

Whelp came at me gripping his hands around my throat and with ease, began constricting the life from me. I tried frantically to reach the bones but the force from his strangulation made it impossible. My blood surged into my head, primed and ready to burst. Already I was feeling faint, with life draining from me, the pathetic mirth of Owell compounded my dulling senses.

"Leave him be!" came a distant voice.

The pressure from Whelp's grip did not relent.

"I said leave him be!" the voice commanded again.

Eventually, Whelp released his strength from my throat and I toppled to one side, spluttering and gasping for breath.

"Who are you?" Whelp called, surveying the immediate vicinity. "Show yourself!"

A long eerie silence lingered and both the men and I searched eagerly for the owner of the stern voice. I hoped it was Treggedon but my optimism waned after another shout roared, unlike his.

"Leave this place or be dead!"

"Who are you?" Whelp insisted.

"I am the Druid."

"That means nothing to me," shouted Whelp in return.

Owell stood motionless with mouth agape.

'Impossible!' I thought. 'Elcris is at Wendatch, I put him there myself so it could not possibly be. I transported him into the wall of the prayer room that night, knowing Talteth had it sealed many months prior. The Druid is isolated within the mortar because the lord is not a Christian.'

"Sire," I called softly to Whelp, "if he is the Druid then it would be prudent you obey his command. He is capable of strong magic."

"Bah!" dispelled the thin man.

"Listen to the boy. He speaks the truth," confirmed the voice.

"Magic? Druids? Only the sword and the might of men have significance in this kingdom," Whelp contested.

"Be away from here before I inflict doom upon you," the Druid continued.

Owell took heed, dropped the leash from his grasp and the mule sped off into the thicket, followed by the mumbling hunchback.

"I will stand and concede to no man," Whelp enforced stubbornly, drawing a dagger from his boot in readiness. "I am not as easy as that pathetic cripple!" he shouted.

"And I am no ordinary man," claimed the Druid.

If this was so, then I feared for my life. Not only would he want revenge for his incarceration within the praying room but moreover, for me escaping with the king. I had made a fool of him and thought he would allow Whelp to throttle me, but in retrospect, he would want the satisfaction of killing me for himself.

At this moment, I was full of self-doubt and brimming with bewilderment, and contemplated slipping away but as always felt compelled to stay for the safeguard of the missing prisoner.

"Show yourself!" Whelp demanded.

"Let the boy be and I will spare your worth," responded the Druid.

"You fail to understand. You are in no position to bargain," Whelp maintained.

"Then," said the Druid ultimately, "you leave me with no alternative."

David Greely

A dreadful silence lingered in the air as both Whelp and I looked for the Druid. I clutched the bones and in an instant, a mist rolled through the trees as thick as raging storm clouds. At first, I could see nothing other than the mournful grey blanket sweeping in, but in my concentration, the haze slowly splintered to reveal a figure fully robed in white with a purple sash hanging loosely about the middle. His face remained secreted under the shadow of his hood.

My heart raced, anticipating what was to follow and fearing Whelp was about to set upon me again, leapt to my feet in readiness. I ran toward him lunging with fists clenched, lashing out with all my might and we both toppled to the ground in the ensuing struggle. Somehow, I succeeded in rolling on top of him, grabbed a boulder lying beside him and smashed his head with it repeatedly as if possessed by an unknown force egging me on. The dull thuds of the stone cracking against his skull resounded in the stillness, yet I was unable stop myself and continued to pommel his head until assured of Whelp's bloody death. I studied my hand saturated in his blood and turned away sickened at my impulsive action.

As soon as the encounter ceased, the vision swiftly melted and the thick mist recoiled into the undergrowth. I shook my head vigorously, trying to rid my thoughts and return to my sanity. Sweat dripped from my forehead as I cupped my face in my blooded hands and under me Whelp laid with his bludgeoned head a mass of claret. I cannot remember any further detail other than my pathetic whimpering prior to collapsing into an exhausted heap.

"Welcome back," said a voice stirring me.

Slowly I opened my eyes, focusing on the face of the prisoner.

"What happened?" I asked.

"That was very impressive," he said.

"What was?" I quizzed trying to recollect my thoughts.

"Killing the stranger," he said.

"Oh merciful Lord what have I done?" I cried.

Legacy of Bones

"You have rid the land of an evil man that is what," smiled the prisoner.

"But I was only dreaming it, surely it cannot be so?" I argued.

"Sure as hogs are hogs Whelp is dead," he confirmed.

"He was not who I saw in the vision. I saw…"

…Whom I saw, I did not know. I caught neither sight of his face nor did he utter words of recognition and I assumed it be the Druid.

"What of the fog?" I asked him. "Did you see the fog?"

"There was no fog little man," resigned the prisoner.

Tears filled my tired eyes as the dreadful occurrence re-entered my mind. 'I am no better than Whelp and nothing other than a murderer.' I feared for what force drove me to such compulsion. I was a Christian and would never conceive doing such a thing.

"Hey, console yourself lad. What you did saved your life and mine."

"But the Druid, what happened to…?"

"…He is here," the prisoner smiled warmly.

"Where?"

"Talking to you."

"But you are not…"

"…I am Ulcris the Druid," the prisoner claimed.

"But your robes have gone. How did…?"

"…Enough questions for now, one thing at a time. I will make a fire and prepare some food. Sleep now and reawaken refreshed."

His passive words met my closing eyes and dreams proffered the moment his steps trailed away. I deliberated my action in saving him and reconsidered everything from the moment of discovery in his cell. If he is the Druid Ulcris, what am I to face when he gets word of my killing his brother? His allegiance needs confirming and I had to seek a method to establish it before disclosing the king's death to him.

I woke shuddering and watched Ulcris, bent, tending the fire. He continually poked a stick into the core of the flames encouraging huge sparks to shoot skyward and as my gaze followed these spitfires, noticed the shard of moon. The smell of cooking meat filled the cold night and my nostrils with a delicious beckoning. I was hungry, though still tired and lifeless. My anxiety at the loss of the bones rapidly quelled when I felt them tucked safely inside the pouch about my neck and with that appeased, wanted no more dwelling on Whelp's death.

"That smells good," I said, softly rising from the ground.

"Ah, you are awake! Here have some rabbit."

'Rabbit,' my master's term of endearment and a sudden gush of sadness overwhelmed me when repeating it to myself. How I was missing him, I still felt hell-bent on vengeance for Treggedon's death and I swore yet again, to see it through. Nothing, despite how deplorable, would satisfy my yearning for justice.

"Hey, cheer yourself lad, come and eat heartily," beckoned Ulcris. "God knows you look like you need it."

"God?" I asked him. "Do you believe in God?"

He took time in replying as he sat away from the fire.

"Why yes, I do," he eventually confirmed.

"What of your Druidism? Does that not go against our Father?"

"On the contrary," he advocated, "the two go hand in hand."

"I fail to grasp," I said pulling a piece of meat from the spit and joining him.

"There is nothing to understand. We Druids preach of God and probably more so than others do. Druidism is, after all, a heavenly order of disciples," Ulcris declared.

"Then what of the tales that involve preaching under the shadow of the devil?"

"I cannot deny their existence. My brother does the order this dishonour."

"Elcris!" I exclaimed, although I meant to ask.

"Ah, you are learned lad. He only tends in tight niches of acquaintance so how is it you should know him?"

He sounded a little surprised.

"Treggedon told me of him and of you too."

"Treggedon you say?" Ulcris pondered. "No, his name means nothing to me."

"He was my master and adviser to Talteth of Wendatch and others before him."

"Talteth," Ulcris spat out a bone, "that man taints my appetite."

"You have no regard for him?" I urged.

"I have more regard for a whore! You forget it was he who imprisoned me and if it were not for you young man, I would probably be long dead by now. For that I owe you."

I greedily ate the rabbit, eagerly pursuing our conversation between mouthfuls.

"I am perplexed my lord. Your brother, what bearing does he have on the matter?"

"None, well at least none I am aware of. Apart from his indulgence in the black art, I fail to think of affairs in connection with Talteth."

I swallowed hard and took time in choosing my words, fearing not to disclose the outcome of his brother's fate.

"The night we left Wendatch, Elcris was there and eager to gain access into the walls that very night."

"He must have got word of my plight and came to rescue me," he offered.

His assumption was feasible but I doubted it, for if Elcris wished to free his estranged brother, surely then, he would have done so a little more discretely.

"How would he have known of your imprisonment?" I asked him somewhat lethargically.

"Come now," he replied, "word travels as fast as the wind."

"Well, I knew nothing of it and I was there!"

"Then I confess I do not know," he said.

"Why were you being held prisoner? And why were you being tortured?"

"Why all these questions?"

"I have the right to know," I insisted.

"Oh?" he smiled, throwing the remnants of the rabbit into the flames.

"Then answer me this. What of your allegiance? Is it with the almighty and the kingdom or Talteth, your brother and the pleasures of the devil?"

"Arbereth of course," he confirmed readily.

"The king is dead," I disclosed sighing.

"Dead?"

"Yes, slain by the sword of a horseman. He lays buried within this forest."

"Whereabouts?" the Druid urged urgently. "I must go to him and seek solace"

"I do not know exactly. Several days and nights have passed since I buried him, besides it is too late for that."

I believed the Druid's fealty when tears fell down his face.

"What of the realm now?" he asked solemnly.

"That is up to you and me my lord Ulcris…"

He looked at me curiously.

"…Why yes," I enthused, "we must quell Talteth and his intent."

"And how exactly?" Ulcris doubted. "Just you and me?"

"And why not? I was set an errand by Treggedon and out of my failing, renewed spirit proffers. It is ordained that you and I will avenge the almighty's death."

"Already you have a plan of action?"

"Indeed I have," I replied. "I shall go to Greddick and muster my kin. You will head south and raise an army against Talteth. When we are prepared we shall send word to each other."

"You make it sound relatively simple."

"It is," I confirmed to him.

"Do not underestimate Talteth, or indeed my brother."

"I still fail to understand where your brother fits in the scheme of things."

"So do I!" remarked Ulcris. "But if he is in collusion with him then I fear dread. Do you not think for a moment that I may not be able to muster such a force?"

"Of course not," I said disregarding the Druid's anxiety. "Arbereth was powerful and has many strongholds in the south."

"I will be hunted and killed. Everywhere I go the enemy will be seeking me out and the same applies to you too."

"If you do not wish to rise up against him then I shall do so alone," I insisted resolutely.

"I am not saying that. It is just not possible."

"We have the Good Lord on our side," I offered.

"And your magic too I would suppose," Ulcris added. "But that will not be enough, besides; my powers have all but diminished."

"Where is your faith Ulcris?"

"I wish I could share your optimism lad. However, I have little option in the matter. I owe you my life and will do what you ask of me but I cannot swear allegiance to a person that will not even disclose his name."

"Arton," I smiled.

"Then Arton, as God is my witness I put my life before you."

"Bless you Ulcris then we will set off in the morrow."

The Druid said no other words and walked away, leaving me to sleep peacefully.

The early morning rain woke me though Ulcris seemed very oblivious to the inclemency. I made a humble fire and waited patiently for him to stir, staring into the flames, concerned selfishly for my impending loneliness for already I was regretting my plan of parting from the Druid. The new day however, was to be one that holds a treasured memory within my heart. Just as I turned away from the fire, my master whispered to me.

"Rabbit," he uttered, "take heed. You must leave this place and get out of this forest."

I called out to him in uncertainty rather than disbelief.

"Danger lurks and you must take your leave now," he said finally.

I did not falter on my master's warning, much as I wanted to capture this moment searching for his spiritual form but his pressing urgency had me complying immediately by waking Ulcris.

"Do not question my motive lord but we must leave now. Danger loiters and we must be gone from here."

Within a few minutes, the Druid and I were parting company.

"I shall get word to you when all is ready," I called to him as he walked off into the thicket.

"I await with eagerness. Fare the well lad," he gestured, idly raising one arm before disappearing into the forest.

My mind burdened with the guilt by failing to admit to Ulcris the fate I instilled upon his brother, but if I confessed the truth would he not have cut me down?

I turned westward heading toward the ocean and though uncertain of the distance, knew the forest would end eventually. The desperation sensed in Treggedon's warning spurred urgency within me and where terrain allowed, I ran swiftly. Morning wore tirelessly on with unrelenting rain and the bare canopy of the trees did nothing to shelter me from the drenching. The land rose and fell like gentle waves, with patches of oak standing firm in grace amidst never-ending birch and gorse. The smell of decay all too often caught my breath causing involuntary fits of coughing. I took rest around noon and with a slow meander, gathered what nuts and berries the sparseness nature offered me. I finally came to rest upon an earth mound and ate greedily at my feeble collection, sparing nothing to fall to the ground. A gentle brushing in the blackened dead ferns stirred apprehension and hastily I forced the rest of the food into my mouth, searching eagerly to seek what skulked. Immediately I thought of Treggedon's admonition and whatever stalked me, feared it poised to attack. The horseman, Owell, Elcris or perhaps Talteth himself, I considered them all. I felt the piercing gaze contemplating my vulnerability waiting to strike with the coldness of steel and puncture my heart. I reached for the bones preparing to make a wish, refusing to die without a struggle. The rain turned into a torrential downpour, forcing me to shield my eyes by persistently blinking and rising from the ground, I stood to face my adversary. He approached tentatively with thick red coat matted by the rain and ragged brush dragging on the sodden woodland floor. His deep brown eyes gaped full and firm upon me with his head cocked, as if in pity of my dilemma.

"Hello fox," I greeted warmly.

It stopped and sat regally poised with his bulbous hazel eyes transfixed.

"I am glad of your company," I said. "Perhaps you are lost too."

The creature blinked, turned his gaze to the thicket and then returned his attention back to me.

"Are you the work of Elcris?"

It sounded a pathetic question but a Druid of his calibre was capable of anything such as this and could well disguise evil in such an animal of beauty.

"What is your business? Are you a messenger from Talteth?"

It was all very unnerving. No wild animal, even a gentle fox such as him, would dare saunter this close. There had to be something amiss.

"I am here to assist you," barked the fox.

I dropped the bones in astonishment. Had I wished inadvertently for the beast to converse?

"Follow me if you please," he barked again, turning about and melting into the ferns.

Despite my anxiety, I followed, though sceptically at first, but as time eroded felt growing confidence in my decision and if the fox were here on Talteth's behalf it would squander little time in trickery and strike keenly and swiftly without dwelling on gamesmanship.

Eventually the rain eased to a fine drizzle and icy blasts whistled their intent through the trees, concealing the rocks pronouncing the boundary of the forest. Gulls and terns soared gracefully above, swooping and gliding with impressionable

David Greely

ease. In my preoccupation, I lost sight of the fox and although calling and whistling it never showed itself. Though cold, the smell of the ocean was a refreshing alternative from the suffocating stench of leaf mould and decay of the forest. I clambered high on the rocks and surveyed the land from my vantage point. Directly west an uninterrupted view of the never-ending ocean: a dull grey-green sea whipping up white torrents against the jagged rocks below. To the south, my eyes followed the rising and falling cliff edge with groins of rich black rocks lying like open talons tearing into the water, sinking and rising with the motion of the swell and though not visible, Wendatch, I predicted, lay deep inside one of the many valleys encased by the vast forest. The north offered nothing in contrast and the dullness of the drizzle blocked any view of the mountains, let alone Polran, so I presumed I had not yet ventured far enough to witness it.

I remained determined and sank deeper into perplexity over the fox. Could it have been but a dream? An imagining conjured up subconsciously or perhaps the work of Elcris, nevertheless, I cared to think it but the kindness of nature with the guidance of God aiding me.

Eventually, I clambered off the rock, continuing northward keeping to the edge of the forest, stopping several times in hope of glimpsing the elusive fox. It was not until darkness fell did the beast come trotting out from the undergrowth bold and regal. He halted just a few paces in front of me but his accustomed mild manner since turned to that of agitation, if not anger. His tail twitched incessantly and when I took a step closer, the animal bared his teeth, which I took as a warning to stop my advance.

"Come now bold fox, is this a game you play with me?"

He did not respond to my asking.

"Are you a messenger from Talteth?"

The rusty beast still declined to answer and turned, strolling off ahead of me. Dutifully, I trailed him again, leading me through the darkness like a dim beacon weaving in and around trees, over rocks, through crags and down ditches. The fox's determination increased to a trot, forcing my breath to struggle and though I managed to keep the pace for a while his swiftness was too much over the terrain and I lost sight of him once more. I stopped panting and coughing, furiously uncertain of my bearings. The heavy cloud blocked any sighting of the moon or stars for guidance and no longer could I hear the lashing waves of the ocean. I was undeniably lost.

Sweet saviour then it happened. The calling of my name enchanted the very ground I stood upon and the mustiness of decay vanished into an overwhelming piquet of sweet incense.

"Arton. It is me, your king."

If not a wizard, I would have immediately renounced his voice.

The vision strengthened almost to a point of reality without decaying flesh in the canvas I had swathed him, neither rank of death nor air of disconcertedness. The almighty king stood tall in majestic refinement, clean and meticulously groomed, donned in the richest crimson velvet robe with plates of gold and chain mail shimmering with the slightest movement.

I gave the sign of the Lord's cross over my chest.

"You must listen," he said with clarity.

"You have the advantage over me good lord, for surely you are dead and did I not bury you with the toil of my own labour?"

"Go to the shores of Laddia and seek the hierophant. Only then can you avenge me and your master."

"But sire," I objected, "I travel north to raise an army against Talteth."

"That will prove quite useless Arton and you will fail."

"What of my master, is he with you? And what of Ulcris…?"

"…You ask too much Arton. Go north and you will be dead before daybreak."

His image began dissipating.

"Lord I need you! I need Treggedon!"

"To Laddia Arton, it is your only hope."

David Greely

I blinked my eyes to dispel the tears impairing my sight and whilst doing so the fox returned and sat boldly upon a mound staring at me. With hesitancy, I walked toward him. On this occasion it remained, allowing me to stroke his scruff. I sat cross-legged next to him content just to smile at his pant quickening with my gentle strokes.

"Tell me fox what I am in the need to know. You heard the almighty, I must leave this place to seek the hierophant. How do I do that? I know not where to look. Laddia is a kingdom far greater than ours, and an enemy too."

I stopped talking, suddenly recognising the place where I sat. It was the site where I originally met with the beast.

"Curse you fox! You have led me in a full circle."

The animal merely glanced at me, seemingly unaware of my irritation. My anger instantly quelled when noticing the tiny bones at my feet.

"Thank you and forgive me fox. I am guilty of misjudging your wisdom."

I collected the bones and held them tightly before replacing them into the pouch. They were my only protection and stupidly I discarded them, how could I be so thoughtless? Although reassured the bones where back in my possession, I sat in a state of despair with coldness, hunger and exhaustion overcoming me.

Chapter Seven

The day brought further rain and in the penetrating cold, I recited a brief prayer shortly after waking, appealing to the Lord for my safety rather than of worship. My fruitless search for food made me feel even wearier and all too quickly lethargy gripped. I honestly thought such feelings passed but eagerness subsided too, and my aptitude of being a wizard depleted to the lowest extreme. Regardless of my efforts to conjure food by wishing on the bones, such a futile endeavour went unrewarded. I slept most of the day to help stave off hunger, drifting into dreamy repetitions of events, concluding my uselessness in this entire venture and wishing to the powers to end my miserable existence, needless to say, that failed too.

Was I to continue carrying this unwanted burden thrust upon me by my master and the king forever? The truth is I fooled myself in becoming a sorcerer already proving incapable of the demand, for it was indeed Treggedon and not I whom bestowed this high honour. I felt so purposeless and

David Greely

pondered upon my ineptitude, which sent me delving into my very existence, knowing nothing of my short past not even a vague recollection of my kin frustrated me. I was born north of the mountains and my parents along with others were slain by Laddian raiders, well that is what my master told me and now I seemed destined to voyage to the very land that harbours such murderers. Untold questions plagued me as doubt led to further doubt and if successful locating the hierophant, what of me then? My fate looked decidedly bleak.

'Where is my strength O Lord? I appeal to you. Guide me through this day and all others.'

The strong waft of cooking meat stirred me and I woke to face darkness, which had long fallen in the duration of my slumber. Only the glowing embers from a fire offered a comfort I had all but since forgotten, I slid over to it without care as to whom it may have belonged and rubbed my hands together, capturing every degree of warmth it radiated, to rid the coldness overstaying its term in my body. The skewered meat was beyond temptation and eagerly I tore a piece from the carcass juggling it between my fingers to avoid its burning. Sumptuous as it seemed, sudden disgust struck, it may have been the fox and I dropped it contemptuously.

"That's it boy, eat heartily. God knows yer need it," smiled the hunchback.

"Owell!" I screeched in surprise at meeting the hideous man again.

"Does the flavour of wolf not liken to yer belly?" he grinned widely.

"Wolf?" I reaffirmed, comforted by the hunchback's disclosure.

"That is all I could trap but even that is better than the scrawny, fleshless carcass of a rat, much too gristly for my liking."

I laughed nervously; relieved the fox was not his victim.

"To confess, Owell, I am perplexed for surely after me killing your partner you would be only too keen to seek revenge and rid yourself from me?"

"On the contrary boy, you served me a great service in killing Whelp. He was nothin' but trouble and all in all much too tiresome."

"But surely…?"

"…No buts about it boy," he interrupted, "I am deeply in your debt."

He ripped off another piece of meat cramming it into his mouth.

"I must say," he continued endeavouring to speak whilst chewing, "you amazed me with the strength you possess, considering yer size and age. Perhaps you have a certain how can I say…" he stopped briefly to swallow, "…technique. Yes technique, that's the word I was lookin' for."

"Perhaps," I replied, dismissing his allegation rapidly.

"Tell me what is really behind your purpose here and what of your travelling companion?" he asked.

"Companion?" I deliberately doubted to bide further time for a convincing reply.

"The tall man you know, the Druid," he pressed.

"Oh him," I dispelled indifferently, "I do not know. He abandoned me directly you ran off."

"I didn't run off," he rebuked somewhat bashfully. "I was just tired of sticking around for nothing. Anyway, I never see 'im go," he doubted.

"Nor did I Owell, one moment he was there and the next well…" I hesitated, "…he just vanished."

"Does this forest not frighten you?"

"No, not at all," I responded confidently.

I was lying of course and nigh on petrified. Even after the short term spent within it, if I could have got myself away from this forlorn place I would have done so long ago.

"I have the Good Lord by my side," I said.

"Ah, so you must be a preacher's boy and not that of a farmer then."

"No not strictly so. I believe and follow the way of the Lord but preach only to myself and not others."

"I need a boy like you," he continued, biting off another lump of meat.

"I will not succumb to the devious arts of robbery and deception nor indeed murder," I insisted.

"Are you not already a murderer?" he implied smiling. "Besides that technicality, you appear to have me all wrong for I am no thief, nor murderer."

"Were you not prepared to assist your partner in killing me?" I proffered.

"Nah, yer have me all wrong laddie, perhaps I ought to explain. You see, if it were not for Whelp, I surely would have perished. Having saved me a long time back, I felt in his debt and could only but follow his traits as obligation …and for my own survival you understand."

"No I do not understand Owell, and do not particularly want to either. I am grateful for the food but I really must be on my way."

"Way? Way, where?" he ventured.

"North and return to my master."

"You still deceive me boy," he scowled.

I looked at him with renewed scepticism.

"Owell?" I quizzed innocently though somewhat pathetically.

"You have been travelin' south since we parted I have been tracking you."

"Then," I suggested to him, "I am deeply lost."

"Perhaps I think that you too may be seeking the king. The reward for him is quite substantial but I am certain you are aware of that already."

"That is not my purpose Owell and need not the riches of blood money."

"You disapprove then?"

"I have no further say in the matter. I seek only peace and the path of the Lord God."

"Then take your leave!" he raged, spitting a fleshless bone from his mouth into the fire. "Go now and waste none of my precious time."

I rose slowly and rubbed my legs vigorously to sample the last of the heat before taking leave from him.

"May your God go with you boy."

"And yours with you Owell if you have one!"

I turned on my heels and without looking back walked eastward into the thicket. I could not help feeling an element of pity for the hunchback, for truly he must have been a lonely individual and no doubt faced a rekindled prospect of a life of ridicule without his partner. Without premeditation, I suddenly stopped, whether on impulse is uncertain, nevertheless, spun round and walked toward him.

"Owell," I called out, "I have a proposition."

He twisted his head casually to greet my words almost as if expecting my return.

"An offer? You have nothing to offer me."

I stood by him.

"Ah, but I have. If I were to rid you of your impediment would you swear fealty to the Lord God and to the king almighty?"

"If you could rid me of my damnation I would swear to anything but you forget it was your 'Good Lord' which bestowed this disfigurement upon me in the first place."

"What the Lord giveth, Owell, he can taketh away," I maintained.

"I cannot and will not give fealty," he said adamantly.

"Then Owell, so be it." I said turning away.

"Wait!" he shouted. "Perhaps I am being a little hasty, tell me more of this offer of yours boy."

His tone sounded condescending and patronising but I needed him and his strength to assist me on my quest. If I was to cross the great sea to Laddia, I required help in doing so besides, deep down if I were to admit it, wanted the company. Already I had learned how isolated a person can feel treading the way of righteousness.

"Then swear it."

"I Owell, swear fealty to the Lord and king Arbereth."

"So be it," I said, "I shall now execute my charm upon you."

Away from Owell's observation, I clasped the bones in readiness and sat close to the fire.

"Believe with faith Owell and no harm will fall upon you."

He drew his knife undoubtedly caked with dried blood from his countless victims. The compulsion I felt to do the incantation was so powerful within me I could sense the strength of the Lord deep inside my soul. I closed my eyes and wished inwardly, pushing aside the fear that Owell may strike. In retrospect, shutting my eyes was rather foolish under the circumstance but so strong was the energy driving me there was no choice. A might so immense up until now never felt as strong, it exuded a divinity and holiness from me. A sudden shock forced my arms open. Owell remained seated opposite with his eyes straining skyward in horror and his wide-mouthed gape portrayed a look of misery as if expecting some beast to fall from the heavens. The sky cracked open, breaking the dense pitch with a brilliant flash and a great fissure spread across the sky like splitting ice on a frozen pond. The dazzling radiance temporarily blinded me, forcing me to avert my gaze. Then a thunderbolt flashed down onto my victim and for a brief moment I feared it had killed him. Did I really wish the cripple vindication from burden or did I subconsciously want him dead, now adequately capable of such fiendish acts? I blinked repeatedly, adjusting to the darkness again. The fire appeared no brighter than a spill after the great luminescence of the lightening and beside it, Owell lay on his back motionless, obviously stung by the power of the lightening with eyes locked in a trance, insensible to the surroundings or me. My concern relented when he stirred, shaking his head as if hit by some vicious blow.

"Consider your fate boy!" he raged gasping irregularly.

I noticed my deed duly served and pointed to his back as he slowly rose to his feet.

"Incredible! A damn miracle! Ha, ha!"

Owell pranced around the fire with uncontrollable jubilation.

"It's incredible!" he repeated with exaltation.

I sat, pleased with myself while watching the man dance, acknowledging the gift granted to me be put to proper use and for the right reason. I converted a blasphemous villain into a Christian, indeed a miracle and if wine or mead could be got then a celebration for the two of us would have taken place.

"Praise the Lord," he laughed jubilantly. "Praise the Almighty. Praise you boy. Praise all..." Owell ceased his words, stopped dancing and thought for a moment.

"...What is this magic you possess?"

"It is a gift. A gift from God," I replied.

"Well whatever you call it, it is nothing short of miraculous."

Already I sensed his scheming and drafting ideas in his calculative mind to turn my power to use.

"Do you know what this means boy? It means we can earn a wealth of fortune and travel this land and others. People will flock from miles to witness such feats. We shall demand uncountable fees for such healings and within a season we will be rich, very rich."

As Owell rambled on, muttering such schemes as he did, I began doubting my judgement.

"Stop!" I shouted to him. "Enough of this! You swore your fealty."

"Yeah, well that was before," he disclaimed.

"Understand me Owell. I can readily change matters and for the worse too."

"Come lad I was merely jesting. I am a man of my word."

"Then keep it Owell and let this night remind you of it."

He quickly quelled his celebration and sat down.

"Sorry," he said unconvincingly, "but I just can't help feeling happy. Too long have my spirits been repressed by my revolting disfigurement. This night and all nights to come I shall show my gratitude to the Lord."

"Then do so now," I ordered him.

David Greely

"What now, at this precise moment?" said Owell suddenly bewildered.

"Yes, now. Give praise to the Lord in heaven."

The long pause of silence must have been agonising for him. I knew all too well rats cannot rid themselves from fleas, nor can a headstrong villain become a meek disciple of God, but he owed me and he owed the Lord and payment was due.

"I don't know what to say."

"Say what you feel," I urged.

"I feel good," he said.

"Then praise the Lord for the goodness you feel."

"Thank you Lord for this miracle…," he paused.

"…And?" I pressed.

"And …and I am beholding to you. Praise you Lord and the king almighty."

"That was not too difficult now Owell was it?" I asked mocking him.

He shrugged his shoulders in a coy fashion.

"No, I suppose it wasn't," he finally admitted.

"And in the morrow you can give prayer again. And the next day and the next, forever Amen."

"Amen lad. Amen."

I carefully replaced the bones, seizing the chance to do so without the suspicious eyes of Owell upon me. If he were to discover them I would not survive the night and be throttled by his hands.

After his jubilation subsided, we eventually slept and the remainder of the night passed swiftly and without interruption other than diminutive bursts of Owell's excitement. The weariness of my body held me captive and I do not recall dreaming.

The fresh day was bitter and though dry, the daunting greyness brought imminence of foul weather. Upon my rising, Owell was prepared and alert in readiness, and spoke the first words.

"I can't keep calling you boy, boy."

"I am Arton, apprenticed to Treggedon."

"That is of little consequence as to whom you were attached, Arton will do. Well Arton my lad I am your servant, lead on."

To avoid him embarrassment I said a short prayer before leading off westward with Owell dutifully trailing. We trekked for endless miles aiming toward the western coast, and as we walked Owell persisted in whistling a high-pitched invention that was far from melodic and it grated upon me. To break such torture, I insisted he tell me of his quests, some of which I found amusing but most, unsavoury and indeed unthinkable. Sorcery seemed paramount to him but I chose to reveal little despite his asking, though briefly mentioned my trait when referring to the tale of my master's spell in the alehouse at Wendatch, just to appease his unhealthy lust. Without disclosure of events, I eventually told him of my quest to find the hierophant.

"This man you seek, who is he?" he asked.

"I know not who or what he is but Laddia is our destination and once there I feel sure we shall seek the hierophant out."

"But why Laddia? That place harbours nothing but the enemy and there will be no ally for us there."

I dared not reply my thoughts to him. 'Enemy to whom? Not to the king for he is dead but to Talteth, then yes!'

"You are but a boy Arton; though I have to admit you possess a shrewd and clever tongue and the Laddians will cut it from you, mark my words, then what will become of me?"

"You? You are a man are you not?"

Owell did not answer and I stopped, turning to face him.

"With you as my aide, together we will seek the hierophant and once found the perplexity of our problem will be resolved."

"Our problem?" he questioned, breaking a hanging twig touching his face.

"Why of course, after all it is not just for my benefit Owell, it is for you too and all the realmsfolk in this forsaken land. I have been burdened with the task to seek the answer but cannot do so alone."

"Your ambition appears somewhat high Arton."

"Not ambition my friend," I responded, "but an errand bestowed upon me by my master and the king, one of which I must see through for such is the gravity of failure."

"And what if you should fail?"

"Then the realm will wallow in the darkness of despair Talteth will surely cause. Blood will spill and innocents will become victims of greed. He will not be content until he succeeds and God help the mortals standing in his way."

I prolonged posing Owell my next question because I wanted him to absorb the callousness of Talteth and his capabilities.

"Do you honestly think you would have lived to reap your reward?"

I did not give him the opportunity to react.

"No, you would not! You would have gone to him with the king as hostage, high spirits would have deluded your judgement and no sooner would he have paid you the purse with one hand, his sword would have struck you down with the other and you would be dead before the almighty himself."

"Well," insisted Owell, "that hardly matters now, does it? Now that we are off to Laddia I'll leave the measly purse for the king to someone else."

Owell pressed ahead of me thrashing through the undergrowth.

"There will be no finding of the king, Owell; Arbereth is dead murdered by the bloodied sword of a horseman."

"Nevertheless, news of his demise will surely reap some reward," he said, seemingly unmoved by my disclosure.

I could sense Owell was still scheming and tugged at his arm, turning him around to face me.

"Not from your lips Owell, and any such attempt and you will face the agony of renewed disfigurement, I swear it so!"

"Whoa! I was only thinking and nothing more," he admitted, holding up his arms in submission.

"Well then do no more thinking!" I said finally.

He swallowed hard and walked ahead mumbling under his breath undoubtedly cursing me.

In the consequent silence between us, I thought briefly of Ulcris still feeling the melancholy of our parting. He was without question a man I warmed to and trusted implicitly. I wondered too, if ever I would meet with the elusive fox again and the peculiarity of his guidance leading me back to the bones.

The day wore laboriously on. The variegation of the trees remained dense on our path and the forest with its smells and sounds sickened me. Owell did not exchange many words after our rebuff. Only when night fell when setting camp and tending a fire did he choose to speak and we both sat close, huddled against a fallen tree to escape the wind driving the rain down on us.

"In the morrow," he said, "we will reach Fleddon. There we can get passage to Laddia. I have a friend that can help us."

Much as I was tempted to say it, I refrained. 'Is he a thief too?' I wondered.

"I have known Pennypot for years. We go back a long time me and him."

"Pennypot?" I mused.

"He is a beggar and a good one I hasten to add. Been at Fleddon for as long as I care to remember. He and I grew up together and became close, what with our impediments and all."

"He will be surprised to see you reformed."

"Have no doubt, if he could see, he would."

"He is blind?"

"Very," confirmed Owell.

I shuddered at my thoughts of Beladon and for one inconceivable moment, imagined the evil man could be the very person Owell referred. The curse of meeting yet another blind man in this escapade made me tremble.

"Are you alright Arton?"

"Yes. Just tired that is all," I promptly excused myself.

"The day has been sapping," yawned Owell in sympathy. "Pennypot is a good man. Sure he has his moments of well, let's say…" he paused briefly, "…temptation but only to secure his needs for survival, you understand."

"Oh I do Owell, I do."

"After all, men like him and indeed me up until yesterday have to survive and thus put our skills to the test."

"Of course," I agreed smiling, aware of what was about to follow.

"Arton, I was just thinking…" again he dithered, "…if you can perform such transformations in a man, could you not help my friend too?"

"Owell, if it were that simple I would not hesitate but you must understand, I have a gift the mighty Lord willingly gave me, but it is something that cannot be beckoned by the click of my fingers and certainly not a whim called upon to better oneself, it takes much more than that. If God chooses me to act, then readily I do so and not for selfishness besides, if it is that simple would I not have whisked us off directly to Laddia without having to trudge through this forsaken forest? Would I not be enjoying the comforts of a well-stocked alehouse offering the finest mead and food? Look Owell, to be honest with you, I have tried all manner of things to better my plight or situation but nothing happens. Nothing I try to do for personal gain is ever granted, only on God's wish will it occur and that is the truth."

Indeed it was and I came to realise over the last few days exactly that. I only held the tool, but it is God, whom controlled the power.

"So my healing was indeed an act of God?"

"Very much so Owell, you really ought to feel honoured."

"Oh I am, praise the Lord not that I am ungrateful for such a miracle. I was just wondering that's all. What I mean is, if I deserved such miraculous treatment then surely too does Pennypot."

"Perhaps you are special after all, you are helping me are you not?"

"I am," he confirmed.

"And you have been rewarded so."

"Maybe if Pennypot helps us he could have the touch of God given him as well. He would truly deserve so Arton, he truly would."

"Only God can judge it. Only he has the divine right."

"Then I pray it may be so."

"We both do my friend," I said finally. "Now, let us rest."

I threw the stick, used to poke the fire, unwittingly into the flames and curled up by its warmth. Despite my fatigue, restlessness tore at me like a disease and most of the night I remained conscious, watching the first snow that ultimately arrived. In disquiet, I pondered without conclusion whether my thoughts of the king, my master, Ulcris or the fox were really dreams or future visions.

Daylight revealed a thick frosty carpet unevenly extended over the forest floor accompanied by a penetrating wind gnawing at my flesh.

"Do you see them Arton? Wolf prints," confirmed Owell crouching in his study. "They were here sure enough, yet strange I never heard 'em let alone see 'em but they were here all right. I am mystified why we 'aven't been torn to pieces."

I rose to study them and validated Owell's discovery.

"I see but do not believe," I said.

"I was awake most of the night and never saw anything. You're the clever one, you explain it."

"I do not profess to be clever Owell, nor do I have an answer. Like you, I heard and saw nothing."

He was right of course; no pack of bloodthirsty wolves would leave trace of us, and again studied the impressions.

"We have been given protection."

"Protection?" Owell looked at me bewildered.

"Something else here," I pointed to the track differing from all the others.

"Looks the same as the rest to me, smaller perhaps..."

"...Not only smaller but a different shape too. The fox," I muttered softly staring at the ground, "it has to be the fox."

"What fox?" asked Owell.

David Greely

I did not even attempt telling him, conceding he would never grasp nor approve my account.

"Oh nothing," I replied, "it is of no consequence."

"Well whatever it was I think it's time we move on."

Owell set the pace and I followed, continuingly glancing over my shoulder hoping to sight the bold creature again. The contours of the land rose gradually for several leagues and gorse took precedence over the density of the trees. At last, we reached the summit, both breathless after the long and winding incline. Deep in the valley below an arterial bridge spanned a river cutting Fleddon in half. The town appeared larger than imagined, stretching across the valley with its westward point stopping abruptly at the sea. Several ships amid smaller craft lined the small inlet where the meandering river spilled into the ocean.

"It looks welcoming," I said cheerily, excited at the prospect of seeing a new town.

"Don't be deceived Arton, like all places it has its good and bad points. It may seem a thriving community but lurking in its shadows is filth, poverty, disease and despair. It harbours murderers who need little excuse to slit your throat and vagabonds that would pilfer the very drippings from yer nose. You'd be wise to keep your head low; it's hardly a place for the likes of you."

Apart from feeling dejected at Owell's description, I grew anxious and remained closer to him. Within the hour, we declined the hill and walked upon the road leading to the northern approach of the town. The well-trodden road gradually populated with travellers and traders alike and artfully, we mingled amid the throng without drawing attention to ourselves. It was pleasing to be amongst people again, be they strangers. The drone of the merchants swelled in the cold air, calling and shouting their sales of ware, competing with the snorting, bleating and cackling livestock. Wafts of cooking meat and fresh bread filled my nostrils with an appealing temptation but then it struck, a God-smitten stench so foul I could taste death, its abhorrence made me wretch.

"You will get used to it," smiled Owell turning to me.

"What is it?" I asked, trying desperately to breathe through my mouth.

"Depravity mixed with raw sewage," he offered willingly.

"I have never smelled anything like it."

"You probably ain't likely too," Owell quipped. "Only a rotting corpse can boast of reeking worse."

"Can we hurry?" I pleaded.

Gratefully, Owell picked up the pace and eagerly we weaved through the milling crowds, crossing over the bridge before turning sharply away from the harbour area and into countless narrow streets and lanes bustling with beggars and scuffling drunks.

"Pennypot lives here amidst all this?"

"Indeed so," confirmed Owell. "He has to. Do not underestimate him Arton. Despite his appearance, he is a very intelligent and resourceful individual. He begs for his living, maintaining a relatively sustainable way of life and has an uncanny feel for plight and will offer and sell many, shall I say, solutions to those estranged. He will have an answer for your dilemma. He usually trades on the northern side but resides here. Follow me."

Owell darted down a dingy passage and I trailed closely daring not to lose him for fear of isolation and exposure to this inhospitable place. The narrow alley turned sharply with the placement of irregular buildings. Most were low with eaves barely above Owell's head and timbers frail with ageing rot and signs hanging precariously above, advertising all manner of seedy businesses. He suddenly halted, glancing in either direction and entered a door seemingly insensible to care if I still accompanied him. Without any hesitation, I followed. A dark hallway led to several doors one of which Owell tentatively opened and then pushed me in.

In the dimness of the dishevelled room lazed a small ill-kempt individual possessing black, lank hair falling in greasy bunches over his sallow face and eyes wandering like senseless orbs in their sockets, confirming his evident blindness. His clothing was as drab as his abode with tattered cuffs on his sleeves hiding his hands, trews long since seen better days and sandals with more twine than leather binding them together.

"Pennypot?" Owell called from hiding, in an exaggerated whisper, poking his head through the widening gap.

"Who asks?" returned a mild-mannered voice.

"T'is me, Owell."

"Friend, enter and I bid you warm welcome."

"How's business?" asked Owell slowly entering the door.

"Oh, much the same, you know how it is trying to scrape a living," replied the beggar. "You must be desperate, what brings you back to Fleddon?"

"On an errand of mercy," declared Owell.

"My ears deceive me, you, seeking mercy?" the beggar laughed. "Never!"

"Maybe I word it wrong. We come to you for help."

"We?" questioned Pennypot glaring vacantly toward me.

"Yes we," reiterated Owell, "the lad 'ere and my good self. Come Arton show yourself."

Owell silently presented me to the blind beggar by pushing me closer to him.

My nervousness in meeting him reflected in my voice.

"Er ...hello Pennypot, Owell has told me a little of you."

"I hope it was good and nothing ill-fitting or insulting," he jibed warmly.

"Full of praise you can be assured," I said.

"Well enough of the pleasantries, we come to you for help."

I could sense Owell's impatience.

"So be it my friend," conceded Pennypot. "What is the nature of your business with me?"

"We need a boat," Owell declared.

"That is easy enough, anyone down the quayside will grant you one and you don't need my assistance."

"With a crew," continued Owell.

"That should not prove too difficult either. A tad limiting perhaps but nevertheless available at a price," assured Pennypot.

"To sail to Laddia," Owell grinned nervously.

In sudden silence, the beggar cocked his head to one side expecting further dialog from Owell.

"Laddia!" the beggar eventually exclaimed. "Are you out of your minds? Laddia is the kingdom's sworn enemy and nobody would want to go there through choice."

"We have no option," I said.

"Your motive I will not question stranger, but to avail a boat and crew to go there is an impossibility," spurned the beggar.

"Rot!" returned Owell abruptly. "Nothing is beyond your means my friend."

"I'm not sure I can help you," resigned Pennypot.

"Then who can?" I asked.

"There is no other," said Pennypot.

"Why the air of pessimism my friend?" asked Owell.

"There is nothing in Fleddon worthy of such a crossing," advocated Pennypot.

"I saw good ships in the harbour, are they not seaworthy?" I argued.

"The craft may be, but certainly not any crew. They're not sailors but merely fishermen and none of them trustworthy," warned Pennypot.

"Then we shall row ourselves," I said.

"Impossible!" Owell contended. "Come on Arton be realistic. I know not how or where to steer and nor do you. We'd never make it."

The beggar remained seated, smiling doubtlessly at my suggestion and Owell's rejection.

"Let me consider this awhile," the beggar said. "I have a matter that needs attending to so wait here awhile for my return. I shall be back later, and then perhaps we can give your dilemma a little more thought. In the meantime make yourselves welcome, my house is your house. It truly is good to see

David Greely

you again Owell, well if I could, but you know what I mean. I will be as swift as I can. Now I really must be on my way."

The beggar shuffled to the door, fumbled with the latch prior to opening then slammed it shut behind him.

"We should have told him we do not have any money," I said.

"I'll go after him. I know he'll help us with or without it."

"I hope you are right Owell though I do not share your optimism in him."

Owell left directly, muttering under his breath in his usual manner.

Alone in the stranger's place, I sat discontented, awaiting their return and much as wanting to rifle through the beggar's possessions, refrained from doing so, satisfied merely to wander in and around his abode. From a top window, I noticed an alehouse and thought venturing there might give opportunity to meet with someone who could help my plight. I did think at this juncture of Owell's insincerity but dispelled my doubts, knowing full well the outcome of his candour would be proven to me, besides he knew his fate should he wander from his sworn allegiance, and converting back to a disfigured vagrant he could have hardly relished.

Firstly, I washed and sought a change of clothing, settling for an oversized grey smock. Again, I had in mind to delve into Pennypot's possessions but swiftly declined my urge, knowing a man of his attributes would notice my disturbance moreover, I did not want to put his aid in jeopardy, something I could ill-afford to forsake.

Having dressed, I ventured out into the coldness, returning to the bustle of the town's populous and its putrid stench, retracing my steps along the narrow streets until finding the Brass Monkey. Although sombre and filthy, the place appeared an inviting haven amongst the hovels surrounding it. I gripped the door latch, drew a long breath and pushed myself in. The deceptively large room proffered secretive alcoves along one side and a haze of pipe smoke dense as the fog, equalled the alehouse at Wendatch. Several rows of benches lined the wall opposite with tables disorderly sited in front, each tendering a varying length of spent candle stuck in blackened holders. The serving bar littered with pitchers did nothing to conceal the stains of age and at the furthest end a feeble excuse for a fire, spat out a feeble flame to combat the cold loitering within. Three men sat hunched over a smaller table engaging in serious conversation and just beyond them, a woman and her male companion conversed, equally oblivious of my entry. I trod the three steps downward and sat at the vacant table nearest to the fire. The portly owner approached asking my preference.

"Mead, if you please," I ordered.

He returned speedily with a jug and set it on the table. I noticed the grime between his fingernails as he pushed the vessel toward me but with a shrug of resignation, greedily took a huge gulp. It tasted relatively rank by comparison to Wendatch but it had been awhile since imbibing, what I sampled proved relatively potent and resorted to sipping upon realisation. I gazed up at the unshaven and sallow-faced fellow bending over me projecting an age beyond two score, but his pallid complexion and darkened rings around his eyes may have possibly delineated my estimation.

"May I join you?" the man asked softly.

"Of course," I replied shifting along the bench to accommodate him.

"A bit young to be revelling in such haunts aren't you?"

"Perhaps," I said, meeting his question with very little enthusiasm.

"Where you from?" he continued, finally settling himself beside me.

"Nowhere and yet everywhere."

"Let me guess now, you are fair of face so maybe you are a Laddian."

His speculation riled me.

"No such thing!" I retorted adamantly. "If so, would I be frequenting such a place as this and are Laddians not sworn enemies of the king?"

David Greely

"Ah, our beloved king," he sighed. "Are you a supporter of him?" the man asked.

"I am, and praise the almighty."

"Shhh! You do not want to be shouting out your loyalty here, men have died for less. Why, before you know it, you'll be clapped in irons and put on a boat to Laddia."

'That is it, my prayers answered and passage to Laddia!' My thoughts raced ahead causing my inattention to the many questions the man aimed at me.

"You seem preoccupied lad. Share your ale with me and I will tell all you need to know," he said glancing down at my vessel.

"Why would I want to know anything?"

"Come lad," he said focusing his eyes back on me, "the signs are all too obvious."

"Meaning?" I asked.

"Meaning that no one, particularly a lad would dare drink alone in this place. This house is crawling with degenerates and Laddians, and nobody comes into the Monkey out of choice. See Tadpole over there," the man gestured his hand toward the innkeeper, "he has an uncanny knowledge for all who repast here. Look about but do not let your eyes linger. See that woman," the man flicked his head in her direction, "she is a strumpet to whom Tadpole expects half her earnings and the man beside her is trying to evade paying for her services. You are lucky I am here because another few minutes you could have been succumbing to her and all her feminine charms. And those three men," again his head tilted several times, deviously in their direction, "they are the sheriff's henchmen and always on the lookout for a bargain, a bargain such as your worthy self."

"Sorry but I do not quite follow you," I said looking sternly at him.

"Let's just say the sheriff is head of the militia here and makes his fortune on slavery, a youngster of your breeding would unquestionably fetch him a handsome fee and because you are in Tadpole's domain he will receive a substantial monetary slice of the dues."

"Slavery for what purpose?" I asked naively.

"Any purpose you care to think of; rat catching, barnacle scraping, in fact any such mundane chore that pays little or nothing. The list is endless my friend. There are of course other tasks for those that fail to comply and grave digging is another, though I consider it a vocation of higher regard in contrast to feeding the lepers down at the cripples' gate. Shit clearance is considered worse, although perhaps…"

I grasped the essence of his warning and interrupted him.

"…Where do you appropriate yourself in such affairs?"

"A drink?" he pursued.

"Why are you forwarding me the warning?"

"For your own sake," he replied. "I seek no more than a jug of ale and good company. I am destitute and without purpose, coming here day upon day in a meaningless and tiresome existence."

"Then why stay? There are better and more prosperous towns in the realm other than Fleddon."

He leant to me and whispered.

"I have no choice. A drink, please spare me some ale," he asked again.

I took compassion on him and pushed my mead toward him.

"God bless you boy," he thanked and eagerly took a large swig.

"I hope you mean that?" I said sternly.

After smacking his lips, he responded.

"I can be accused of many things lad but blasphemy, no."

"You are a believer of the faith?" I asked.

"Perhaps," he replied as if with disinterest.

"Perhaps?" I quizzed him further.

"Yes perhaps, for certainly I did once."

"And what gave you doubt?" I encouraged him to elaborate.

David Greely

He took another swallow and leaned toward me, exhaling the mead's potency over my face.

"The Lord God took my son, my only son. He would have been about your age. Last summer he was taken."

"Then may God rest his soul," I said making the sign of the Holy Cross on my chest.

"Oh no, he is not dead, least, I pray not."

"But you said…?"

"…The lord saw fit to send him to Laddia, sold by the sheriff to slave for the enemy."

"I have heard nothing of this sheriff's despicable business. The king would never allow this to happen," I advocated sternly.

"Far too many years Gelbor has had his way here but now I await the king's arrival and the chance to rectify matters. News tells me he visits Wendatch and it can only be a matter of a few days before he reaches here, then I will tell him of these unholy acts."

I tested my own judgment but committed myself to the man.

"He will not be coming to Fleddon."

"Ridiculous boy, of course he will be here! He always comes here once his business is done in Wendatch."

"The king is dead!" I whispered.

The stranger slumped back against the wall with a look of apprehension and discouragement.

"When and how?" he asked eventually.

"He was murdered by the sword of a horseman. We had left Wendatch pursued under order from Talteth days ago, I do not recall exactly how many, perhaps five, six, maybe seven…"

"…You confuse me. Talteth…?"

"…I know Talteth is his son and what I disclose to you seems unthinkable but I swear to God it is the truth."

In brief, I revealed the misfortune of my errand without ever disclosing my power or reason for being at Fleddon, merely the slaying of the king and those thick in the scheme against him and the realm.

Our eyes met reflecting the hopelessness we were both sensing. Suppressing the tears pouring down my face was difficult to control and apart from the sadness for me and the situation faced, felt some anguish for the stranger next to me, no matter what he may have done, suffering with the ill of the unknown is an excessive price to pay and surely God's practice is above it.

"Have faith my friend," I eventually spoke. "You will find your son, pray to the Lord. The king is dead, long live the king!"

I rose from the table, bearing toward the door but the gruff voice shouting above the mundane drone of the house stopped me immediately and without inclination, confronted Tadpole.

"Who's paying for your drink?"

The trivial matter of coinage was an imprudent oversight and I glimpsed back at the stranger who sat incognizant of my predicament, staring into the drained vessel.

"Well?" insisted the landlord, puffing out his cheeks in exasperation.

"I have no money sir."

Tadpole tightened his lips with escalating fury.

I cussed having induced unwanted attention and in the intensifying predicament, the alehouse lessened to a murmur, excepting the constant sniggering from the small gathering of men.

"Unless I get payment..."

"...I am not refusing, it is just I have no money."

Judging by his reddening face I sensed I was testing Tadpole's patience.

"I will accept nothing else."

"Run boy!" shouted the lean stranger. "Run!"

Before I had chance to react a hand clawed my clothing, forcing me to my knees and the henchman pinned me tightly against the wall.

"What is your request for this wretch, Tadpole?" he asked, pushing his weight against me.

"Fetch me a good price," he beamed.

Despite meagre condemnation from the stranger, my captor bundled me out of the door and escorted me through the narrow streets of Fleddon amid shouts of increasing ridicule from its townsfolk. Trying desperately to liberate myself from my captor's grip he compensated me with a spiteful punch to my back and whilst shrinking with pain, became hurled headlong into a caged cart, joining others of misfortune. The threatening whip of the rugged mercenary curtailed my shouts, so I willingly complied to remain silent. I sat submersed in dejection and self-pity, though without justification, considering I may have secured what I sought by getting my passage to Laddia.

Along with the other detainees, I remained despondently quiet, cold and hungry in a manner of damnation. My perplexed emotions did little to boost my assurance, for I did not relish the quest still facing me. Even with the assumption of crossing the ocean to Laddia as good as secured, I had to undertake seeking out the hierophant and needed guidance, hoping the bones would provide, yet that aside, I still found myself pleading upon them for liberation though no answer proffered.

The hours in captivity brought darkness until eventually the cart rattled off over cobbles and trenches toward the harbour. Dim lights from some abodes reflected their meagre glow on the thick pools of slurry oozing across the roadway and trickling downhill toward the stinking harbour. We came to a halt outside a large wooden building on the quayside and the five of us chained together jostled inside continuing our compliance in the dark and dampened room.

"A fine consignment Blen," invited the sheriff.

He was sheriff true enough, his manner betraying him so, dressed morbidly in black and full of self-regard with an ego as long as my arm.

"They will fetch a handsome price," he continued.

"Indeed so," confirmed the keeper in a patronising manner.

"Have them ready for tomorrow's auction," ordered the sheriff before taking leave.

"Auction?" I contested in surprise. "I have to get to Laddia, not sold to some wealthy landowner in the realm."

"Quiet lad or you'll feel my whip!" shouted the keeper, twisting and teasing the leather strapping in his hands, keen to put it to use.

I languished in trepidation about the bones and secured the pouch best I could around my manhood, hoping not to be stripped.

"Master?"

My intention was to whisper my appeal to Treggedon and not call out as loud as I did. The flick of the keeper's wrist cracked the whip smartly across my face, its sting venomous as the nettles pulled from Ulcris.

"I warned you about staying quiet," he said.

"Curse you!" I cried.

The keeper cracked his whip again, catching my rising forearm to protect my face.

"Silence!" he demanded.

"Curse you a hundred times!" I retorted rebelliously.

He grabbed my neck and dragged me up against the wall.

"I will not repeat myself to you or any other. Do not push me into using force."

"You cannot hit me," I remonstrated, "the sheriff will be displeased and any blemishes will lower my price tag."

Without warning, he punched me in the gut.

"There," he smiled with immense satisfaction, "he won't see that will he? Now silence!"

He turned about and bolted the door behind him, leaving me doubled up in agony on the floor gasping for breath.

Having recovered from the keeper's blow, I sat with the other occupiers of the grimy room, nursing the sting on my face in renewed silence. Only the sporadic footsteps of Blen the keeper beyond the door broke the otherwise deathly quiet. I drifted in and out of slumber throughout the night, undergoing heady dreams and scattered thoughts.

The shifting bolt stirred me and distorted silhouettes of the approaching keeper and his two assistants flickered against the wall in the brilliance of the flaming torch one of them held aloft. They threw in another victim, which created a dull thud as his apathetic body fell heavily to the floor and with their business swiftly dealt, left their unconscious victim lying in a dishevelled heap next to me. I tried reviving him but failed and eventually slept.

Daybreak came rapidly and the arched grilled window directed a shaft of refreshing sunlight against the door opposite. I glanced at the despondent prisoners in turn, sitting virtually motionless staring vacantly at the floor between their legs, and when my eyes met the latter intern I realised it was he, the stranger from the Brass Monkey.

"Well lad," he said, greeting my fervent study, "looks like I have found you."

"It would appear so. Were you looking for me then?"

"Companionship," he said affording a smile. "I thought we might travel the realm together, once we get out of this mess of course, and find what you seek. There is nothing for me here what with the king being…"

"…Shhh!" I stopped him.

"The king being what?" asked one of the others raising his head in awareness. "What is that about the king?"

"Now you have done it!" I sneered at the lean man.

"What of the king?" demanded another, confirming the surmounting curiosity.

"Quiet now," I pleaded softly. "Say nothing and listen to me all of you. The king is dead. Arbereth has been murdered."

I could hear their sighs and looks of despondency.

"And Talteth was his father's killer and I shall avenge him. Talteth's treason must and will be accountable."

"Listen to the boy," said one man in mocking tone, "he's going to avenge our king. You talk little above treason yourself. Talteth is a worthy king and you talk false."

"It is true," I implored. "I swear to God Almighty."

"That means nothing here; in fact it means nothing anywhere. Where is the Good Lord now, has he not deserted you? Has he not deserted us?"

"Our time will come, you see."

I was not offering them false hopes for I truly believed the Good Lord would redeem us.

"Hey, what goes on in there?"

The opening of the door and Blen's' booming timbre quickly silenced us.

"Come on you lot," he continued. "It is your big day so look lively now."

I stood with the others awaiting instruction while the keeper began eyeing us all in turn, his malevolent gaze sent shivers down my back. I promised myself this man needed a lesson taught and I would be the one to administer it as soon as the chance availed itself.

In single chain-clinking file, we followed the front guard into the daylight, stopping on a platform by the side of the building. Here, a crowd of several dozen men and a handful of ladies gathered, scrutinising us with their fascinated intentions. The sheriff appeared directly, clad in a rich blue and grey robe and ascended the four steps to the gantry to initiate the proceedings.

"I will start off today's sale with an offer of no less than thirty gold pieces. Who'll give me thirty for this man?"

Blen pulled the lean stranger forward.

"I'll pay ten!" presented a bid from the congregated horde.

"Sir, I will take no less than thirty or there will be no sale this day," said the sheriff.

"Twenty!" shouted another bidder.

"Come now, I know I am renowned for my generosity but I am not foolhardy. Who will bid me thirty?" the sheriff prattled on undeterred.

"Twenty one!" shouted the first bidder.

"Blen show them the boy," the sheriff ordered taking displeasure from the appeal.

The keeper cracked his whip in the air, gaining better attention and pushed me against the stranger.

"Here now," the sheriff said, "this man and boy here, I will accept fifty pieces for the two of them."

David Greely

"Fifty ...I bid fifty!" yelled the first buyer raising his arm energetically skyward.

"Fifty five!" demanded another further back in the crowd.

"Sixty!" called the first bidder.

The sheriff grinned with satisfaction at the two buyers locked in their bidding.

"Sixty two!" yelled a fresh bidder.

"Sixty five!" yelled the first in determination.

"Seventy!"

There followed a momentary lapse awaiting an overbid from the man at the rear until it eventually came.

"I will give you one hundred and sixty for the lot!"

His bid met silence and after the long pause, the sheriff spoke.

"Two hundred and they are all yours."

"One hundred and seventy and that is my last and final offer," shouted the buyer.

"Look at these fine specimens, are they not worthy of two hundred pieces?"

"One hundred and seventy," yelled the bidder confirming his ultimate offer.

"Then so be it, one hundred and seventy it is. Your name sire?"

"Oban. Oban of Laddia," the buyer proclaimed.

"Saints be praised, a Laddian!" I whispered to the stranger.

"You jest lad!" he remarked.

"On the contrary, I have been praying for passage to Laddia."

"This is not good lad and may well cost you your life. Don't you realise what sort of plight you and I are in?"

"Indeed I do but do you not see this is our opportunity to seek out our desires. You for your son and me..." I paused before committing myself further.

"...Well?" he persisted.

"Well what?" I replied.

"What is it that you seek help?"

"To rid our realm of Talteth."

"You will not get that from Laddia. You'll be wasting your time."

"Maybe so," I acknowledged, "but as things stand I have no option, Laddia is my only salvation."

"Quiet and fall back in line you lot," blasted Blen fidgeting with his whip.

We conformed to his order and the six of us were led off in file down from the gantry and handed directly over to Oban.

He looked a nasty piece of creation, standing tall and intimidating, ageing on three score with a toothless wry grin full of loathing. He inspected us in turn by tugging our ears, pulling on our hair (for those that possessed it), and prizing open our jaws with his filthy fingers, peering into our mouths whilst exhaling his poisonous breath over our faces. On concluding inspection, he turned to face his cohort.

"A bargain for sure. Take them aboard while I settle with the sheriff."

We were bustled away and led down a narrow path winding to the quayside. Further ridicule from Fleddon's inhabitants greeted us as did rotting vegetation thrown by some of the onlookers, the stench of death crept over me yet again when we neared the jetty. The chains around my neck and ankles began ripping into my flesh and the pain caused me to curse aloud.

"Damn Talteth and his allies!"

The whip across my back terminated my brief outburst.

We boarded the Valdemar, a craft far bigger than I imagined and the largest in the harbour with three towering masts and twin sails on each. Crewmen engaging in their menial tasks appeared disinterested at our arrival save for one securing barrels to the side rail. He smiled and motioned a cut across his throat with his hand, a sign that was all too ominous. There was no dallying and no sooner the grill hatch screeched open, forced one at a time below deck into the hold. Before ducking my head below, I took one last disconsolate look back at the realm. Once locked to the central bar running the length of the hold our neck chains were thankfully removed. The smell of seawater and human sweat overwhelmed the deathly reek of

David Greely

the town and dithered what I considered be the worse. We joined other prisoners sitting hunched in dejection, making a total of nineteen, though yet to see their features because of the dimness.

"Tell me your name?" I whispered to the lean stranger from the alehouse.

"Hebren," he replied.

"I am Arton, apprenticed to my late master, Treggedon."

"Well Arton my young friend, now you have landed us in this serious predicament what do you propose?"

"I propose nothing well, at least not for the moment. I need time to reflect then will find a solution."

A bucket of seawater gushed over us thrown from the hatch above.

"Silence down there! There is to be no talk. Save all your energy for the rowing," the crewmember laughed.

I sat discouraged, taking no comfort of having Hebren as a friend knowing it could not possibly endure because, as with all my companions they had a tendency to disappear or desert me. 'What of Owell?' I thought, 'and his friend Pennypot where were they? Why did they not search for me? Running to Talteth no doubt and revealing the fate of the king. I hope they get there just reward by the sword of Talteth! What too of Ulcris, did he escape to the south? And what if he should fail?' The mere thought of Ulcris dead set the fear in me as I did not want to fight Talteth alone; I needed him and his strength. Hardly did we speak but gladly I warmed to him. My thoughts lingered as to why I felt so compelled to save him without knowing at that earlier juncture, yet an unprecedented urge forced me to. I grieved for my master of course and dearly wished to see him if only for the once and such disappointment flooded my eyes.

"Why, such sorrow Arton?"

"Owell, is that you?"

"In the flesh lad and true as you sit there."

"Thank God! I thought that …well never mind now, I am so relieved you are here."

"I wish I could say the same. Good for you, maybe…"

"…Me neither," added Pennypot, "what a God forsaken hole! We'll be damned lucky to live this through!"

Owell whispered how he and Pennypot involved themselves into the affair by going to the harbour, seeking a boat for the voyage and recklessly Pennypot, despite his guile, failed to recognise he had unwittingly confided in Oban's second commander. 'Sure' he said, 'you can have passage aboard at a price,' the price being slavery!

The other captives were equally hapless victims of circumstance, resulting by being in the wrong place at the wrong time and left with choice of imprisonment in Fleddon at the whim and the mercy of Blen and his sheriff, or a new career in Laddia.

After five buckets of seawater, we established our misfortunes and learnt to be silent. The boat finally set off at dusk, slowly drifting out of the harbour on the ebbing tide. Timbers creaked as the northerly breeze gradually crammed the sails, a thankful blessing considering we could have endured the arduous task of rowing. While others lay pondering their own future, I dwelled in discomfort with the pouch of bones gnawing into my groin, questioning why Laddians had somehow, been allowed to infiltrate the shores of Aeria.

I did not know whether to laugh or sob having Owell back as company, in the perplexity of it all considered I had indeed learnt another lesson this day, that from the depth of solitude and fatigue how one values the magnitude of friendship.

Chapter Eight

The night passed monotonously, I sat miserably conspiring a hundred useless schemes of escape each shattered by the creaking timbers as the craft rode the heaving waves, though none worthy of action. The following morning brought us water and hard bread served by a crewman taking the opportunity to check some of our shackles at random, prior to leaving by the ladder through the hatch. Needless to mention I never sailed before, the rolling and tossing of the vessel made me quite delicate. None of us had any concept how long the crossing would take, with estimates ranging between three days to six weeks and the latter speculative guess by Hebren was very demoralizing. I miscalculated the original number captive in the hold and eighteen of us wallowed in its putrid depth. 'Hardly an army,' I recall telling myself, nevertheless, felt confident if riled or spurred, they would offer an adequate display of resistance. We were chained into two teams and given numbers: Pennypot number eight, Owell seven, Hebren three and I, number two, at midday, summoned to row and taken to the adjoining galley. I sat positioned on the port side as third oarsman, procuring some consolation at placement next to a porthole and sample daylight, though it added to my queasiness. I prayed wind would return but it never did, I rowed in mundane unison goaded by the demands of the pacesetter's drum. His monotonous voice incessantly echoed through the galley and never surrendered, except when a brief changeover occurred. Still my head schemed of ways to escape and only the unfolding plan of mutiny seemed feasible, though doubted how to confirm my plot to the others. The crewmen never averted their sterile gaze from us, any talk instantly thwarted by the crack of leather, remaining apart in split shifts also made collaboration difficult.

For three days and two nights, I hardly ate, and slept even less. So physically exhausting were the rowing periods, calluses developed upon my palms, aggravating the enduring stings of the nettles. No longer prepared to tolerate the suffering nor anguish over the uncertainty enveloping the realm, I chose to act, and on the approach of the third night decided upon a simple plan. Just rid my chains, unlock the others, wait for the changeover of crew and stifle them into surrendering. It was time to use the bones, confident my wish be granted because it was a plea to help the realm, not for self-gratification, and after the change of numbers and the pacesetter restructuring his dulcet tone, I gripped the bones pleading for guidance. As on most occasions, nothing happened, but on the third time of wishing, a chilling spectre clad in a hooded robe materialised. The grey shroud covered it entirely and in the gloom of the hold I could see no feature, flesh or bone. I feared this ghost more than any other image seen before, perhaps not knowing whom or what it was, provoked my dread nevertheless, I cried out in fright as it drifted toward me with arms folded. It spoke unhurriedly and very softly.

"Why do you show dismay, did you not wish for me?"

"I wished only for help," I replied.

"Then I am as you wished," it said.

"I did not expect ....what I mean is, I thought my master or the king would come in answer."

"If I disappoint you…"

"…No!" I called out. "Please stay and aid me?"

"I am here as you wished," it repeated.

"Then why do I fear you?"

"You tell me, Arton. I am only a messenger of the Good Lord and his divine spirit has sent me to you. Perhaps I reflect what you fear, but I am what you see not how you want me to be seen."

"I fail to understand."

"Because you sense fear then ultimately so shall you see it as such."

"Then why have you not visited me before, for I have always had fear within me?"

"Your need," the voice continued, "for seeing your master and the king are greater at this moment."

"Nothing has changed," I insisted. "I love them now, no greater than before."

"That is so and I do not doubt you, but only when your fear subsides will this be."

"I just want help," I sighed.

"Why? You do not need it, you only think it so. Look to the obvious Arton."

"Like what?" I urged.

"What obstructs you from escape?"

"These wretched chains!" I cursed rattling them at him.

"Are you so blind of things that surround you? Remember what your master told you and look to the obvious…"

"…Arton, are you all right?" Hebren whispered, shaking me.

The spectre dissolved instantly.

"You must have been dreaming."

"Yes, I …I am fine."

Wiping the sweat from my brow, I cursed at Hebren's intervention.

"Some dream," he remarked.

Legacy of Bones

"I am fine now," I smiled, telling him to return to his position.

I replaced the bones, tying the pouch back around my neck where they truly belonged and recalled the brief apparition to mind.

'Was I that blind of my own surroundings?' I repeated again. What did it mean?

I shook the chains fastening me and the clasp uncannily clicked open and fell with a thud to the deck.

'How stupid!' I called out in my mind. 'I never thought to check the lock. Surely it had not been unfastened all this time?'

"I am free!" I declared, loud as I dare.

I clambered across to Hebren and quietly pulled the irons through the rusted bangle. Soon enough our elation heightened as we hauled the joining chain through the shackles of our fellow captives.

"We will take over at the change of shift," said Hebren, "be ready my friends."

The impending minutes seemed like hours, and those hours passed like days. Every man waited in anticipation, reflecting his fate, acknowledging no doubt, the looming altercation that death maybe their final, and ultimately, their only resolve and would I be spared from these fears with God on my side, but if it were so, never felt accordingly.

After the lengthy wait, the hatch opened and a crewman directed the spent shift through.

"Now!" I whispered sharply.

Hebren leapt to his feet wrapping his chains around the Laddian's throat while the others speedily overwhelmed the second Laddian. I motioned for immediate silence, removing the keys from the crewman and after freeing prisoners numbered nine to seventeen, made for the rowing galley where the pacesetter sat inattentive with his back to us. Slowly we trudged along the gangway as if still encumbered in our locked irons, rattling the empty chains to avoid raising alarm.

"Look lively you lot and hurry to your oars."

The Laddian said his last words as Owell's strength wrenched the Laddian's neck forcing his head to flop forward like a broken flower.

We had no estimation of crew numbers on board and the element of surprise our only weapon. Splitting into our two groups, we chose to climb back up through the hold while the others clambered up from the galley. One crewmember was at the helm and yelled out his surprise when we trod across the decking toward him. More Laddians swarmed from the hatches and doorways, brandishing knives or swords, so we used our chains as means of defence when the fighting broke out. I crawled up the rigging, not to avoid combat but to call out strategy to my kinsmen in efforts to overpower the enemy.

Owell fended for Pennypot, thwarting any advance aimed at him and Hebren proved an able fighter gaining a sword from a dead crewman, his tenacity and power killing four of them in his relentless swathe. Bodies from both parties fell to the deck screaming and others locked in combat falling overboard. Blood spilled in a desperate onslaught for survival and as each Laddian gradually fell and weapon seized, armed ourselves to do better battle against them. Hebren threw me a sword and though grasping it eagerly felt reluctant to put it to use. With every thrust of blade, another Laddian collapsed until there were no more and the battle stopped as swiftly as it had begun, with no enemy spared. We made a thorough search of the vessel ensuring we won over our captors.

"The ship is ours!" I shouted with elation. "Praise the Lord and praise the defenders of the realm," and with the twelve survivors, shoved our arms skyward in deserved jubilation.

We threw the dead and injured Laddians over board and organised ourselves to handle the craft. As it transpired, we all lacked experience in the art of seamanship but made do, and Pennypot, with limited use, settled unwillingly to row with the others, none of us escaped the gruelling task. We ate heartily and drank freely for several days and nights making amends for the meagre existence endured under the enemy's control. I was surprised the men took to my commands but in retrospect, Owell may have had something to do with their passiveness, remembering my capability and obviously relaying such talent to them.

The calmness of the ocean continued for three days and nights, everyone including myself moaned about rowing and gradually our spirits plummeted. We never sighted any other vessel, land or seabird, and I feared we steered incorrectly, for surely Laddia could not have been this far, I pondered on whether to abandon the quest and sail back to Aeria. The fatigue and the growing impossibility of the task rapidly eroded my already dwindling determination.

Owell and Pennypot sat opposite Hebren and me on the main deck while others sprawled themselves unceremoniously about the vessel. All rowing ceased on this new day and the sails dangled torpidly, hoping to snare a friendly breeze to carry us to land. No longer could I inject enthusiasm into their hearts and indeed, how could I when I too felt the scourge of such mounting dejection?

"This is hopeless Arton," complained Owell.

"What do you propose we do?" I asked.

"You're the one with all the answers, you tell me," he moaned.

"I am only guided Owell, you know that."

"Well we can't just sit this out forever. Food runs short and if we don't find land soon we'll all perish. Look about you Arton; it is not just I who is dispirited."

"Then we shall have to raise them. Summon the men and I will speak."

With an aspect of reluctance, the men began gathering on the deck to listen to my oration, and in the time it Owell took to motivate them I obtained brief solitude at the prow, gazing at the horizon in a last fleeting hope of seeing land. I held the bones and wished not just for help but strength too, strength to guide me through my new ordeal. I closed my eyes and gave a short prayer.

"Arton."

The whispering of my name broke my immersion. It was so faint I thought it perhaps a trick of my imagination or the trick of the flapping sail above me. I looked about but saw no other than the silent men standing assembled behind me. I returned my gaze seaward, staring hard and long across the deep water toward the horizon, listening intently for another call when a vision unexpectedly intensified. A boat equalling the size of the Valdemar transpired before me, bobbing perilously on enormous waves set by the turbulence of the increasing wind. A bolt of lightening struck out from the tempest, splintering a mast and sending the rigging crashing down onto the upper deck, broadcasting splintered timbers and tattered sailcloth. Screams from the hapless sailors emanated amid the howling storm, tormenting me with their haunting cries of pain and as the stricken vessel fragmented, witnessed them succumbing to their deaths. Those defying the falling debris and abandoning their post jumped overboard but the swell was equally ravenous and it engulfed them.

"We are ready for you Arton," Hebren called, breaking my vision.

"If this be our fate oh Lord, then so be it. No longer will I suffer the burden of this cruel existence you bestow upon me," I cursed, walking back to the main deck.

"What is wrong? You look like death."

"Do not concern yourself Hebren, all is well," I replied with feeble assurance. "It is with God to whom I speak."

"Then speak to us!" Owell prompted with scowling eyes.

"Men of the realm," I said sharply, "not all is favourable, for I have seen disaster; a raging storm set to engulf this craft and all of us with it."

"Then we are doomed," resigned Pennypot, staring vacantly and open-mouthed.

"Alas, it is the way of the Lord," I confirmed.

"Do something Arton, you have the power," begged Owell.

"Yes," confirmed number three, "we know of your magic powers, you must be able to do something."

"I cannot and will not fight against the Lord."

"Then all our suffering has been in vain," resigned Pennypot pitifully.

"I wish it were otherwise," I conceded to him and the others.

There was anger in their tongues, discontentment in their hearts and they were surely justified, but I had nothing else to offer them other than the prophecy of the approaching doom. With hindsight, I would have been wiser to say nothing of the fate awaiting us but feeling demoralised meant no consequence in being forthright with the truth.

An eerie silence prevailed on the vessel and in the lengthy impasse, every man sat in disquiet, pending the dread of what was preordained. Then it struck and misery let itself upon us. The approaching storm clouds engulfed the sun and the sea whipped up in fury, together with the icy blasts of the northerly wind, lapped enormous swells at our boat in a persistent frenzy. Snow fell as did thunder roar and all the men escaped the rage below deck, leaving me to face the ruthless elements alone. The sails, despite sodden, billowed out in defiance in the fullness of the wind, timbers creaked and ropes snapped under the increasing strain, disseminating the worthless cargo lashed to the side rails. Squinting from the biting gale, I shielded my face from the flying fragments and regardless of the inevitable outcome, ill prepared to surrender, I rushed to the wheel. I clung to it in resignation, steering the boat headlong into the wind. The bow rose and fell with the torrent like a bobbing apple. Survival was my strength at this moment and instances of the suffering and disappointment marred my vision; just anger and revenge prevailed above the ensuing terror. Lashing the wheel tightly, I crawled toward the hold, struggling against the crashing waves and the strengthening storm, and shouted out in the lamenting wind, doubting myself at first, but in the near distance the ship seen in my discernment strived to remain afloat with its sails in tatters. The driving snow impaired my study, initially considering it an uncanny reflection of our own plight, but true enough, the Laddian vessel head for disaster, the realisation of my vision began to unravel and I yelled to the men bellow deck for assistance

"Come and help me, we are not yet condemned!"

David Greely

I clambered back to the wheel, turning the boat westward away from the jagged rocks protruding from the surf. Owell and Hebren joined me and assisted steering.

"You see, it is not us!" I said, pointing to the distressed boat. "I was wrong and the vision was a warning. We have to steer away from those rocks."

The other men finally scrambled on deck hastily securing ropes and loosening the sails and when secured, watched the unfolding misadventure.

The rugged caps dodged menacingly in and out of the furious swell like rotten teeth eager to bite into its hull, lightening struck the boat's mast as foretold, sending it crashing onto the lower deck. Its stern whipped around and struck the rocks, causing it to list. Waves pounded constantly and on each impact began shattering the hull of the luckless craft into eventual fragments. I could openly hear the cries of death upon the wind and if thoughts were not for our own safety, their screams would have freely sickened me. Voices yelled out briefly, engulfed by the storm's rage. It seemed hours for the confusion to subside and it was not until the tumult quelled and the sun began setting did I finally release my grip from the ship's wheel.

Miraculously we survived with minor cuts and bruises as testimony of such an ordeal, we sat or lay exhausted. I stared up into the heavens, praying aloud, thanking the Lord for his mercy and our deliverance. I lay motionless and full of remorse for my outburst at the earlier vision, acknowledging I was wrong to doubt what God gave me privilege to witness and swore never again to take the Lord's name in vain.

The cold night passed without incident, taking my turn at watch, only the flurries of snow falling gently onto my face stopped me from slumbering.

Shortly after the early morning's snowfall Owell sighted land, though my elation marred at the possibility of it not being Laddia, for if not the enemy's land, then surely the others would jump at their joy. We previously deliberated landing during darkness but like the rest of the men, favoured landing immediately, besides, we were in all probability already observed by our foe and conceded with no doubt in my mind our arrival would not undergo detection, no matter when we decided to go disembark.

We tacked along the coastline, continuing westward until finding a suitable cove in which Owell steered us, running the boat straight onto the steep shingle beach. Walking on land again was great relief; I had had enough of the sea for a long while and if ever to go afloat again, would have been all too soon!

The inlet lay exposed, surrounded by steep chalk cliffs and serrated weed-covered rocks led inland, trailing the long sloping incline. An abandoned bottomless craft with matted nets strewn across lay on the high tide mark. From the eastern edge, several barnacle-infested wooden posts marked the remnants of a collapsed jetty rotting with decay and age, and the furthest pole barely touched the water on the receding tide. There was little to salvage from our boat so we took any remaining provision along with our weapons, and hastily ran up the beach to the perimeter of the maram grass, panting in our hurried spurt. A small tributary spilled from an inland marsh, un-worked and overgrown with neglected reed beds where shingle yielded to blackened silt. Once away from the shore the stiff cold wind surrendered to a gentle breeze though maintaining the bite of winter. Little snow fell here, much to my wonder, after the recent storm. It appeared deserted with just the footprints of wading birds confirming any life, and here at the edge of the marsh we took respite to gain our breath.

"It is time for some strategy," I announced.

"What do you suggest?" asked Pennypot, staring expressionlessly skyward.

"That is for you to decide, all of you. I have my own task to consider."

"And that is?" prompted the blind beggar.

"To seek the realm's saviour, the hierophant," I confirmed.

"Where are you going to find him and what purpose is he going to serve? And besides that, how can you be sure we are even in Laddia?"

"Faith Hebren. The Lord has delivered us safely, now it is up to me. I admit I know not where to search for the hierophant or how to identify him, but somehow I will seek him and find my answer."

"I think you are setting yourself an impossible mission," Hebren continued.

"If I thought that, I would not even be here," I said stubbornly.

"You had no choice, you were captured for slavery like the rest of us," said number twelve.

"It is with God's will I am here," I insisted to him.

"God? Your God has a lot to answer for. If God has the power, would he not have seen the events that have transpired and stopped Talteth?" number twelve asked.

"I cannot answer for the Lord, I am merely his servant and chosen for this quest, but nevertheless shall see it through."

"And what of us?" asked Pennypot. "We cannot pass as Laddian; we will all perish in this land."

"That is why I propose we stay together. Surely, between us we have the guile and courage to survive. One saving grace is we speak their tongue."

"I will remain with you Arton."

Hebren's fealty was both timely and welcome.

I turned to face Owell.

"And what of you and Pennypot?"

"I am with Owell," said the beggar, apportioning his decision onto his friend.

"And I..." hesitated Owell, "...well, I am with you lad, of course!"

Owell sighed heavily, yielding to my expectancy of him though no doubt damning the good Lord and me.

"And the rest of you?" I asked turning to each one in the long lapse of silence. "Who will speak for you?"

"I will show fealty to you and the kingdom," confirmed number twelve.

"Then I give thanks to you and praise to the Lord," I smiled.

The remaining men either nodded or muttered half-heartedly their unconvincing allegiance to my cause.

"Now the matter is settled we will head inland and seek food, shelter and the hierophant. Direct us Owell and find us what we seek."

Owell led off, with Pennypot tagged with rope closely at his heels. The others and I followed, with Hebren falling back to the rear. We trekked for the remainder of the day taking well-earned refuge in a hollow for the night. Owell lit a fire and cooked the mullet trapped by the ebbing tide, though hardly a mouthful for us all, nevertheless, savoured. Every man took his turn at watch and our first bitter night in the enemy's clutches passed peacefully.

I knew a diminutive amount of Laddian culture from Treggedon's' teachings but never saw a draft or map of the domain, I could only but imagine the enormity of this strange land. The Laddian's are an aggressive creed and readily take what futile laws exist into their own hands. They have no king or queen, nor indeed any one ruler, just numerous councillors answerable only unto themselves, enforcing their own ideals on how their territories be managed. Killing is rife amongst their kind, only the Laddian militia have control over the many acrimonious citizens, and conscription is unchallenged regardless of age or ability. Some hold religious belief but it is not in the Good Lord Almighty, at least not according to my master.

For five monotonous days we trod wearily across the sodden marsh never encountering a soul or beast, I come to recall. It was not until the sixth day did we stumble upon any evidence of civilisation, a small native hamlet with three abandoned dwellings and wheel-less cart confirmed our being in Laddia.

The weather, since our arrival, worsened to the extreme and snow fell with vengeance, unequalled back in the kingdom thus making our progress impossible. We agreed, though with my show of reluctance, to remain until the spring thaw.

The long winter months passed tediously, only our scheduled hunting trips broke the tedium of our isolation. We feasted well on rabbit, hare and fish with occasional wild potato where

David Greely

ground yet yielded to frost. I managed to convert most of the men to the way of the Lord even though it seemed hypocritical, for I knew no sooner when we would continue our journey all such regular praying would deplete. I looked for signs to assist locating the hierophant but as with my unanswered prayers, met no reward. Neither vision nor spell on the bones come forth and in the solitude of winter, I schemed and re-schemed a thousand times over, my course of action. My prominent objective never escaped my thoughts even though seeking the hierophant seemed somewhat impossible, nevertheless, I pursued it and we agreed to remain together until that moment, so discretely pledged to Hebren, whatever the outcome, I would remain with him until we found his son.

At last, the weather broke and our doldrums melted with the snow. We gathered our frugal stock and set off westerly, electing to travel by night knowing all too well we would eventually encounter the enemy. We began striking at small settlements to obtain food and clothing, under the sworn promise I made them honour, nobody was to kill wantonly, alas, the vow broke on our first raid but it was kill or be killed, as God is my witness. The further west we travelled the populous increased, only one or two nights passed before we stumbled upon another hamlet. Most places we fringed, to avoid confrontation and again, only resorted to aggression when meeting our needs.

A tavern at Bendoria sent us northward on my mission to find the hierophant, and the loose tongue of a drunken farmer told of a hermit delving in unnatural practices, dwelling in the hills east of Nopi, but to our horror, as we were to discover, he omitted to mention Nopi is the capital town of the wretched land!

We eventually approached the city after several weeks of travel from Bendoria, stealing and dodging our way along the heavily used road, avoidance of our enemy rapidly became impossible. Our acquired clothing did maintain our inconspicuousness, separated by travelling singularly or in pairs, only to regroup closer to the city. To our thorough distaste, gibbets lined either side of the roadway with degenerates dangling with lost causes and for those still breathing, a wait, bringing an inevitable prospect of their inescapable demise. Those long dead were without flesh; just decaying corpses with expressionless bleached skulls and parched bones, with tattered rags stained in black, congealed blood. As for the dying man I stopped upon, I could offer nothing other than prayer, while he drew his last solitary breath as residue in his struggle for freedom from his agony.

"Come lad," consoled Owell tugging my arm, "there is nothing more to be done here."

He was right of course, yet I felt useless even with the power I seemingly possessed, but Owell quickly reminded me of our task and with a heavy sigh, resigned myself and turned away.

"Does such a crime warrant that?" I asked him.

"I cannot lay judgment but perhaps it was what 'e deserved."

"Perhaps," I proffered, "he is innocent, just like all the others."

"Then call them victims of circumstance. Ain't anything worse being in the wrong place at the wrong time," said Owell, distinctly wishing to close the matter.

Nopi was disagreeable, with dilapidated buildings reflecting the city's oppression, the perimeter walls protecting commoners from the encroaching wilderness lay in disrepair. Farming appeared less intense here and most folk resorted to free trade, though judging some characters witnessed, thieving seemed probably the most successful vocation. Life seemed underprivileged save for the councillors, and most wore drab ill-fitting clothes that would compliment rags. Regardless of the earliness of the day people scurried about their business with haste, although, I did detect an air of sadness about its people as if their hearts hung heavy. A continuous market filled most of the inner streets with anxious voices peddling for much-needed trade, and cries of incarcerated animals bawled in the breaking day. Several patrols of militiamen ambled about as if uncertain of their mission, causing us to keep well out of

David Greely

their way, and with their oppressive menace, chose to break into two groups, needless to say I opted to remain with Owell, Pennypot and Hebren, giving ourselves six hours to regroup north of the city.

"Arton?"

I looked at Hebren who portrayed anguish across his wrinkled brow.

"What is it?" I asked.

"I fear this will lead to our death."

"Have faith my friend," I assured him, "we will see this through."

"What of my son?" he suddenly asked sadly.

"We will find him and hopefully this is also where we find my solution, trust me."

"I do Arton, implicitly, it's just that…"

"…We will succeed Hebren; we have to, now my friend this way."

My smile seemed to do nothing to lift his spirit and reluctantly Hebren followed as I led us through the twisting streets not really knowing where to begin our search. For hours, we wandered through Nopi looking for a situation that may reward us with the information we sought. For Hebren's sake, we inquired about slavery camps but none of those we asked proffered any trail to follow, equally, no one knew of the existence of the elusive hierophant.

As we trod down yet another dismal alley, a monk suddenly appeared, his stout frame stood immediately in front of me blocking the low sunlight from my eyes. Directly at his side clung a small boy gripping his dusty robe as if in desperation. Slowly the Holy man bowed his head in greeting and nervously I returned the gesture.

"You have come at last," he said in a slow and muted voice.

"Are you whom I seek?"

"That would depend on whom you are seeking," he replied ambiguously.

"Are you the hierophant?"

Legacy of Bones

"No, I am not," the monk smiled, mocking my speculation.

"Then who are you and who is the boy that clings to you in torment?"

"I am precisely what you see, and as for this unfortunate, he is abandoned and without cause. He has nothing …and yet he possesses everything, freedom and the way of God. You believe in God do you not?"

He gave me no time to respond.

"…And your name, it is Arton?" he speculated.

"Yes," I confirmed with surprise. "But how…?"

"…The fact I know your name is of little importance. You do believe Arton?"

"Of course!" I confirmed resolutely, perplexed at his knowledge of me and why, amidst these detestable Laddians he should preach the way of the Holy Father.

"That is good. Now tell me Arton, would you have a mind to take this unfortunate and lead him through the path of righteousness and forsake everything for him?"

"No, I could not," I answered reluctantly, looking down at the boy.

"Could not or would not?" he pressed.

"Could not I suppose. You see I already have an engaging errand that must be seen through and cannot afford the necessary demands for his welfare."

"Think on Arton, do you suppose your master would have refused you?"

"Sorry but I fail to understand."

"When Treggedon and I met, you were as this soul; wanton, desperate and very much alone yet he did not refuse me and willingly took you into his guidance. You were given a chance of mercy under the eyes of God and yet now you are in a similar position to do so you bluntly refuse."

"But what of my commitment? The whole kingdom depends upon me," I said in defence.

"Do you think yourself far and above such asking?"

I felt bemused to say the least. My master never told me of such a thing and certainly no monk or handing over, nothing. I

David Greely

was born at Polran, north of the mountains sure enough and my kin slain.

"I know what you consider Arton but think on and be it very wisely. Where would you be now if Treggedon had refused?"

I could hardly summon the gesticulation of a shrug of my shoulders.

"Deprive this foundling and you will deprive yourself of everything you strive for."

"Then I have little choice."

"I despair Arton, I truly despair. Has not all those years with your master taught you anything?"

"Yes!" I replied tersely.

"Then prove it so," the monk persisted.

"I profess I know not how."

"I will tell you this Arton and let it be a grim warning. Turn yourself against this boy and you will turn yourself away from the very thing you seek, including God!"

"Arton?"

Owell's hand shook my shoulders vigorously.

"You look awful," said Hebren.

"Where did he go?" I asked searching for the monk.

"Who?" Owell quizzed looking for nothing.

"The monk," I insisted, "the monk!"

"Monk, what monk?" Owell continued, doubting.

"Then it was a vision," I sighed, cupping my hands to my face in exasperation. "What happened?" I asked softly.

The sudden realisation of the boy's hand clasping my elbow gave self-doubt of my own merit and contrived what I had just observed. Of all the visions and images yet experienced, nothing seemed this realistic. The killing of Whelp although it transpired true enough and with my bare hands, appeared simply as a transcendental affair and the despatching of Elcris too, neither gave the significance of this reality because this was so very different. The boy was mortal, living flesh and blood, holding tightly to me, and I could feel and smell him. I lowered myself to his level to question him.

"Who are you?"

The boy remained silent and somewhat alarmed.

"Come Arton," Owell persisted, "we ain't got time for picking up waifs and strays."

"Be patient," I enforced.

"To whom do you belong?" I asked the boy.

"No one," he replied softly.

"Then take my hand, you are now with me."

"I really don't believe this!" Owell retorted with disdain.

"I have little choice, the boy comes with us."

"Our situation is grave enough without the need to nursemaid a kid," Owell contested.

"It has to be. I have witnessed a vision and the boy stays with me."

Owell spun sharply on his heels, noticeably enraged. Pennypot erstwhile cocked his head, no doubt full of question to my action but wisely chose to utter nothing. I was unwilling to accept judgment from anyone, least of all from the blind beggar who created no worthy impression on me whatsoever. If adept in bureaucracy then getting himself and Owell captured was far from proving it. I began realising he was more a hindrance than an aid in my struggle.

With time pressing, I clasped the boy's hand tightly and followed Owell who subsequently stormed off muttering, with the beggar in tow. I quizzed the boy while ambling through the city streets, asking question upon question, bearing fruitless answers and establishing nothing other than his name, Tolin.

I close my eyes now overwhelmed with self-pity, though not in sadness but deep regret and if more stubborn, Tolin would be here with me now, continuing the practice I felt certain he would master, but I digress.

Without drawing any attention to ourselves we mingled with the Laddian people, avoiding the militia, listening and asking where possible my need of the hierophant's whereabouts and the hopelessness of locating Hebren's son. I even offered my free services to the landlord at an alehouse in an effort to glean information on the hermit but swiftly departed after raising unwanted suspicion over my magic. We dodged about in the depths of the shadows between the deteriorating buildings until finally reaching the northern road. We were the last to arrive.

I took comfort we all survived but feared the difficulty ahead in consoling Hebren should we fail in his want, and handed Tolin into his care in the hope of a pathetic substitute for his lost son.

We continued northward with ponderous tread, hungry and extremely vulnerable. The sun sank as low as our hearts and to the east, a bank of broad cloud threatened the imminence of rain. We trod the winding road toward the distant hills, dispersing on numerous occasions from the roadside and hid in ditches or behind trees, avoiding unwanted confrontation. I wished for the luxury of a warm bed and a sumptuous feast for us all but more than realised now wishing for selfish gain will go unrewarded.

On the long and lonely road, I drifted from one daydream to another, dreams of my master, the king and Ulcris, and began questioning my own wisdom in making the correct decisions and if indeed trod the correct path in my effort to save the realm. My final dream was of the fox and how he suddenly abandoned me, bewildered, my heart raced furiously at the thought of the beast. If it were not for the tracks in the snow I would have renounced the fox as a figment of my imagination and doubted it was he, whom saved Owell and me from the wolves.

Hebren called out from behind.

"Arton we must rest, the child is tired and hungry."

"We all are," moaned Pennypot clinging to Owell's sleeve.

"Soon we will rest but we must reach the hills first. It can only be a matter of a few more hours. Follow me, I will set the pace."

I expected a drone of rebellion but they complied faithfully, or so I thought.

With the drizzle came a heavy mist, impairing my vision to all but a few paces ahead, it took all my concentration keeping to the road to avoid the Laddians. Hearing Hebren's footsteps behind me was confirmation everyone followed. On reaching the foot of the hills, I slumped back against a grass bank and waited for each of them to arrive. Hebren came first with the child wrapped in his tunic, and then Owell with Pennypot still attached to his arm, followed by Maddox, number twelve.

"Where are the others?" I asked him after a few minutes lapsed.

"They took rest a few miles back."

"Then we will make camp here for the night and await them."

We took haven in a small copse a short distance from the road. I stressed to Owell, who had already gathered wood, to keep his fire to a minimum and set a roster for watch, thankfully I went first while the others slept, and gazed into the misty night hoping to spy the others. Unrewarded and several hours later I changed with Owell and nestled close to the pathetic fire. The night passed quietly, save for a loud scream, which I readily dismissed as an unfortunate beast meeting its match.

The next day brought showers, with an icy wind whipping up the rain into frenzy, branches creaked and boughs groaned under the strain of the forceful gusts. Owell managed to dig up a few wild potatoes and voluntarily prepared them on the fire. We ate greedily and sat patiently for hours awaiting the rest of our men.

"This is hopeless Arton; we can't just sit 'ere. Maybe they are already ahead of us," suggested Owell.

"Maybe they have deserted us," offered the beggar.

"Some of them were talking about returning to the boat," said Maddox.

"Why?" I asked him.

"Disillusioned I suppose," he replied.

"Curse 'em!" Owell stormed.

"That is a matter for the Lord to judge and not you," I reminded him sternly.

David Greely

"Well I've had enough of this and yer Lord God! It's led us into hardship, unnecessary suffering and in a place I wouldn't even waste my piss on!"

"Enough!" I demanded. "That is all you ever consider Owell, yourself!"

"And why not, eh? I have nothing to gain from all this," he ranted.

"If I adopted the same attitude as you, how do you think our kingdom will fair?"

"No worse than it does now," he argued.

"Have you no conscience or pride?"

Owell refused to answer me.

"Then there is little point in your continuance," I fumed, turning to face the beggar.

"What of you Pennypot, have you a say in this?"

"Put it this way lad, if it were not for your pressing I would still be revelling at Fleddon."

"You fail to grasp what I am trying to achieve here. You all do! All I want is for the kingdom to be whole and peaceful and enjoy the tranquillity that life offers."

"I was content at Fleddon," continued Pennypot.

"Yes but for how long, a year, a season, or maybe less? How long do you expect Talteth to allow you or anyone come to think it, to wallow in self-gratification? Why, within weeks he and his army would wipe you and your kind out of the realm. Already the kingdom is changing …did we all not witness Laddians at Fleddon?"

"I only got caught up in this because of you," Pennypot remonstrated.

"Get to your point," I impelled angrily.

"Then I will say this," he continued. "You and hardly a man beside, pretend to yourself and others you can change everything just to suit your own whims and manipulate people to swear fealty…"

"…so this is where it is leading to."

I looked sternly at him before facing Owell.

Legacy of Bones

"Owell told you of my power and you came along for your own selfishness. You wanted me to rid you of your blindness did you not?"

"Give it to me and I will remain."

"I will not succumb to blackmail," I said.

"You practiced it on me," goaded Owell. "Was I not deformed? Did you not push me into travellin' with yer?"

"It was done by the way of the Lord and performed under his divine eyes."

"I doubt you Arton and I doubt your God."

"Do not blaspheme Owell."

"Do not threaten me boy!"

"Remember your fealty to me and the Lord," I reminded him.

"Too late Arton, I have had enough of this and I'm returnin' to the kingdom."

"And me too," Pennypot supported.

Both men rose, away from the fire.

"Then face the consequence Owell, I have warned you."

"Yer don't scare me with yer words or yer sorcery."

"Your memory is short my friend and your vision is as blind as Pennypot's!"

"You can't hold me captive. I'm cured of ill and shall walk away from yer when it pleases me."

"Then go now," I raged, "and take the useless beggar with you. Do not expect any leniency from the Lord. You will never survive without me."

"You overvalue yer power lad and can hold nothin' over us."

"Then let time be the final judgement Owell. It is the way of the Lord and make no mistake."

"The only mistake I made was running into you in the first place. Rot to yer God, Arton! I will seek Talteth, tell 'im of the king's death and reap the handsome reward."

"You will not live to receive it," I warned.

"Come Pennypot; let's take our leave from this eccentric."

Owell steered his friend back toward the northern road without casting back a single gaze.

"You'll never succeed boy, never!" Owell shouted from the distance before commencing his doleful refrain.

His piercing whistle drifted on the wind as I watched the pair disappear from view and with them gone turned to Hebren.

"What of you?" I asked him dejectedly.

"I believe in you and want to believe in your God too."

"Then trust me," I said.

"I do, it is just that I need to find Pecos."

"We will find your son my friend; it has been my promise from the start and remains so."

I gripped his shoulder offering some reassurance, wishing God could have done the same to me at this moment.

Despite my sincerity, most of my supporters had now abandoned me and how long before Hebren and Maddox left too? And what of the young boy, am I destined to be no more than his guardian? Not for the first time I endured God's desertion, my depleting task developed into a fruitless struggle and seemed I was about to face it entirely on my own.

"God!" I yelled in frustration. "Does no one have a care what happens?"

"Come now Arton," assured Maddox, placing his arm across my shoulders, "all is not yet lost. You have my word this day I shall remain honourable to you and your cause until the hierophant is sought."

"And I will remain until I find my son," confirmed Hebren.

"I take heart in your allegiance my friends," I smiled though a little encouraged.

"Then it is time we ventured on," said Hebren taking hold of Tolin's hand.

We trekked two days into the hills seeking the hierophant without reward, doubting the tongue of the vagrant from Bendoria. We were all disillusioned and exhausted with few words spoken whilst the ill current of dejection overcame us. The young boy remained under the watch of Hebren in the makeshift shelter whilst Maddox and I searched for food. The weather turned against us too and heavy rain with accompanying strong winds battered continually. I returned to the encampment with my thrifty collection of berries and nuts and sat opposite Hebren and the boy close to the fire. I warmed my frozen hands with vigorous rubs and stared into the crackling flames leaping skyward in defiance of the falling rain, attempting to quell its heat. I noticed a soft green light emitting from within the fire, if I possessed the energy would have stood in amazement but my fatigue allowed such response to falter. Gradually the green hue turned into a deep blood red and spitfires crackled violently as I remained mesmerised. The waning confusion produced an enchanting glow, beckoning me closer, whether I entered physically or mentally, remains uncertain, nevertheless I fully entered into the exuding light. It felt as soft as gossamer on my flesh and a haven safe as a mother's womb. I drifted in the now colourless void, floating weightlessly and succumbing to the heady warmth it radiated. I saw not the source from whence the soft voice uttered.

"Arton," she whispered, "why the need for despair?"

"Who is this that calls to me?"

"It is I, the one you seek."

"But you are a woman I thought…"

"…Does being female make me less worthy?"

"No, of course not, it is just that I was told to seek out the hierophant…"

"…And you assumed me to be a man?"

"Well …yes," I confessed awkwardly.

"Forget the irrelevance of my being. Now you have sought me, what is it you want from me?"

"I am uncertain."

"Is it that you may fear what you are seeking?" she asked softly.

"I truly do not know what I am to ask."

"Perhaps you have forgotten after all, it has been a long search for you. When you can recall what it is you desire then so shall I return."

"Please," I implored hopelessly, "do not leave, not now that I have found you. Will you not present yourself to me?"

"There is nothing to hold me here and I must go."

"How do I reach you?" I asked.

"As before."

"Please, it has taken me an age to find you and to lose you now will bring me nothing but sorrow and anxiety."

"Then it is up to you Arton, until you ask of me what you desire I must depart. No longer can I linger here."

"Wait please, I beg you!"

She spoke no more, despite my calling and begging, silence returned to the void.

"In the name of God Arton, what are you trying to do to yourself?"

Hebren's shout conveyed me to reality and his sodden tunic dampened the flames around my head. The panic in his voice also brought the sensation of the burning pain.

"Are you alright?" he asked.

"Yes, well at least I think so."

I breathed heavily to help combat the sting on my head. The smell of my singeing hair wafted in the smoke as he dragged his garment off me.

"What possessed you to do such a thing? You were in the fire!"

"I do not know. Maybe I fell asleep and dreamt, or perhaps it was a vision.

Did you hear her?" I asked. "The woman? The hierophant?"

"No, nothing, other than you falling headlong into the flames."

"Oh Hebren, I am so confused."

"You're lucky not to have been cooked alive. Best you rest now. I will collect some water and bathe your face."

I glanced across to Tolin who returned a smile, a welcome consolation for my wretched state. Soon enough Hebren returned and eased my burns.

Legacy of Bones

"Sleep now Arton. Tomorrow will come soon enough and perhaps when Maddox returns he will have a more cheering bounty of food for us, eh?"

Hebren's calming words blended into my much-needed slumber.

Maddox's shout of excitement woke the three of us with a start. He came running down the hill with the fear of the devil hard at his heels and his breathlessness made it impossible to decipher his explanation.

"Catch your breath for a moment," I instructed.

"God Almighty," he gasped. "Beyond the third hill and out to the east. Dead, all dead, every single one of them."

"Who?" I asked.

"The men. Owell, Pennypot. The whole damn lot!"

"How?" asked Hebren.

Maddox stood motionless, staring at the hills and openly snivelling.

"How?" I repeated shaking him to respond.

"Murdered," he eventually said dropping a handful of pig-nuts.

"I knew something like this was going to happen," I said with disdain.

"Then why didn't you do something to prevent it?" Hebren retorted.

"How could I if I was not there to protect them?" I defended angrily.

"You say you have these special powers, the powers of the Lord so why did you not avert it?"

I sensed Hebren's words of doubt and replied swiftly in justification.

"You heard Owell and the beggar, as well as the opinions of the others, they chose their own destiny. Did I not warn them all?"

Hebren remained silent.

I did consider briefly that I brought about their misadventure, but rapidly convinced myself it was the Lord's work and justice perhaps, for their own transgressions.

"Are you sure they are all dead?" I asked Maddox, knowing it a feeble question, but he may have been mistaken.

"Did you witness who did it?"

"Damned obvious it was the Laddians," Hebren interrupted.

"Let Maddox speak," I insisted to him.

"I did not see who but oh, the suffering they must have incurred hanging in those cages like fodder for the crows. I could do nothing and they are all dead."

"Could you be mistaken?" I asked.

"There was no mistaking what I saw Arton. No man screams in such agony and then stops voluntarily. There were others too, not just men but women and children also subjected to premeditated slaughter."

I wept beside Maddox, full of inconsolable grief. Yes, I felt anger at their mutiny but never wished this upon them. At this point, I doubted the Lord again, in allowing the senseless killing of innocents, even the women and children, be they Laddians or not? Everything God amassed against me was rapidly sickening, if I were the one preordained in bringing justice to the kingdom then surely, he would not burden me so with such thoughts.

"We will go to them at daylight and give prayer before continuing our search."

The men said nothing at my suggestion and ate on the paltry hoard until sleep harboured our own thoughts.

We rose with the sun and tracked east over the hills. Later in the morning we reached the northern road and turned south on Maddox's' instruction. The way weaved between mighty oaks laced with bramble, and on the western edge, a tall bank, sheltered us from the wind blowing against the rippling grasses unperturbed by its bitterness. The sharp decline in the road displayed the cages ahead and one by one, they came into view, clinging to the wayside on shaven posts, swaying and creaking with the weight of their content. Crows skulked around the ground fighting over the draping entrails and littering the ground beneath the gibbets. Certain as Maddox said, they were all dead. Some with their guts torn from their stomachs, some dismembered and quartered, and others garrotted. Women and children bleeding from their slashes and several too, decapitated. I was physically sick at the gruesome sight and in mind to keep Tolin away from the carnage, but if he did not witness this Laddian atrocity now, then it would only delay the inevitable, besides, I wanted him to see this testimony as proof of their despicable capabilities. Someone was to pay for this and I swore to the Lord God vengeance would be mine, but like all the things I uttered in anger, my act of vengeance on this occasion will join the list behind Blen the keeper, the horseman, Beladon and of course Talteth.

We walked the line of corpses, stopping briefly at those we recognised. I did see Pennypot with eyes plucked and mouth slit and immediately became filed with remorse, knowing I could eventually have warmed to him. I saw the stooped remnants of 'number one' laying limp in his pathetic encapsulation but could not distinguish Owell or indeed any of the others, among the pile of mutilated and decapitated bodies. I prayed for them all till my throat hurt.

Eventually, we turned north again, back into the hills and neither Hebren nor Maddox need remind me of their fealty for they dutifully followed without question. We walked in an agonising silence but having bore witness to the slaughter it was understandable, to think the night past, the distant cry I heard may well have been this misdeed and not the fate of some wild animal I adjudged it to be.

On our return to the encampment, Hebren and the boy made hot broth from the pignuts they unearthed whilst Maddox and I collected rushes to replace those threshed by the high winds. We eventually sat together and spoke of the kingdom we all so desperately missed. Hebren told us of his life in Fleddon, from the hardship and the misadventure of Pecos.

To be truthful I did not hold much hope of finding him, let alone still living. We just witnessed the abomination our enemy is capable of and felt sure Pecos would have realised a similar fate, nevertheless, with sureness in his heart and a deep love for his child, Hebren spoke as if no doubt existed in his mind.

The fullness of the moon silhouetted the rolling hills surrounding us and pitch shadows clung to the ground with a deep forbidding emptiness. I remained on watch while the others slumbered, poking at the meagre fire to generate any additional heat from one so pathetic. I searched its heart to summon the flames that might again engulf me and lead me to the hierophant. Our next meeting I felt confident I would be able to seek the answers so desperately needed. I held the bones tightly in my grip and prayed when my palm burned, but it proved hopeless and no dream, utterance nor vision came to bear. I remained on vigil throughout the night as sleep failed to beckon me.

The next day brought a crisp and sunny start, and the deep shadow of the hill dispersed with eagerness on the sun's rising. I hoped this day would bring a fresh approach to my dilemma but alas, transpired into another lacklustre day, a day of useless meanderings and cogitations with unenthusiastic chatter sinking us still deeper into despair. I sensed the dejection across Maddox's face, predicting to myself his allegiance wore thin. Keeping his spirits raised became challenging and even my words of encouragement in what the future held, back at the kingdom, left me unconvinced and whether the strife endured be worth anything. 'Perhaps,' I thought, 'the next day will be more giving' but no, and neither too the following eight days. I did not think I could sink so low with dejection and self-neglect and felt the right to question the virtues of God in allowing us to struggle on so. I gave everything to prove my worth as a Christian and still the Almighty refused answering my prayers. I cried to the heavens with rage in my soul.

"God has deserted us," whispered Maddox.

"It seems so my friend," I admitted.

"Then what are we to do?"

"I wish I knew."

"Perhaps the hierophant does not exist."

"But I have heard her," I said smartly, convincing myself I did actually speak with her.

"Maybe you only thought you did," suggested Hebren. "It may have been just one of your dreams."

"I am not sure," I sighed. "Then again, I am not sure about anything any more. No longer do I know what is real and what is not."

"Well if you're not sure, then how can we be?" posed Maddox.

"I need time to think. Please leave me be, I will find the answer, I have to."

Hebren and Maddox adhered to my wish though Tolin remained seated by me.

"Come boy," called Hebren, "leave Arton to himself."

"He is fine with me," I said.

This is the closest he and I had been since our first meeting and sat looking at the bright skyline. It was some while before he spoke.

"Arton," he suddenly asked, "why are you so sad?"

"I am sad for everything. Not just for the kingdom but for Maddox, Hebren and even you as well."

"There is no need to be sad for me, I am content."

"I fear for your future."

"My future is secured, now we have each other," he said calmly.

"What do you mean?"

"I have the need for you and you the need for me."

"I do not understand."

"You never do, do you?"

"And what is that supposed to mean?" I argued.

"All the while you never grasp the meaning of things. You look too deep for the answers and yet they never become obvious to you."

"For instance?" I asked him.

"Look about and tell me what you see."

I turned my head idly looking about the hills.

"Hills, I see green hills," I said.

"And?" he prompted.
"The sun. Blue sky."
"What of the hills?"
"Like I say, green."
"Can you not see the bright yellow of rape or the vivid crimson of the poppy?"
"Well yes," I replied weary of the pathetic conversation.
"Then the hills are not green. Look by your feet what do you see now?"
"Fungi."
"And?" he prompted further.
I looked idly down again.
"Growing in a circle," I added, uncertain my response met Tolin's seeking.
"Precisely," he validated, "now what of the circle?"
"I do not know."
"The circle is there for a purpose."
"It is?" I questioned.
"Of course! Everything within this world is here for a reason."
"Then why a circle? I pursued.
"It is a faerie ring. It is said these pixie cups grow, following the moon rotating the kingdom."
"And what do you say Tolin?"
"It is the work of the faeries sure enough. You see, within each ring dwells a faerie or elf in some instances. The stools mark the domain for which the nymphs set. Step into the ring and the kingdom of magic can be gained."
"Could I gain this now?" I humoured him
"No, this circle is already complete. You can only get it when the ring is being created around you."
"What bearing does this have with my problem?"
"Very little," he replied.
"Then why talk of it?"
"To make you wiser and help you try to understand."
"Well this much I do know. I have to save the kingdom and seek out the hierophant in order to do so."

"And you shall, but not with the misgivings you hold."

"Where do you fit in the scheme of things?"

"I am uncertain."

"What of the monk?"

"What monk?" he said looking perplexed.

"The day I found you at Nopi the monk insisted I took charge of you."

"I think you are mistaken Arton."

"Then I am at a loss. Perhaps it is all in my mind or maybe the work of the Lord."

"Perhaps," the boy repeated.

"I am puzzled by your wealth of knowledge. You seem very learned for one so young."

"What I have learnt I learned myself. "

"Then how do you acclaim such knowing, like the faerie ring for example?"

"From the faeries," he smiled.

"This leads nowhere," I sighed heavily.

"Why don't you ask me what burdens your mind?" the boy suddenly invited.

"And that would be?"

"The hierophant of course! You need to seek her do you not? Well I can help you find her."

"How?" I asked with rapidly waning fervour.

"By asking the faeries."

I must stress at this point I did not believe in faeries, goblins and the likes nor did I believe a peck as to what Tolin told me, but remember, I was alone and in a state of self pity without answers to my problems. I continued to accept what the boy said more as a gesture of compliance rather than a solution.

"These faeries know of such things?"

"Certainly!" Tolin was adamant.

"Then we shall seek them and ask of the hierophant."

"It isn't quite that simple. First you have to believe in them."

"Oh! I do," I confirmed flippantly.

"Then you will find your answer but be warned, for they have a knowing of preference. If you say you do believe but really you don't..." the boy paused. "...well the circumstances will become obvious."

There was an air of certainty in his voice and it scared me.

"I will return to Hebren now."

"What about the faeries?"

"All in good time Arton. All in good time," he repeated walking away.

I remained staring at the faerie circle unaware of Maddox's gaze and uncertain of how long he stood there.

"Ah, Maddox, I think it is time we moved on. These hills hold nothing for us."

"But what of the hierophant?"

"I will find her but not here, when the time is right our paths will cross."

"How can you be certain?"

"I am not, but a solution will always be there and I will find it eventually."

"And in the meantime?"

"In the meantime the choice is yours my friend. You are welcome to go as you please. There is nothing more you can do apart from being my protector."

"Then," he confirmed, "your protector I shall be."

"Do you not want to return to the kingdom?"

"What, and face the rule of Talteth? No, I shall remain at your side, your number twelve."

"You could find Ulcris and aid his raise of arms."

"I am no warrior Arton."

"Then so be it," I pronounced. "For one frightful moment I thought I would be travelling Laddia alone."

"You would still have Hebren and the boy."

"For what needs to be faced, Hebren and Tolin will fair better away from here."

"Are you suggesting they go back to Aeria?"

"Yes, once we have found Pecos..."

"...We may never find him."

"Oh, we shall, although between you and me, I fear for his welfare. That is why I gave the boy to him; he is going to need him for support."

"But you wanted the boy."

"I know but let us just say I have no choice in the matter. I am hardly a man myself let alone having experience in child rearing."

Maddox smiled and shook my hand, consolidating our friendship.

Chapter Nine

Later that afternoon we crossed the hills, striding northward along the roadway and although none of us knew where it led, such a well-trodden road must eventually lead to a town or hamlet, sure enough after the stern pace I set we arrived at Crosshall at first light the following day. The town looked inviting by comparison to Nopi and a tree-lined road fanned out into a square riddled with compact wooden lodgings. Passageways fingered off from the main square, equally crammed with similar building and the smoke trails from several potted chimneys petering off into the still air afforded us welcome. Chickens and domesticated boars ambled about, scratching and snorting respectively in their industrious foraging, and a cackling cockerel sounded its early morning reveille to resurrect life into the slumbering residents. The streets would soon fill with the presence of folk and jostle by us preoccupied with tasks and chatter, and hopefully oblivious to our being. From the southern side appeared a contingent of down-and-outs shouting

Legacy of Bones

and wailing, breaking the peace that prevailed prior to their arrival.

"Well what have we here?" shouted one of the seven vagrants on their approach.

We chose to ignore them, turning off the square into one of the passages but they followed us through the maze despite our quickening pace, and misfortune led us into a blind alley forcing us to turn and face them. Hebren and Maddox were prepared to contest our way back through, both gripped their swords but with my concern for the boy felt it prudent otherwise.

"We will not fight," I told them, "there are too many of them. Wait and hear what they want from us."

"Trouble for sure," said Hebren waving his sword at his side.

"Please let me control this," I said, moving toward the madmen while motioning my arms for calmness.

The wild bunch came to a stop a short distance away, jostling and goading with an intimidating urgency. Without premeditation, I reached inside my pouch and grasped the bones tightly in my right palm. I took another step forward slumping to my knees, with my free hand selected one bone from my clenched fist and lay it openly on the ground. I scuffed a few paces sideways, placed another in similar fashion and continued until all five bones where displayed in front of me creating a dividing line.

"I warn each one of you, step across these bones and face the consequence," I called out, rising to my feet.

Two of the vagrants laughed at my words while others dared to motion forward each goading the other to get closer.

"And what if we cross your pathetic barrier boy?" yelled the tallest of the group.

"Face the outcome," I returned.

"The threat you behold so strongly," he continued, "won't stop us."

"Then cross it but at your peril," I warned again.

Despite the vagrant's flippancy, reluctance overshadowed any imminent confrontation.

"What do you want with us?" shouted Hebren moving aside me.

"Your valuables," replied the taller one.

"We have nothing," Maddox contended.

"Then we will take your lives in exchange," said the man tensing his hands.

"Hardly a proposition," I said.

"There is to be no bargaining," he returned.

"Ah but there is, I will spare your wretched lives for our freedom," I offered, adjusting my stance.

The man laughed, drawing closer toward the line of bones.

"Get the boy!" he suddenly shouted.

Three of them rushed upon me and I instantly closed my eyes, calling for Treggedon.

"Help master where are you?"

"I am here Rabbit."

The vision of my master grew beside me, giving me the necessary confidence of my conviction.

"Then die!" I shouted out to the attackers.

The vagrants lunged at me simultaneously, and in turn, the rowan staff of my master met each of them. He swung it across the face of the first, felling him instantly to the ground and his second swipe bludgeoned the next attacker forcing him to wince to his knees. Treggedon twisted deftly on his heels and leapt into the air, cracking his stick down squarely on top of the third man's skull and splattering blood over me by the intensity of the impact. The man collapsed by my feet and lay motionless. The second vagrant rose and dived at me again only to meet with the point of my master's pole, lunging deep into the pit of his stomach and as he writhed in pain Treggedon's final thrust cracked across his neck. The three strangers lay sprawled at my feet smothered in blood and very much dead.

"Who will be next?" I shouted defiantly, taking a cursory glance down at them. "Who will dare cross these bones?"

Although the taller man called for his cohorts to attack, they chose to scamper off leaving him alone to face me.

"It appears your friends have seen sense, will you not do the same?" I urged him.

"You do not frighten me boy."

"Then cross the line," I challenged.

Insolently he did so though slowly and never taking his cold stare off me. His sudden lunge caught me by surprise and his punch to my jaw knocked me to the ground. I managed to twist to one side and as he came at me again, my master's staff whacked him across the shoulder. Before the man could regain his stance, Treggedon aimed his rod and hit him in the face, repeating the same doleful swipe as the vagrant toppled forward. I crawled on top of him and clamped my hands around his neck before throttling what little life remained within him.

Maddox pulled me off him.

"Enough!" he shouted.

The anger within me immediately quelled as I regained my breath and I stood silently staring at the last victim, wiping the sweat from my face with my blooded hands.

"I have never seen anything of the like before, you killed them all as if possessed. Where did you summon such might?" asked Maddox.

"From the strength of my master," I gasped.

"Is this then a sample of your magic?" he continued.

"I prefer to call it wizardry, but yes."

Maddox turned and smiled.

"I have heard of your gift and now have the good fortune to witness it. And these bones…" he pointed to them, "…are they a part of it?"

"Yes," I confirmed, "but I admit I know not how or why."

"Such power in something so innocuous eh?"

"It appears so," I smiled.

"We ought to rid ourselves from this place," pressed Hebren, taking hold of Tolin by the scruff.

"Indeed so," I agreed, picking up the bones and replacing them inside the pouch.

David Greely

I accepted my master's assistance because I saw him and used his stave, which materialised in the enchantment, thus confirming his existence within me and surely too my companions would have been convinced of his intervention had the rod not suddenly dissolved.

A distinct weakness overwhelmed me as I followed my friends, I felt dizzy and bleary eyed as if intoxicated by the strongest mead. My mind enveloped with flashes of the deepest black and sporadic shards of sunlight danced between the visions of pitch. Squawks and cries deafened my ears as I tried frantically to continue walking and though concentrating on my footing, stumbled and fell to the ground as if in an animated state of slow motion. I witnessed myself turning and stood over a decomposing body; a hideous cadaver with ragged torn flesh and eyes plucked from their sockets, with cheeks ripped away displaying rotting teeth. A bloodstained neck with draping sinews carpeted the earth beneath him in a fleshy web. I tried averting from the macabre sight but the flashes of blackness lingered, scattering around me, and the relentless squawking made me linger to witness the inopportune death laid at my feet. Was this to be my fate?

I woke next to Tolin who remained asleep in the straw, breathing rhythmically and peacefully, taking this moment to study his babyish features and pondering over the recollection of our talk in the hills. He seemed wise and certainly portraying a strong awareness far in excess of his age. I grew fond of him despite his hindrance, the apparition of the monk, puzzled me somewhat, and this shadow of doubt persisted over me. Was he yet another figment of my testing imagination?

At this time the countless occurrences were now in an order of perspicuity, but areas of misgiving gnawed at me and although fully aware of the power invoked within the bones, I still could not understand their untimely resurgences nor too, if I possessed any power without them.

Maddox arranged an overnight stay at an alehouse on the outskirts of Crosshall, both he and Hebren aided me there after my collapse. Rumour was rife since our fracas with the vagrants, with talk of a young sorcerer casting spells and killing innocents. Innocents indeed, it was either do or be done by! I became a very much-wanted tyrant and passing through Laddia as an alien fearful enough, but hailed a warlock would certainly worsen matters.

I remained hidden until we set off in the early hours of the following day, heading westward with a bright waning moon high above us. The warm night made travelling comfortable, save for the rapid pace set by Maddox who continued at an unrelenting rate until dawn. The wilderness changed from the vast openness of rolling hills to a forest saturated in dense growth. The fullness of ash trees matted with holly and bramble entwined with a profusion of old man's beard, and where the light penetrated through the thick canopy, ferns grew in bright green pockets gently swaying on the waves of the slightest breeze. Eventually we came to a stop, giving me the opportunity to question Maddox on his decision to head west.

"I did as you instructed," he replied.

"When?" I doubted him.

"Yesterday you said we are to make for the blackness."

"I said no such thing," I argued.

"Well I didn't dream it. Hebren, you heard him say it did you not?"

"True enough Arton and as plain as day," he confirmed.

"Is this some sort of conspiracy? I really cannot believe this!" I raged.

Moreover, I could not and strived to recall the order, but memory, since using the bones evaded me.

"Before you collapsed in the alleyway you shouted to us to travel westward and find the blackness," afforded Maddox. "Not that we had a clue as to what the blackness referred. Maybe it is this forest."

His speculation was wrong.

"Did one of you not think to question me, how could you be so stupid?"

"Hey hold your temper Arton; you said it, not me!"

Maddox was furious.

David Greely

"Did you not realise I could have been delirious after the fight?"

"To be honest Arton I never know what is real and what fantasy is anymore. You talk in riddles and function as if you own the kingdom. You are continually drifting in and out of reality and I cannot comprehend the truth anymore."

The words from Maddox were cutting.

"Surely you must have adjudged my condition and questioned it?"

"No and no longer care to."

"Maddox is right Arton, you have altered so," continued Hebren. "Your purpose is lost and we amble about this woeful land without a sense of reason. I know why I am here and that is to find my son…"

"…And for me to find the hierophant," I advocated abruptly.

"Then do just that! You have found her once and now you must find her again. Get your answer and return to the realm. You, out of all of us know the urgency at hand; God knows you have told us enough times!"

"Am I so lost Hebren?"

"It does appear so lad and you must find the solution. Fail and the kingdom which is so dear to us all will wallow in the foulness and the blood from Talteth's reign."

"I had all but forgotten of course, the almighty. God help me!"

I sat with tear-filled eyes, ashamed and steeped in self-pity. I lost my purpose and strength but worst of all, lost faith.

"What am I to do? Will you help me Hebren?"

"I know not how Arton."

"What say you Maddox my friend?"

"I can only be guided by you. I have neither the power nor the insight into such matters."

"And you little one?"

"Arton," responded Tolin, "much as I would it is far from my reach too."

"What of the faeries, can they not help me?"

"Faeries are for believers," reminded the boy.

"Faeries are for fools!" exclaimed Maddox with eyes turning skyward.

"Do not underestimate the powers of the faerie folk," advocated Tolin.

"Have I missed something? Did someone mention Faeries?" Hebren asked. "Oh, this is all too much for me. I struggle enough coming to terms with sorcery and now you talk of pixies and the like. I will tell you now and for all time, as soon as I find Pecos our friendship terminates!" Hebren muttered traipsing off, shaking his head in exasperation.

I dearly wished not assenting to help find Pecos, apart from wasting precious time it deviated from my purpose.

The boy followed Hebren's trail through the bracken and shortly after Maddox and I shadowed them. I heeded their words and thought hard for answers in a much-needed resurgence of haste, but no sooner restarting our trek the vision returned, the same dense pitch and the bright flashes. The cries almost deafening in their tone continued to drown my thoughts, the wretched victim lay discarded with tattered clothes stained in blood and stiffened sinews draped across the grass and ferns. About me, the flapping of the pitch, crying and calling in uncontrollable frenzy. Again, I sensed vacating my body and drifting aimlessly in the strong sunlight on the light breeze. I tried blinking to rid myself of this profound prescience but it lingered and lodged within me, voices whispered in beckoning manner daring me, testing my strength and encouraging me forth.

"Where are you?"

"Arton?"

The calling voices of Maddox and Hebren broke the vision and I woke swamped by ferns with the feeble aroma of mould, rising to witness them thrashing about in search for me.

"Over here!" I called to them.

Having caught their awareness, I walked toward them heading for a small clearing sparse of trees save for a handful of willowy saplings. The bracken thinned with clumps of digitalis forcing their heads through the grass. I approached warily, fully expectant as to what followed and was not wrong. The black madness came at me like a drawing curtain, this time however, very real. How stupid of me not realising the evil blackness is the work of crows, dozens of them took flight at my arrival, flashing into the air in alarm, flickering against the sunlight cackling their deafening and contemptible cries. I waved my arms to shield myself from their frenzied flight and when dispersed, remained the sickening aspect of what I dreaded.

"Oh, my God!" I exclaimed, examining the ragged victim at my feet. "This cannot be, pray tell me this is not so."

Hebren fell to his knees beside me and wept.

"Is this who…?" began asking Maddox swiftly curtailing his obvious propose and bending to witness the atrocity.

"…Yes it would appear so," I confirmed softly.

"In the Lord's name what a way to discover …what I mean is…"

"…Say nothing more Maddox and let us leave Hebren be."

We both reluctantly turned to allow Hebren time with his son.

Maddox was able to stop Tolin venturing too close and gathered him up under his arm.

"Come," he said, "this is neither the time nor place for you."

"But I want to see," the boy remonstrated.

"No!" said Maddox emphatically, carrying the struggling boy across the meadow.

We sat a little distance away waiting for Hebren's return. It transpired a lengthy stay, several hours in fact, before he eventually rejoined us. He needed no reason but Hebren failed to hide his grim face and bloodshot eyes; the epitome of a grieving father. I could offer him very few words of comfort.

Somehow, I felt selfishly toward the situation because none of them seemed aware of the suffering endured throughout our search for Pecos, nor the visions sapping my mind and strength, and nor the guilt. Perhaps I should have clarified my vision to Hebren and save him anguish but in hindsight I did not know the victims' identity. I should have realised, although in my own defence would Hebren have believed me? Would he not want to witness it for himself? Any man would want that, certainly not I, or the Lord God could deny him that right. I felt pity for him of course. He demonstrated kindness and factors of righteousness, so did he not deserve a better outcome in his destiny? Hebren's sworn allegiance alone earned a far richer reward and if it is the Good Lords' doing, I doubted his worthiness.

Eventually Hebren spoke.

"I have buried him."

"Then I will give prayer," I offered.

I rose sharply, gesturing to the others to follow. Little Tolin stood close to Maddox and I next to Hebren opposite, I slowly closed my eyes, clasping my hands in front of me.

"I call upon you Lord to take our beloved Pecos into your realm. May he rest within your loving arms and be shielded from the smite of his enemies. Grant him peace and life eternal. Lord, give Hebren your comfort in this, his time of compassion, watch over him and guide him through his term of torment. Gracious Lord I beseech you."

I remained silent, thinking in vain for further words to comfort Hebren yet none came readily. I presumed Hebren sensed my floundering.

"Thank you Arton," he said, "now may he find peace with the Lord."

"For that I am certain my friend. His suffering here will have no bounds of reward with our Heavenly Father."

"I pray it be so," Hebren said finally.

Maddox gently gripped the youngster's shoulder, turned and walked him away.

"It is time we left," I said softly to Hebren, daring not to force urgency upon him.

"Yes of course, I had forgotten about your quest, forgive me."

David Greely

"There is nothing to forgive Hebren, my journey can afford a few more moments."

"There is no more to be done here, I have found him now let us take our leave."

"As you wish my friend."

We returned to Maddox and the boy sitting in silence on a fallen tree.

"I am sorry Hebren," Maddox commiserated as we approached. "I dearly wish this outcome not so."

"Thank you for your sentiment," he responded, "it is done now."

"What is to happen now?" Tolin enquired innocently.

"We must part," I said.

I had mulled this decision over and though uncertain of my wisdom, told him.

"You will accompany Hebren back to Fleddon while Maddox and I continue our search for the hierophant."

"I do not want to go," the boy said obstinately.

"There is little option," I maintained.

"But I want to stay with you."

"It is better you return to the kingdom with Hebren."

"I will not go!" he wailed, bursting into tears.

I went to him and held his head against my chest knowing I had to convince him.

"I want to stay with you," he sobbed. "I want to help."

"But you are helping, don't you see? Hebren needs your companionship right now and he cannot possibly venture back alone. You can help by getting yourselves back to the kingdom. He needs the strength and guidance you can provide."

"But it is not helping your quest," the boy argued.

"Far from it. It is all a part of my scheme," I assured him.

"It is?"

"Why yes of course, let me explain. When my master first sent me on this adventure I felt exactly as you do, unwanted, unimportant and pushed aside but now look, see how everything alters? What I do in the near future will change the outcome, this applies to you too, because your progress will alter the course of fate for all of us."

"It will?"

"Most certainly. If you or Hebren fail to reach Aeria, I shall have no one to welcome me. I need you and Hebren to establish the progress within the kingdom. I will not have time to find out for myself what transpires, I want to come directly to you for my answers."

"Then I shall go with Hebren," he agreed finally.

"Good, now look lively!" I smiled and patted him on his head.

He broke from my restraint, cuffed his nose and walked to Hebren.

"I will see that we get us there safely," he said to him.

"See that you do," instructed Hebren.

"We shall go now," the boy urged.

"Well you heard him," laughed Maddox, "you'd best set off!"

I smiled at the boy's enthusiasm and even Hebren broke from his sorrowful grin momentarily at Tolin's fervour.

We retraced our steps back through the forest stopping only to find food and rest. We moved rapidly with refreshed exigency caring, to take risks previously not chanced. Hebren exhibited some light-heartedness despite his sorrow and Tolin amazingly portrayed an air of confidence and defiance that somehow wore onto me. I still felt perplexed by his maturity and knowledge, and imagined the strength of his attributes when much older. Maddox steered us competently and never once faltered nor hesitated in our return to Crosshall. We agreed not to enter the streets for fear of certain reprisal, opting to avoid the town and rejoin the road south to Nopi.

The days shortened and the nights grew colder as autumn began to wield its drape over Laddia. I did not relish another winter in this inhospitable land, fearing it would be far worse without a greater number of companions and with this determination in mind took the pace from Maddox. I proposed Hebren and the boy remain on the road to Nopi when time arrived for

David Greely

Maddox and me to set off into the hills in renewed search for the hierophant. I felt sure with the incumbency of Hebren and Tolin lifted I could be more affordable in my objective.

Two days travel from Nopi we parted company and it was a sorrowful affair. Not one of us withheld our grief at separating and Tolin, despite his previous confidence, sobbed openly, pleading with me to remain, I had to convince him all over again of his necessity within my plan. I hugged him, kissing his brow.

"Remember," I whispered to him, "Hebren needs you, and you must be strong and have faith in all you do. If you fail then we all fail."

Strong words perhaps upon a juvenile but I said them for encouragement, not fright.

"I will not disappoint you Arton. I will do it and it is my promise."

"You have no need to pledge, Tolin; I know you will be successful. Remain at Fleddon with Hebren and I will come for you. Take no risks in your return and find out the fair of lord Ulcris for I shall need to know."

"I will."

"Then go with good spirit," I said.

We hugged each other again.

"Good fortune Hebren," I said, turning to him.

"You too young fellow. The kingdom needs you Arton so be swift in your labour and return to us soon."

"That I shall friend."

We patted shoulders and looked at each other. My heart hung heavy and I could find no fitting words at our moment of parting. The feeling of great loss overshadowed me, I feared for him and the boy, already doubting my strategy of our separation.

'Maybe if we all went back into the hills it would be safer. How were they ever going to get passage across to the realm? Would they get through Nopi without Maddox and me?'

"Come Arton it is time to go," Maddox encouraged, breaking my hesitancy.

Legacy of Bones

"Yes of course," I sighed heavily.

I felt like defying my action and calling them back but the strength of God kept my will from faltering, I lingered to watch Hebren and Tolin amble along the road, purposeful in their stride. Occasionally they turned to wave and duly Maddox and I responded, not until they were distant specks in the dimming horizon did I turn west, aiming for the hills. Maddox loitered a moment longer before hastily following.

"How long do you suppose before they return to the kingdom?" he asked, gaining breath.

"As long as it takes," I replied.

"That is not an answer."

"Then I do not know," I admitted.

"What if they don't make it?"

"Hebren is strong, they will succeed."

"What if …?"

"…There is no if my friend. Be assured for I have seen it in a vision."

I lied to him well enough, in fact I felt more pessimistic than Maddox but if I portrayed the same scepticism and discernment where would we be other than lost and without cause.

"We shall return too, immediately I locate the hierophant," I offered him.

"What is different this time in assuring your success?"

"The desire, passion and yearning, and the belief, yes the belief."

Moreover, it was very much so. For too long I drifted aimlessly in self-doubt, hesitant and apprehensive but now, with no other burden hindering me certain I would achieve reward.

Maddox looked dourly at me and I sensed the reservation in his mind, but no other words could I proffer to convince him that our forlorn journey be a short one, but oh, how wrong my speculation would have been.

We traced the setting sun westward and already the distant satanic hills loomed again, shrouded in a damp mist, casting an eerie orange haze. We eventually came to rest and lay under

David Greely

the deep canopy of a lustrous night, wondering what fortune lay ahead of us.

Chapter Ten

The following morning covered the land in a crisp light frost, the first of the season and accompanying it a cold snap that penetrated my bones. Despite our growing fatigue, we kept a stern pace throughout the day until finally reaching the bottom of the hills. Although having previously spent some while in the tors, we failed to locate our original encampment and after trekking south for another two days made station by a small river lined with willows. The differing heights of the lush green tors towered high above in a great magnificence, and though seemingly tranquil, I sensed an element of disquiet.

On our first day, I took the opportunity simply to study the enormous hills, though never venturing beyond the sight of our camp. Just slow wanderings up and down the gentle slopes, digesting and I suppose, inwardly searching out the hierophant, looking for indications of something different or out of place, a sign to show me the way, but my searches proved discouraging and our term in the hills stretched into weeks. Every day I

David Greely

would venture off forever hopeful and Maddox did much the same, though he became more intent on hunting and gathering fuel. At night, we would rest, eat and talk of the kingdom, beside a fire.

Maddox, by far, in my opinion, secured an easy life though his words portrayed an air of reticence, only his misfortune meeting the sheriff of Fleddon suggested he suffered any kind of torment. He cared not to mention his woman other than once and I did not question him further about her. Until the previous year when fever saw to the death of his father, they drifted about the realm selling earthenware at townships as far south as Farning and north to the mountains, securing a decent enough existence to fend off the trait of hardship that many peddlers succumb to. Here before me, sat a large man some two score plus, proficient in fortitude and astutely aware, who begged no trifling with yet possessing a kind and gentle manner, moreover a willingness to offer his support in my bid to salvage the realm. I doubted the reason for his fealty, but like any man or woman akin to Aeria, conceded it was in his blood to sacrifice himself for it, a quality uncommon in my early years. I was envious of him for having met the king on three occasions. I questioned his experiences, accordingly begging him to summarise his intimacy with the almighty, but he could not elaborate, for it transpired in our discussion he had never actually spoke with him. At least I could, and did boast of such fortune. In return, I told Maddox of my escape from Wendatch and of the king's death, though daring not to interpret my vision of him, nor subsequently the elusive fox. Nor did I disclose the king's site of burial as this remained sacred to me, and until able to assemble a shrine, nobody, not even this dear friend was going to know and if I were to perish before completing such a task, then so be it, nobody would ever know where he lay.

I slept lightly that night, deviating in and out of reality, dreaming of the realm, my master and until it had arisen in our conversation, sudden thoughts of Talteth emerged. I dreamt too of the hierophant and how equally elusive she became, and least of all, I dreamt of Tolin's damned faeries!

Morning brought a thick blanket of grey cloud and the imminence of rain. I said prayer with a feeling of guilt, having not recited one for some considerable time, I felt purer of heart for having done so but suspected the Good Lord was not of the same stance. I set off into the hills in a sprightly manner leaving Maddox still in slumber, and opted venturing northwest, though not for the first time however, determined to search much wider and further into the night if necessary.

I became curious at not sighting anyone all this time in the hills, any traveller, farmer, hunter or ensuing Laddian bandits. No homesteads did I stumble upon, this perplexed me somewhat, because the hills appeared fertile and rich enough to sustain a good existence yet there was nothing, no one except Maddox and me.

I took my first respite around noon, sheltering on the leeward away from the lashing rain. I sat sodden and cold, though not downhearted and my morale remained as high as the clouds. I ate from my hoard of pignuts to stave off the hunger churning in my stomach, yet wishing for a feast, a feast as large as those in the great hall at Wendatch.

'Ah Wendatch,' I sighed wistfully.

I sojourned and thought for a lengthy while of the place dearly cherished and missed, suffice to mention my thoughts inclined toward Treggedon and his gruesome murder. My hatred for Talteth did not wane, I reassured myself though ungodly, and to seek my revenge upon him whence I return. I considered the fate of Ulcris too, hoping by now he resided in Collington and having amassed a great army in readiness against the realm's transgressor.

'Perhaps,' I smiled, 'the good deed had been served already and Talteth lay rotting in hell, the kingdom at peace once more.'

"Long live Ulcris," I shouted at the top of my voice.

A sudden reflection crossed my mind.

David Greely

'What of Elcris?' I broke into a self-assuring grin, knowing he lay in a shrunken heap of dusting bones in a cavity of the castle wall; death deservedly for the traitor! I cared not to give Hebren or the boy any consideration because my anxiety of their welfare would set off doubt again.

The sudden change of fierceness in the rain negated my wonderings, and rising from the ground I walked to the apex of the hill and stood looking across the vast land before me. To the north and west, the gigantic hills intensified, almost touching the sky and in the east, their contours flattened into a flat mass of amber and brown, announcing the edge of the forest. I turned south facing the carpet of the green planes, broken by gentle fissures of the many streams fingering their course toward the distant coastline. I wished I knew more of this land and its rulers and what made the people the way they were. Apart from their lust for greed and unequalled brutality, there was nothing I could call upon to aid my survival against them.

A small band of Laddians travelling westward summoned my attention, whether they were the remnants of the vagrants from Crosshall or mere traders, I could not determine, but regardless, assumed the worse. It would have been futile to return to the encampment because they would have reached it long before me, I hoped Maddox already spied them and made safe his escape. Tentatively, after they passed, I continued my search for the hierophant and ran down the hill, slipping on the wetness before ascending the next tor ahead of me. Though fearing my friend's welfare, I promised just one more hill before returning to him. I clambered up the last tor before collapsing in a sodden and breathless heap at its pinnacle, and lay contemplating my dilemma, unwittingly pinching a grass blade and chewing upon it. Though I recall my action vividly, knew not why I did it. I was famished sure enough but the satisfaction from a single thread of grass never staved off the hunger, perhaps I did it for the sake of concentration.

"God in heaven!"

I gasped at the crown of the mushroom suddenly appearing before me, and lay mesmerised observing the matted constriction of grass yielding to the fungus extending its wiry stalk. Next to this grew another, and simultaneously a third. Instantly I considered Tolin's tale of the faerie rings and shielding my face from the driving rain, bowed my head closer. I crawled nearer, restraining my eagerness to touch them. Suddenly a wave of unequalled enchantment swamped over me, unlike the visions accustomed, this was something greater and more fantastic, unrivalled in its warmth and opulence. In my bewildered circumstance, more mushrooms sprung up around me, breaking through the thick grass and boldly venturing into the cold wet air. Though sporadic, a captivating ridge of them encircled me, some large, small, tall, thin and some daintily minute. Within the confine of the ring, strangeness overwhelmed me, the rain ceased suddenly as did the wind and a shaft of sunlight beamed from a hollow in the clouds, illuminating my entire body. Gently it warmed me with its enticing glow and with this light came faint whispers like heaven's own breath, tantalising my ears with its beckoning. In my bewilderment, I remained motionless save for my eyes flickering continually at the unfolding spectacle, relishing it as if in entitlement of my own presence. The mushrooms floated beside me, agitated by the sun's increasing glare, then a soft chanting echoed in my head, sending me dizzy. I tried blinking to curtail this preposterous vision but the circle continued to compress around me, I felt myself rising as if pulled by threads, then only to plunge like a leaden ball. Deeper and deeper I sank, gripping the soil in an effort to halt my falling. The ring dispersed as I plummeted heavily into the ground with the shard of sunlight accompanying me. I clutched at the bones and closed my eyes, begging on them for rescue. My body twisted and contorted in uncontrollable spasms until I came to rest. Panting nervously, I took courage and opened my eyes and before me a cloudless blue sky, with the sun penetrating warmth equal to a midsummer's day. Hills radiating a lush green filled the scape as far as I could see, broken only by a trickling brook meandering aimlessly near my feet, mirroring deep crystal water with a diamond-white effervescence dancing tirelessly on the surface, exploding into vapour on contact against the smooth black stones steering the river's course.

"You are not Tolin," disputed a mellow voice startling me.

"Where is Tolin?" the strange voice spoke again.

"Who are you? What is this place?" I demanded of him, rising to my feet.

"There is no point you shouting. Shout all you want, you cannot be heard," said the voice. "There is no one else around to hear your wailing."

I rubbed my eyes and wished again upon the bones firmly in my palm.

"Help me!" I screamed. "Take me from this place. Awake me now from this vision, I implore you."

The dwarf appeared from nowhere, his bulbous green eyes looked sternly at me equally scrutinising, as I did him. His faded brown leathers hung shabbily over his podgy body like a discarded turnip sack. His drab brimmed hat flopped across his head, tilting to one side and casting a deep shadow engulfing his enormous nose. His thick hands had clutch of a wooden pole, poised and ready to poke me.

"Who are you stranger?" he wondered.

"Might I ask the same of you?" I said briskly.

"Why aren't you Tolin? I do not understand," he ranted, releasing grip of his stick with one hand to rub his chin in perplexity.

"I thought my judgement was accurate," he added, still rubbing his chin. "You should have been Tolin," he rambled on.

"Sorry if I disappoint you," I offered him a feeble smile.

"On the contrary my friend, it is refreshing to see a new face. I never get the chance to meet fresh faces in these times. It gets very lonely you know, because nobody ever seems to come here any more."

"Are you from these hills?" I asked him, pointing lazily to the horizon.

"Oh, gracious me no, and yet…," he suddenly pondered, "…yes, I suppose I am."

"I do not follow."

"I do," he said, spinning full circle with the aid of his stick. "I always follow."

"Sorry?" I quizzed.

"I follow. I always follow."

"Follow what?"

"Tolin," he said.

"The boy?"

"Boy?" the dwarf laughed rolling his head backwards. "Boy?" he repeated continuing his incorrigible laughter.

"He is no boy," he eventually said, having calmed from his excitement. "Why, he is nigh on thirty or is it forty? Oh, I forget," he rambled.

"Impossible," I asserted, "he is but a young boy, certainly far younger than me."

"No stranger, you have it all wrong…"

The dwarf stopped suddenly and began approaching.

"…You know him?" he asked, looking directly into my eyes.

"Yes," I replied.

"How?"

"How what?" I questioned.

"How do you know him?" he questioned, halting a little distance from me.

"We have travelled together and parted a few weeks hence."

"Weeks? What is weeks?" he probed.

"A week is duration of time. Seven days," I did my best at explaining.

"Days?"

"One day you know…"

"…No, I don't or I would not be asking you!"

"Well, let me just say, some time ago," I sighed in resignation.

"Where is Tolin now?"

"I am not sure."

"I must seek him. Was he alone?" he continued to question me.

"No."

"Then he is still with the monk. Saints preserve us, that is good news," the dwarf laughed, spinning full circle around his pole again in the opposite direction. "So long as he remains with the monk no harm will befall him."

"He is not with a monk," I declared.

"Argh, then he is surely doomed. Another one of us good folk abandoned without hope and left to wander aimlessly, all because of that stupid monk! I knew he could not be trusted."

Realisation struck me and brought to mind my meeting with him at Nopi.

"Then the monk is real, but why did no one else not see him?'

"Thinking aloud? Perplexed?" asked the dwarf.

"It is nothing and of no consequence."

"Come now," he urged, "say what is on your mind."

"Very well. The monk you refer to, is he real or just a figment of imagination?"

"That would depend on how strong your imagination is and whether you believe or not. You see, to ordinary folk the monk is not apparent, but to those who believe and understand, he is very genuine."

"And if I said I saw him?"

"Then you must be a believer," he replied smiling.

"A believer in what?"

"Why in faeries of course!"

I kept striving to grasp the dwarf's confusing revelation.

"You obviously accept us or you would not be able to see me. Why, you wouldn't even be here!"

Again, the dwarf broke into laughter and danced around his stick.

"And…," he quickly paused, returning to a more sombre state; "…more importantly it proves you are no ordinary person."

Legacy of Bones

Well that was very evident to me, having undergone the spells, divinations and all; of course, I am not ordinary!

"This monk," I pursued, "who is he precisely? What is his purpose and whom does he serve? And why do you seek Tolin?"

"I am not sure I want to answer those questions."

"Then, little man, who can?"

"You ask too much. You have no entitlement for answers and I am not a little man. I am a faerie and very proud to be one!" he ranted.

"I meant no offence."

"That is all very well but you had best change your attitude if you want to remain breathing!"

"Come now, there is no need for aggression."

"No need? Us folk do not liken to inquisitive bombardment, especially me!"

"I am sorry."

'Sorry?' It was the last thing I felt. I wanted to grab the goblin and throttle him until his head turned blue. All my questions and surmises went unanswered and he infuriated me. I wanted to establish where I was, or if I was undergoing another vision, all he kept doing was evading answers and firing questions back at me.

"I have to proceed now and find Tolin," he said, having regained his calmness.

"What about me?"

"That is entirely up to you. You can stay here or accompany me to find Tolin."

"I can do neither."

"You have to choose an option."

"I need to return. You see I am seeking someone too, and can ill-afford the time to neither help you, nor, can I stay here and wait for your return. I must get back and now."

"There you go, demanding again," sighed the dwarf.

"Very well then I shall demand. I demand you get me back!" I contended strongly.

"I am afraid it isn't that simple. You see, unless I find Tolin I cannot take you back."

The dwarf twisted around his stick again.

"You got me here did you not?"

"Of course I did."

"Then return me!" I pressed.

"For the sake of goodness I can't!"

"Why not?"

He sat on the ground crossing his legs and, plucking a blade of grass, chewed upon it. I stood over him in the prevailing silence wanting to lash out at him to cease the petty conversation. He must have acknowledged my annoyance for he then spoke.

"Tolin has that power, not I. He possesses the Western Crescent, and me, only the Eastern."

"Western? Eastern? Crescent?" I repeated dumfounded.

The dwarf fumbled about his neck producing a small flat metal adornment; a crescent shape with the lustre of pewter and the thinness of gold leaf.

"This is the Eastern Crescent," he said, quietly twisting the amulet which reflected the sunlight.

"And that holds power?" I asked somewhat derisory.

"Do not mock!" he warned. "This has the power to transport any living form from any place I care."

"And the Western Crescent?" I urged.

"The power to do the opposite and transport anything from here back to reality."

"Where is here exactly?"

"What you see belongs to the world of Keld, the land of ancient faerie folk, and all what you see in this land is ours. It stretches for untold leagues and as long as a hundred summers filled…"

"…So," I interjected, "you hold the power to get in and Tolin holds the power to return."

"Precisely!" confirmed the dwarf. "And that is why he must be sought. He needs to be brought back and be amongst his kind."

"Then I am as eager as you to find him but I must leave here."

"You are welcome to join me in my search," offered the dwarf, "though I think it wiser you remain should he return, then on the other hand he may not pass this way again."

I gave this weird situation consideration and tempted to journey with him, but my own task had to be my priority, and apprehensive if not more so now, for the plight of the kingdom and the wellbeing of Ulcris. Whilst accompanying the faerie may probably be salvation, my heart urged me to stay. If I were to journey with him, where would I end up? Doubtlessly a lot further away from the hierophant and the realm.

"I shall remain here," I said emphatically.

"That is your choice; I hope you find what you seek."

The dwarf rose, replacing his talisman inside his robe.

"I shall return with Tolin," he said confidently.

"I may not still be here."

"Oh you will," he smiled mordantly, "you will…"

…And that was it, our encounter curtailed swiftly, without wave or goodbye. He just vanished in a plume of smoke, leaving me hopelessly floundering with a deepening sense of resignation, more so than any other time since leaving Wendatch. Deserted by God, my master and missing the company of Maddox. Already, after only but a few minutes since the dwarf's departure, I regretted un-accompanying him, proving yet again I allowed my heart to rule over my head. Treggedon warned me and still I failed to learn the lesson.

How long was I prepared to await the dwarf's return? Was I to linger in this solitude forever? Was I foolish, surrendering to the strange faerie magic and being enticed into this eccentric void, afflicting me with such distress? I did not nor could not consign any solutions to my questions, despite proffering logic to my situation, and all too soon, the shroud of decadence gnawed, to endorse the feeling of becoming my own worst adversary.

Hours turned into days and in the extent I wished constantly on the bones, though aware such desires would go un-

David Greely

fulfilled. Hunger drew my strength and despair my sanity, I dared never to venture far from the place of the dwarf's encounter for fear of missing his return, and thinking by doing so would commit me to Keld forever.

    I took to eating weird root crops, although some resembling those of the kingdom tasted quite different, I even gave them names such as 'hog bulbs' and 'orange stems,' but it is no longer important. You see, within my time in Keld I had little else to think of and naming things such as the vegetables I ate, was a way of passing through the boredom. Firstly, I would study, then taste and then name them. The same applied to the fish I caught too, when fortune prevailed. I constructed a dam across a river and mastered the art of their capture, though nothing of worthy size, appreciative for what I trapped.

    Each new morning I clambered up the tor overlooking the river. I gazed ardently over the horizon in the hope of espying the returning dwarf but each day met disappointment. My return from the hill became increasingly laboured with dejection, even more so than the upward climb itself. Throughout the many hot days following, I gathered materials for a shelter and the large branches and mud-packed grass offered a prudent abode, although my night fires did make up for the inadequacies of comfort. Early evenings, prior to the sun clipping the hills, I said prayer in hope of respite in my isolation. Being alone tendered morose, unwanted feelings and too much opportunity to think over the squandered chances, the mistakes and of the disappointments, all of which bore heavily upon me. I even became weary of the bones hanging about my neck like a millstone, and at one time considered tossing them into the river to rid myself of them for good. They never really proved worthy and I can only proffer I retained them as a link to my master.

    At first, I took to bathing regularly, but like all things in Keld, time saw I became idle and slovenly, and with no other to sample the pungency of my body odour I had no need to bother. The only objective keeping me rational was my relentless study of the wild flowers and for the lengthy duration to follow, began creating my own stock of herbs and seeds. I dared now to venture further a-field to find new species, and took to wandering through open meadows and wooded glades far beyond the hills deep into the forest. Although most were familiar, I discovered an array of new varieties. Some with delicate petals, others with heady perfumes and others so diverse it is impossible to imagine their creation. Massive flower heads larger than cabbages, hung like globes from trees, wiry stems piercing the damp wooded floor with the tiniest of flowers excreting a sickly foulness; all these and more grew in this strange forsaken land. I ate, cooked, blended and dried all of them in my relentless studies and welcomed the day discovering wild potato, although my first harvest was sparse I eventually managed to farm successful crops. Fish apart, meat was a luxury; I made numerous endeavours to hunt but the scarcity of prey along with my ineptitude, left me wanting. I did trap an injured rabbit, although reluctant to kill it, did so to ease my hunger, although as recompense when dining, it brought poignant memories flooding back to me.

Oh, my beloved master, was he so wise to have chosen me as his underling? I felt a torrent of pretentiousness acknowledging my failure in a simple task: mishandling and successfully bringing about the king's death and then to cast my only true ally Ulcris aside, in a hopeless self-possessed dream to restore goodness to the kingdom. Moreover and undeniably irrational, sending Hebren and Tolin back into the clutches of uncertainty, and abandoning Maddox, my true friend, in a land full of vile and contemptuous people. I missed them all, not one day passed without giving them thought, nor did I forget Owell and Pennypot's betrayal, although never wishing it upon them or the others, it did seem ironic their demise served just reward for their mutinous action. Harsh judgement perhaps, but such is the way of the Lord, had they not strayed and remained solid in their pledge to me, then surely their fate would have reaped better fortune. My thoughts of them led me into many hours of digression; I set off each day in keenness with my plants, only to submit to the sorrow and anger of the recent past. At night I

David Greely

dreamt often, though little of the future, often waking in cold sweats aside my shouts into the dead of night, facing adversaries and wild imaginings. Each new day brought fading hope and every night a stronger and heavier burden of despair. Would I ever see the dwarf again? Would Tolin be beside him to rescue me from Keld and return me to my realm?

Chapter Eleven

I could gloat the cultivation of the crops and flowers in Keld but it is of no consequence despite the importance it instils in my heart. I gained sufficient quantities of herbs and made potions now considered to be treasured, and though worthless in the land of faeries, would make any merchant a wealthy man in Aeria. It was however, to lead to an experience of deep regret.

I experimented by taking potions that left me either intoxicated and swathed in a sea of madness or in some instances with renewed strength, vigour and importance. There were times however when I sank into the shadows of oblivion, uncertain as to what was real or imaginative: hallucinations, convulsions and sickness, all of which drained my waning sanity, yet others gave strength of a hundred men, creating a resurgence of wisdom and belief in the very attributes all too often lacked.

David Greely

My term in Keld remains uncertain to me and at periods feels all but a few months, but it transpired into years. I lost sense of time and for that, perhaps the land's trait is responsible. I long surrendered counting days and the seasons; only seeing my mirrored image in the still water by the river did I unexpectedly become aware of just how long the term must have been. The shock at seeing my reflection; a full beard with matted shoulder length hair is somewhat of an awesome awakening. At first, I failed to recognise myself and duly turned around expecting to see some stranger standing there in pathetic tattered rags long outgrown. How could I have been so blind never to notice my own state of welfare? Primarily, I assumed my haggard condition the result of the self-administered concoctions but along with the duration in Keld, it was a combination of the two. I wept, unable to control my feelings and trod for hours in what became my domain, inwardly cursing the wretched place. My fields, once delicately furrowed, heaving with vegetables and flowers lay forlorn in neglect, overgrown with bramble and nightshade. Eventually, I returned to the river, sinking my head into the icy water in a bid to revive myself and wash away the coat of pretence hanging upon me and in ridding the realisation of my haggard reflection I sank my sallow face into my bony fleshless hands.

What had I done and what had I become? If I were not so faint of heart, I would have taken my life. I did not pray any longer because I had forgotten how to, the meaning of God and his wisdom deserted me. The magic bones, long discarded, lay in their pouch in a darkened confine somewhere in my malodorous hovel, now bereft of roof save the ribbing spars, listing like the skeleton of some old fisherman's craft.

It is paradoxical when all appears lost; fate comes to bear and if not witnessing it myself, would denounce such likelihood. Cocooned in my own degenerative and piteous state I failed to realise my experiments coerced my mind into thoughts of misgivings, straying off the path of the Lord and wallowing in a fruitless indulgence fit for those lesser mortals unprepared to resist and face the harshness of their own realities. Surely, I was stronger and wiser, yet by allowing myself to slump to their extreme, can explain it only as thus.

I woke on a night without moon feeling cold and feverish, huddling by the flickering golden flames of the near-spent fire. Within the dark chasms of the shelter, contorted shadows of morbid shapes threatened as if by a demon's dream, unholy and frightening: hideous creatures with penetrating eyes and dripping fangs hid in the corners waiting to take me with gnarled claws, poisonous talons poised to strike when daring to close my eyes. Rancid wafts of their death hung in the quiet, sickening my stomach and paining my head, they came at me inching nearer and nearer as I lay on my back. Covering my face with my hands did nothing to fend their continual advance and I screamed aloud in anticipation of my imminent death.

"God help me!"

"Why should he?" questioned a voice from within the gloom.

I dared not remove my hands covering my eyes and lay rigid and motionless but for my involuntary gasps.

"Am I not a disciple of the Lord?" I called out.

"Are you questioning your own faith?" asked the voice.

"No," I proclaimed, "I am a disciple of God!"

"You do not appear so," the voice spoke again.

"Who are you? What are you?" I shouted in the darkness. "Just leave me be. You are not welcome here."

"That I cannot," returned the voice.

I shook my head rigorously to dispel the voice and wake myself from what I perceived as a nightmare.

"I am still here," continued the voice.

"You are the work of the devil! Cast yourself from this place, I command you!"

"You are not worthy of command," the voice endorsed. "Look at yourself."

With dread, I slowly opened my eyes, peeled my hands away and stared into the pitch searching out the sinister visitor.

"Is that you dwarf? Come show yourself," I laughed nervously.

"Tolin, why you little sprite come forward and let me see you. Maddox?"

There was no response from any of them and I called out again.

"Hebren? Owell no, that cannot be."

"I am none of whose names you call," the voice eventually said.

"Then who?" I urged fearfully.

"If I were to disclose myself you would not have a care to believe."

"Test me," I said rising off my back.

"No!"

"Very well then," I asked, "what is your purpose with me?"

"I have no purpose. I am here merely because of your demand."

"I want for no such thing, now go away from me."

"Too late my friend."

"Friend?" I doubted. "You are not my friend."

"If I were not, then do you not consider I could have slain you whilst you slumbered?"

"God in heaven who is this that torments me so?" I yelled.

"There you go again, calling for the Good Lord or to be more precise, demanding. Do you never contemplate to give instead of want, Arton?"

"How dare you and how do you know of me?"

"Think for a moment Arton, what have you given the Lord?"

"He is my testament and knows all too well what I have given."

"What you perceive and what he regards, are they not very distinctive?"

"I cannot answer," I conceded.

"Then answer this," continued the voice, "why is it the Lord deserts you?"

I gave it thought but conceded to no reason.

"Until you find the answer Arton, he will not accompany you."

"Perhaps then," I offered, "there is no God."

"Search within yourself and perhaps you will find him."

A daunting silence prevailed like an eternity and I drifted back into slumber.

Upon waking, my head pounded relentlessly in disquiet of my intruder and after slowly rising, staggered outside the hovel, staring blindly into the strong daylight. The despicable creatures had vanished, as had the owner of the voice whom dared question me. No footprints could I see when walking the frosted ground or broken ice on the frozen stream edge to give evidence of any visitor. I returned to the dwelling when the sudden realisation struck; I had found my answer. There was no demonic visitation, it was my self-indulgence and addiction creating the nightmare, and withholding any realism lacking, since taking the samples. The voice was my own; the small wooden hollow where I once stored seeds, now diminished, confirmed it so.

I could not recall the last time I ate or a day when possessing a clear head, the brightness of the winter's day forced me to remain seated under cover, avoiding the sufferance of the sun's glare. For several days beyond, I was unable to challenge the daylight and drifted in and out of slumber, submitting to the pains of withdrawal, confusing day with night, hot with cold and sanity from illusion.

After some eventuality, gradually rid myself of the unholiness in which I resided, regaining my judgment along with my belief and resumed prayers; something I had dismissed for as long as I could recollect at the time. I prayed morning and evening, each and every day regardless of my bodily condition, for many things; a better shelter, food, warmth, clothing and even companionship but above everything, I prayed to the Holy Father for forgiveness. Ultimately, I learned to pray to the Lord and not for me realising that to better oneself, one can only enhance it alone, not entrust to reliance upon others. It was all too simple to ascribe others for my delusions and misgivings rather than accept them as my responsibility, a judgement taking me far too long to discover.

'What of me, now that the dwarf has not returned? Am I to become a sad individual, undeserving of rescue and if never to meet with the hierophant again, remain a lost soul without sense of purpose or destiny?'

"My God, the hierophant!"

My wail resonated in the dwelling's emptiness.

"The bones," I cried even louder, hastening on all fours to the dingy corner in an urgent escapade to locate them.

I had disregarded them yet then again, forsaking everything, including, which I loathed to admit at the time, the kingdom, if it still existed. I endeavoured to understand why I stooped to my addiction and reached plenty of logical conclusions. Loneliness, boredom and as always, self-pity but these were all just lame excuses to enjoy the experience, in an effort to overshadow the underlying problems I refused to confront. It was too easy, and then wanting more and more, until I spent my stock.

I sat facing a field of wilderness with no crops and no seeds to sow, which in retrospect was good, for more seeds would have meant more potions. My dwelling became an unholy hovel and I hated it, the deathly rankness and my own putrid excrement equally abhorrent. I chose to bathe despite the icy water, cleansing myself in an effort to revert to the path of the Good Lord, and with severity, strung the pouch of bones around my neck and set off into the hills. Leaving my encampment was simple, but departing the only place of known contact with the dwarf was not. I debated whether to remain and restart my wait in earnest or leave to roam the land of Keld, powerless to return to the kingdom, never knowing if Ulcris succeeded in deposing Talteth or never seeing anyone again.

The rain and wind lashed at my near naked body and the ground lacerated my feet as I journeyed away from the encampment, tempting though it was, I did not stop to glance back, fearing alteration of choice. I did my utmost to remain cheerful by ruminating the lost days with Treggedon, recollecting our cosy evenings by the hearth, avidly watching his delicate tricks in the comfort and warmth of the apothecary, but with hope of returning to the realm all but dead, proved increasingly testing.

Stumbling upon a projecting stone roused me from my reverie, and cursing as I did, failed to ease the pain shooting through my toe and up my shin. Whilst sitting to attend my injury, the inclemency abruptly ceased, surrendering to a warm breeze. Slowly I rose, looking skyward to greet the radiant shaft of sunlight upon me, promptly accepting it as work of the faeries but while standing in studious awe, the awareness of an imminent vision struck, and the soft voice of the hierophant spoke.

"Arton," she whispered.

"Praise heaven and praise the Lord!" I said excitedly, instantly recognising her sweet voice.

"Arton, you have returned."

"Returned?" I questioned excitedly.

"I thought you gone forever."

"I have been here searching for so long, I thought it I who had lost you."

I fell to my knees and wept.

Her elfin body came into view, drifting toward me on the gentle breeze, I squinted to rid the tears and focus on her heavenly body. Her delicate outline shimmered in the warming wind, trailing a white gown, waving like a dragon's flame and snapping at the air in wild confusion simultaneously with her long black hair. I wanted desperately to affirm the hierophant real, confirming her a prophecy and not another withdrawal-induced concoction. She seemed real, as ever a divination could be, with dark emerald eyes effervescent as a spring pool, captivating and beckoning me to gaze directly into them. High cheekbones complimented her narrow lips beaming a caring and warm smile. Milky flesh, as if cosseted from the sunlight, flowed gently with her movement and at her effortless approach I noticed the finely trimmed gold filigree on her gown, adding to her veneration. Continually the vitality rippled portraying her elegance, unequalled to anything I have seen. She was holy, nay; godly, nothing created other than by the Good Lord could define such exquisiteness and grace. My anxiety waned at her overwhelming calmness; no apprehension, no condemnation, just the air of simplicity as if subliminal of her own fetching resplendence. She spoke again.

"Oh, Arton, why did you forsake me?"

"I beg your forgiveness my Lady."

"Your neglect of God has clouded your belief."

I bowed my head in guilt.

"Then I am at your mercy, gracious Lady."

"Now you have sought me, perhaps a little wiser you must assert yourself in your objective."

"I am at a loss."

"Indeed?" she questioned smiling.

"I do not comprehend anymore. Why this lengthy duration since our last meeting?"

"I think you are aware as to the reason."

"I am…?"

My doubt was undeniably stupid of course and I knew why. Because I did not have the courage or commitment of my own admission, because I deserted my faith and if I remained honest and true with the Lord, then no suffering would have ever transpired.

"…Yes I am," I reluctantly agreed," but why did I have to find you?"

"Can you not recall the words of your king?"

"Yes, but I had to seek you in Laddia and this is not Laddia," I appealed.

"Of course it is you stand upon its northern hills?"

"This is Keld," I disagreed.

"Oh dear,'" she sighed, "it would seem you have met with Mullyfoddy."

"Mullyfoddy?" I repeated, suddenly realising my misfortune. "The dwarf, can you explain?"

"This is becoming tiresome Arton."

"Please I need to know."

She clarified accordingly.

Legacy of Bones

"Mullyfoddy is the hermit frequenting these hills. He is untrusting and disliked by everyone and everything. All in all, he is a despicable character and his irritating antics cause immeasurable pain and suffering."

"But…?"

"…I know, you think him a faerie. He says that to most."

"I saw the mushroom ring and was taken to Keld. I know it happened."

"You only thought so," she quashed my resolve.

I felt perplexed to say the least and cajoled into believing the dwarf, even though sane then. If I had my addiction at the time of our meeting, then certainly I could have understood, but knew it to be real. Tolin told me of the faeries and the pixie rings.

"I still cannot understand all this," I admitted.

"Think on Arton. What potion did you imbibe to ready your belief in Mullyfoddy?"

"Nothing that I can recall."

"Did you not eat the grass?"

"How preposterous! Why would I want to…?"

I became mindful.

"…But I hardly even chewed on it."

"Enough to coerce you into his bizarre fantasy. He is artful, he smites everything to capture anyone who ventures and though appearing amiable, his trait is nasty, devilish and often fatal. Think yourself fortunate Arton, you survived the ordeal."

Thus it was. The dwarf whom I thought a faerie portrayed nothing other than a charade by upholding Keld as his imaginary land, but it was Laddia and these were the same hills I first sighted when leaving Nopi. No beast, no bird and no people wander into them because the place is swathed in his unholy marinade. The Bendorian farmer's reference was truthful; the hermit was very much real and delved in unnatural practices. I scoff considering at that time in referring him as the hierophant.

"But what of Tolin?" I asked her.

"He is factual enough. He strayed into Mullyfoddy's path, and but for the priest, would have succumbed to his wiles too."

"So the monk is real?"

"Did you ever doubt?" she returned.

"But no other saw him."

"Tolin accompanied him, is he not real?"

Arton, you have become misguided. The truth is, whatever you judge becomes insignificant, a wizard is to believe in everything no matter how strange by turning improbabilities into actualities, dreams into realities and visions into occurrences.

Tolin is an orphan and faced similar peril as you once did. You were abandoned after your parents died so I sent you to Treggedon."

"My master never disclosed it."

"Surely that is no surprise, would you have believed him anyway?"

"No probably not," I conceded.

"Then you have your answer. Take heart Arton, Treggedon never quite grasped it either."

"Why the priest?"

"He is my aide and a disciple like me. He selects the adoptee, where as I choose the guardian."

"As in the instance with Treggedon and me?"

"Precisely, and the same as Tolin and you. It is a legacy each chosen subject inherits and only those chosen can see the priest."

"Is this then what makes me a wizard?"

She openly laughed and if she were not of holy countenance, I would have taken offence.

"Partly, Arton. Being destined a wizard is one thing, portraying it, however, is another. I think you will make a fine wizard though a little hasty, perhaps too headstrong for your own good, but time will eradicate such excessive quirks."

"Why here though, in Laddia?"

"Unfortunately, I cannot be in two places at once. My task was to rescue Tolin and bring you both together. I had to rely on others to guide you here. Remember the fox, did he not help you?"

"It was the king who sent me here."

"Did the fox not guide you to the king?"

"What of my master?" I asked impatiently.

"He is with our Lord."

"Can I see him? Speak with him?"

"Not until your work is done."

"And when will that be?"

"I am sure you do not wish to know, not that I am able to reveal it anyway, for it is the Lord's proclamation and not mine."

"The fox, please tell me more of him."

"There is little to tell."

"Come my Lady, surely a talking fox possesses a gift worthy of explanation."

"Your persistence is gratifying Arton, very well. When in the realm, during the winter prior to his death, the king and I walked the forest, sat in a grove overlooking Desseldor and passed many hours with idle chatter. Our conversation became flighty, full of wishes and wonders…"

"…You knew the almighty?"

"But of course. He called upon me often for guidance to help find the Lord when needed."

"Did he stray like me?"

"Yes, but differently."

"And the fox?" I pursued again.

"Arbereth wished upon his death to lead the life of a fox. Experience the freedom, the wisdom and the guile of such a creature. I granted his very wish."

"So the fox is the king."

"Exactly," she confirmed.

"If you hold such power why then have I been entrusted to save the kingdom? Surely there exists a greater person rather than me to fulfil what is expected?"

"You are but one piece among many Arton. You, Ulcris, Hebren, Tolin, Maddox and soon others besides, all have the destiny of the realm in their grasp. Even with my learning and power, I cannot withhold the evil Talteth brings upon Aeria. My purpose is to guide, not avenge and can only recruit and serve those chosen."

"Then without me…"

"…There will be no kingdom," she resigned.

"But Ulcris, Tolin and the others, they have the strength and loyalty, so surely they will succeed?"

"Not without you Arton. Faith, no matter how strong, cannot overcome the prevailing tyranny. One has to be like their enemy think, believe and act like them in order to succeed."

"Surely to be the devil and to fight the devil is unholy," I advocated.

"It may appear so but as with all things in life, it is God's creation, only he has the divinity to eradicate."

"But killing is against the vows."

"That is so Arton and far too many innocents are slain for the sake of greed or glory, but this is different."

"It is a contradiction," I judged.

"Arton, you have to try and perceive. Look, if a crop has the foulness of blight how would it best be cured?"

"By burning what is affected."

"Precisely," the hierophant confirmed, surprised at my awareness.

"But this is different. I mean, these are men, women and children."

"Nevertheless, it is of the same principle. God created them therefore he holds the justification to obliterate, moreover, whether he does it or you do, it shall and will be done.

Did he not create the great flood and wipe out those offending him?"

"Yes, but…"

"…There is no but Arton. He created you as he did me, we both serve because we love him and for all he represents. Defy him and be smitten. There is no life eternal other than in God's heaven and do not be fooled by those choosing to follow under the shadow of evil."

"I want to believe. I do believe."

"I know but more importantly Arton, God knows. Without his consent do you not perceive you would have perished along with your kin?"

"Then what is to be done?"

"I think you know the answer."

"But the king, he told me to seek you."

"And you have Arton."

"Is it not for instruction?"

"If it was then you have received it. Go now Arton and with haste. Find Tolin, restore the kingdom and return to the faith of our Lord."

"I know not how," I admitted.

"With purity of heart, with faith and with strength," she advised.

"What if I should fail?"

"With the eyes of God looking down upon you Arton, you will not falter."

Her image and parting words dissipated along with the return of the cold blast. The meagre shaft of sunlight vaporised into the oncoming rain and I remained alone once more staring up into the heaven, calling for her return. She never did.

Chapter Twelve

I lingered upon the tor for some while cold and sodden, digesting meeting the captivating hierophant and considered whether she be just another ambivalent dream. I recognised the potential of my mind and its competence in creating such imagining; her sagacious words somehow confirmed her realism and feeling in possession of the truth concluded her appearance to be genuine. My thoughts altered to the period spent in the confounded hills and the foolishness to even dare believe in Tolin's faeries. How was I going to recapture the wasted time having woefully subjected myself to such deplorable debasement? God knows Ulcris and Hebren would probably have conceded to my ill fate. Moreover, what of Maddox? I abandoned him in this forsaken wilderness equally alone and vulnerable and wondered if he escaped the Laddians. Thinking of them spurred me into action and regaining composure, pushed all neglect aside in readiness to return to the kingdom. Nothing was going to prevent me and swiftly embraced a resolute and confident temperament, which I lacked for some considerable time. Now I wanted to move on.

The forest came into view just as darkness fell. It looked uninviting but my want in ridding myself of the hills quelled such dread and thoughts of a good fire and long sleep overpowered trepidation. I trod wearily down the last grassy slope forsaking regulated steps in my scurry to reach the outlying trees. I contemplated the greater yearn and gathered fuel to tend a small fire heaping cones and bark in a stockpile, appeased with the blaze, I sat against a tree staring into the crackling flames, unconcerned with neither the possibility of being watched nor giving care of the beasts stalking in the night. Sleep came in an instant wave of submission and I slumbered long and heavy without dream. If the enemy were to stumble upon me now then let it be, for I preserved no regard.

My eventual wakening, presumably later the following day, met the waning sun sinking behind the trees in the west; the elongated shadows cast a sudden chill, impelling me to remake my fire which had long since expired. I resolved staying another night before moving on though my stomach ached for food and my heart yearned to rid the solitude, the vivid recollection of the hierophant with her comforting words accompanied me while I slept.

The following day was mild for a winter's day, with a hazy blue sky enriched by the stealth of the sun and hearing birds chatter about the trees proclaimed abnormal tranquillity. I glanced back at the hills for the ultimate time with surprising diminutive abhorrence, perhaps the combination of high spirits and my reformed faith in the Lord since seeking the hierophant caused this. I did not even assert any bitterness for Mullyfoddy, the culprit answerable for my seasons of abandonment and the pitiful mortal I became, though I had good reason; he, above all deserved some disdain yet could but smile at his whimsical antics. I recited a short prayer, smiled inwardly with a sharp inhale of breath and set off eastward into the heart of the forest.

By singing and talking to the Lord, I overcame loneliness on my travel, resorting to thinking of my friends and invoking

David Greely

images of the kingdom. How was is to unfold upon my return, though more appeasing, scheming the downfall of Talteth and Ulcris, sweeping from the south with magnificent armies, wiping aside the pitiful resistance of the pretender's untrained and ill-equipped soldiers. Smashing them then driving north, forcing Talteth to the brink of the realm and beyond, and in the final battle, the fatal blade piercing the devil's heart, draining his life in an instant. The grand feasts and celebrations with me seated to the right of a new king and Tolin beside me. To the left of Ulcris, Maddox and Hebren in equally high spirits, holding our regal revellers transfixed with our chronicles of courage and fortitude. Telling every one of them how it was the Lord's work and that we should praise him. Oh, how Wendatch looked; its outer walls emblazoned with banners and pennants of a new king, fresh straw carpeting every piece of piece ground in welcome. 'Long live the king,' wailing from the heights of the wishing tower amidst the constant pealing of bells, and endless chants singing out across the land praising the Good Lord of our liberation. From every township and city, the populous amassed upon the new capital of Aeria with harmony and peace going hand in hand, grand speeches by the lords swearing fealty to Ulcris, with cheers of acceptance from the common-folk humming in a never-ending furore. Tolin residing with me in my master's old apothecary experimenting, teaching and revelling in a life so rich within our magical sphere.

    I ate sparingly on the futile offerings of the forest while trekking and stopped only when the necessity for sleep exhausted my strength. I travelled by day and night compelled by my haste to return to the kingdom. Every day that passed, I anticipated the morrow would bring sight of the road that would lead me to Nopi, and though disappointed many times, my eventual reward transpired. By noon on the fifth day, the road came into view. Meeting with any strangers in my forlorn condition would certainly raise suspicion, wary of such confrontation I took actions of avoidance. I walked south, adjacent to the track, keeping an ever-watchful eye for any Laddian. My tired and frail body kept going, fed only by the strength of my resolve. My feet were ulcerated, hands numb, still sensing the stings of the nettles and my head pained from the withdrawal. Not that anyone would rejoice at such a sickening sight but observing the gibbets aligning the waysides, heralding my arrival to Laddia's capital.

I cast my gaze into the redundant cages one by one when passing by. Flesh no longer filled their confines and unrecognisable bones bleached by the seasons, lay matted with rotten cloth hanging by soft thinning fibres. The greedy crows; the callous birds of Satan had long since satisfied their appetites and vanished, undeniably feasting upon the sinews of some other hapless victim elsewhere, sentenced by the ill-deeds of the Laddian regime. I stopped briefly at one cage and stood wondering if the carcass before me may be the remnants of Owell or Pennypot, giving the sign of the Holy Cross in hopelessness before moving smartly on.

Heedfully, I entered Nopi fully expecting to mingle with the lesser fortunate, yet the city was stark, completely void of life but for the odd scraggy chicken and the pack of scavenging dogs scurrying about the alleyways and open doorways, barking and yapping at my presence. Although a welcome sight, I felt immensely disturbed by the lack of people and passed through hastily, stopping only to renew my clothing, take a drink and gather stale discarded food into a bundle.

Having travelled this far without confrontation, I thought it wiser to flank Bendoria rather than test my luck further. Under kind skies, I was in better fettle though remaining perplexed by the city's emptiness. Nothing dampened my rising spirits as I continued south-easterly, knowing every step was a step closer to the kingdom, I even dismissed contemplating my passage across the sea as trivial by overcoming it when an opportunity presented itself. The feeling of nausea endured, sailing to Laddia was by far an experience I wished only upon my enemy but if to incur again in order to secure my return, I prepared to suffer it tenfold, even though swearing never to venture the ocean again.

David Greely

    I relished the wilderness surrounding me; spring awakened Mother Nature early, with trees bursting into bud and clumps of pixietock in full bloom, dancing about their roots. Birds contested for partners, wild boar thrashed in the undergrowth snorting their haughtiness at my intrusion, hares boxed in open meadows and rabbits darted through their runs along the embankments. I forfeited awhile to savour their antics and chance too, to delve into my feeble food stock. Although stale, the bread was a tasty alternative to nuts and frost-withered berries, and in my frivolous mood I shared my meagre hoard with a pair of majestic jays.

    The nearer I got to the coast the fewer the trees, only sporadic copses stood with some defiance against the encroaching salt marsh and the gentle contours of woodland depleted to a mundane mud-covered flatness. If in comparing the bog with those in the realm then it would be all too willing to drag me into its stagnant deathly abyss, and in caution I sought only to travel during daylight.

    Although it was not my intention to seek it, the settlement we inhabited in the first winter appeared before me. I had in mind to stop but with only a few hours of daylight remaining, continued on my path of intent. The lengthening shadow in front of me signalled my halt, I walked haphazardly until finding a suitable dry mound where I eventually rested amongst the tall rushes. I checked for the pouch of bones, said my prayer and quickly surrendered to sleep.

    Strangely, I dreamt of the marsh village and in all the excitement of returning to Aeria, my lost years under the influence of addiction and even the beauty of the hierophant, could not thwart consideration of the settlement. An astonishing delusion, so real that it felt as if it occurred as I slumbered. Dead bodies lay strewn on the ground, fresh and un-smelling save one smouldering carcass, as if the event transpired as I arrived to bear witness to the massacre. No face did I recognise, nor implement of destruction could I see. No marauding gang punching the air in jubilation, nor assailants fleeing from the horror they beset, just seven lifeless bodies lying with heads bludgeoned and limbs bruised, then as I turned away a voice called to me, fragile, straining to be heard above the quietness of dawn. I stopped and waited for the call again, 'perhaps a trick of the wind,' I dismissed it.

I woke with a start, ridding myself of the macabre dream, glimpsing at the sun breaking through a thin bank of cloud. I crouched behind the rushes and leered back at the village to assure myself the nightmare did not endure. With relief, I rose, stretching my arms skyward to sample another fine morning and broke off a lump of bread, continuing south, eating as I went.

Later that morning I stopped beside a silted river, its tide had ebbed and I followed the meandering course, twisting like a giant snake to the ocean, with my eyes. The bubbles breaking the surface in midstream caught my attention; gently at first, like a fish snapping for a fly, then without warning, a sudden gush burst into the air. I stood open-mouthed watching the rising spout. The vision came simultaneously and the marsh appeared with exceptional clarity, almost as if in front of me. Round lodgings perched on wooden stilts, each accessible by its own ladder. Discarded boats lay in the mud like floundered fish caught on the receding tide, and then one by one the vagrants from Crosshall appeared, snarling with rage, mercilessly dragging a man tethered by his ankles, who called my name. His cries dispersed as the waterspout eased and the river returned to its gentle ebbing flow.

I stood shaking and breathless, uncertain of the vision or its connotation, this gift given to me by the Lord needed attention, so without dither; I twisted sharply and sped back toward the settlement, abandoning my bundle which hindered my pace. I never considered wrong footing or falling into the mire, nor did I give care at the noise emitted in my dash, and sprinted as if the devil gnawed at my heels. It felt an age before revisiting the tussock I had previously slept on; I leapt it with ease whilst remaining focused on the village ahead. My approach gave witness to the activity foretold in the vision, seven scruffy individuals, some of whom I recognised from Crosshall whooped

David Greely

and jeered at their captive, pulling him in unison along the ground by his feet and dragging him across the open fire, whipping him and lunging flaming torches at his near-naked body. I let out a wail of defiance, charging at them with my master's stave reincarnated in my hand.

"Dogs of the devil!" I shouted, swinging the staff around my head without considering how it came to be.

Instantly they stopped, firing words of irreverence at me and making themselves ready for attack. Without premeditation, I sped into their midst arcing the rod directly down onto one vagrant and striking him squarely in the face, the impact of the dull thud trembling along the rowan into my arms. I swiped again, catching another under his chin and as they dispersed and gave chase until tangling with them all. My third victim received a timely crack to back of the neck, collapsing him to the ground, as he struggled to gain his feet, I followed with a hefty prod deep into his gut. As if in the same swift motion, I spun on my heels whipping the pole across the chest of another. The remaining Laddians struggled to flee but my pace was too rapid and cracked the staff over the head of the fifth. Another felt the end of my weapon into his jaw, the resounding bloody impact shattered his teeth. The last member screeched in horror as I gave chase and stopped squaring up to me with sword drawn. Undeterred, I leapt at him with staff gripped at either end and pushed him to the ground, forcing my weight upon his throat, not relenting until his final breath drove out his tongue. Discontent with his death, I scythed the pole across his head, cracking his skull open. The fight quelled. I gasped for breath whilst examining the carnage dealt; watching one blooded vagrant crawl blindly across the ground into the raging fire, screams of agony billowed loud as his body submitted to the inevitable death richly warranted.

"Arton," a breathless and faint voice called.

I ran to the bound man lying on the ground and my stomach churned noticing his body riddled with burns, cuts and gaping wounds. Slowly I bent down and cradled his head.

"Maddox!"

Legacy of Bones

"Arton, you are alive," he whispered breathlessly. "I hardly recognise you. Where have you been? I have been searching but thought…"

"…Silence my friend and let me help you."

"I am afraid you have come too late."

"Quiet now," I instructed. "Let me tend your wounds."

"Listen to me."

I bent over, wiping his blooded brow and tears flowed too easily as I continued to cradle him in my lap, rocking him and stroking his hair for comfort.

"Why this?" I sobbed.

"It was either you or me Arton. The vagabonds followed us into the hills and I kept them away from you. I have fought them off for countless seasons yet still they trailed me, I eventually led them to this place in the hope you would be here."

"I am here now my dear friend."

"Do not go south Arton, the might of Laddia is gathering."

"What do you mean?" I quizzed.

"Laddia is sailing to the kingdom. You are too late."

Maddox took one final laboured breath.

"You came back, I knew you would. I never doubted…"

His words tapered into a smile.

"…Maddox I am so sorry, if only I realised."

His head flopped to one side.

"Maddox?"

I closed his eyelids gently with my fingers and continued to rock him.

"Oh Maddox, why?"

I cuffed my face, averting the tears from dripping onto his face and looked at him sombrely, aspiring on the bones if I could take his place. I cursed my deviation, damned the hills of Nopi and condemned the bones.

"When wished upon you grant me nothing thus you are worthless to me and the kingdom!"

I still did not know their intent, strength or method of summon, to control their power. They were fake and fickle, and did not deserve me nor I them. They were useless. I wrenched the pouch from my neck breaking the thin leather strap and threw them to the ground in condemnation.

I looked down at Maddox, crying further, and offered a feeble prayer between sobs.

"Dear Lord, please take him into your heaven and see he wants no want, nor feel no pain, forever eternal. He has earned his keep and your trust, a worthy disciple. Amen"

Maddox deserved much better but I did not have the courage or inspiration to find such words with grief so strong.

It is strange, the feeling of penitence. When one shows sorrow at the death of one so close, it is sadness not for the victim but for oneself. A selfish attitude of being abandoned and no longer thought of, it is the mourner that suffers the anguish and loneliness.

Using a piece of broken timber, I dug a grave for my friend as deep as my energy allowed and positioned his head facing the kingdom; the least to offer for his eternal rest, though an unjust and pathetic reward for a good friend who sacrificed his life for the realm and me. I wished he would receive his just compensation in heaven, before covering him with stones and boulders, though dissatisfied with my friend's internment. I searched vainly for my master's stave amid the strewn enemy, contriving Maddox's slayers deserved nothing, then left them to the pleasure of scavenging crows, but again the authenticity of the rod eluded me.

Chapter Thirteen

Certainty of my course of action needed thorough reconsideration, if it was as Maddox disclosed and the Laddians already poised to invade the kingdom then I needed to be even hastier in returning. My originally conceived plan relied heavily on Hebren but now with the death of Maddox, I doubted as to whether he or Tolin ever made the crossing to Aeria and dreaded the struggle without them. Yet I needed to remain positive and resolute, and upon my return to the realm seek them, glean the welfare of Ulcris and his endeavour in raising an army. I was confident he would achieve it but dubious he would still be waiting for me.

It took seven days to reach the coastline, seven long days of inner hell. I fought battles with myself and guilt clawed me constantly, though not just for the death of Maddox or my abandoning him, but also for Treggedon in failing to avert the king's demise, and for Owell too, pushing him and expecting far too much from him. Even for Pecos by arriving too late to save him, ruing if only I valued and understood all of my visions, not one of them would be dead now.

I recalled the misadventure at the marsh village a hundred times over, yet prolonged and bewildered as to why the vision, the strongest hitherto witnessed, came much too late. Surely if God bestowed the bequest of inner sight upon me, why then did I not possess the power to differ the outcome?

I prayed for solace and forgiveness, swearing the curtailment of my selfish ways by reaffirming my fealty to the Lord. This time differently, with veracity and the belief it had taken years to achieve, now ready to accept Him but would God acknowledge and lift the burden of guilt off me?

The only deviation from my remorse occurred three days later when considering the wishbones. Perhaps I acted in haste, for I was angry and no longer wanted them. Their power, no matter how intense, was of no use to me if unable to control it, if I were to seek help, 'then God,' I confirmed to myself, 'will provide it,' and this became my conviction from that moment on.

To contemplate my strategy I rested upon the stony shore, looking south at the far horizon and beyond the lashing waves, tempted to go east by following the coastline and see the Laddian force gathered, but commonsense told me to take Maddox at his word even though I knew not either their strength nor when they may strike.

'Gadzooks!' I thought, 'what if they had already begun their invasion? Surely the kingdom would fall. No doubt the realm already frayed with civil war, the might of the marauding Laddians would easily overpower it and Aeria would capitulate.'

I scoured the beach, optimistic of finding an abandoned vessel, but with the lapse of time knew whatever I discovered would now be a wreck or reclaimed by them. I even searched for a trusting sole too, with whom I could bargain. If not to acquire a boat then at least to secure a passage across the ocean, but these aspirations went unrewarded.

"How stupid," I confessed aloud, "there are boats back at the village."

I did not hesitate in my return there; I immediately backtracked through the marsh. I made swift progress each day, running when availing the strength and walking in the darkness of night, risking the bog in effort to save time. I ate only when faintness struck, baked frogs were not a delicacy I likened to, but it meant survival. The weather remained meticulously kind and only did it rain one late afternoon; the same day I spied a mass of Laddians filtering south toward the coast, delaying me several hours in having to flank them.

Early, on the sixth day saw my arrival back at the settlement and with the certainty it appeared as I left it, I ran into the enclosure with a buoyant surge of eagerness. My entrance set the feasting carrions into harried flight, vacating the strewn bodies of the vagrants with plucked eyes and flesh oozing from pecked holes. I took consolation at seeing the stone mound of Maddox undisturbed but with my need for a boat pressing, spared little time for reflection and merely gave my friend the sign of the Holy Cross.

Ahead, on the river's overgrown western bank lay three vessels, one small and ill equipped for open sea, one lodged up the bank and impossible to move alone, and a third lashed to a post at the end of a dilapidated landing stage with its bulging hull listing in the silt on the ebbed tide. I boarded it and scurried around looking for any holes, throwing apprehension at a split, just above the waterline near the prow, but with no other means of returning to the kingdom, convinced myself it would suffice, despite the added doubts of a broken mast bent to stern and cabin all but demolished.

With some hours before the floodtide, I returned to the dwellings to collect anything useful for the voyage. The scarcity of food worried me, as did the shortage of vessels to take fresh water aboard. The availability of items was equally frugal, managing only to find a hayfork with a split handle, a coil of rope and an array of swords from the dead enemy. I renewed my clothing; I hacked at my hair and beard to make some resemblance and myself presentable to a Laddian. With everything aboard, I returned to the land for the ultimate time, giving prayer at the feet of Maddox, again reciting my final farewell to him. Doing so alas, brought back the sadness of his death.

Oh, I almost forgot, I also collected the pouch of bones lying on the ground close to him, though unsure as to why I did it, perhaps on impulse or a change of heart.

I made an oar from the pick handle by lashing together pieces of wood from the cabin roof and by mid morning I was ready to sail. Anxiously, I checked the boat for holes again as high water approached, pleasantly astounded when it finally rose off the muddy riverbed. I cast off with the makeshift paddle, steering the boat against the flow of the incoming tide and though strenuous, gained some headway until the tide turned, enabling greater speed.

Cheerful at the prospect of sailing home across the sea, I started singing an inventory ditty to display my rare moment of happiness. It went something like this:-

'With a derring-do, derring-do I sail the sea.

A friendly breeze accompanies me.

With a derring-do, derring-do I sail the sea.

Away from the might of the enemy.

With a derring-do, derring-do I sail the sea.

To the kingdom I am set, majestically.'

I repeated the tune countless times then whistled and hummed it until growing thoroughly fed up.

The boat drifted with the ebbing current from one side of the river to the other, but once mastering the rudder I was able to steer the craft adeptly round the tighter curves, keeping in the deeper and stronger flows, though I confess to running aground twice. Smaller tributaries connected into the river course creating a faster flow, often sending me colliding across to the opposite banks. The lowering ebb left but a shallow trickle and the vessel gradually drifted to a miserable rate, scraping the hull on the slimy shale. Before long, it came to rest on a mud flat in the middle of the river's winding course and a good enough reason to take rest. Working the boat proved very exhausting and my arms ached from use of the tiller. I surveyed the marshy flats from my low disadvantaged point, not that there was much to observe, the high sedge banks and the lowness of the water level obliterated any worthy sight. I scrambled atop the broken cabin to obtain a beneficial position but the marsh stretched as far as could be seen, and so dense the rushes, impossible to follow the river's course beyond the next turn.

I felt vulnerable stuck in the mud and anxious for the floodtide to get the vessel mobile again, but what I failed to expect when it arrived was the thundering gore crashing upon me like a tidal wave. The swell drove the boat back some way, almost capsizing it with the impact and water seeped through the split causing the boat to sit lower. I rowed best I could against the tide and not until it peaked did I start making headway south again. Navigating in the dark proved intricate, I chose to hug close to the banks should I need to abandon the vessel if it took in more water, I would swim to shore. It was much the same the following day and night, barely advancing on the flood yet more than compensating with the ebb. I ate little and drank sparingly hoping my supply would last. I knew the river would end eventually and my estimation of a couple more days could not be far off.

At the approach of the following dawn on the second day, fate delivered a savage blow. My earlier fears secured their claim; I floated aimlessly into the midst of the Laddian force. Hundreds of vessels faced seaward lining the mouth of the open estuary and in midstream, floating platforms moored with provisions and countless armouries awaited loading. Crewmen and warriors alike engaged in varied tasks set by a cacophony of orders blending with the general hubbub of clattering, scraping and banging in preparation for their invasion. The eastern shoreline was flanked with tents brimming with what seemed like ten thousand men, and fires nearly expired littered the open ground beyond, casting a gentle orange glow in the early morning.

David Greely

I swallowed hard at the awesome sight, lubricating my dry throat and pondering over my strategy. It seemed I had two choices of action, abandon the boat now and swim ashore in the hope of stowing aboard a vessel bound for the realm, or continue to drift along and chance going unnoticed amid the commotion. Surely, they would never suspect an infiltrator arriving from their own land, so this latter scheme I elected to do.

My boat continued to float in the deep channel toward the Laddian might, despite my hopeless effort at controlling and maintaining my course.

"Hey you there!" came an undesirable shout from a crewman standing on a pontoon.

I waved half-heartedly at him, keeping my eyes fixed on the bow of my vessel.

"Call yourself a sailor? Look out!"

'Look out for what?' I thought.

I should have heeded his words. With a resounding crack, my craft struck another anchored in midstream, I fell forward by the impact and was almost forced overboard. Excited shouts sounding high above the general melee of the loading bellowed in the air.

"What's happening here?" demanded a man whom I assumed to be the captain of the stricken boat.

"Humble apologies," I called back.

"You nigh wrecked us, you damned fool!" the captain admonished.

My craft came to a halt and a line was cast to me to secure. The captain swung himself confidently over the railing of his vessel, landing squarely on the deck, facing me with justifiable agitation.

"Well?" he probed.

"My steering failed and I could not avoid you."

He studied my pathetic vessel before speaking again.

"By the look of things here your whole boat has failed. That is the trouble with you farmers, pretending to be sailors. You should be steering cattle not boats!"

"A hundred pardons," I said remorsefully.

"You have a strange accent, where you from? Pender? Effra? No don't tell me, you're from Issen, all farmers come from there-a-bouts."

Well, wherever he thought I be from I was going to take him at his word.

"How did you guess?" I replied.

"By your manner. You should be tending fields. Well now you're here you'd best come with me."

I did as asked without choice and followed him across the line of tied vessels at the pier-head, and entered the command house overlooking the inlet. He rambled on tirelessly, muttering under his breath and cursing the farmers and their likes.

"I warned them conscripting you farmers is a mistake, but did they listen? No!" he tutted aloud, flinging his head backwards. "And to think they reckon you're able to fight. If the enemy see the likes of you lot as an army they'll split their guts with laughter!"

We entered a large room where a group of Laddians stood hunched at one end of a long table. Charts lay neatly coiled, pinned by heavy candlesticks and table boxes with elaborately curved legs.

"Your Grace," blasted the captain, "this man here nigh on sunk my boat and the crew with it!"

One of the men turned gazing disdainfully at the intrusion.

"Why must I always be interrupted?" he scowled.

"This man is not fit for manning a vessel," maintained the captain.

"I will deal with you momentarily," said the man, returning to the others in conversation.

Within a minute, he broke away from the table and walked to me.

"Now," he said, "what is the problem here?"

The captain inched forward wasting no time replying.

"He ran straight into me. He could have wrecked us!"

"My rudder broke," I said feebly in defence, "I could do nothing to avoid it."

"What is your business?" the man asked.

David Greely

"I have come to join the force…"

"…We don't need farmers," interrupted the captain contemptuously.

"I am in command here and I will decide who we do and don't need, Smeeks."

I laughed inwardly at the captain's reprimand.

"Take him to Almet and see that he gets him displaced."

"Sir," the captain obeyed the commander with a salute.

Under instruction from Almet, I joined a crew of three, managed by captain Molwen aboard a craft anchored offshore on the western bank. Preparing to sail proved hard toil, I spent beyond two hours fetching and storing supplies, and appeasing the selfish whims of boarding soldiers. We set off later that morning laden with fresh water, provisions and a score of heavily clad warriors.

The gruelling work-rate persisted; I pulled on guys, secured blocks and climbed sails until my hands bled with pustules. My distress went rewarded with wholesome food -a luxury forgone for some while.

Being in the midst of the enemy was intimidating, though nothing they said or did could quell my high spirit in the prospect of my return to the kingdom. I kept a keen eye and sharp ear on the passage across, seeking any hint of the Laddian scheme, but it seemed no one aboard including Molwen himself had an inkling of their objective or when or where, we would disembark. I had to be content with a safe crossing and concern myself later with the invasion, as and when we landed.

Altogether they were an amiable bunch, bantering and singing shanties most of the time, although I did get bitter when they talked idly and schemed of their landing. What they proposed to do with the womenfolk does not bear mention; I wanted to kill them all after such talk, but to dismiss my resentment on these particular episodes, opted to excuse myself.

Over the emerging days at sea, more vessels joined us, gradually forming a great flotilla with pilot boats scurrying between the larger ships conveying messages and orders, as well as personnel. The Laddians proved their seaworthiness and sped the ocean handsomely, though difficult to judge the speed with the wind behind us, I would have guessed it to have been in excess of twelve knots.

In my quieter moments, I gazed across the dipping eastern horizon hoping to sight land, eager too for a vision to foresee the curtailment of the voyage, but one never came. By now, my palms had hardened but worrisomely developed a rasping cough that often winded me.

The crossing had been uneventful up until now and the weather much favourable for my stomach. Late in the afternoon on the fifth day at sea, we sighted land and fulmars flew acrobatically overhead confirming the nearness of the shore. We hauled sail and anchored, and just waited, watching the pilot boats ferrying commanders and captains to the ships in unrelenting frenzy. Word finally reached our vessel the landing and the invasion will commence on the forthcoming night, but even hearing such fearful news failed to quash my excitement at reaching Aeria. It had been so long, and I praised God this day for my emancipation.

Molwen instructed me to join one of the pilot boats as oarsman and for some while, rowed without rest other than awaiting a new commander, to transport to another vessel of his desire. Whilst tarrying for such a senior officer a vision enveloped me so strong and vivid it caused me to faint. I witnessed a gathering of cloaked men whose faces were featureless and without expression; they came out from a mist swirling with their movement, perhaps Druids or priests from some other holy order, judging by their finery of the purest white, embroidered with gold tessellated trim. They proceeded stealthily toward me with their fine gowns shimmering in the wake of their tread and I begged them to stop, but they did not listen, perhaps they could not hear. Their rapid advance was upon me, I wanted to shut my eyes, refusing to bear witness, but something compelled me to look, forcing me to an awareness and anticipation. In file, they walked straight through me as if I did not exist, I turned the moment the last man strode through me yet they disappeared. I retracted my stare, looking

David Greely

ahead of me and from that same mist, noticed the raised banner of the almighty; the black eagle set on the deepest of crimson. Beyond, a flame so furious I sensed the intensity of its heat from where I stood and farther still, a ruin from whence haunting cries of dissolution roared louder than the fire's intensity. The water splashing into my face roused me and I eased myself onto the boat's spar shaking my head. The boat lay broadside on a steep beach with waves lapping against the hull, the evening sky forcing away the last of the sun into the sea. I scanned the shoreline and the horizon for the armada but there were no ships. I listened too for the commotion of their advance, the clanging of weapons, battle cries, but there were no Laddians and nothing prevailed, other than the incessant lapping waves.

I can only speculate on the consequence, perhaps the boat became unhitched in my slumber, while awaiting a commander and drifted unnoticeably in the fading light, but it is of little significance however, I'm eternally thankful to the Lord for my freedom. Now with my feet firmly back on Aerian soil I could set about my quest to find Ulcris and undo the misdeeds of Talteth. Already I planned to go to Fleddon and doubtlessly onto Collington where Ulcris would be, it was just a simple matter of establishing my whereabouts, even with the threat of the invasion I felt elated at being home again.

I ran up the beach dubious of my position, more distressingly, uncertain of the intent of the Laddian force. Had they seized the chance to overpower the realm while it lay in chaos and in civil war? God knows there would be little or no defence against them, perhaps they were in coalition with Talteth combining to crush the loyalists in the south, if I could reach Ulcris in advance of the enemy then at least the avoidance of an otherwise certain massacre could be achieved.

In the twilight, I looked out to sea once more before ascending a dune and set off bearing inland high with hope of locating Ulcris, confidently reliant upon my prudence of orientation.

Chapter Fourteen

After sleeping for most of the night, I set off early the next morning under the pleasantry of the spring sun, passing only a few isolated and long-deserted dwellings, clambering tors and crossing rivers in my eagerness to reach Hebren or Ulcris. Though tired and weak, I pressed on day and night with the necessity of locating either of them. At every turn, I feared coming face to face with the Laddians but just kept going and had, in my need, to apprise everyone of the imminent onslaught. Least of all it was my duty as a fellow realmsman and not accept the land to become overwhelmed, least not without a challenge and contemplated Talteth's fate, if he were to die in battle against the marauders, what then? If Talteth is all the realm had for a monarch, then surely, better him than some sadistic Laddian.

On the third day, I met with somebody. The early evening mist refreshingly scented with pine obliterated the trace of dampness in the air, and out of the exhilarating haze came the silhouette of a robust figure. His astonishingly large and solid frame carried a huge adze, slung upon his shoulder in a somewhat lethargic fashion. With his free arm, he gestured a wave, signalling me to approach. His attire was as sombre as a spent autumn yet his face, in contrast, ruddy and bright as a summer's day, possessing a welcoming smile that cracked his weathered face. The lone woodman was ignorant of the danger that loomed and admitted not sighting or hearing any Laddians. He did offer however, a useful contribution as of the realm's welfare, stressing the existence of several differing stories none of which proved to be factual. He was vague of his estimation as to how long Talteth reigned and could only confirm since hearing of the almighty's death to be some years since Talteth became king. The cheery woodman also validated Ulcris continued waging war against him, upholding Talteth killed his own father.

"Some," he said, "choose to believe, some do not and others do not give the slightest concern. The land," he continued enlightening me, "remains divided and has been so for many years. Talteth in the north, Ulcris in the south and us innocents stuck in the middle. Talteth's armies have been sweeping eastward and now they move south again from the mountains quelling any resistance on their march to Collington. The battle of all battles threatens."

As to how far south Talteth had reached, the woodman could not account.

'Ulcris lives and has raised arm against the pretender in readiness,' his words, I repeated, were heaven sent. Now I needed to establish the whereabouts of Hebren and Tolin. Curiously, I sensed fortune, despite previously doubting their success in accomplishing the crossing, but if they had faltered, surely I would have sensed it. They both knew the importance of reaching Ulcris. I did ask the woodman if he spied them but of course he had not, and not for one moment did I think he would have, but it cost nothing to inquire.

"Rest awhile with me," he offered.

"I am obliged but cannot afford such comfort however if you could spare a little food I am in your debt."

"If that is your only want."

"It is," I confirmed.

"Then follow me."

The woodman and I strode off through a narrow track overrun with bramble leading the short walk into an open pasture where, in the northern corner, lay his modest abode. On our approach, the heady aroma of burning wood filled my nostrils, earth mounds with open tops funnelled acrid smoke clinging to the stillness and strewn on the ground dishevelled piles of hacked wood, amid shavings and clippings both old and fresh. Inside the woodman's dwelling were mud walls washed with flaxen and woven tapestries more befitting nobility were pinned to the ceiling amid the craggy oak beams. In all corners hung polished stone pots containing wax and wick, suspended on thin chains waist high from the floor. An oak table with three accompanying chairs lay off centre to the modest hearth on the opposite side.

"I have bread and wine," he said.

"Woodman," I acknowledged, "your welcome exceeds all others."

"It is little often I have visitors but when so, I liken to think that I, Matlock, made them comfortable."

He offered me a chair and pushed the bread across the tabletop.

"I am grateful for your hospitality," I said breaking off a piece.

"You look awful," he remarked, seating himself and pouring the wine.

"Just fatigue," I admitted, positioning myself opposite him. "Where is this place?"

"Scullycrag Fen."

I'd never heard of such place and it left me no wiser as to my location within the kingdom.

"And tell me," I asked between mouthfuls, "where is the nearest town?"

David Greely

I took another eager bite from the bread and chewed greedily awaiting his reply.

"Now that is debateable," he pondered briefly. "Caer Tal is two days south and Vledor Beacon is three days east."

"Why ponder, for obviously Vledor Beacon is closer."

"Not if you cannot locate the ferryman at the inlet. Old Bravitt Dettel is an elusive goat and sails when he chooses and never crosses the water 'til his ferry's laden to get his value out from his toils, you understand. And if he is in the mind to go scurrying, you could be waiting a whole damn season."

"I profess knowing Caer Tal but nothing of Vledor Beacon. Then Caer Tal it is, I shall leave for there shortly."

I was a long way off from Collington, some forty days travel at least and much farther still from Fleddon. Despite my earlier promise to Hebren and the boy, I had to head to the capital, they would understand, given the circumstances. If I possessed a horse the duration could be halved but they were an expensive commodity and very scarce too, since they would have been availed for the armies.

"You appear anxious my friend," observed the woodman. "Will you not rest awhile? You are most welcome to stay here."

"I know Matlock, and I am grateful, but matters press that will not withstand any idleness."

"Will you not tell me your name and purpose?" he asked.

"I am Arton of Wendatch, as for my purpose, well…" I hesitated, "…that requires a lengthy explanation. Let me just say I travel along the path of righteousness and raise arm against the enemy."

"Where lays your fealty Arton?"

"With few people and many things."

"That does not answer my question."

"I am loyal to those displaying the same trait in return, but if you require names…"

"…Indeed I do," emphasized the woodman sharply.

"You will not know their names other than that of the king's…"

"...Talteth?"

"Merciful God no," I quickly corrected him, greedily gulping the wine, "the almighty, Arbereth."

"But he is dead," Matlock confirmed.

"Yes he is dead. Long live the king."

"You show no support for Talteth?"

"None whatsoever," I responded emphatically.

"Then you are his enemy."

"Equally as he is mine."

"And these others?" he pressed further.

"They are but names and will mean nothing to you."

"Nevertheless I want to hear."

"Ulcris, Hebren and the Good Lord of course."

"Ulcris?" he challenged in surprise, spitting out the wine he had just sipped.

"Yes," I confirmed.

"He is a worthless Druid and delves in the black arts."

"On the contrary Matlock, unlike his brother, Ulcris does not practice in devil worship," I contended sharply.

"Who's to say? I have heard many tales of that pair, none of which are very warming."

"Many stories unfold as distorted rumours, measly fabrications of half-hearted whispers uttered by the tongues of foolish gossipers and scaremongers. If in mind to believe all I hear then surely I would be petrified at my own shadow besides, such accounts are age-old now. Elcris has been dead since I was a lad and as for Ulcris well, he is a good man, believe me, and is the realm's only redeemer. He will be king and deservedly so, and not Talteth."

"What matter is it to me as to who is king?" he resigned.

"Of course it matters!" I contested sternly. "Without Ulcris there is no future for anyone, however humble and insignificant we may think we are. If Talteth is not overthrown, the land will engulf in continual war, bringing death, destruction and decay to the kingdom and its people forced into slavery, a sample already thriving at Fleddon. Land and possessions stolen but worse still, hearts of men will become discouraged, fouling our minds from the goodness of the Lord's way. Wish towers will be burned; our towns and cities will be put under siege and our soil smitten with decay."

"How can you be certain? How do you know?"

I was disinclined to proclaim my gift of the prophecy but his pressing would not relent until his curiosity met.

"I have seen what the future could hold and all I state will transpire, unless Talteth is stopped. The whole of Laddia raids our shores, with realmsmen locked in civil war the invaders will meet no resistance, they'll laugh with bellies full whilst watching us destroy each other, before seizing the land for themselves."

The woodman stared vacantly across the table cuffing a residue of wine from his lips.

"Are you a seer? A bard?" he quizzed.

"I cannot boast of either."

"Yet you say you can see into the future."

"Indeed so but I cannot control what I see, nor am I certain at the time of the happening what the event will lead to. I just know from these images the compulsion impelling me. Talteth needs to be stopped."

"And you are going to act solely on some dream?"

"I have no option Matlock."

"But you do," he smiled, offering more wine and bread. "You can forget about your dreams, these false visions of yours and live a life of fulfilment."

"Can you honestly say your life now, as you live it, is content?"

"I am comfortable," he smiled.

"That does not answer my question."

His eyes looked sternly at me.

"Then I will offer this. I have no choice either."

"Woodman, you have a greater alternative than I. Destiny is already laid out for me and I have to tread that path."

"And my destiny?" he asked.

"Whatever you desire. You can remain a woodman and live day to day for the sake of it or become a man full of virtue.

Linger here and be sure to die by the sword of a Laddian. Come with me…"

"…No, I will not raise arm with you."

"Then our meeting must end."

I slowly rose from the table savouring the last of the wine and breaking off a final piece of bread.

"I will not linger on your hospitality Matlock."

"Will you not stay till dawn at least?"

"It will be of no use. Whatever I say will conflict with your own morals."

"Am I not entitled to them?"

"Most certainly," I approved, "but it leads nowhere. My urgency to reach Ulcris is of far greater importance than wasting words on a selfish individual. If the kingdom consists of men like you then God in Heaven help us. You are a stubborn fool woodman and for it you will be killed."

"There is no invasion, I do not believe you."

"Then die the fool, for I shall not tarry to witness your death."

There became a sudden gentleness in his words.

"Look," he sighed, "I would like to help you but my heart is not with your cause. Do not think me a coward nor a selfish man; I cannot live on ifs, buts and maybes."

"If in your heart you regard yourself higher, then your conscience will clear away the doubt," I concluded.

I slammed the door in anger when leaving, though not at Matlock but at myself. How presumptuous was I to assume winning over a stranger that easily? I told him few facts and in retrospect, it was witless. Goading others to my aid succeeded in the past, but now to suffer refusal made me feel bitter and certainly very disappointed. I stood outside the door for a moment collating my thoughts before charging off eastward to find the ferryman and get passage to Vledor Beacon. I am uncertain of my change of heart for if Dettel were missing at the lake I would be squandering valuable time, but nevertheless, saw it as a possibility worth chancing.

My concern for Ulcris grew ever more apprehensive and apart from Talteth approaching from the north with God knows how strong an army, he is going to have to defend himself against the Laddians too, but if I could get to Collington first, then at least he could slip away and have time to contemplate new tactics. Running away in this instance would not be an act of weakness, it is commonsense, and in fact could prove a solution. Imagine Talteth's determination in destroying Ulcris then, upon arriving at Collington end up falling directly into the laps of the Laddians.

I walked off into the cold night heading for the thicket across the meadow, turning briefly to see the dim light from Matlocks' dwelling through the window. I could have used the sleep for a full night but anger denied me that comfort and my heavy gait reflected it so. Although fed and carelessly light-headed from the wine, it was little compensation for my tiredness. I battled through the undergrowth fighting against the whipping gorse and protruding tree roots hindering my progress, throughout the night I passed numerous coppices undoubtedly the results of Matlock's toil.

In the crispness of dawn, I found the inlet of Matlock's reference. A vast tidal lake lined with trees on the western perimeter before me in the distance, a ridge rose and dipped as if a dragons' back was spreading across the entire edge from east to south. I turned and followed the water's edge. If the ferryman was missing then at least I was progressing toward Collington by skirting the lake and crossing the ridge to Vledor Beacon.

The advance of the morning sent the sun high above the hilly crest, reflecting the grey mass onto the still water. If it were not for the task I would have blissfully spent times revelling in the beauty beset and idle with nature, perhaps make camp and hunt. I kept close vigil, still expecting pike heads and banners of the enemy; I listened too for the thunder of their tread and the clanking of their armour. I stopped but once to wash in the cool water to keep myself alert. Upon every high mound, I peered intently for the elusive ferryman and at each turn, looked again but feared the woodman right.

For half the day, the shoreline never broke until in the distance, set between two of the craggy ridges, a wooden landing stage pierced the lake. I neared with apprehension, eager nevertheless to seek passage across the lake. I clambered on a rock encompassing the pier and glanced down. There was no commotion and Bravitt Dettel with his ferryboat absent. I slid down the rock and dashed onto the pier, entering the small lodge sited at the end. Inside, empty nets hung matted over the beams, disused cork floats with tangled ropes thrown into a dim corner, and on a dust-covered bench against a wall, empty cups rested beside dirty bowls. Spent candle wax moulded to the flatness of the table confirmed it a while since the place was engaged. I turned cursing my luck, making for the door.

"Arton?"

The call stopped me walking out the lodge and twisting my neck, caught sight of the woodman fully laden with pack and menacing axe propped over his shoulder.

"Matlock!" I yelled, unable to control my delight at seeing him.

"I have come to assist you," he shouted. "Your words got me thinking."

The woodman walked smartly along the length of the pier to join me.

"Your good sense prevails, I'm truly glad to see you," I welcomed him.

"I'm not sure why I am doing this," he resigned, squeezing my greeting hand.

"Laddians perhaps," I smiled. "Come; let me convince you a little more."

We vacated the lodge, opting to sit at the end of the jetty dangling our legs over the edge. I explained everything to him at great length, including the deception of Talteth and his followers, my plight into slavery, the journey to and from Laddia and ultimately meeting the hierophant. The magic I possessed, the visions and the inexplicable wishbones with the exception of my addiction, plus the misfortune of Elcris. He listened to my reason, my feelings and my belief in God, avidly, without questioning any account in my lengthy dialogue.

After my chronicle, we remained silent, gazing at our floating shadows on the water below. Now I entrusted my secrets onto the man sitting aside me and felt good for it, almost as if a burden of guilt had been erased, freeing me of the doubts kept locked for so long within.

'Maybe,' I thought, 'once Matlock sifted through and absorbed all that I had divulged; he may be able to offer some logic and assemblage of my much-needed understanding.'

"Well," he said eventually, flicking a piece of wood into the water, "I must be a bigger fool than I thought. I have never believed in magic but do believe my own eyes and ears, and what you have stated is either remarkable or false. I will choose the former and accompany you on your quest but will say if this proves to be the work of your dexterous tongue, I will not hesitate in slitting your throat! I am not a man to be crossed Arton."

"There will be no need of such action Matlock, for my words are the truth."

"Then let it be so," he said. "We must not dwell here, let us press forward to Collington this instant."

The woodman stood gathering his pack and axe, and walked back along the pier never taking his gaze off the lake. I followed directly and approached him when he unexpectedly stopped.

"Why the sudden rush?" I asked.

His thick arm extended to the lakes' horizon.

"That is why," he said.

At first glance, I could see nothing other than the sun's haze but to my horror, they appeared, and out from the mist they came. It was impossible to estimate how many vessels, but if they were but a part of the Laddian invasion fleet that had crossed the ocean, then heaven help us all. My worst fear disconcerted me for already their assault commenced, without perception of their ultimate intent, or speculation of their scheme I prayed inwardly to the Lord for guidance.

Legacy of Bones

'My God,' I shuddered, 'protect us and the kingdom.'

"We best leave now," maintained the woodman.

"What about the ferry?"

"Wait for Dettel and you will wait an eternity."

Mattock's words trailed off as he sped from the pier, I ensued frantically, almost tripping in my haste.

We edged the lake, running whenever the terrain yielded, which at times were all too often for my liking. His pace was swift considering his build and the belongings he carried and I soon found myself flagging. Eventually, we came to rest by a huge rock and I fell against it in a heap of rasping breathlessness.

"How far to Vledor Beacon?" I asked, trying to recapture my breath.

"Tonight and perhaps another full day at best," Matlock speculated.

"Can we not get there sooner?"

"Not without the ferry."

"But we must get there before the Laddians; they will strike tomorrow night for certain."

"Then we will arrive at the moment of battle."

"Not if we get there first," I said rising to my feet.

"Impossible!" insisted Matlock. "We won't reach there in time."

"We will. We have to," I urged, setting off immediately.

"I don't know why I'm doing this," groaned Matlock from behind me.

"For the kingdom and for your life," I shouted back without turning.

Soon enough the woodman caught up and passed me by with ease.

"Never say die eh? Well," he said enthusiastically, his words broken by grunts, "if you've got the stamina my friend I will get you there by the morrow's end."

"That's the spirit," I gasped.

Matlock injected more haste into his running by leaping rocks, jumping crags and cutting through the water to avoid any climbing. I did my utmost to remain close behind but my chest rattled and feet bled at the continual pounding against the tricky ground. My confounded cough impaired my breathing so much so, I came to a breathless termination in a deep hollow.

"Matlock," I yelled with all the breath left in me, "wait!"

The woodman returned and peered down at me.

"It is no use," I said gasping, "I cannot maintain this pace."

"We will rest awhile."

His words were cheering. I wiped my mouth after spitting the phlegm of my cough and closed my eyes awaiting return of my breath. Sleep conquered me, too strong to resist and too deep for dreams.

Matlock woke me, it felt like I had only blinked and I sat pensively in the darkness awaiting the snake cooking on the small fire. While the juicy wafts filled the air, I pondered on the enemy's tactics. If my notions were correct the landing force would have moved easterly across the peninsula and probably struck at Caer Tal by now, then they would move north and join a second detachment before marching on to Vledor Beacon. We were just ahead of them and any further dallying would no doubt resort with our clashing, a confrontation I did not savour. I suspected they would have encountered little or no resistance at Caer Tal, with their element of surprise being by far their greatest weapon.

Under Arbereth's rule, there was no need for strongholds, only at Collington was there such a body of men equipped to quell such an onslaught but since his untimely death, most men if not all, would have shown fealty to Talteth and moved north. As to how strong Ulcris's army was, I could only but speculate.

Matlock tossed the cooked snake at me, intruding my deliberation.

"Here, eat this then we must move on."

Rising from the hollow was difficult because my limbs ached so, after grappling over the rock I sat by the small fire sampling the warmth, content to watch the aromatic wisps of the cooking meat. I ate and dressed my sores and before long, we set off again.

I was apprehensive of Matlock's pace, knowing all too well I would be unable to sustain it, and was right. Only a short time elapsed before feeling the tightness across my chest, again labouring my breath with the distance between us increasing. I did not shout for his attention for fear of alerting the enemy as much as I tried to enhance my rate, I lost sight of him as he descended a distant ridge ahead. There was only one direction to go and following the perimeter of the lake could not be simpler, but by the time I reached the apex of the hill, Matlock was already disappearing beyond another. This was to be as the night wore on and the stretch between us distended wider.

I took respite and sat upon a craggy rock protruding into the lake, coughing and gasping between irregular breaths until finally clearing my congestion and cuffing the drip from my nose. Sinking my feet into the cold water of the lake was blissful and it sent my mind into an unperturbed state. I pondered vacantly, just staring at the skyline, following the hills that now became closer since the arrival of dawn, then onto where the sky touched the lake in a nebulous blend and to the west where out of the haze, trees and rocks disputed the shoreline. There were no enemy ships nor could I see any advancing legions. The fog rolled calmly though swiftly across the water, increasing in density as it drifted toward me and within it, a deepening perceptible shadow. Gradually the darkened mass of the ferryboat appeared, bursting out into the diminishing sunlight. At the helm, a shrouded figure stood carelessly as if disinterested, I watched intently as he navigated to shore, sampling now an intelligible representation of the craft listing starboard with heavy freight. There were no other people aboard, just the ferryman working with accomplished precision at the wheel, surrounded by barrels big as hogsheads, crates and livestock jostling unsteadily for balance. I stood on the rock and howled to him, forsaking exposure to get his attention.

"Dettel! Bravitt Dettel!" I wailed.

His silence compelled me to call out again yet still he failed to respond to my call.

When, just a short distance from the shoreline he walked to the prow equipped with a long pole and as the ferry drifted closer, navigated with ease, bringing it to a slow calculative halt. So skilled was he, the craft never scraped the shale in the shallows. The cowering figure returned to the stern, standing proudly as indeed any seaman would at such proficiency.

'A little late,' I thought, but could not contain my excitement at seeing him.

Nevertheless, soon I would be able to float across the lake saving hours of toil and warn my people of the Laddian invasion.

The ferryman detached the tie from the gate and encouraged the beasts to move by tapping his pole against the deck. Goats, pigs and a renegade cockerel, butted, grunted and flapped respectively in their eagerness to reach dry land.

I yelled to him again though still it went seemingly unheard.

'Perhaps', I considered, 'it is not Dettel.'

"Ferryman! Ferryman!" I repeatedly called.

The caped figure continued his business oblivious to my calls. I moved from the rock and jostled amongst the animals, prodding and tapping them in an effort to reach the ferry.

"How fairs it?" I asked him.

He stood from his bent position as if hearing my calls for the first time.

I approached the landing ramp and spoke to him again.

"Greetings, Bravitt Dettel."

Without utterance, he gestured a wave for me to advance and on doing so his arm continued to beckon me.

The woodman never mentioned Dettel's deafness, not that he had reason to, but when folk describe somebody they usually make point of any abnormality or affliction.

I stood in front of him not an arm's length separating us, yet still he waved me forward. His robe covered him entirely, black as pitch and sinister as the shadows of the deepest chasm, neither flesh nor feature could I see, just the cloth enwrapping him. His body stench was vile, no doubt brought about by his toil, yet strangely, an odour I recollected and similar to the sickening reek at Fleddon.

I chose to remain, advancing no further and with my outstretched arm made notice to him of my being. A chill caught the back of my neck causing me to quail at its iciness. Although I heard nothing, something coerced me to turn about and on the shoreline, a bedraggled stranger stood with shoulders rounded in a dispirited hunch. Torpidly, he boarded the craft and shuffled slowly toward the ferryman and me. I moved aside and observed with incredibility as Dettel beckoned him ever closer to him. The ferryman plunged his pole into the water, swung the ferry about and began drifting away from the shallows. After several stabs with his pole, the ferryman faced me, raising his head and what I witnessed chilled my flesh. He pulled back his mantle to reveal a besmirched skull of dingy yellow. Irregular set teeth clung to his jawbone like discarded tombstones, eye sockets with an emptiness epitomising the very death he was. His emaciated hands became noticeable as his sleeves fell back to his elbows. I was too horrified to scream much as I tried and stood transfixed, unable to move or hide from the wraith as if caught in a nightmare. It seemed an age before finally averting my gaze, in doing so I faced a new terror in the traveller standing beside me, for his face reflected that my own self.

"God have mercy upon me," I invoked all my energy to shout aloud.

The expressionless face of the dejected wretch stared vacantly at me as if I did not exist.

"This cannot be, I am here. Here within my own body, you cannot be me!"

My intractable avowal sounded piteous, I glanced back to the abhorrent ferryman for further confirmation, his loosened shroud revealed yet more of his skeletal body. This nightmare impeded any reality, thwarting me from breaking away from the macabre torment that seemingly embellished.

I felt the vessel riding the water, drifting further from the shore into the forbidding mist from whence it came. My regenerated effort to break from the ordeal set me into alarm; I swung my fist into the empty gut of the phantom, anticipating its bones to shatter. I swiped a second time, which proved equally futile as the first and nothing I did prevented its advance. I closed my eyes briefly in submission, fully expecting my defeat, waiting for my life to deplete and praying to the Lord for mercy. The spectre was upon me and then, as if I did not exist, drifted straight through me. I staggered to the platform and stood in wonder at the occurrence.

Within the fog, drums began pounding a dull and daunting beat, initially sporadic before suddenly bursting into a crescendo matching the angry roar of thunder. I plunged into the water and swam furiously toward shore daring not to look back until finally reaching the shallows. The incessant din of the drumming muted my gasps and I observed breathlessly, the ferry proceed across the lake and pierce the fog, which continually thickened until it finally yielded to the dense grey mantle.

"Arton!"

I turned and watched the woodman's approach.

"There's no time for bathing what are you thinking of?"

I was far more concerned with the ferry than Matlock's pathetic questioning and returned my scrutiny onto the lake.

"What is this about?" Matlock asked, resting against the projecting rock.

"I saw Bravitt Dettel," I eventually responded with dismay.

"Then why be cheerless my friend for it is good fortune he arrives now."

Matlock's excitement quelled when scanning the horizon in search of the ferry.

I knew well enough it had been a vision but this time feared its outcome. Seeing myself, set me contemplating, knowing it could lead to my expiration.

"Ah, now I see it!" Matlock said keenly.

The woodman pointed to the western edge, some way back along our trail and from the shore, the ferryboat appeared.

"I will have word with him and catch him before he is too far off. Bravitt will see us across the lake."

"No wait!" I insisted, rising out of the water. "There is death at hand, we must not go. I have seen a divination and there will be no good from it."

"How are you so sure?" he asked, brushing away the flies congregating about his head.

"If you want proof of my warning then wait."

Although Matlock joined me and took me at my word, letting him witness the fruition of the vision would dispel any doubt he harboured, and even more convincingly, establish to him the powers I truly possessed. One thing I learnt back at Wendatch is that idle tongues carry the venom of aggrandisement, so if the woodman and I should ever terminate our partnership, I could at least have assurance of prominence.

Though we could ill-afford to tarry, the evolving situation would prove my strength. I needed the woodman; forsaking time now would instil the gravity of the situation to him, even if it meant jeopardising our arrival at Vledor Beacon.

We sat for a while avidly watching the ferry's approach to shore. It all came to be and a boat appeared from the confounded fog, followed by another and more still. I ceased counting beyond seven as the confusion welled. The vessels cut through the water at great speed, along with those deathly drums beating their dulcet tones of denunciation, elated shouts overwhelmed the throbbing beat as the fleet confronted the ferry. The pilot vessel ran headlong at Bravitt Dettel and splinters of shattered wood burst into the air on impact, cascading and splashing into the lake. Cries from the beasts on board made my stomach churn, I am certain I heard the ferryman's wail above the din, defying the onslaught now upon him. Barrels rolled into the water, bobbing like dunked apples in a trough and from the other boats, flaming torches arced at the stricken ferry, some fizzling out as they hit the water, others hitting their target and bursting into fireballs. The craft was ablaze, sending a plume of acrid smoke heaven bound. The Laddians seemingly content with their strike turned their boats sharply and disappeared back into the thick mist. All was silent now, save the gentle lapping waves about my feet. No beast cried and no defiant wails from the ferryman. The drumming ceased too, leaving an eerie calmness as the ferry sank and only the bobbing barrels in the water remained as its epitaph.

"How could you just let us watch, knowing it was going to happen?" the woodman snapped.

"Do not be angry."

"Angry? I am seething! How could you?" he questioned me again.

"My vision was a warning. I knew something was to happen for there was death aboard the ferry and if boarded, we would have been killed along with Dettel."

"Is this your own doing?"

"What are you implying?" I returned sharply.

"Did you make it happen?"

"Of course not!" I fumed at Matlock. "What advantage would it achieve?"

"Perhaps you want this invasion. We had the ideal chance to get to Vledor Beacon and you made me sit and watch Bravitt's destruction."

"You still fail to understand."

"What is there to understand eh? As far as I am concerned, your mind is warped with this magic of yours. You conjured it just for your own pleasure."

"Damn you Matlock, that is not so!"

How could the woodman even consider such a thought?

"If it were not for the vision you would be dead," I said, incensed by his words.

"So where does this leave me?" he asked.

"Wiser, because you were in doubt of me. Now you know the Laddians exist and fully aware of their intent. It is up to you and me to warn the kingdom."

The woodman sighed and returned to his passive trait.

"What of these visions of yours? How do you invoke them?"

"I do not have control over them whatsoever. They strike unexpectedly and without warning but now I am beginning to comprehend."

Moreover, it was so. When hope was absent, a vision would come to me as in the instance of the storm-raged ship before reaching Laddia and the blackness of the crows rejoicing the death of Pecos. The fight with the vagrants, the killing of Maddox, the flying cart and others, all bore the characteristic by advancing a solution in my moment of anguish. Others at this point however still lacked insignificance, as my master with the almighty and the burning ruin, but perhaps I dismissively conceded they were just dreams.

"Well Arton," said Matlock gaining my attention, "I cannot say I understand it too clearly, I would like to dwell on the matter but we best consider getting to Vledor Beacon before those Laddians."

"Indeed so my friend, lead on."

We set off again keeping to the water's edge where feasible. My sodden garb impaired my running from the outset, though in truth, made little difference to my pace if my clothing had been dry. It was late in the afternoon when the land changed to a gradual incline signalling that we had finally reached the eastern perimeter of the lake. Shale and rocks surrendered to sharp ridges and steep edifices where ferns filled every crevice, displaying their fronds in contemptuous defiance against the dull granite. The plummeting sun clipped the outlying trees, transmitting the familiar and daunting orange glow onto the rocks we clambered.

If left to Matlock alone, I felt sure he would have made it to the town by this time and in hindsight, should have organised it so, instead of my hindering his tread but alas, could not alter what was already done.

We passed moored ships before our approach early the following morning and ascended the high tor overlooking the small town. The carnage was very evident, fires raged through the streets and wooden outbuildings collapsed before us. The wish tower sited on the plateau had all but fallen, with its

David Greely

crumbled stones scattered over the ground. Despite having trekked cumbersomely through the night, we arrived at Vledor Beacon too late to proffer warning and too late to save anyone.

The woodman and I looked at each other signalling our synchronised dash, we tore down the hill in senseless abandon, me with sword drawn and Matlock with axe swinging. The striking Laddians wasted little time. Dead and dying littered the streets and haunting cries of pain and suffering reverberated in our ears as we walked cautiously through the town. Hands of the injured made feeble attempts to grab our ankles, seeking redemption from their senseless misery but we could offer them nothing, the bitterness felt at witnessing them corrupted my desire for vengeance even more so. There seemed little testimony of resistance with only a handful of the enemy laying dead by comparison. The Laddians had struck keenly and had left atrocities far and beyond the imagining of any sane mortal. Many men bore deep gashes to their chests and in numerous instances, arms severed if not ripped from their torsos. Of those of obvious prominent ranking, their bodies impaled on pikes through the anus to the chin, with their genitals stuffed in their mouths. If there could be a greater sufferance, then the womenfolk endured it by undergoing depravities to satisfy the lust of those barbarians, where wombs gouged and spread like tattered sheets across their bodies, breasts hacked off and strewn, axe handles forced between their legs and the poor children too decapitated and butchered beyond recognition.

Matlock and I were physically sick, powerless too, to summon any words to quell our revulsion and anger at the horror lying before us. I knew the capabilities of these Laddians and now too did the woodman.

I demanded from the Lord the reason for bestowing such an occurrence, for if the people of Vledor Beacon were guilty of anything, was this then his answer to their repentance? With all the mercy of the realm, I certainly could show none toward a Laddian now.

Sadly, this was the allegory in the following days, every settlement we came to had suffered similar carnage, and there was no exception. No individual escaped, no beast tore loose, nor abode unburned. We collected scraps of food eluding the pillaging, although sparse. This raiding army was precise, swift and thorough. Each day that passed, we hoped to catch them by travelling long into the night, listening for the distant cries of conflict or the rumble of their battle drums. So determined were we, Matlock with his fine speed ran ahead in search of them. We even doubted our own course despite the continual evidence of slaughter. They were fast and evasive, did they never rest?

It was not until the eighth day from Vledor Beacon did we finally near them and this was with thanks to Sangalpraise.

The Laddians pride themselves in their worship days some four in all, over the seasons; summer and winter solstices, Elkinmorg and Sangalpraise. I later learnt Sangalpraise is the Laddian equivalent to the realm's Easter, legend recalls on this day late in spring their god Sangal prophesised the end to their suffering. A day when after feasting all would rise up and slay their foes, to live a fullness of life without want and a purity of mind that will guide them to the side of their god. The celebration of Elkinmorg is three days later as an act of confirmation.

'Where now is the sight of my guidance oh Lord? Must I suffer more to prove my worth and must I continue to witness this savagery to honour you my fealty?'

I was angry with the Lord and felt justified in being so. If I am the saviour to his kingdom then why must I be subjected to witnessing these sorrowful torments and atrocities put upon by others, and for how long before Matlock would take his leave from me? He has gone beyond the cause of any man to demonstrate his allegiance. It is equally his matter sure enough for he is a realmsman, but not to observe the continual acts of unholiness. He would be wise to depart and go south, well away from these troubles and thus I told him so, but mercifully, he laughed at me for suggesting such a thing.

"I am converted and you converted me Arton. I will stand where you stand and fall where you fall. No greater desire do I possess than to serve you Lord Arton and your God, our God."

David Greely

    Praise him. What sweet words of comfort and me a Lord! I had no right to doubt him and from this day forth never did so. It was warming to pray together and greater the feeling of ridding the isolation from my quest.
    I acquired many allies now, none greater than Ulcris of course, though very indebted to the others and wished they were all with me now. All of us together, to travel the realm and raise our army to rid the kingdom of all its perpetrators once and for all.

Chapter Fifteen

Matlock and I did not discuss any plan other than to pass the enemy and reach Ulcris, presuming he remained at Collington, as much as we were prepared and eager to avenge our folk, it would prove a futile bid with such numbers against us. Killing but a handful of Laddians would not stop their advance, besides, what use would we be to the kingdom dead?

Torches and fires lit the vast encampment where thousands of Laddians women and children included, began celebrating their unique festival. Smoke plumes whisked on a light breeze in a dancing array, amid the drone of pipes and drums cheerily playing to the mass. Men, the same obdurate men that attacked our towns and killed our people, were dancing clad in their battle dress, banging sword against shield in a resonant din scorning the music and pennants waved with exhilaration held in unison by the circle of on-looking pike-men.

I could not perceive their premature glory. They were not celebrating Sangalpraise but goading themselves into belief

David Greely

that they had already won battle over the realm. I spat on the ground in abhorrence and distaste of their merriment.

The woodman and I sneaked by though tempted to linger and watch them, fooling myself that if I were able to infiltrate the camp I would glean more of their purpose. We began running once we were passed and Matlock took up his usual inflexible pace. The land changed dramatically, from rocks and hills to easing slopes amassed with ash and oak.

Matlock assured me we would reach Dunleigh in all but a few hours; the time needed to warn the folk of the Laddian advance. We continued eastward and finally found the road leading from Vledor Beacon. Though it made our progress considerably easier, the continual running was all too much for me and again I staggered to a halt collapsing with exhaustion at the roadside. My breathlessness precluded me from calling to the woodman and within seconds, he trailed the road's bend disappearing from sight. I closed my eyes voluntarily.

As if it were a mere blink, I awoke in a fit of coughing and sudden awareness of strange surroundings. My head pounded, throat dry as a rasp and eyes gritty. In the idiosyncrasy of this weird new setting, I sensed shaking and jolting where I lay, amid nauseating clangs of pots and skillets. A lantern hung precariously overhead, dancing to the uncoordinated rhythm of a wagon. I sat bolt upright in sudden unease.

"Steady lad, steady."

The calming voice of a realmsman reassured me of safety.

"Where is Matlock? What have you done with him?"

"I cannot help you there. I know nothing of whom you refer."

"He is my companion, the woodman."

"You were alone when we found you."

"Where am I? And who are you?"

"Slow down, one question at a time," the man paused, contemplating his answers.

"My name is Ebden…" he paused again.

"…My partner is Fallan, he found you lying on the ground. Nigh run you over. Lucky he was navigating for I would not have seen you. He has eyes acute as an eagle and don't miss anything."

"Arton," I volunteered, offering my hand, which he shook limply.

"Well Arton," he recommenced, "you look the worse for wear I must say. I will fetch some water and food."

My eyes followed him as he slipped under the canopy, leaving me to familiarise myself with the new surroundings. Among the dangling array of pots were trinkets, coils of rope and discarded sacks stained with dried blood strewn about my feet, expelling a strong and sickly odour? I was uncomfortable to say the least and kept jostling on the rough bedding to rid a stick poking in my back.

"So," he said re-entering, dipping his head in habit to avoid the hanging pots, "what is a cripple such as your good-self wandering alone for?"

I turned on my side and felt my master's staff, surprised of its re-emergence and immediately thought of the bones. Without caution, I felt for the bones as if scratching my chest to hide my purpose, relieved they were secure within the pouch. I shifted again and leant on my elbow in preparation for the food and water. He handed me a wooden bowl and a piece of bread, which gave me time to consider a reply. I drank greedily and tore the bread in my jaw. I had tasted better but when little else is available, one is very thankful, as I was.

"Travelling," I eventually answered, taking time over my mouthful, "but I am not a cripple. My stave belonged to someone dear to me; I always carry it with me.

And your purpose?" I asked him.

"Travelling," he replied smartly with a wide grin.

He seated himself by my feet.

I studied him briefly before he afforded his next question. He seemed an alert and quick-witted, robust man boasting around thirty, with straight cut mid-length hair though somewhat dismally dressed.

I wanted to be certain no harm had fallen upon Matlock by this man or his partner, for he also portrayed an air of mistrust and my head echoed at my conclusion of him.

"How long have I been here?" I asked.

"A short while perhaps an hour. Forgive me," he resumed without pausing, "you look very dishevelled, did you run into some trouble along the road?"

"No, just exhausted," I said.

"Then you are lucky we found you. There are few people who'd give aid to a stranger these days."

"Then I am indebted to you Ebden."

"Not many use this road and wandering about alone can be perilous."

"Like I said, the woodman accompanied me."

"Tell me of this woodman, Matlock you say?"

"Yes, though there is little to tell. We were travelling the road together but his pace is stealthier than mine and I lost sight of him."

"So there was urgency in your pace?"

Ebden's questioning started to agitate me.

"Yes and thank God you came along. Are we heading for Dunleigh?"

Ebden laughed aloud raising his head upward.

"Dunleigh?" he scoffed openly. "We have long passed there; we're on our way to Vledor Beacon."

"Vledor Beacon?" I queried with a shout.

"And why not? It is the only place in these parts where we can fetch a decent price for our wares."

"Do you not know of the invasion? Turn back now!" I insisted, rising to my feet.

"Invasion?" he sneered.

"Yes, Laddians have stormed the town and set torch to it. Vledor Beacon is completely decimated."

"Outrageous!" remarked Ebden.

"It is the truth I swear. They have landed upon our shores and you are aiming straight for them."

"Yes," he teased, "and I suppose there are thousands of them running amok."

"Do not ridicule me Ebden; I am a man of merit."

"Oh come Arton, don't you think if such a raid be in progress we would have heard so?"

"No-one escaped their onslaught because they were swift and very precise. I have seen the results of their attack Ebden and never been so sickened. It happened in the still of the night, that is when they always strike and this night will be no exception. Now for God's sake turn the cart about!"

"You must be wrong, there can be no raid, besides, Talteth would have seen to it and wiped them out before they could even tread upon our soil."

'Not if I know Talteth,' I thought, recalling an earlier mystery surrounding his battle in the southern islands, those years ago leading to his command at Wendatch. In my opinion, the truth was unsubstantiated and until proof forwarded, my judgment of him will never alter and even if testimony existed, nothing will convert me otherwise since his action against his father.

Ebden turned his head and shouted out to his partner.

"Hey keep an eye for an army of Laddians, our friend here says they are invading."

"I think the stranger is right," Fallan called back, poking his head through a slit in the canvas. "Look at this lot!"

Ebden scrambled to the front of the wagon and peered through.

"Mother of Christ!" wailed Ebden. "Quick, turn the damned cart!"

Immediately Fallan drew the horse to a halt and began backing the wagon off the road. I leapt from the cart, glancing along the darkened road ahead if only to confirm to myself what I had already seen. A flickering glow highlighted the distant trees by what must have been a hundred flaming torches advancing up the sharp incline toward us.

"Come on," urged Ebden anxiously, "this isn't the time to stand gaping, lend a hand here!"

David Greely

I assisted the travellers by turning one of the cartwheels labouring in a deep rut, though my eyes stared transfixed on the oncoming glow and as the brightness grew, heard the thunder of their clambering feet. Fallan's whip cracked loudly above the horse's head demanding full compliance from his order, the frightened creature choked in resistance from the incessant tugging on the reins. I told Ebden to extinguish the lamp, which he did before jumping off the cart to grab the horse's bit and goad the reluctant animal forward. His action revolved the wheel over the furrow and the cart finally rolled into motion. I clambered aboard and crawled to the front snatching the leashes from Fallan's grip, whipping the stinging leathers against the hesitant steed, spurring it to move quicker.

"Climb up!" I shouted to Ebden.

He clung to the side of the cart in desperation, reflecting dread upon his face.

I dared not to look behind for fearing the closeness of the enemy, knowing our falter at turning would have consumed the meagre distance separating the Laddians and us. I imagined the torchlight shining their awesome path and awaited the spears, arrows and slingshot to hail around us. I continually flicked the leathers to urge the animal on, but with the weight of the wagon and the road's rise, it maintained the same burdensome pace.

"They are gaining ground," Ebden yelled from the back of the cart. "Stop for nothing!"

I did not intend to do otherwise.

The rumble of the cart put in mind my escape from Wendatch, the horseman with his relentless pursuit of me and how Treggedon, though at the expense of the king's life, whisked me away to safety.

The cart's wheels trembled as fearful as I and failed to cleave in the deep mud-filled tracks. Even the tiring horse found little adhesion in the centre ground of the road, yet I demanded more from it by whipping the air above its flanks, but the creature could give no more, its breathing became erratic and heavy, with froth exuding from its mouth.

"How fairs it Ebden?" I asked, eager for an appraisal of our predicament.

"I can still see the glow but it is farther off."

"Saints be praised!" I yelled back with nominal contentment.

Instantly, I relinquished my demand off the horse and though our distance from the Laddians was far from comfortable, it was far enough to offer a little respect for the exhausted animal.

Whether sighted by the enemy or not I can only speculate, but regardless of the gap, we maintained our travel without light for hours, at times barely at walking pace, allowing the steed to guide us. The three of us kept our eyes firmly fixed behind, waiting intently, until finally the glow faded into obscurity and the pitch of night returned. Perhaps it was the disappearance of the torchlight but the night seemed exceptionally dark, and with the intensity of the trees blending into the blackness made it increasingly maladroit to differentiate between land and sky.

Now the immediate danger quelled, Ebden rejoined us, sitting next to Fallan. I had all but forgotten Matlock in the current crisis and until Ebden made reference, the woodman did not come to mind.

"I fear for your friend. We should have caught with him by now," said Ebden shuffling uncomfortably on the bench.

"Dunleigh will soon be upon us," said Fallan, pointing to a faint glimmer some distance ahead.

I was confident of Matlock's safety, surmising he bedded somewhere hospitable within the approaching hamlet and told Ebden so.

"Dunleigh," he remarked, "is a small inhospitable place and not many folk would welcome taking in a stranger."

"On the contrary my friend," I insisted, gazing behind, "with the tidings Matlock bears, he would have a compassionate listener offering him shelter."

Fallan suddenly turned to face me abandoning his concentration.

"I doubt that," he said. "If he describes anything like what we have seen this night he would only succeed in vacating the place."

"That alone would be welcome," I said averting my eyes from him.

"How would it be so?" he asked.

"Because once they know of their attack, word will spread quicker than any plague and reports will reach Collington faster than me."

"Are you travelling to Collington?" Ebden asked, peering over Fallan's shoulder.

"Yes," I confirmed sharply.

"For what purpose?"

I chose not to reply directly and feigning a cough, gave a feeble reason.

"Relation," I replied.

"Relation?" doubted Fallan.

"Yes, my father is sick and not expected to live through the coming autumn. I go to him in his moment of need."

"But Collington…"

Ebden nudged his associate before he could utter any further words.

'Why the doubt?' I thought. 'What is so unfavourable about Collington?'

"…What conspires here?" I upheld, looking directly at Ebden.

"Nothing," he said evasively.

His response was as shallow as a puddle and I challenged him.

"You do not convince me. What is the doubt surrounding Collington?"

Ebden glared at me and I witnessed hostility on his face.

"Answer me this Arton. What do you know of the king?"

"That," I said superficially, "is a leading question."

I was uncertain whether his asking was a deliberate ploy to goad me or if he genuinely omitted naming the king.

"Just answer me!" he demanded.

"Then have it so, the king is dead," I countered with equal irritation. "Long live the king," I added defiantly.

"And your fealty?" continued Ebden.

"With the king of course!" I exclaimed.

"Long live Talteth!" he hailed.

"You do not hear me correctly Ebden. I said 'Long live the king,' the rightful king and not the fake. Talteth is not creditable and never will be."

"Such words will get you killed," maintained Fallan. "You utter treason."

"Treason!" I raged. "What do you know of treason?"

I refused to allow either of them a moment to consider my rebuff and continued.

"Hear me you two and heed my words well. The king almighty is dead, killed by his son's treachery. When I left Wendatch, the king was already as good as dead and regardless of my effort to save him became hunted then slain on the pretender's authority. I am blameless of betrayal and probably one of an insignificant handful who knows the truth and I remain honourable to Arbereth."

"Words of such doing never reached our ears, the king's death was confirmed to be an illness brought upon by age," believed Fallan, choosing to speak. "Even a grand requiem was held in his honour and distant kings, lords and realmsfolk gave tribute."

"Did you see the king for yourself? In fact, did anyone see the king?" I invited.

"Don't be preposterous, how could we when he lay incarcerated in solid marble?"

Ebden flapped his arms into the air readily dismissing my challenge.

"Did you not think it odd? Previous kings of the realm have lain in state so why should Arbereth be treated any less so? Was he not a popular monarch? Does this not give rise to suspicion?"

"No, I cannot say that it does," Ebden continued, repudiating my scepticism. "Not that we went to his interment but for those that did, witnessed for themselves a marble sepulchre with ornate gold carvings."

"That does not prove the almighty was in it," I contended harshly, breaking my gaze to look behind again.

"Neither," declared Fallan adamantly, "does it prove he was not."

"This discussion leads nowhere," proffered Ebden.

He was right about our disagreeing but I did not want the truth slipping away, it needed telling, and the falsehood the realmsfolk were living under, over the king's demise, fully exposed.

"I am merely attempting to assure you despite your belief Talteth killed his father."

"Mud or shit," added Ebden, "it is of no consequence now."

"Far from it," I contested, "the truth needs to be declared."

"And you have elected yourself to be the one to tell it," Ebden said flightily, directing his attention on the road ahead.

My annoyance at Ebden's words did not abate, so much so that I pulled on the horse's reins bringing the beast to a halt. Anxiously, Fallan flicked his head, glancing backward, anticipating without doubt the enemy would be on us again.

"For the Lord's sake Arton," he pressed, "get us moving!"

"Not until I make you both realise. We will venture no further until I have convinced you of the truth in this matter."

I had in mind to tell them everything, not only of my sufferance but the visions too, the way of the Good Lord and more importantly, the necessary security for the fate of the kingdom.

"Can we discuss while on the move?" suggested Ebden fidgeting uncomfortably.

"No!" I opposed emphatically. "This cart is not moving until you hear me out."

"But the Laddians!" reminded Fallan.

"Then I best be quick in my explanation," I smiled calmly.

They both watched me ardently, I perceived they were scheming to overwhelm me but I gripped my stave in readiness. Admittedly, they could both overpower me although not without fight, yet they developed some reluctance between them. It must have irritated them, considering they rescued me and then within a few hours, suffered my dictatorship.

"Then say your piece Arton but in God's name be bloody smart about it!"

Ebden's fury did not decrease.

"God's name?" I repeated, turning to him readily. "It is in God's name that I am doing it. I did not elect myself for any of this, I'm just the one chosen to restore the realm for the Good Lord."

The awesome glow returned and the night sky began brightening around us, confirming the advance of the enemy. My chest raced with urgency, goading me to flick the reins upon the reluctant horse and be on our way, forgetting briefly my argument with them. My dilemma needed a hasty resolve. Was I to stay firm and convince Ebden and Fallan facing the onslaught of the Laddians or flee now and abandon my need to control these two much-needed allies?

My heart won battle over my head, I chose to sojourn and was quick to explain. I cared to refer my decision as instinct, by far a more flattering description than just a mere gut feeling and in my fluster, the two men were shouting at me, insisting I give leather to the horse. Ebden, in his instant of trepidation tried seizing the reins from me but to avoid any physical clash, I threw the straps forward over the animal and leapt from the cart. I glanced back along the roadway, watching the increasing glow of the enemy's torchlight baying to consume us, and to become three further hapless victims undergoing superfluous death just to appease their gruesome appetite. I could not, nor would not let it befall upon me, I was worth more and destined to progress further.

As had arisen before, there seemed no premeditation in my forthcoming actions and what transpired was by impulse or if not, then an unknown hidden force, but found myself staring at Fallan with the wishbones firmly in my burning grasp. A possession forced me to shut my eyes and without resistance relented to the influence conquering me. In the black void, the

David Greely

fox sat boldly at my side with his big hazel eyes keenly fixed upon the advancing enemy, to my right Maddox, my long trusted friend stood undaunted and prepared to sacrifice himself yet again for my cause. Even with eyes closed, I could see the shimmering torchlight increasing as if in a newfound exigency, as it grew brighter and undoubtedly nearer, I steadied my feet to defend my ground. The fox never blinked nor so much as flicked his brush and Maddox too remained composed and well set. The worthless shouts of Ebden and Fallan aboard the wagon vaporised until I could no longer hear their plight, as the vision developed I felt my command strengthening; a force up until now I did not conceive imaginable. Of course, I had felt power before and used it, but this experience was so incredulous though not daunting, but ardent and welcoming and I seized the energy willingly to do battle. I ordered the fox to assault and as he sprung into the light, his mass increased eightfold to an incalculable magnitude. At every stride, the fox neared toward the enemy with his size amplifying, screams of their frenzy resonated in the still air. Shortly their cries of anguish turned to that of pain and I watched satisfied while the majestic beast tore into them. Maddox vacated my side swathing at the Laddians, without weapon he tore at their throats with his hands, throttling them and casting them aside like discarded pigs bladders. The Laddian's responded, hurling spiked orbs and spears at him but Maddox was invincible, evading and deflecting all they threw. Then he advanced into the diminishing light and haunting shrieks of death echoed in my ears. I followed in Maddox's wake scything at the futile advance of the enemy with my rod like a blade cutting through parchment. Their shields proved inadequate protection, their strategy incompetent, and Laddians fell in contorted piles, either dismembered or decapitated and none in our trail escaped our uncompromising advance. The fox ravaged them voraciously, snatching groups of them in his mighty jaws and with shakes of his head scattered his victims in disregard. Many scrambled up the wayside into the dense undergrowth to avoid the colossal fox and for those not swift enough, were scooped and flung high into the air.

Their numbers were diminishing rapidly, as was their torchlight and within a short while; the bloody confrontation subsided, exposing a lone torch held aloft defiantly by a Laddian clad in weighty armour. I approached him cautiously while sensing Maddox and the shrinking fox return to me. I was eager in wanting confirmation of the enemy's expiration but unwilling to avert my gaze from the bold warrior, should he strike. The taper reflected a cold blue shimmer upon the awesome blade he gripped, his full beard and brow pronounced the hostility he possessed yet out of my wariness of this character, my heart remained calm and mind alert. No sound prevailed now, for the din of battle befell into a hush and in this remarkable stillness, I ventured another step closer.

"Come any nearer and you will be headless!" he warned.

His admonition was peculiar, as God is my witness his mouth never moved in utterance.

"Take heed Arton," barked the fox at my side, equally intangible as the Laddian warrior's voice.

Then veracity struck, the words proffered were from within my own mind. I knew not how or why the warning developed, yet nevertheless it forced me to listen without preference. Again, the enemy's voice pealed his caution.

"Slay me and you will be destroying yourself."

In my stupefaction, screams filled my head, pounding and scratching inside like an ensnared animal gnawing at the back of my eyes for means of escape. Blood began dripping from my nostrils and dizziness fell upon me: the nausea, unparalleled and far beyond my experience with the sickening sea; I endured this until the pain eventually expired along with the divination.

I woke at the back of the wagon, again suffering the incessant clattering of pots with a welcoming gentleness compared to the breath of the enchanting hierophant. I blinked many times to accustom my eyes to the bright daylight filtering through the many gashes in the canvass, though electing to keep them closed a while longer to recollect the vision, debating with myself as to why I spared the remaining Laddian. God knows with the atrocities I had now seen, slaying him was the least he would have deserved, yet finally concluded I had allowed him to return to his warlords to tell of the massacre befallen them. The battle was sure to slow their progress, acknowledging our capable resistance and perhaps under the circumstance of the phenomenon, breed among them their want for retreat.

The conversation between Ebden and Fallan infringed my thoughts and though no intent to eavesdrop, meant my exhaustion led me to linger before rejoining them.

"And what I saw," maintained Fallan, "is not possible."

"When he wakes we shall found out more."

Ebden's words continued conveying their mistrust.

"I still can't believe what I saw," continued Fallan in exasperation. "I have heard of such matters but those tales are legend, born on the tongues of bards. No good shall transpire from this necromancy and I want no part of it either!"

Fallan, I sensed, went to stand but halted by his partner.

"We will get to the heart of this. The stranger has more explaining to do. Come," Ebden persisted, "let us not allow some trivial incident mar our friendship, after all we have been together…"

"…Ebden," Fallan interrupted him, "if I thought for one moment any good is going to transpire out of this I would be the first to remain. You witnessed it too and it is not natural. The devil's work is at hand here I tell you."

"A little bit of magic shit I grant but…"

"…No Ebden I will not be a part of it! Don't you think it a little bizarre that one individual could wipe out over thirty men with a gnarled stick as a weapon?"

"Like I said," Ebden resigned, "perhaps it is some type of magic."

"Not good magic that is for sure!" added Fallan.

"Just give it a bit more time. We will get to the truth of all this as soon as he wakes."

"And in the meantime...?"

"...In the meantime we wait," Ebden said calmly.

"Supposing there are more Laddians, then what?"

"There are no more. Where is your sense Fallan? If there is such a huge invasion as the stranger speaks, don't you think the kingdom would be in readiness? Why, Talteth would have wiped them away long before all this. No, they were just a band of speculative raiders and easy for a small group to land with a boat or two, but the size Arton claims is impossible."

It was evident Ebden was going to question me no end but if I volunteered the knowledge first could dictate the passage of my terms. I considered it time to consolidate my purpose to them again and would do so when drowsiness ceased to besiege me.

Slowly I rose and ambled over to the fire, helping myself to a leg of the cooking badger. I sat between the two realmsmen and spoke confidently and precisely between succulent mouthfuls.

"What I am about to divulge falls upon your ears only, if anything of what I say is repeated I will cut you down and cast you aside in a hell of suffering. You have been witness to my power and its capability, so impede my intent and you will both face the consequence of your perfidy. Now before commencing I must insist upon your sworn fealty."

I deliberately looked studiously at the two travellers, almost relishing my confidence.

"Our fealty to whom?" asked Fallan softly.

"Why, the king of course," I confirmed sternly, scorning at both of them in turn.

"But Arbereth is long dead, even you admitted that," remarked Fallan.

"His spirit lives on and not just in me but within the kingdom. Without him this land and its people have little hope of survival."

"What if we chose not to swear fealty?" invited Ebden broadening his smile.

"Then perish along with the others," I condemned.

David Greely

"What others?" Fallan probed.

"The folk who tread the unfavourable path following Talteth. His methods are devilish and those supporting him will be smitten by the Lord."

"You forget Arton," pursued Ebden, "there are those that have no choice as well as those having no regard."

"God will consider everyone and those in servitude shall be saved from his damnation. The Lord's kingdom has no room for those choosing to follow the adversary."

"And you are going to see to their deaths, just you alone?" Ebden asked, retaining his wry smile.

"Far from it," I replied. "It is not I but the judgment of the Good Lord as to who shall live and who will suffer."

"Where exactly do you appropriate yourself in this matter?" Ebden continued.

"I am his messenger; it is with his spirit and guidance that leads me."

"If this is part of the outcome by following God then I for one want nothing to do with it. Being hunted down is not my idea of proving one's faith."

"You are prejudging Ebden, and without certainty. Hear me out; if you feel the need to denounce God then so be it."

Fallan said nothing and sat contemplating my words, staring into the flames of the exhausting fire and poking it idly with a thin twig. Ebden by contrast, continually fidgeted and his eyes pierced mine, etching at me like acid. I wanted to avert from his gaze but it was essential to overpower my will against his and if I submitted, would have undermined my strength.

"Enough!" Ebden blasted. "Enough of this charade!"

"Why the agitation?" I posed calmly.

"Who are you to question my belief?"

"I am merely establishing my situation, no less than you have been doing. I give honour by quizzing you in person and not behind your back when in slumber."

"Then you heard everything," conceded Fallan.

"Yes."

Although listening to the tail of their debate, I wanted them to think I overheard everything they discussed and assessing their look of guilt led me to suspect that a plot had been instigated between them.

Ebden stood towering over me.

"There is nothing more I want to hear from you Arton. You go your way and Fallan and I will go ours."

"Suppose I stay with you."

"You are not welcome," Ebden replied fervently.

"If you are travelling east I can protect you," I suggested to him.

"We have survived on our own up till now," added Fallan, rising to his feet.

"What, even against the might of the Laddians? You saw how many there are and they were only an advance party. There are thousands between here and the coast, how long do you think you can survive? You know my strength, I can lead us to safety and consider also, if it were not for my intervention you would have trundled helplessly into their midst."

Fallan glanced submissively across to his partner.

"He is right Ebden we won't have a chance without him."

"Very well Arton you can travel with us but do not assume it as an allegiance nor a token of any friendship, it is only because we happen to be travelling in your direction now the west is threatened. I will say this, now that we have no intention of going to Collington, as soon as the road becomes favourable with a lengthy distance between the Laddians and us, we will part company, is it understood?"

"Perfectly," I confirmed smiling. "Now perhaps it is time to travel on."

Fallan kicked dirt over the fading fire as I gathered the last of the meat and followed Ebden to the cart.

"Fallan can take the reins and steer us to Dunleigh and I shall observe from the back."

"And me?" I asked Ebden.

"Whatever you choose, just so long as you are away from me."

David Greely

Assessing his manner toward me, Ebden was going to prove very difficult to win over so at this moment I decided to manipulate his associate first.

Once aboard the cart Fallan gave command to the horse setting it in motion and once impetus gained, applied a good rate. I adhered to Ebden's wish and sat on the front board with Fallan. I did not want to force any conversation from him and thought it wiser to let him volunteer, however, if I knew it to be a lengthy quiet that would lead into the following morning I would have contemplated a different scheme. In the prevailing silence I looked idly at the road ahead, hoping each bend would announce our arrival at Dunleigh.

Chapter Sixteen

My continual thoughts of Matlock left me pondering for his welfare and extremely anxious to locate him. In my heart, I was certain of his safety but then again my heart was not always right. He was brimming with resourcefulness and sufficiently able to survive 'and wise too!' I smiled, inwardly deliberating how quick he understood me. His decision in joining my cause would have banished any lingering doubts about me or my intentions. Fully assigned and dedicated to the realm, a commoner I openly and readily trusted, though more importantly a man I knew would put his life before mine. Did I deserve such a faithful disciple or earn such dedication? I likened to think it not the fear of my power that won him over, for that I knew was pure folly, but to assure myself his support be simply out of love for the kingdom. Comparing his loyalty, even after the brief span of time to that of Maddox was never my intent but I confess my incredulity in his ardent faithfulness, yet in those same moments of wonder though rapidly ejected, felt doubt of him abandoning me. In the time that dragged in my melancholic suppression, I could think of nothing other than of his welfare.

Our approach to Dunleigh devoured my muse and the hamlet lay as expected, beset with sporadic dwellings both vulnerable and deserted. I feared that somehow the Laddians had beaten us and had already attacked, but on closer examination my dread allayed and no feeble whimpers of defeat, cries of anguish or degradation were evident; just a calm silence subsisted, accompanied by a lone cockerel scratching for edibles. Farming implements and wicker crates lay discarded and fully exposed to the air, small bundles of dampened crops were stockpiled close to the mill-house, all however, evidence of a hurried departure.

The three of us be it briefly, scurried through the vacated buildings in hope of finding something. Fallan, discontent with his short sword, eagerly sought an upgrade but a pick as reward was no test against broadsword or mace. Ebden's exploration for another cart proved as useless as my forage for food. Within minutes we reassembled aboard the wagon, travelling hastily eastward in the hope of finding the evacuees. The wind stirred a haunting whistle through the trees and the sun now well passed its height sent a blinding glow dancing between the horse's determined stride.

The gratification of witnessing the emptiness of the small town surprised me. Selfishly it confirmed Matlock must have come this way, and warned them as well as assuring Ebden and Fallan of my earlier caution of such trepidation.

The silence between us continued, Ebden remained on watch at the rear and Fallan with God's fear spurring him never relented from flicking the horse's leathers. The prolonged rise in the winding road slowed the animal's pace to an exhausting effort and its weary trudge echoed against the turning of the wheels. In the hours that evaporated, we each took turn at guiding the horse, not that it was an arduous task but allowed the opportunity to eat and slumber. Throughout the shortening day into twilight, we proceeded slowly east.

I took consolation, even with the many leagues ahead, that my long awaited meeting with Ulcris would only be a matter of a few more weeks and this prospect after so many years of our pending tryst became unendurable; what once seemed distant and remote aspiration was rapidly becoming reality. I was thrifty in my thoughts for Hebren and Tolin but as always, did not want to dwell on the outcome of their plight nor sink into the depths of melancholy, for would life without ambition and reliance be a life without hope? Hence, I chose to cling to my wishes and not succumb to their uncertainty for I felt confident if either of them suffered ill fortune, I would have sensed it. I openly smiled, thinking of the boy though now a young man and aspiring to guess his age, impossible, having no recollection of how long I spent in the Laddian wilderness. My thoughts turned to my final confrontation with Talteth as if like a fantasy drafting images in my mind, yet each one different and with its own outcome. Some I favoured and others I dismissed rapidly, but overall none that could depict the verity of the future.

"Hand me the lamp," called Ebden breaking my reflections.

I responded and scurried inside the cover taking the rusting lantern hanging above me.

"Here," I said, handing it to him.

"Tell me Arton, what is your opinion of all this?" he surprisingly asked mildly.

"I have said my piece Ebden and it turned you against me. Does my opinion really matter to you?"

I scrambled by his side and like he, dangled my legs over the bouncing tailboard.

He did not reply forthrightly and pressured me to speak further. I wanted to win his favour and this became an opportunity to do so. His lighting the lamp gave me the brief opportunity needed to select my next words to him.

"Look," I agreed, "I know what happened seems impossible…"

"…Work of the devil I'd call it."

David Greely

"Please Ebden," I implored passively, "let me give you my account before you go concluding again. You have asked me, now let me explain."

"Very well Arton have your say," he agreed, hooking the lantern above us.

I knew I had to be prudent with my words for Ebden, apart from being headstrong was very untrustworthy. He was shrewd and not to be fobbed off with words of impulse, so in the brief lapse decided to tell him my chronicles, though not all.

I told of Talteth's plot resulting in the deaths of my master and the king, and mentioned my visions and actions within them to help him understand my strength in battle against the Laddians the previous night. I began to explain my search for the hierophant but felt reluctant, in fear of announcing my addiction in those satanic hills would undermine my strength of character. I managed to avoid it and swiftly narrated events up to the present, though a trifle erratic with times and dates what with my lost years, but it all came to a neat conclusion.

"…And that is the way of it," I said terminating my account.

I glanced at his face, which reflected the flickering yellow glow from the lamp.

"Well?" I ventured.

"It is quite fantastic and in truth Arton I know not what to say."

"Try," I urged him.

He sighed and kept his eyes transfixed on the road.

"I have," he said, "travelled this kingdom both length and breadth, there are not many territories I have not roamed yet I have never heard of such doings. Sure, I know of witchcraft and Druid shit, why, it's as common as farming the land but what disturbs me is trying to grasp what is the truth. Men have said the strength of our king is in his words and he promises new wealth and freedom for all. Songs even praise his efforts."

"Songs from the mouth's of his own bards. They are just words," I admonished.

"And so are yours Arton," he countered sharply.

"Then it is your choice as to whose you wish to believe in. I will say this however, idle over your conclusion and you will discover your answer when it is all too late. Heed my words Ebden for soon reckoning will fall upon us."

I was irate at the traveller's incertitude and duly leapt from the wagon and made my way round to Fallan who was surprised to see me jump up from the road.

"You have had words then?"

"Yes." I confirmed, though not wanting to elaborate.

"And?" Fallan persisted.

"Nothing really, we just still beg to differ. I have put my point and he his."

"Where does it leave things?"

"Purely as a matter of disagreement but he will see sense eventually," I sighed.

"I know what you portray is unnatural Arton, God knows I have seen it with my own eyes and not from the tongues of rumour…"

"…Then why is it hard for you to accept?" I questioned finally and snatched the reins from him cracking them against the horse for more effort.

The narrow slither of the moon gave little comfort to me on the cold night and the cloudless pitch seemed to intensify as the hours passed. I steered the horse along the narrowing road and increasingly challenging, beech trees extended their huge boughs in resistance across the canopy, and brambles whipped their spiteful fronds against the steed's legs, attempting to thwart our progress. Fallen twigs snapped under the weight of the wheels, entangling the spokes which eventually drew the cart to halt. I grabbed my staff and alighted begrudgingly, after unravelling the wheels I guided the horse by the bit. In the unexpected loneliness, I began talking to the animal, offering words of encouragement as we dragged up another steep incline.

I was yearning for sleep and warmth. Hot broth and freshly baked bread then came to mind and such thoughts drifted to obscure luxuries I was missing. The hearty glow of the fire in

David Greely

the great hall at Wendatch, the tantalising wafts of cooking expelling from the kitchen and the generous gossip from the revellers filling my ears with rewarding expectancy of the joyous night ahead; bards competing for the king's approval, with their sweet laments of courage or fearlessness of long-gone heroes. Dancers, tumblers and illusionists too, performing to a careless audience, following the plenitude of wine and ale with fruit and succulent meats. Whimpering dogs join the throng with tails a-wag almost smiling at the opportune morsels falling to the floor. My master laughing…

"…Treggedon I miss you," I lamented softly.

"And so you should my boy."

"Master," I whispered in wonder, "is that you?"

I gazed into the darkness uncertain whether he spoke or my mind tricking me, knowing it was all too willing to summon such uncertainties and imaginings.

"It is me lad. Come and bear witness with me."

His bony hand reached out for mine and though gentle, a compelling intensity in his grip feared me not to resist. He released his grip when he drew me away from the horse and immediately my confusion waned at the sight of him, although unable to catch a much-needed glimpse of his features, his voice, manner and dress confirmed it was he. Slowly he drew from the road, forcing me with diffidence to release the horse's leathers. I was enveloped in his summoning and powerless to resist and the animal tottered to an easing halt as I walked away. Without sound, Treggedon's silhouette drifted like a delicate zephyr into the darkness of the thicket and no creature stirred, nor did a single twig snap in his wake. Not wanting to lose sight of him, I ran into the undergrowth in eager pursuit, thorns and gorse ripped at my clothing tearing at my flesh like the slave master's whip, yet I felt no pain. It transpired into a nightmare, like a dog chasing a weasel. I was getting so close that another stretch of my fingers would touch him and just as I was about to, he pulled away from me, maintaining a greater distance. Now I could hardly see him and in eventuality I lost him.

"Master, please wait for me," I called, slouching breathlessly against a tree, coughing. "Master!" I repeated in a broken gasp.

I peered into the pitch of the night endeavouring to distinguish trees from the fearsome shadows, trying to determine the pathway to take me back onto the road. I slid down one tree in despondency, sitting with my pounding head sunk low in my hands. My eyes felt aflame with soreness and with immense disappointment, my heart shattered.

"Arton," my name whispered on the wind, "remember my words."

I raised my head slowly, cuffing away my tears, no longer thrilled at what transpired. Reality or illusion, I wanted no further part in it and called out to him with despise.

"You play games with me master, games I no longer wish to engage."

His hollow rejoinder echoed on the increasing wind.

"You still do not understand do you?"

"You are right master, you are always so right, and no, I do not understand, nor do I possess the yearning."

I did not suppress my vexation any longer.

"Too many times you raise my hopes and too many times you leave me discouraged. I cannot and will not endure any more."

"Save your anger for the foe Arton."

"I am beginning to think you are my enemy."

"Nonsense lad, I am here because you summoned me."

"I did no such thing!" I contested.

"Oh, so you think I came here out of choice rather than sit by a hearty fire feasting and supping wine? Have you ever given a momentary thought it is you, when in a state of distress or hopelessness, call upon me? Not that it is I who complains. I have been watching over you Rabbit and admit, I'm deeply enthused by your progress though must confess frustrated at times, in your moments of diversion. I feel the same pains you do Arton, suffering the same disappointments and dream the same dreams so try considering me for a change. Feel my feelings, understand my needs, yearn for my desires and suffer my agonies.

Remember my words Arton?"

"Words? What words?"

"Can you not recall the day of our parting?"

"Of course, as if it was just yesterday." Truly I do.

"Then recite and heed them Arton."

In recollecting what he said, my mind immediately recaptured the sorrowful day and reconstructed the early morning of our parting.

"In every colour shine a light."

I recited the very words he had uttered delicately and slowly, without feeling any apprehension for misquoting them.

I cuffed my nose again wiping away the final residue of my tears and repeating the words, louder a second time with added confidence. No sooner replicating the first passage a green light emanated out of the darkness, I rose swiftly, breaking my thoughts from Treggedon and stood a moment, content merely to gape in wonder. The light rapidly dimmed to a flicker as if aware of my watching it, and drawing me as if a beacon on a night of tempest, with energy far more persuasive than my wanting to remain with my master. I could not resist and walked toward it and at each step, a narrow path opened out, enabling me to concentrate on the flickering light I feared I might suddenly lose. Trees with their cumbersome gnarled branches eased away from my stride in gentle sways as if pulled back tenderly by invisible hands, I took care not to break or damage any as I ventured. My footsteps made no sound, silent as a creature of the night stalking its hapless prey. The incline submitted to a sharp dip overlooking a rocky outcrop and on all sides, steep fingers of sandstone pierced through the ground grasping for the stars in heaven. Their tops tinted with bright green halos generated a mystical reverence and within the shadows of their feet, lichen grew rich and vivid, and beyond further where more rocks lay. Some much taller and mightier, aged monoliths shaped since the beginning of time. The entire expanse portrayed an undisturbed gentleness yet seen by inquisitive eyes. I felt an impostor encroaching on this sanctuary, daring not to step closer in apprehension of breaking some mysterious ancient myth; desecrating what seemed a holy place might result in sacrament I wished not to serve, yet the warming glow coerced me until my feet stood confidently at the wall of rocks and then the light vanished. I felt temporarily marooned, waiting now for the insurgence of God's wrath to strike me down. The faint muttering of my master's words continued to echo in my mind and after semblance I repeated them softly.

"In every stone sleeps a crystal."

It was upon me and what demonstrated as an impenetrable wall of stone was but a deception of nature, merely single stones displaced to give the appearance of solidness, yet a multitude of stones ingeniously blending into each other. I rounded dozens of them to hearken upon whispered opinions, and then as the voices spoke louder, angrier became their din. Still I failed to decipher their scrambled words. Upon my first glimpse, two men temporarily ceased conversation, as if disturbed at my approach before recommencing content at the falseness of their ears. Though one sat with his back to me, they were strangers and I did not know them. One, a thickset man and judging by his shoulders, strong and in contrast, his wiry framed cohort had long grey hair matted with grime, touching his shoulders in a turned out curl. His lengthy nose hooked toward his mouth pronouncing a hair-lip within its shape, and a narrow pointed jaw added to his profound ugliness.

I had become a good mediator of character over the years save for the blind man when a lad, and this man before me, in my conviction, was a conspirator.

I loitered, satisfied just to listen and be enlightened perhaps as to the significance of their being. Strangely, my body cast no shadow nor did any sound emit when moving and I crept carelessly nearer defying the act of eavesdropping. Venturing closer still, I sat between them as if enacting the spirit of a dream, fearing without hurt and witnessing without outcome.

David Greely

What I saw and heard meant nothing, just two men conspiring, but against whom I had no notion. No names, dates or places gave mention, nor any motive instigated. The iridescent shades caused by the fire impeded my chance of scrutinising the second stranger fully, his long dark hair and full beard added to what I had already determined. Their outlook drifted skyward with the smoke and whatever they agreed now seemed absolute. Their gathering had to signify something, perhaps a warning or an opportunity for assessment but it meant nothing to me.

Treggedon's words returned, breaking me away from this dilemma.

"With every night a dream, with every step treads hope."

Wise words for certain, yet seemingly out of context in my current circumstance. Of course, I know now though I feel ashamed for not grasping their meaning then.

'In every colour shines a light…' My master was providing me guidance and when surrounded by the blackness of the night, offered me a guiding light.

'…In every stone lies a crystal…' Here Treggedon demonstrated truth, the sandstone wall was not as it seemed and the hidden exactness came to bear.

'…With every night a dream…' Within my vision came inspiration, the resurgence of my desire to bring curtailment to the misery and put right the ills the realm was undergoing.

'…With every step treads hope.' Every vision was presenting a resolution and forwarding me the prospect to strive further in my duty.

"Arton?"

The feeble calls tossed inside my head multiplying the confusion I felt and I tried waking from the dream to expel the unwanted feelings.

"Arton?"

This time the voice sounded normal, not distorted and I blinked rapidly to bring myself back from the vision.

"Fallan?" I finally responded, smelling the sweat of the horse.

"You fell asleep," said the traveller, holding my weight up against the animal.

How I managed to stay upright is a mystery, I shook my head in a concluding attempt to rid myself from the dream and my eyes readily filled with the awareness of the breaking dawn.

"We must set pace, look!" Fallan's dread re-instilled reality and his outstretched arm confirmed approaching Laddians.

Feebly, I tugged at the horse's bit to encourage some motion.

"Here, let me take it."

Fallan snatched the leathers easily and pushed me toward the cart.

"Where is Ebden?" I asked.

"At the back of the wagon," confirmed Fallan, straining against the horse's stubbornness.

Uncoordinated, I boarded the wagon, dipping my head under the canopy, collapsing onto the strewn sacks and much as I wanted to re-enact the vision, slumber as always dominated.

It was dark when I stirred, light rain penetrated through the splits in the canvas and dripped on me. Gusts of wind billowed inside the cart with a composition of weathered creaks resembling full sails of a sailing vessel. Hunger twisted my stomach into a dulling ache, my head throbbed, my throat rasped and my chest rattled at another fit of coughing. I scrambled to the rear fully expecting to see the ominous glow of the enemy that continually haunted our journey. Seeing only the dissipating blackness of the night, the thick outline of the wayside trees was welcoming and I gave thanks to the Lord. I expected to see Ebden where I left him the previous night, with his legs dangling over the tailboard still contemplating upon my words and mulling over the truth. His booming voice confirmed him at the front seated with Fallan.

"Ah!" he exclaimed as I settled between them, "our wizard has arisen."

"No thanks to the confounded rain, I am soaked!" I cursed with a reflexive shudder.

David Greely

"You have slept through the worst," added Fallan light-heartedly.

"Where are we?" I asked, directing my question at Fallan though his partner chose to respond.

"Less than a day from Belthorpe. There we can get food and shelter."

His words felt gratifying.

"What of the Laddians?" I asked.

"They are far behind us now, Fallan smiled, with reassurance in his voice. "We set good pace and this weather I suspect, has dampened their zeal."

"Not far enough for my liking," maintained Ebden nervously glancing behind.

"Have you seen anyone?"

"Not a sole," he said.

After several minutes silence, Ebden submitted a question until this point I had not contemplated.

"What is the plan once we reach the town?"

Without forethought, I told him my objective.

"I see it as this. Assuming Matlock has not reached there, we shall take stock of food before we even utter any warning of the Laddians. It is essential when telling them, to do so calmly and avoid any panic. Rushing in there with cart wheels ablaze will get us nothing. We must organise matters with the best resources available and perhaps make a stand against the enemy. We shall seek council to inform them of the gravity and they will surely help us set up resistance."

"Supposing your friend has beaten us there?" Fallan asked.

"Then the place will probably be deserted like it was at Dunleigh," I sighed impatiently.

"You overlook one small factor Arton; these people are not warriors, just common folk that have never seen a cockfight let alone a battle! They are farmers, herdsmen and peasants the lot of them."

"That may be so Ebden but they still have the right to fight. This is their land too and their town. Believe me they will fight."

"And how so?" Fallan urged.
"You my trusted friend, you will see that they fight."
"Me?" he retorted, turning his head with a doubting scowl.
"Trust me it will be simple." I concluded.

The damp night and most of the following day gave me all the time needed to speculate on the immediate future. Despite the Laddians being close behind I could not help feeling excitement at nearing Collington. Each revolution of the cartwheels were one closer to my aim, thoughts of the feasts and merriment, and the embrace of Ulcris after so many years accomplishing knowledge of the state of the kingdom, establishing everything necessary to plot Talteth's downfall. As always, my muse drifted into reflections of the past and I mulled over my entire life from the day I left Wendatch.

Though light drizzle persisted, the sun finally broke through the melting clouds as we climbed the last tor winding into Belthorpe. Fallan was to give us an hour's start before rushing into the town announcing the Laddian advance; enough time for Ebden and me to gather our needs. On Ebden's insistence at navigating, we ventured into Belthorpe. Under the normality of casual travel, I would have sighed a hundred breaths at the scenic approach to the small town. Belthorpe lay sheltered in a small vale between two hills in the region of Terren. Amidst a network of spindly tributaries, tree lined edges cut through lush and prosperous fields bursting with ripening cereals. The embellished bridge lay ahead of us, built with six pillars and each carved with hideous crouching gargoyles depicting my mind's worst adversaries. It pierced the town's heart and beckoned anyone to take respite within it. On crossing the river, unique wooden houses boasted a thriving community that seemed completely uncharacteristic in these turbulent times. We trundled over the cobbled road margined with steep grassy banks dipping gently along its meander until reaching the first dwelling. Ebden pulled the wagon to a slow stop.

"Greetings!" said the rotund man seated on a bench, sheltering under the eaves from the fine rain.

In return, I called back the compliments of the day.

"I trust you come in peace?" he proceeded.

"Indeed so," I smiled looking over to him. "We seek the sheriff."

"Ah, then you have not ventured here before?"

"I make you right my friend," I said retaining a false smile, wondering what he meant.

"And what might be your business here?" the fat man enquired.

His red and bloated face scrutinised me as if doubting my words even before having the opportunity to reply.

"Simple trade. Wares in exchange for food, water and shelter," I answered.

"Good," he said struggling to raise his heavy mass off the bench. "It is always refreshing to see new wares. I hope you find a good bargain. The water incidentally is both plentiful and free here."

I retained my grin as he approached and asked him again for the sheriff's location.

"We have no sheriff here."

Ebden returned a shrug of his shoulders after my quick glance at him.

"You seem surprised," said the fat man.

"A little," I replied, "for surely every town has a sheriff."

"Things are different here at Belthorpe. Here we have a collective council and find matters of the town run much smoother administered by a panel, rather than left to the thankless task of one individual."

"Then perhaps you would be so kind to direct us the way to this council."

The fat man pointed to himself with his podgy forefinger.

"Ah, then you are the council?" I could not refrain from surprise.

"No," he laughed aloud, "not just me, I along with others."

"Of course," I acknowledged.

"May I ask of your business with the council?"

"Permission."

"Permission?" he pondered, "permission for what?"

"For trading," I said.

He continued to snigger.

"You are in no need of a permit to trade, at least not here my friend."

"Forgive me, but often we experience certain resentment when calling at places unannounced, as it often riles the locals."

"You will not sample that attitude here. You and your friend are most welcome."

I displayed my gratitude with a nod of my head, which signalled Ebden to flick the reins. The councillor revisited his bench as we moved off.

"Well it confirms we have beaten your friend," said Ebden. "This place looks hardly a town ready to wage defence against the Laddians."

"Indeed so," I readily and cheerfully agreed, "and fortune is on our side. Nevertheless, we must scurry, Fallan will be here soon enough and there is no telling when and if Matlock will show."

Ebden drew the wagon to a terse halt outside an alehouse.

'How convenient,' I considered, guessing the years since last sampling mead.

"Why here?" I queried.

"Good a place as any. This, my friend, is the very hub of any community and certainly the centre to do any business."

No sooner had he finished speaking, Ebden leapt from the cart and rummaged around at the back of the wagon. Having gathered a sack full of wares, he proceeded with energetic haste up the steps and entered the alehouse. I laughed inwardly at his petulance; an enthusiasm I would not have thought would ever surpass my own. Who was I to contest? I followed him with equal enthusiasm.

Nothing was untypical within and a long serving bar heavily stained littered with a manner of vessels greeted us. Benches and tables filled the room to the extent of appearing cramped. Aged straw remained unkempt on the cold stone floor

David Greely

along with empty barrels and discarded sacks. We sat among the commotion at the only vacant table beside the door and soon enough our needs were attended to and a pitcher of mead was eagerly served with two clay pots.

"Innkeeper, bring us some food," demanded Ebden. "Me and my friend here are famished."

"Very well sire," the man obeyed willingly and tottered off beyond a secondary room, presumably the kitchen.

"I am in much need of this Ebden," I admitted, savouring the mead in front of me.

Without further utterance I swiftly filled the vessels, casting care aside of spillage and greedily gulped at the ale.

By the time I poured our second fill, the innkeeper returned laden with a board filled aplenty. He transferred the contents to the table while I teased myself at his generous offering of bread, wedge of cheese, meat and fruit laying in tempting readiness. In my moment of idle torment, Ebden tore at the bread and meat with both hands and not to be outdone, grabbed the cheese and the remaining bread for fear of missing out. We ate heartily, washed down by the rapidly draining mead.

"Another pitcher please landlord!" Ebden ordered with mouth fully stuffed.

"That is all very well sire," said the keeper with some disdain, "but I insist on money first. Not that I distrust you two gentlemen but I have been victim of absconders in the past…"

"…Not from the likes of us you haven't," Ebden contended rudely.

"Sorry sire but with all respect I must ask upon payment first."

"Then have this," offered Ebden, kicking out the sack of rattling goods toward the proprietor.

If all it contained were the hanging stained pots from the wagon then it would have been a diminutive return as payment.

The innkeeper pulled the sack open and peered apathetically at the contents. His face broke into a broad smile.

"You jest," he laughed before looking grimly. "I will take your horse and cart as full payment for my services."

"Now you jest!" said Ebden raising his laughter at the keeper's exorbitant demand.

Fellow revellers ceased their activities and musty conversations modifying until an expectant hush descended upon the place. I have observed this sort of consequence many times in the alehouse at Wendatch, and often the outcome would be for the scrounger to get swift expulsion by way of a boot up the rear from the innkeeper, yet here it was different. None of these characters looked affable and little encouragement seemed warranted for any one of them to assist the keeper in expelling us.

"That is all we possess," Ebden claimed protectively.

The keeper continued to be amused.

Now I know why Belthorpe flourished. If his demand was typical of disbursement due, then they must all be rich and so much for Ebden's 'herdsmen and peasants!' I could ill-afford the affair to escalate and acted swiftly.

"Very well, let me resolve this futile predicament," I said, rising from the chair, looking directly at the innkeeper. "Now be realistic and name your price."

He moved closer to the table tossing the stained cloth over his shoulder before placing his hands on his hips.

"Very well," he responded, "I will just take the horse."

"Come; is there not something else you want for?"

"Either money or the horse," he reiterated.

Ebden gripped my sleeve and rose from his chair.

"There is no point in bargaining with him, let's take our leave."

I considered smartly and thought of the little tricks I used to perform at Wendatch.

"A horse you say?" I shouted, endeavouring to be heard above the increasing drone.

"Would you not settle for a pig? You can eat a pig."

"It would need to be big and fat," insisted the innkeeper.

"Then it shall be so. How does eighteen stone sound?"

He rubbed his hands, relishing at such prospect.

David Greely

"Delightful," he said, "but impossible. I will settle for your horse."

"The pig!" shouted one of the onlookers.

"Yeah!" agreed another. "Show us the porker. We want to see the pig."

"Where is this pig of yours?" asked the landlord with an impulsive change of heart.

"Momentarily," I assured him.

I glanced at Ebden who looked bewildered and completely unaware of the trickery I was about to render.

"Before I produce the pig we must clear the way here. Lend a hand and make room."

With excitement, men scrambled from the middle of the room dragging with them benches and tables, dropping vessels and spilling their ale.

"We are waiting," snarled the keeper.

I rolled back my sleeves and clapped my hands together in readiness for my caper.

"Here is your pig!" I announced.

At this precise moment when about to produce the animal, the door burst open and in walked the fat councillor. The room fell into uproar.

"Your payment," shouted Ebden, "for the food and ale."

"What transpires here?" exhorted the fat man aware of the laughter but oblivious to the reason.

"These two here are refusing payment," moaned the innkeeper.

"Nonsense!" I snapped, returning to my seat. "He was offered a fair exchange but refused. Greed is his only price."

"He wanted my horse," Ebden griped.

"Be calm, all of you. Fezzel, I will settle their account later now fetch more ale and look lively about it!"

"But...," persisted the innkeeper.

"...Now Fezzel," the councillor demanded.

"Yes, lord Weigel," he responded obsequiously.

The fat councillor sat between us.

"Disregard old Fezzel, he means no harm. Good living has altered his character a little."

"He was ready to do battle! We are indebted to you," I said.

"Please," he upheld, "you owe me nothing, nothing that is, until you have told me of your purpose here."

"It is as I said, we come here merely to trade but in retrospect the standards set in this town are far and above our expectation."

"Oh come now," he grinned at me, "you both look like men of experience surely the places you have frequented differ in parameters of bargaining?"

"Indeed so," I acknowledged, "but a horse for food and ale is beyond any man's means."

"That is the price level of things around here. Did you not think to enquire first? Nevertheless, in this instance your account will be settled by me."

"I am dubious of your intentions Weigel."

And I truly was. No one, not in all the years I have watched the comings and goings of an alehouse, has anyone been willing to aid a stranger, least of all without good reason.

"Why so? I am an honourable man and a man willing to assist another."

"Yeah and at what cost?" Ebden goaded.

His question was founded and I fully agreed with his scepticism.

Whilst the councillor chose to ponder, I glanced around the room. Calmness had returned and most imbibers re-seated, and apart from the insidious glare from Fezzel, the three of us went unhindered in our trite conversation.

I was becoming increasingly distressed over Fallan's arrival. Shortly he was going to come bursting through the door proclaiming the invasion and still Ebden and I had yet to organise matters. I did consider forgetting the scheme and walk away to leave the town to face the enemy. Persuading this lot to make a stand was going to prove an arduous task.

"Knowledge," replied Weigel, eventually breaking my deliberation.

"Knowledge of what?" Ebden queried.

Weigel's eyes became narrow slits, devious, sly and scheming.

"It is time for the truth. Now then my friends, I am still mystified somewhat by your authenticity…"

"…And I of yours," Ebden interjected.

"My needs are honourable gentlemen," responded the councillor with an insignificant twisted grin. "Firstly I must establish for myself that your intention is upstanding. You see, here at Belthorpe strict laws are enforced and 'no man shall act in a fraudulent manner' is number six on the charter, by doing so lends itself to punishment and your deception has already broken that law."

"Our needs were genuine," I claimed. "Refreshment for wares is widely acceptable."

"Yes at the right price, but it is by the by. I have seen to your debt and you owe Fezzel nothing."

"But now we owe you," I conceded.

"Precisely," confirmed the fat councillor.

The innkeeper returned, placing a further pitcher of mead and an extra cup on the table.

"If…," Ebden asked, pausing until Fezzel departed, "…our wares were unacceptable to the innkeeper then how can we pay our debt to you?"

"By way of service," replied Weigel.

"What service?" I asked with deepening suspicion.

"That," he continued, "is open to discussion."

The fat man bent forward and whispered his next words whilst looking cautiously around.

"You see I have a problem too. There exists on the council two members strongly opposed to our king. I and the others mean to see them eradicated and establish new members who are true advocates to Talteth."

Ebden looked straight at me anticipating my retort. I remained silent however, choosing to hide my derision and take a gulp of ale.

"Then," I said, replacing my vessel on the table, "perhaps we can help each other."

"It is refreshing to know some men exist in the south still showing loyalty to their king."

I cringed at his words.

"Too many subjects have strayed of late, just look about you. Half of this lot do not give a bushel or peck who rules over the kingdom. To them Talteth is just a name, so long as they get their ale they remain impartial."

I needed to investigate the councillor. Did his allegiance stop with Talteth or was he also involved with the Laddians? Perhaps he was a believer in the tyrant because of ill-acquired knowledge of the truth.

"Tell me Weigel what of the old king?" I asked him.

"Arbereth?"

"Yes," I confirmed. "You see, we have heard so many conflicting tales on our travels over his death and cannot establish fact."

"The fact? The truth is what has been spoken from his son's lips."

"He died then of old age," I conceded falsely.

"Did you ever doubt?"

Of course I doubted, damn him! I knew the truth; I was there and buried him. The whole matter was a lie, so too was the kingdom under Talteth.

I found it difficult to quell my anger; if it were not for Ebden's awareness of my feelings and his timely interruption I may well have committed an act of murder in rage.

"Of course we never questioned it," he said. "Some southerner's possess bitter tongues."

I was grateful for his intervention and his show of solidarity.

Weigel continued.

"I must rid the committee of these rogues and rectify the harmony Talteth deserves. To be blunt gentlemen, I want them both dead."

David Greely

"What if we do not comply with your need?" I asked, leaning back into my seat.

"Then you will leave me with no choice but to hand you over to the assembly. Your act of deception will see you locked in irons and thrown into the pit at Awar then perhaps quartered, depending upon the councils' resolution."

I did not know such things went on. Awar in particular is a large town of tranquillity so surely it could not sink equally low as Fleddon. Of course, there exists penal reform and any wrongdoers accordingly punished, but quartering…!

"…Then we have little option," Ebden surrendered.

"Good then it is settled," smiled Weigel. "Fortune will shine upon us all.

In the morrow there is to be an assembly. The council will of course be presiding and all you have to do is choose your moment. The two seated to my left will be the heathens in need of elimination and when the council retires to the chamber for deliberation, this will be your opportunity to strike without fear of witness. My two cohorts will be aware of the scheme and should there be a need for assistance, will aid you accordingly."

Weigel's grin broadened confidently at his transpiring accomplishment.

I sojourned with two men, one an enemy of the true king and the other a comparatively new ally, neither of whom I would trust to hold my sandals. I felt justified to doubt everyone from now on. No one since my arrival back to the realm displayed an ounce of honour and even in this moment of disquiet, I had new doubts over the woodman. Was he ever eager to get to Collington and seek Ulcris on my behalf or just suffering intimidation with the threat from the Laddians? My glance met Ebden's stare, sensing he identified my mood of agitation.

"It is time to take leave; I have much to prepare so until the morrow gentlemen, the chanting hall at mid-morning."

The fat man rose, swigging the last dregs of ale before turning sharply and walking to the door.

"Gentlemen," he nodded and immediately left.

"This is all too harrowing Ebden. I mean, I cannot wantonly kill two supporters of Arbereth and defenders of the kingdom. I cannot and will not do it!"

"Then I will," he said smartly.

"You are missing my point. They support us and God knows we need them."

"Have you not grasped the gravity of our dilemma? If we fail to comply with Weigel's demands, we might just as well stand by the two men swearing our fealty along with them, what consequence then, eh?"

"You are right but I will not be a part of their demise," I insisted.

"I will do what's necessary."

"What if we were to run?" I offered pathetically.

"How foolish you are, besides, what of your friend Matlock? And possibly you can see it in your heart to give Fallan some consideration too!"

"My God, Fallan! The Laddians!"

My exaggerated whisper could have caught anyone's ears above the inconsequential din.

"His arrival has lapsed and I fear for him."

My dismay in thinking of the suffering he may have undergone at the hands of the barbarians brought foreboding, and I contemplated Matlock's fate too, for both could now be dead.

"What now?" I asked Ebden, turning to him for support.

"Remain here and I will find Fallan and cancel your plan."

"What about the Laddians?"

"Relax my friend," replied Ebden, his face breaking into a perceptive smile. "Tomorrow is Elkinmorg."

"Elkinmorg," I repeated discordantly with relief, "why of course!"

The entire contingent cast their eyes upon us after my loud outburst but I did not give a hog's hoof. With times of elation rare, this was one realisation worthy of merriment and knowing the Laddians lay twenty-four hours behind gave justification for drinking.

"Give everyone ale," I ordered Fezzel.

David Greely

"Not on your worth stranger," rejected the innkeeper.

"Do not concern yourself with trivialities man, the councillor will be settling our tariff," I laughed.

"And" added Ebden, "you would not want us telling him of your refusal of his custom, would you?"

A great furore throbbed from every musty corner of the alehouse fuelled by the realisation of their gratis libation.

"I will search for Fallan," said the traveller and without dally promptly supped his ale.

Ebden's insistence on finding his partner superseded my want for further discourse and he immediately departed.

Chapter Seventeen

My head pained me the following morning and my stomach, full of fermenting mead was ready to burst. I could not recall our slumbering arrangements, nor did I give a care to. Ebden was already awake, washing in the horse trough just beyond the stable door. The smell of rotting hay and ripe horse droppings impelled me to rise immediately and on standing regurgitated vomit over the luckless horse tethered near my side.

Though peculiar and never questioning it, Ebden said nothing of Fallan's fate when I first rose and naturally I assumed all was well. Perhaps he had told me the previous night but the fourth pitcher served was the last I could recall. I took it too, that he had not found the woodman for surely Matlock would be here to greet me; however, the silence suited me what with the sufferance of an immense hangover.

The day started brightly enough but with the gathering cloudbank in the southwest, threat of more rain looked very

David Greely

likely. After a quick rinse which did nothing to refresh me, I ambled slowly toward the chanting hall following Ebden's tread, relying heavily upon my staff, contemplating what lay ahead. I passed the many abodes jutting into the lane, caring to peer surreptitiously inside any open window or door, daring to proffer anything in the way of fortitude. It was not far to the meetinghouse and the grand stone and oak building, set away from the road, beckoned with open doors. I plodded along the short and well-trodden track, doubling back across the narrow section of the river by way of a rickety footbridge, listening to the dull peels of the bells reverberating as I approached the steps. Other townsfolk fell in behind, urging me to move quicker in their eager compulsion to enter before others and once through the iron-hinged doors, ushered to one side and told to remain. I searched for Ebden and Fallan among the large congregation but it was hopeless with so many people jostling for a prime position, I stood firm, doing my utmost to sustain my footing amid the pushing and shoving. Folk demonstrated no concern having a stranger amongst them, though in retrospect, with the amount of people gathered most were probably unfamiliar, even to themselves.

The hall was refined and delicately carved with cloisters running the whole width of the far end, concealing a small door in its shadows and from the timbered roof hung silken tapestries depicting the realm's legends, with Talteth's standard of the green and white chevron in the centre. Directly below it was a marble altar furnished with two gold candlesticks with lengthy tapers flickering in the draughts. Blue and gold filigree complimented each stone column in a descending helix to the floor, and on each side, row upon row of pews fashioned in oak laid the length eternal. Above the entrance hung a cluster of three brass-cast bells precariously poised to fall at their next toll. In all, the splendour of this place made the great hall of Wendatch seem like a cellar by comparison. There subsisted an air of holiness within and so intense the feeling I secretly drew the sign of the cross across my chest, although not ashamed in doing so I did not wish to draw unwanted attention to myself.

The peacefulness impressed me, everyone stood hushed and motionless with eyes closed as if in their own silent prayer and yet, I could feel their icy stares piercing me through their lids, tearing my flesh like the talons of the Melca, the fabled blue erne. Twisting and pulling, ripping and scything in a moment of frenzy. The sensation eventually abated leaving my whole body tingling, the ardent sentiment felt like the commencement of a divination but no, not here, it was too blessed. I felt servile, almost insignificant and equal to any of those standing with me. Men, women and children, the frail, crippled or smitten, I was not superior to any of them, least of all by the power possessed and it is God's way of course, we are born as equals and thus die as equals.

The massive doors creaked, closing to a thunderous shudder that rippled under my feet and signalling the proceedings to commence. Five men clad in deep blue garb appeared in file from the far door. Long hoods with draping muslin masked their identities and each with arms folded across their chest burying their hands into their sleeves. They were the council.

A small girl dressed in white led them to the altar stone, gently swaying an incense bowl, expelling gentle smoke trails delicate as marble stains. The men, on stopping, formed a semi-circle and bowed their heads. The central councillor leant and kissed the stone, which set the assembly into a morbid chant, at first softly and scarcely the pitch of a hornet's wings, before increasing and changing key to a melancholic drone that resonated around the hall. As time lapsed, the pitch increased to a nauseating threnody piercing my ears and just when reaching my threshold, stopped almost as if knowing the limit of endurance. The place echoed and vibrated for several moments before fading back into silence.

"Ubar Ontenium. Saxin Ubaris," wailed one of the shrouded councillors, sanctioning the inauguration.

'These were sacred words used by monastics centuries past,' I thought, 'and long since used in the realm.' I racked my memory in an effort to accurately translate them and have done so ever since. It refers to being a moderator under the guidance

David Greely

of a divine justice, in other words, the council had given their selves the right to adjudge anyone or anything without fear of recrimination.

The same councillor spoke.

"Proffer yourselves those seeking resolution and forward those of sin to be heard by this council."

Out from the throng a man and a hoary woman jostled into the aisle and pensively stepped to the front of the altar stone. I screened the crowd once more for Ebden and Fallan, in need of a signal from them to dictate my next action but still could not locate them. This had to be my opportunity to near the council and probably the only method of demoting suspicion of the foreboding ahead. Seizing the moment, I pushed through the crowd with my stave and barged out into the aisle joining the man and old crone. As we walked together in procession behind the congress, the deafening chant took rise again and continued as we entered the shadowed door.

'Where are you Ebden? Fallan? Matlock, you should be here!' My doubt added to the feeling of increasing vulnerability and I felt myself shaking with tension.

The door closed with a gentle click, stifling the monotonous lament from the hall and I stood with the others, fearing their trepidation; already beginning to scheme my departure from the claustrophobic chamber, sceptical of my decision. The lingering silence availed me time to gaze about the small, dank and gloomy room. Four pathetic tapers as a means of light illuminated oak-panelled walls with bevelled edging embellishing simple designs. The floor was cold stone with a small tattered bearskin arranged off centre in front of a table and bench. Then the smell struck me, not fusty but a sweet redolence I had tested elsewhere but despite endeavour I failed to recognise it, before me, assembled the council of five.

"Tochra, what is your purpose here?"

Immediately I recognised Weigel's voice.

"Sin my lord," the docile man responded timidly.

"And this sin?" urged the fat councillor.

"I have stolen two sheep," replied the man, twitching his fingers.

"The reason being?" asked Weigel.

"Well your worship, they strayed onto my land and I knew not to whom they belonged."

"Do these strays have brandings?"

"No sire," the man substantiated.

"Well if no man or woman claims their loss by the termination of this council they will be yours to keep."

"Thank you my lord," the man smiled fretfully.

The farmer dipped his head in respect, turned sharply and departed speedily from the chamber, temporarily rekindling the doleful drone when opening the door.

"Hessan, you again, what be your purpose on this occasion?" Weigel asked somewhat belligerently.

"Resolution," she squeaked, shuffling her haggard frame closer to the table.

"The resolution being?" sighed Weigel, displaying his growing impatience with the old woman. "Well?" he pressed at her hesitancy.

"Sire, could it be granted I be bestowed to trade?"

"What is this trade?" he asked.

"Amelioration," she hissed, moving yet closer to the table.

"Means nothing to me, define it a little more."

"Potions, elixirs, medicines for the sick and needy."

"That is the devil's practice!" Weigel renounced.

"No, you do not understand…"

"….Quiet hag, I will do the talking!"

An uneasy stillness skulked while the council hunched closer to each other, expelling their muffled whispers, nods and sighs. Eventually Weigel raised his head to speak.

"Well it would seem you have caused indecision among us, therefore a vote will be cast.

Those in favour of the granting?"

Two councillors to the left of Weigel slowly nodded their approval, the same two men Ebden was set to kill.

David Greely

"Your resolution is denied by three to two, now take your leave from us, woman."

Weigel's words were final and Hessan departed after emitting an icy glare at him.

"Arton..." announced the fat councillor pulling back his hood.

'My God he knows my name, but how?' I was startled.

Admittedly, it was no close secret but knew I did not disclose it to anyone at Belthorpe, and Ebden never mentioned my name in our conversation at the alehouse. Having already regretted entering the chamber I felt a challenge over my identity, objective and detestation for Talteth was about to be tested.

"...What is your purpose?"

Weigel knew damned well and needed no reminder! I had to think sharply.

"Resolution," I returned dismissively.

"And the resolution?" prompted Weigel with a pathetic grin.

I clutched the bones through my tunic hoping for immediate salvation.

"I wish for Ebden's presence."

"Come, come Arton that is not a desire warranting the attention of this council but nevertheless," he sighed, "I think we can afford such granting under the gravity of these circumstances."

The councillor to his right raised his head and pulled back his shroud.

"Ebden!" I shouted in absolute surprise. "What transpires here?"

Both he and Weigel smirked knowingly at each other.

I had fallen into another elaborate ruse; a trap I should have suspected all along. My gut feeling was right about the traveller and foolishly, I had disclosed everything to him in my bid to win him over.

Was I now to meet my death along with the other two councillors? I was bewildered of their intent after having gone to such lengths to capture me. Surely Ebden could have killed me anytime on the road, so this scheme could only have arisen from the previous evening but then again, I pondered, it may have transpired whilst I slept. Time ran its course and I had to show my strength.

"You are forcing my hand and continuing this charade will only lead you into dire consequences," I warned, purposefully not wanting to appear intimidated.

Weigel turned to Ebden.

"What does he mean?"

"It is nothing," rejected Ebden, "he talks in riddles, in fact, he always talks in riddles."

"Enough of this!" I stormed, taking firm hold of my gnarled stave. "You know what I am capable of producing Ebden," I hastily reminded.

The traveller rose with anger on his face.

"You are nothing but a fake Arton and as demented as the old hag. You conjure some illusion and have the impudence to acclaim yourself sorcerer, expecting everyone to believe in the shit! Your cause is lost and no one believes in your God anymore. Look around you, can't you see the change? Talteth is our king and not some distant ghost from the past. The wishing towers are redundant, they fall into decay and in time, Talteth will see them all demolished. Your dream is dead Arton, along with your wretched God."

In the momentary silence following Ebden's outburst, I glanced along the row of councillors and the three opting to remain shrouded never stirred by what was unfolding. With Ebden's involvement in this dilemma, Fallan had to be apportioning himself to it.

"I have another purpose with this council," I said, inching toward Weigel.

"Sin or resolution?" he asked scowling.

"Sin," I replied.

"And your sin?"

"Plotting to kill the pretender to the realm and his despicable disciples!"

David Greely

"You are too late for that," mocked Weigel, "Arbereth died years ago."

"Oh, but you miss my point, the almighty lives in the hearts of his people," I said.

"Talteth is king and it is he who is worshipped. You are on your own Arton."

"I will see to it I swear!" I cursed.

"And," he asked, "How do you propose to eradicate our king unaided?"

"You still underestimate my strength and more importantly, God's will. The divine Lord has the ultimate power Ebden; he will undo these sinister workings and if I fail there are others. Ulcris will see to it!"

"Ulcris indeed," scoffed Ebden, "he is nothing but an insignificant Druid."

"My words are not a threat..."

"...Enough!" shouted Weigel. "You are nothing but a sinner."

"Yes, I have sinned and a thousand-fold too, but no sin shall reward me greater satisfaction than in slaying Talteth."

"Prevaricator! Cut out his tongue!" yelled Weigel.

Ebden leapt across the table and lunged at me, scattering the candles to the floor. With my left hand clasping the bones I thwarted his advance and dodged to one side, calling for Treggedon's aid. Weigel and another councillor rose and made their move. Now I was cornered and despite my frantic bid to reach the door, Ebden's fist struck me square on the jaw. My face tingled from his heavy blow and before I was able to recover Weigel and the third councillor pinned my arms down. Again, I sampled the odd aroma.

"Show yourself!" I demanded of the unknown councillor, but the shrouded man did not comply and nor did he speak.

Weigel thrust his dagger to my throat forcing me to drop my staff. The cold blade touched my skin nullifying my breath.

"Utter another word," he said, "and you will face your God!"

I felt ineffectual with his dagger ready to strike and remained rigid, inwardly cursing my ineptitude of not conceiving what transpired, wondering why Ebden betrayed my trust, speculating at Fallan's involvement, concerned for the woodman's welfare and curious for the identity of the third councillor. Moreover, what of the remaining two men, were they also to be murdered after me?

I looked over to them, trying with my eyes to warn them, but they remained seated and unmoved, seemingly dispassionate with my plight and insensible of the fate laying in wait for them. I wanted to yell out the danger and tell them to run but Weigel's blade foiled me. Too late now for my dreams, my passions, my hopes and my yearning for vengeance for everything was about to wither.

My hand dropped away from the wishbones and I dared not to try wishing again. Any movement now would ignite Weigel's temper and undoubtedly sever my life. The last two councillors stood and calmly walked the short distance towards me and my transgressors, ready now to join their brothers in the deed to follow. At their approach, they drew their daggers.

"Drop it!" ordered the fourth man, driving his blade against Weigel's back. "Drop it!" he repeated, adding a further threatening push with his blade.

The fifth counsellor grabbed Ebden's throat in preparation to slit it.

"Move away!" he commanded him.

Although his words were distorted I was elated upon recognition.

"Woodman!" I yelled in surprise.

"In the flesh my friend," he confirmed, pulling back his hood.

Matlock revealed a hearty smile, beaming from ear to ear and though a thousand questions sought explanation none came from my lips.

"And who...?"

Before I had finished asking, Fallan revealed himself, in my amazement I could only smile.

Weigel dropped his dagger, backing away beside Ebden and the third councillor, who continuing his silence, wilfully joined his devious confederates. Assessing the expressions upon the conspirators' faces, they were equally as astonished as I was, and not one moment did I conceive the woodman and Fallan being in this together.

Though I was prepared to offer forgiveness to the three rebels and settle for them locked in chains, Matlock viewed it very differently and despite my shout for leniency, wrapped his massive hands around Ebden's throat. The strength of Matlock was astounding and his victim by no means a small man. He administered his power so effortlessly. Feeble was the traveller's resistance against the might of the woodman and gradually his life constricted from him. Ebden's body went limp and slumped heavily to the floor.

"No!" I yelled. "It does not have to be like this."

"Too late my friend." he said, turning his attention to Weigel. "It is a matter of do as you would be done by."

"But you had no right that was murder!" I contested.

"No less than what he was prepared to do to you. Compassion Arton is not worthy for those who live in enmity, he deserved it."

"And so do you Weigel!" said Fallan.

Before I could offer any debate for clemency, Fallan drove his blade deep into the fat man's heart and as he withdrew, pushed the dying councillor forward, forcing his head to slam against the wall. He sank to the floor with eyes rolling. Fallan intervened on Matlock's want, stopping the third councillor's demise under the throttling hands of the woodman.

"Wait," he said, "leave him to me. Get into Ebden's robe Arton and I will do what needs to be done. Now go quickly!"

To hear him speak as he did was out of character for him. In the short while of knowing him he personified a passive and sensitive logic yet now, equally as barbaric as Matlock with his words.

Under his insistence, I donned Ebden's robe. Taking the clothes off the dead man was not easy but I eventually managed. I refused to forsake my master's rod and secreted it inside the loose-fitting garb.

Matlock tied the hands of the third traitor under Fallan's protection and even after the captive's struggle I was never rewarded witnessing his identity, however it meant little now considering he would not attend my company again. I surmised Fallan was about to secure his fate and it would be useless to plead on his behalf. I yearned for Fallan and Matlock's exegesis but despite want, suffered deference at the current situation and until the time came, remained suffused in speculation.

The chamber door slowly opened and two shrouded figures entered. They briefly introduced themselves as Nalos and Imesh, shaking my hand with the warmest of greetings. They were Weigel's intended victims and judging by their response grateful of our intervention. I felt warmed in the knowledge of gaining another two allies opposed to the rule of Talteth. I pulled the hood over my head, fell behind Matlock and upon his command followed him out into the hall, sharply closing the door behind me.

The chanting persisted though somewhat softer now. The woodman and I joined Nalos and Imesh by the altar stone. Shortly, Fallan reunited with us and to the assembly appeared as the five original councillors, though we feared exposure of our identity. Nalos clapped his hands bringing the soft chant to a slow and disorderly curtailment.

"People of Belthorpe heed my words for danger skulks in our realm. Laddians of a vast number invade our shores and already we have lost councillor Weigel and a traveller by the name of Ebden to them. Hundreds more besides from Vledor and Caer Tal are confirmed dead, thus we must prepare ourselves."

A gradual furore of disbelief culminated from the magnitude drowning any supplementary words of Nalos' warning. Questions were fired anxiously and consternation began eroding their earlier calmness. Anger and panic became evident and the five of us looked at each other through our gauzes, floundering in the growing uncertainty. It was time to perform; I felt it up to me to take management of council. On impulse, I pulled back my hood, releasing my staff simultaneously and held it aloft. Aiming directly at the bells hanging over the doors, I fired a blazing globe which arced across the hall, and on impact sent a resounding and deafening peal. It had the desired effect and immediately acquiring their full attention spoke my mandate deliberately and resonantly.

"For those gathered, hear my words, for I Arton of Wendatch proffer an omen of death that looms over us. God has been kind this day and it is with good fortune the enemy takes brief respite from their plundering but the morrow will bring dissolution, vileness and death to Belthorpe. You must flee from this place and save yourselves. Spread the word of their coming. Run north or east, but save yourselves and your kin."

I do not know why but when announcing my name I half expected an integrated gasp of surprise, after all was I not now famous, at the very least would they not of heard of my incredible deeds.

The subsequent rebuff I anticipated for I knew my words sounded frail and unfounded, with no proof to offer other than what my confidants witnessed for themselves.

"I am Newing," announced the approaching man, "I shall with consent, act as spokesman."

"So be it," I encouraged him, "but let this issue proceed with haste for time is precious."

"If what you say is true then swiftness is indeed wise," he agreed, coming to a halt at the front of the altar stone. "What foundation do you have of the Laddian invasion?"

"Proof exists, my friend though dead men cannot speak of it; I have seen abominations beyond imagination. Men, women and children felled by our adversaries," I confirmed.

"It is only your word," he pondered stubbornly.

"Every place west of here is decimated, I have seen it so."

Newing turned and faced the congregation as if awaiting confirmation from them to continue his voluntary undertaking.

"Impossible!" he claimed bluntly. "The Laddians would not dare venture into the kingdom."

He laughed falsely but I suspect out of the fear of my tidings.

"Only yesterday did I venture on the western road but saw no Laddians. In fact," continued Newing, "I saw no-one. Weigel and the traveller were in the alehouse with you last night so how is it they are not in this company of council now. Their absence provides me fear they are dead and if my supposition be founded where are their bodies?" he asked accusingly, turning on his heels to face the multitude again.

"Weigel is not dead, I have spoken with him not moments ago!" echoed the voice of the farmer out from the congregation.

Inwardly, I cursed the farmer's intervention, choosing to ignore his declaration by hoping my weak story would appease Newing, but he possessed guile and strived for further validation.

"I can only speculate, for obviously you have not witnessed the workings of these murderers. I saw both their heads with eyes plucked but could not locate their bodies."

"I have seen him in the confession room and talked with him!"

The farmer's persistence was unnerving me.

"You are mistaken my friend for it is I you spoke with," said Nalos sensing my dilemma.

"Then where are their heads?" pressed the spokesman choosing to ignore the farmer's challenge.

"Suspended high from a bough of an elm. I did not dally, especially with those marauders about," I continued.

"Then how is it you managed to escape them?" Newing insisted.

"I was a little intoxicated and Ebden thought it best I take some air, so accompanied me and met up with Weigel. The three of us walked the roadway beyond the bridge and next I remember there were shouts in the night. Slingshot whistled around us and in haste I sped off and fell down an embankment. That is all I recollect until waking some while later and when walking back along the road saw their heads swaying in the tree above me. It was dreadful."

The assembly stood in a momentary disquiet for my thin story set fear in them.

"Then answer me this," pressed Newing, "why are you dressed in council robes?"

"I am chamberlain and council at Wendatch."

Lies of course, but I had to employ something in order to avert growing suspicion.

"And these two?" he asked, pointing to Fallan and Matlock.

"They are brothers of our faith."

Newing stood silent, considering my words.

"If we linger you shall have your proof for certain but by then it will be all too late. I have seen the enemy," announced the woodman, "and all what Arton states is true.

You must believe him."

"Must?" refuted the spokesman. "There is no must!"

"The people of Dunleigh heeded my warning and fled their homes to escape the Laddians. Join with them and spread the word of the enemy's coming."

"I have seen the Laddians too," confirmed Fallan taking discourse from Matlock, "thousand upon thousand. I can also give testament to Arton's power. God's touch it is and so powerful it can strike any mortal…"

The last thing I wanted was a debate on my wizardry and surreptitiously cursed the traveller's declaration. The enemy's advance was of far greater importance at this moment and I needed to gain support.

"…People of the realm," I interrupted, "I stand beside men who have seen their atrocities, will you not therefore give credibility?"

"Like you, they are strangers to us, how can we honour their words?"

"Accounts as honourable as mine!" I admonished angrily.

"Then I remain in doubt of you, councillor Arton," said Newing turning to the mass.

"You have no right!" blasted Matlock. "Arton is of great worth and potency."

"Again," announced Newing, "this power of Arton is given mention. If he is as mighty as you claim then let him stop the enemy threatening us."

The hall erupted in support of their spokesman and the woodman looked over to me, dithering in his crusade for words.

"Let us test his power!"

The crone's unwanted proposition hissed like a giant cobra, thwarting my intent with its dripping fangs poised to puncture my skin. Amid the overwhelming jeers and shouts, Hessan approached, directing her icy stare filled with the darkness of Satan into mine, although I tried averting her gaze I dithered helplessly, transfixed and induced into submission until forcing myself to blink. Whatever influence she possessed, it was fervent with a strange capacity I reviled immensely. I finally broke away.

"Ah Hessan," I greeted, "so you want verity of my power?"

"Aye," she squeaked through her blackened and decaying teeth.

"Are you not above these others congregated here? Does the testament of my brothers not satisfy you?" I asked.

"I am superior to these pathetic souls," she cackled, edging her ugliness closer to me. "It is apparent you have the instinct but what fortitude do you hold eh? Shall we test it now, fake?"

"Oh, do not doubt my potential woman?" I warned.

"I know you are not of the elite. Power of magnitude is created from within the mind, body and soul, not in some pathetic wooden pole," she contested.

"Did you not witness the ringing of the bells? Did it not warn you of my magic?"

"Anyone with practice can demonstrate a simple deception as that," she disputed.

"Trickery?" I smiled. "My ascendancy boasts a little more than simple deception."

"Prove it," she hissed.

David Greely

"Then let it be so," I shouted above the din, raising my arms to receive attention, "but before I commence, do I have the guarantee from each and every one gathered here they will support me and my congress?"

"You are the wizard," laughed Newing, "arrange it so."

The petulance of Newing was wearing and I decided it was time to act. As with most spells, I chose to give no forethought this instance, I did not grasp the bones for their secret continued to elude me and conceded relying upon them as source for assistance. I grabbed Newing by his cuff, my valour proving far greater than his resistance.

"Come," I shouted to him, "I will give you your proof."

Instantly we stood in a vast open meadow, a place where I had yet to travel and judging by Newing's stupefied expression, equally unknown to him. In the diminishing light of dusk we both bore witness to perdition; a manifestation brought about by the drone overwhelming us; flies, thousands of them flittering around indiscriminately, the size never seen nor dreamt, some larger than the span of my palm. They crawled in our hair and over our faces, prizing their legs into our mouths and nostrils. There was no pain however, just unequivocal repulsion proving ineffective to fend off. The grass at our feet blackened as our slow tread crushed those flies that crawled, and broken wings of refined lace drifted into the air like weightless feathers. I raised my staff, discharging mordant smoke into the air and agitating the insects into a funnelling swarm that spiralled upward like a black tower toward heaven. For those flying into the smoke death was instant, their bodies dropped rapidly to the ground, at first a negligible drizzle of spent bodies but at its height a torrent befitting a raging storm. Those escaping the cloud continued flying up far beyond my view; I strained my eyes to watch the last remnant of the pestilence dissolve into the greyness.

Newing's face reflected fear I had not witnessed on any man and it sent his complexion ethereal white. He stared long and intensely at the lifeless mass beneath his feet, full as I in disbelief of what transpired and much as I acquired a certain loathing for the man, I bestowed some pity by putting my arm around his shoulders.

"Come," I said faintly, "we must journey on."

I sensed he wished to speak and voice his repulsion of the manifestation but his lips were frozen. We continued a little further into the meadow until Newing suddenly stopped and hesitantly pointed to the writhing mounds littering our way. His body began shaking as if in consternation of his own death.

'My God!' I wailed in a stupefied hush, and though it felt like I had shouted my words, only my mind could here them.

The people of Dunleigh lay butchered. Where open wounds availed, maggots rejoiced in the repulsiveness, the victims eye sockets flinched with the grubs and every torso moved at their avid gyration.

Newing had right to bury his eyes in his hands, appalled as I, at the grotesque affair and finally as testament, beside my feet lay a Laddian with tainted leathers housing what was almost an empty carcass.

"Here is your proof Newing, now go tell your people!"

He turned away in obvious disgust, utterly confused by all he had seen and though repulsed by my vision I succeeded in convincing him.

The time elapsed was but a blink of an eye. It drained me and temporary feebleness forced me to lean against the altar stone.

"Well," I urged breathlessly, "what say you now Newing?"

He looked across the hall with a vacant stare, irrefutably pre-possessed of the sight I had shown him. At last he spoke, breaking the dulcet whispers igniting among the throng.

"I know not who or what he is but he embraces the divine power, I have seen it and am abhorred. Listen to Arton for he is honourable in his words."

"Hog shit!" the old hag cursed.

"Is Newing's testimony not confirmation enough for you?" I asked.

"No," she claimed, "it is not enough!"

"Then what more proof is needed?" I advocated.

"Evidence you are not a fake."

"God will damn you woman!"

"Too late for that," she cackled, "God has already done so!"

She spun full circle emitting a putrid vapour at me from her mouth.

"Pretender!" she screeched.

To avoid the noxious haze I dropped to my knees and aimed my staff, conjuring a bolt that propelled her high into the air and right across the aisle. She came to an abrupt halt hitting her back against the far wall.

"Say what you observed Newing," I instructed.

"Arton speaks the truth of their coming. I have seen the aftermath of a bloody battle confirming what will be."

"Rot!" stormed the hag shaking her head back to consciousness. "Are you all blind to his evil trickery?"

"It was real," confirmed the spokesman, "I smelled the sickly death and sensed the forbidding. It surrounded me…"

"…It's deceit you fool!" Hessan repeated, charging at me, defying the restriction of her age.

Our eyes met again no further than arm's distance and any mortal would have feared her, but not me, I was stronger than her, my power mightier and purer with God on my side.

I stood my ground, knowing winning the confrontation would demonstrate my purpose to everyone. I did not want to sink into the depths of petty spellbinding but resorting to it was the only method to use on the witch. She was hindering my progress and with time rapidly waning, needed eliminating.

I flicked my wrists, generating a rapturous thunderclap that vibrated the timbers of the hall and the people of Belthorpe cringed in stillness at its potency, staring at one another as if awaiting some eventual consequence. The witch laughed at my spell and spat phlegm at my feet in derision; a vile green glowing serum illuminating the shadows of the hall and with it a putrid stench reminiscent to Fleddon. Gasps of horror and bewilderment trembled in a continual appeal from those people too petrified to move, though others began edging toward the door. Woman and children sobbed and screamed aloud, clinging to each other in what they sensed their final day of judgment. I needed the people's support but did not want to win it by terrorising them with such actions and had to cease. To reinstate calmness required me making them fully understand the forthcoming peril and more importantly, tell them the truth behind Talteth's folly.

"I will offer you redemption Hessan if only you accept me."

"Never," she shrieked back at me, "this has gone beyond the bounds of bargaining."

I gathered up the generating spittle with the tip of my pole and flung into her face. It slapped loudly on impact and began dripping like puss from a festering ulcer, slowly down her neck and then creeping over her body. Before she could counter, I swiped my staff across her forehead with incredible might and the hag fell with a muted gasp, clutching at the gaping wound. I was tempted to administer another blow but the first was enough and I stood watching her blood pump from her skull. Slowly her form disintegrated, decomposing like a leaking goat bag and within moments, only the smouldering shabby mantle of Hessan remained. I kicked it in reassurance of her death.

An uncanny suppression arose from the remaining multitude more out of disbelief than repugnance. I had no intention of slaying her; it was an action in which I had no control over. The mystifying force was far too potent to resist, I had no option other than to comply. I turned to face the discernment from my associates. They knew it would end in some way like this but it was too late for reasoning and beyond any evaluation too, what occurred could not be altered. I was ready to face any verbal rebuke yet the people waited silently and with this opportunity I gained authority.

"Perhaps now you will take consideration of my warning and the veneration of my capabilities. We must rally and make a stand against our foes. Now, are you all with me?"

For those agreeing readily it was out fear of me and how fickle was I to be elated, gaining their allegiance successfully

David Greely

by such means. In defence, I consider fealty be gained by two manners, one is out of love or trust, the other out of trepidation. I was confident their adoration would eventually oppress any apprehension of me.

In my weary condition, the woodman's intervention heartened me and gave instruction like a warlord. Steadfast and unmoved by any qualms fired upon him, brushing aside the numerous doubts deserving explanation and castigating any pockets of feeble resistance. It was torpid and painstakingly laborious but eventually he won them over, so resplendent were his words that in the final moment of his conclave roused those cheering in support, something I would not have dared aspired.

Chapter Eighteen

Along with Matlock and Fallan, we collectively swayed our address to the assembled, focusing on strategy and after an hour of continual deliberation, formulated the defence of Belthorpe. I appraised the enemy would follow the western road and if my calculation erroneous then God help us all.

It felt good to be back in control of my own destiny even though it may not endure, but far more importantly at this moment was accomplishing the support of my fellow men. Now was the time to catch my breath and dig my heels in. Not having to rely upon the decisions of others was in itself my definitive motivation.

Though time, as always, was pressing and opportunity scant, I was thankful when Fallan eventually told me he spared the last councillor. He bound him in the confession room hoping to extract any useful information from him later. I was eager to discover the timely intervention of Fallan and Matlock,

David Greely

but the imminent onslaught of the Laddians moderated my yearning for a later conclusion.

Fallan, by his own appropriation was to make stand ahead of the bridge, taking some eighty men and displacing them along the western bank. Knowing an attack could arise any time after dusk, they engineered several deep pits on the road's approach with wooden spikes displaced at their bases. To the north, where the river was wide and shallow, Matlock gathered forty men, each armed with a weapon to help defend the town. Under my instruction, Nalos and Imesh departed leading the women, children, old and frail eastward following the edge of the wood and beyond. I remained with fifteen young men; nay boys, clean-faced and petrified, but nevertheless prepared to stay and offer their support at the looming confrontation with the enemy. I offered every one of them a change of heart and join the vacating itinerant but they unselfishly chose to remain and in the short time together I got to know their names.

It was quite uncanny, every lad proffered some type of skill and those boasting strength carried and dug, those lean and supple climbed, and those with guile schemed alongside me. Between us we spread cow-spikes the length of the road from the bridge, sunk pointed timbers knee height at varying angles, strung nooses from beams and trees, built barricades of discarded carts ill-fitting the exodus and set straw stacks soaked in poppy oil poised for ignition. Deadliest of all was the shrapnel engineered by the tubby youngster Ablett, with glowing iron fragments white-hot from the fire of the smith's forge. He continued relentlessly all afternoon cutting and shaping hand-sized pieces ready to slow the Laddian progress, with a trowel primed at his side to transfer the heated metal into the rigged catapult.

Despite the afternoon's foulness, our dedication drove us to completion and before night fell, we were ready. Though the rain eased for several hours, a torrential downpour fell at dusk sure to hinder the enemy's attack and poignantly prolong our inevitable confrontation. To ease their torment whilst waiting, I told the boys of my early childhood at Wendatch, re-enacting in my mind the illustrious days with my master. I even conducted a harmless spell, sending a pair of white doves fluttering off into the darkening sky, we watched avidly as the birds flew overhead and far off into the eastern horizon.

Then it came, the portentous faint glow of the enemy's torchlight. Not that it needed announcement from me, everyone recognised it almost simultaneously. Some of my charge openly wept in trepidation and if I were as callow then surely would have joined them in their sobbing. I could do little to offer them comfort other than to say I would take care over them. I gave a short prayer and begged the Lord to watch over and deliver us through the impending battle.

Under protection of the forge's wooden canopy, we waited pensively, watching tirelessly as the distant glow intensified. The heavy raindrops highlighted at the ever-increasing brightness of their torches looming along the road. The stomp of their feet preceded their chant, rolling like thunder in our ears and oppressing the noise of the rain. I feared for the lives of the youths, feeling responsible for each one of them, and had I been alone to face the enemy would have given full attention to the transpiring battle but their dependence upon my leadership preoccupied contemplation, and at this confluence I decided whatever may befall, their safety was to remain paramount.

The strength of the torchlight was penetrating now, seeking out the darkest shadows hiding within the trees just beyond the river. The interminable dirge suddenly ceased at their approach to the bridge as if intensifying their concentration to their attack. At first, I thought they spied what lay in wait for them but the forerunners dispelled my alarm, and a band of Laddian warriors came running down the road with clubs aloft swiping at the air in careless abandon. More horrifying was the main war host that followed. Outnumbered tenfold, I feared Fallan's slaughter, yet his tactics proved shrewd and rewarding. The deep pits proved useless and inadequate save for ensnaring a few scouts because all the others ran around them in avoidance. Fallan's men hid until the last Laddian reached the bridge and on his command attacked. Several hundred already crossed the

David Greely

bridge facing the unsteady headway of the traps we had set and before realisation struck them, Fallan and his group charged from the rear. Screams fuelled by the incessant din conveyed death and bodies fell at Fallan's onslaught. Flaming torches hissed into submission as they struck the water joining those bodies fallen in conflict from the bridge.

The adversary's breakthrough into the town forced me to act and no longer was I just an observer. I signalled to Ablett the smithy's boy to load the shrapnel into the catapult and while he darted from the furnace I organised others to light their spills.

"Now!" I commanded softly.

My boys acted like soldiers. No show of reluctance, just a performance of enduring duty and one by one they filtered out into the wet night to face their tasks. Calmly they slipped the canopies off the straw bales and on instruction by waving my rod, simultaneously ignited the oiled stacks. Great fireballs suddenly roared if only for a brief minute, yet suspending the perpetrators advance and exceeding the brilliance of their torches. Clouds of crackling acrid smoke fused by burning stubble melted into the night briefly quelling the rain. Whilst Fallan and his men fought tirelessly at the Laddians backs, the woodman joined the battle from the north, forcing the enemy to divide. Undeterred, the Laddians advanced, running at us like hell was breathing down their necks and although plenty fell at the pains of our traps there were too many, and wave after wave penetrated deeper into the town with every surge, closing in on my lads and me.

When the last boy returned, Ablett released the first hail of burning metal into the path of the pressing foe. High into the air fragments arced, hissing as they cut through the rain before plummeting on them with cruel menace. More shrieks resounded as bodies fell, clutching their heads or shoulders in hopeless restraint from the biting metal fragments. We fired another with similar consequence, only this time, it made them hesitate. They broke formation, fanning out in avoidance of the third shot and some turned back only to face Matlock and his men.

The combat was bloody and fatal. It was difficult to assess who gained advantage until a second legion of Laddians came at full flight along the road. We could not defend ourselves against such a multitude so it was time to call a retreat. We did all we could and meritoriously too against such a formidable army, but remaining would see to all our deaths. I shouted to the lads for order and ushered them along the shadows of the buildings and out into the fields.

"Follow the others to the wood and tell them to turn north."

Having reassured myself of their escape, I returned to the battle to reach Fallan and Matlock for they faced total encirclement. I dived into the river, swimming amongst the dead and dying and though my rod was a hindrance I dared not release it. It was part of me now, even if it meant a choice of surviving without it or dying with it, then let demise strike me swiftly. Somehow, I managed and found myself crawling up the steep bank under cover from the bridge. I saw Matlock first, his big frame wielding his axe in tireless swipes at the enemy. My calls to him were in vain amid the loud cries of the battle, my only option was to get nearer to him. I rose from the slippery ridge onto the road muddied and dripping with robe hanging on me as heavy as armour. I stood at the mouth of the bridge devoid of any able man and turned westward on impulse. Behind me, Matlock and Fallan engaged in heavy combat yet I could not go to their aid, I was forced to stay, facing the second advance alone with terror trembling in my every nerve. The torchlight hallowing their threat was almost as bright as if it were day and their thundering feet came to a sudden standstill as they approached. Out from the drifting smoke came the warlord I had seen before and though it took some while to see his face in the shadows, I was certain it was he, the Laddian reprieved in my earlier vision.

"Halt!" I commanded him, readying my stave. "Another step and be smitten."

David Greely

"I admire your pluck realmsman but this time it is I who will be victorious in this battle."

His words were strong and purposeful and his gait frightening.

"You made a fatal mistake in showing compassion toward me. A warrior cannot afford to give leniency. You stand so bold against me," he continued.

"You have been witness to my power, does it not unnerve you?" I asked.

"Why should it? I have observed sorcerers at work and seen warriors fight. The two will never be equal," he replied.

"Then you have underestimated the forces of wizardry, fool!"

"It is you the fool, whom dare stand alone to face me and my legions."

"Alone?" I laughed openly. "I have God on my side and he gives me the potency of a thousand men."

He spat on the ground.

"That to your God!" he glanced aloft and continued to speak mordantly. "I look but I do not see him. If your God is all powerful then how be it he let us take your land so effortlessly?"

"Every man, even you my enemy, is given a chance to prove his worth and let no man who walks this land ever doubt…"

"…Oh, stop! I cannot abide preaching! You are an insignificant being, as are the rest in this forsaken kingdom."

"Let the Lord be the arbitrator of your blasphemy!" I endorsed.

"Neither your words nor your magic scare me."

"Then you are ignorant!"

I chose to move a few steps closer, if not to prove my courage to him, then it had to be for myself.

"'Ignorant. Fool.' What other names befit me wizard?" smiled the Laddian.

I could have replied a hundred but the look of wrath upon his face warned me to act swiftly.

"Prepare to die for your senseless cause!" I wailed, raising my staff above my head.

"Slay me and you will be destroying yourself," he warned.

His words were cutting for I had heard them before proffering warning, yet I did not comprehend their meaning.

I had to destroy him. Doing so was my only chance of slowing the onslaught and displaying an example of my capabilities would surely have them fleeing. Not just for myself did I have to act but for Matlock, Fallen and all the townsfolk too. If I were to fail in doing so, we would all be dead the moment the enemy crossed over the bridge.

Then I contemplated. 'Death need not be the propagator of testimony; it does not have to be this way. Forcing terror could be equally rewarding in its outcome and invoking something to strike fear into their hearts, large and grotesque enough to make them hide under rocks, scatter and force them to flee back to their ships.'

Before priming my incantation, the shrill bark of the fox announced his presence to me and sat at my side with long tongue flicking at his breaths. I bent a little, stroking his crown in welcome, never leaving my watch from the Laddian. I half expected Maddox to appear but alas, no. I could have done with him now.

"Do it Arton!" barked the fox. "Sow the breath of the dragon!"

My staff became warm and weighty to the juncture of almost dropping it, from its tip expelled a dense white mist of the dragon's breath, cleaving to the foot planks of the bridge before spilling over the sides in a cascading billow, touching the water and wafting in both directions along the river. In its drift, the floating dead and dying became overwhelmed, as too those victims clinging desperately to the steep banks. The mist rolled gently, unfolding and extending its gossamer swathe along the bridge toward the warrior ahead of me. It touched his feet, coiling its tendrils around his legs and heaved its weightlessness up to his waist. I witnessed the Laddian's distress and consternation.

David Greely

"Here is a sample of my power!" I shouted defiantly.

The mist continued to creep along the bridge and onto the road, encapsulating the feet of the stupefied enemy by clinging to their ankles in a contorting rhythm, sapping their efforts to flee. An extraordinary suppression came from the foe, their eyes stark at the approaching fog, and only the remnants of the concluding battle behind me confirmed any materiality to the otherwise bizarre circumstance.

Matlock's approach established we had won the first contest and his face did little to hide jubilation. My concentration needed to be stern much as I wanted to shout to the heavens of our triumph, I instructed him to take the remaining men immediately and join the exodus, with reassurance I would shortly follow.

Out of the night sky came the winged serpent flying with the grace of the albatross, pushing away the clouds that had lingered all day, swooping and soaring ever closer. Its green and orange body scales gleamed in the enemy's torchlight accentuating the perfection I created. Short darkened wings with rusty undersides beat effortlessly and a long tapering tail traced its own descending course. From its mouth exhaled steaming vapour, suppressing the falling rain to an insignificant spit. Heads strained with looks of anguish fearing its nearness and every Laddian waited for his fellow to make the first cowardly gesture to flee.

"Run!" I shouted to them. "Run for your lives!"

I watched contentedly as the dragon infused hysteria into them all and compelling them to scatter.

"Hold fast!" demanded their superior, still entwined in the woven mist.

"Run!" I yelled again, countermanding his order for calm.

There was nothing to keep them other than their deaths and they dispersed like a herd of sheep, fearing to look above them at the diving serpent. Weaponry fell willingly to the ground and torches slung pathetically at the ensuing beast in a piteous bid to impede its ravaging plummet. Adding to their plight echoed the cries of despair from the dying and wounded, and within moments the Laddian host dispelled into the night, leaving me with the fox to face the warlord.

"There," I posed immeasurably satisfied, "have you ever seen such might?"

He said nothing and moved forward. The mist swirled in his steps, flowing as if to make a path for him. He stopped close to me.

"Clever I grant you, but your dragon does not fool me," he maintained.

Somehow, I knew it would not have done. The man before me was no dolt and probably more intelligent than the whole of his army collectively. An illusion even as powerful as this was not going to deter him.

I lowered my staff and thumped the end hard on the foot plank signalling for the dragon to withdraw. With splendour equal to its arrival, the huge beast soared over us and continued up into the heavens, discharging a radiance befitting a shooting star. Up it flew until it became impossible to trace, blending with the many stars now bursting through the clearing sky. The mist started disentangling its puffy tendrils from the banks, receding along the river, exposing the stricken victims of this superfluous war and retracting its mantle from the bridge until funnelling back into the tip of my rod. The fog vanished and so too did the fox.

"I admire your courage Laddian."

And I truly did.

"And I, your magic, realmsman," the Laddian remarked.

He stood unnerved with his sword poised in keenness for my next action.

"Fate," I continued, "has dealt us a different outcome to this. My physical strength is no match to yours and though I have the gift, I cannot slay you."

My words were as frail as my energy and if he were to make a challenge against me now, then death would be my only honour. I was physically and mentally drained, incapable of making a stand against him and nor could I contemplate any aspiration to fulfil this impasse. I feared nothing I could create, even if having the necessary strength to do so I would foil his menace and this he must have known.

"Where is your might wizard?" his voice boomed with resurgence.

"In my heart," I replied "in my passion and in my soul."

My response was immediate but hollow and the Laddian's perceptiveness of my predicament gained him confidence.

I wanted to stop him but could not summon any more potency and clutching the bones proved pathetically futile. Fleeing from him would be pointless too for he would cut me down instantly, and in bewilderment, turned and looked for Matlock or Fallan or indeed anyone to assist me, but only the dead and dying remained. The Laddian approached closer and I could almost feel his breath. He hesitated and stopped as if with renewed apprehension before delivering his final swipe of his blade. His following words shook me as he relaxed his sword to his side.

"I fear your death more than your existence realmsman and wonder what torment you are capable of if I were to slay you."

"Many things," I submitted with immense relief, "things far stronger than any mortal's imagination."

"There is within you something more potent than I envisaged, something deeming to dominate my purpose, as if possessed by another sense and I admit it is all I can do but comply. I cannot kill you and leave myself exposed to your fury."

His admission to my powers was unexpected and perplexing, but exceptionally welcoming.

"Then you would be wise to turn away," I said.

The Laddian shrank his head into his shoulders in preparation of smite.

Of course, I would haunt him and his confederates until banishing all deceit, wickedness and needless death thus associated. Attack them when they could offer no resistance to me, go to them in their moments of loneliness or when sleep their only sanctuary and drive them to despair in a continual nightmare.

"Go!" he demanded. "Walk away from me before I have change of mind."

His empathy bewildered me for I am the warlord's most ardent adversary, I should be killed without vacillation, not allowed to leave. If his words were founded then I could only conclude fear was within him and the greater compulsion.

My eagerness to leave must have reflected in my pace for though my legs felt like leaden anchors, I briskly stepped back along the bridge toward the burning town. I tried to restrain myself by attempting to demonstrate an air of composure and confidence but failed, I contested with my urge to turn and look back at him as well as fighting off my compulsion to run. Slowly as dared, I walked under self-restraint until the wooden planks of the bridge finally conceded to muddy ground. I relied on my staff to aid my weakness and wound through the deserted smouldering streets caring not to linger at the decimation of the battle. I had witnessed it before and this instance was no different. Fires raged, engulfing buildings, fuelling the flames for its hungry continuance with putrid wafts of burning flesh stifling my breath. Groping hands of dying realmsmen feebly grasped at my sodden and tattered robe in attempts for salvation, calling my name and imploring me to help deliver them from the inevitable.

It pained me to listen to their pathetic whimpers but I needed to be stern, stopping to aid one would lead to helping others, much as I loathed ignoring them. I had to rejoin Matlock and Fallan to engage in strategy, stopping now could unwittingly be surrendering the kingdom, and everything strived for would be in vain. I could not save them all and who was I to decide who shall live and who shall perish? I did not want that responsibility for it is God's work and his alone. The best I could offer them was prayer, this I did whilst staggering through the town, offering my free hand that ached, making the sign of the holy cross so many times. My mind became weary too, repeatedly declaiming prayers of salvation.

It seemed an age passing through Belthorpe and not until the sun shone through the distant trees piercing my eyes, did the realisation strike that my current nightmare had concluded. I stopped and turned back, looking at the distant plumes of smoke rising up into the new day's calm. Alas, Belthorpe no longer existed and the wish tower had collapsed and sunk to the ground without resistance, inexorably succumbing to the madness of this absurd war.

I was ambivalent of my feelings, physically enervated and unable to sustain my own weight. My chest was splitting with the hurt from the acridity inhaled and my cough reinstated its clench, hindering concentration to any importance I ought to have been considering. I surrendered willingly to my fatigue and fell to my knees releasing my ebbing grip on my rod. If the enemy regrouped to find me now, let them, for I had no defiance left within me, nor did I have a care and the force once inspirational truly forsaken. My mind felt saturated with the emptiness of confusion unable and unwilling to grasp any reality or projection, content to waiver everything for a respite from the cankerous expectations demanded of me. In my current perplexity, the insignificant wonderings deserved no justification of being like the welfare of Newing, why should I possess any concern for him, for he is irrelevant now and only hindered my appeal. Others too with similar unimportance; the remaining councillor bound in the dingy room, what of he? His bodily odour though familiar, still lingering in my nostrils, elusive and distant from recollection and of Mullyfoddy, what of him now, was he still searching for Tolin?

'Tolin!'

My sudden recall of the boy dispelled the absurdities churning in my head and caused me to jolt. Then others precipitated Hebren, Maddox, the beautiful hierophant, Matlock, all of them, even the fox and Treggedon. I felt a sense of shame not recollecting my master first for he deserved it above anyone. No doubt, he witnessed my deep remorse and that was punishment enough.

Slowly I rose, relying once again upon my staff to lift my weight. I glanced back for the final time at what was once Belthorpe fully expecting the marauding throng of Laddians dashing through its dying embers, but with the assurance of their wanting moved on apathetically. With the encroaching day, there would be no Laddian movement until dusk and this had to be my time to reach Matlock. If I were to be alone at nightfall then I would be as good as dead. Having the fortune of meeting an adversary scared and witless does not occur twice and the next Laddian I encounter will not hesitate in killing me.

Though there were ample hours of daylight, I feared my pace no match to the enemy and no matter how far I progressed, the Laddians would be upon me before the stars set. I had to devise a method of distraction in order to give the refugees some chance of survival. The path they led was an obvious one, wheel trenches and discarded belongings left a trail even a blind man could follow. I drifted eastward, fringing the wood until it met the hills of Drin where the road divided.

I was hardly a mile along the northern way before my ears responded to their babble and sensed disappointment they only reached this far, though a little unjustly perhaps to expect them to have ventured further. I called out to the hoard and it was not long before Fallan and Matlock dashed to greet me. To say they were surprised to see me is an understatement, Matlock with his compelling enthusiasm hugged me as if a long lost brother and Fallan shook my hand so vigorously it brought back the stinging pain of the nettles. We found space in an open cart toward the front of the vacating journeyers and the three of us sat together plotting our deeds. I told them my account of the conflict at Belthorpe, as did my two friends, but was more fervent to learn the truth behind Ebden's betrayal, which almost ended everything, including me, and this was the way of it.

Matlock had dashed into the shadows of the thicket at the approach of Ebden and Fallan's wagon, unaware I lay unconscious back along the way. He assumed I too would have evaded them and if awake would have done so readily. He decided to enter Dunleigh where he quickly won their favour, then took them several leagues north before backtracking in

David Greely

search of me. Needless to say, by the time he returned onto the road I had been found by the two travellers heading westward back to the clutches of the Laddians. He assumed I made haste to Belthorpe and continued easterly. He was astute enough to realise my failing to reach there, confirming something was amiss. He waited beside the bridge and slept, missing my crossing aboard the cart with Ebden; in fact, it was the rumbling of the wagon's wheels that stirred him. He met with Fallan shortly after and having forced my plight from his lips changed his tactic. He and Fallan overheard Ebden's conspiracy with Weigel, which brought about by the change of council's membership and on the night in the alehouse, Ebden did not go looking for his partner but schemed with Weigel to arrange my termination for a handsome price.

This confirmed someone knew of my return to the kingdom, perceptibly troubled by my presence. I ought not to have felt delighted, after all, I was now worth more dead than alive and my list of enemies grew rapidly, but finally achieving recognition by becoming a potential threat to Talteth I failed to thrive upon it. I did wonder at Ebden's motive until Fallan confirmed the magnanimous payment on offer for the deed was too much for his companion to refuse. Weigel on the other hand was under instruction from an unknown and as it transpired a strong advocate of Talteth.

"Arton, I fear for these people."

"And Fallan," I replied wearily, "I fear for the whole realm."

"What is your next plan of action?" the woodman asked.

His question caught me unaware. I did not have opportunity to consider the immediate predicament and surviving my last confrontation still dwelled heavily in my mind. I lacked any resource in my current mood and only slumber would arrest this feeling of nonchalance.

"My friends, you have served me well and have done so readily, without question, but I am truly at a loss of inspiration, so let me rest now or I shall be good for nothing. Lead us north, away from our enemy and despatch the speediest of runners to tell others of our plight and get them to join us. We must get to Collington and..."

Slumber struck me. Having failed to deliver one line of private prayer to the Almighty, I drifted off without contention into a deep dream that seemed from the outset to last forever. The hierophant adorned in splendour, visited, and her soft words melted like a whisper from heaven while she sat aside me, her hands soothed my troubled brow. Although distinctly hearing her sweet manner, could not hearken her words and I floated weightlessly on gossamer clouds, trying to touch her with my outstretched hands, yet as always, a fingertip from reach, content however, just by her being at my side for it had been a long time. Then my recollection of the prophecy followed, the same prediction I witnessed, though yet to come to fruition. I felt the searing heat emitting from the burning ruin beyond, with plumes of dense smoke in a multitude of blending greys billowing out from the stricken structure. Then from this confusion, men majestically dressed, riding toward me and fearing our clash I flinched as they speedily approached. My heavy eyes remained firmly shut as I fell back into a long and heavy sleep.

The brilliance of the midday sun pierced through my eyelids, forcing me to avert my head from its sting and I torpidly raised myself onto my elbows, made difficult by the movement of the cart. The damp air incited my confounded cough forcing me to catch my breath. I laid watching in astonishment, the sight enveloping me upon waking, giggling children clung to the cart staring at me as if I was some type of freak, before turning away coyly to avoid my stern gaze. Along the narrow grassy tract folk jostled to get a glimpse, pushing and shoving in efforts to greet me. Gasps and sighs developed into a lengthening crescendo as men and women with broadening smiles bowed their heads in turn to acknowledge me. Arms pointed or waved, forcing me into a sense of nervousness and although I acknowledged them by feebly returning the gesture, I felt rather bemused by their ecstatic reception.

"Hail Arton!" they repeated unremittingly.

"Hail Arton!" beamed the woodman with his broad characteristic smile.

"What has transpired?" I asked him, rising to a seated position.

"These people are your disciples Arton and supporters of the faith," he smiled continuously.

"But so many, there must be hundreds!" I exclaimed in wonder.

"You have a powerful influence my friend," he sustained, "in fact so powerful, word spreads far."

"Is this the result of the messengers you sent?"

"Indirectly yes but whispers prove louder than shouts, and they convey the tale of the dragon, Arton, your dragon," Matlock confirmed.

Not for one moment did I envisage winning the realmsfolk by some incantation for surely they needed something far more consequential than that.

"Do they not realise it was not conjured for their benefit, I did it merely to save myself?"

"Be that as it may Arton, you have succeeded gaining their fealty."

"But so many people," I remarked.

"They have been gathering for the last two days…"

"…Two days!" I shouted in disbelief, cutting Matlock's explanation short.

"You collapsed remember? However, it is unimportant now, but what does matter is keeping ahead of the Laddians."

"How close are they?"

"I do not know," he confessed despairingly. "In fact I am not certain of anything now. Their strikes are everywhere yet we never see them, and whichever road we take they have already ventured, leaving dead realmsmen in their wake. They have regrouped and now I suspect in fervent pursuit of us. We are being stalked like hapless elks and it can only be a matter of another night's chase before we clash."

"Did turning north not frustrate their search?"

Matlock took long replying and somehow I knew I was not going to like his response.

"We are travelling east," he finally admitted.

"What!" I said, consciously muffling my shout.

"We had little choice Arton. We discovered the exiles from Dunleigh and they are dead, all of them. There seemed nothing much different, slaughtered and mutilated as always and only one lifeless Laddian as recompense. We spent time burying them; it was the least we could offer them and yet what was peculiar..." the woodman paused seemingly recollecting what he was unveiling, "...were the flies."

"Everyone associates flies with death," I said.

"Not of the like I witnessed. I mean there were thousands of them and maggots too. Corpses writhed..."

"...You need not elaborate Matlock," I resigned interrupting his report. "I have seen the atrocity for myself, I took Newing there remember?"

"If that was the evidence you showed him then no longer do I wonder why he changed his opinion."

"Tell me everything what has occurred whilst I slept, and I mean everything!"

I knew continuing east would seal our doom and felt vexed for having not being woken on a matter of such relevance.

"The first night we wandered north, as you instructed, always watching our backs for fear of their torchlight. We despatched several vanguards to send word to others and made snares to foil the Laddian advance.

We feared for you Arton, not knowing if you were going to survive. You lay so frail and still with breath so shallow as if death had stricken you. Our progress became sluggish against the terrain, we were forced to turn east in avoidance of the steep hills, it was later on when we discovered the massacre.

The sight instilled in the minds of those bearing witness to it and now they are afraid, afraid for themselves, their kin and for the realm."

"Perhaps it is good they observed such horror for words can never adequately describe testament of such abhorrence, they now have confirmation of the heinous capabilities of our foe."

"Perhaps," sighed Matlock, unsure of my words and preferring to continue his account.

"During the night we saw the torchlight illuminating the valley behind us and somehow we managed to retain our distance, by the following day needed rest. We knew to keep moving but fatigue was all too overwhelming, most of the day became depleted in idle complacency with talk of your dragon, then bands of realmsfolk straggled in adding to the ambience and increasing the incitement of the people. Word has spread of the Laddian invasion, though more pleasing they acknowledge you because 'Arton and his dragon' is on the lips of folk. They believe that you alone can save them."

Matlock's words were welcome and encouraging though not for the recognition I thought deserved, for that in itself would be sufficient, but for Ulcris and his allies in verifying to them of my return to the realm and better still, the words uttered across the land will filter into the ears of Talteth.

"The next night was strange," the woodman proceeded. "We fully expected an onslaught but nothing happened. With little progress during the day we should have been overrun by the time fullness of the moon shone, yet there was nothing, no torchlight not even a distant flicker and certainly no sound that would indicate their accumulation. The council led the old and feeble and Fallan with me, the main contingent. We weaved through woodland and over knolls in an effort to locate the enemy and surprise them. Not knowing their whereabouts was worse than witnessing their confounded torchlight. Each hamlet either laid abandoned and dwellers, already with us or burnt to the ground, with inhabitants strewn like blooded and discarded rags. We feared our advancement wondering what atrocity would greet us next."

"You have my word Matlock; the enemy will pay for this dearly, I swear it so!"

The woodman was right, the people did need some affirmation and they looked upon me as their mentor, yet inwardly I held reservation. The culpability of the lives of so many people was testing me, what reputation had I if my judgement faltered and my influence lead them to suffering or death? I would become no better and certainly reviled more so than the foe. I needed time to deliberate and the wanting to clarify, if only to myself what the priority should be.

"Where is Fallan?" I asked him.

"He rides at the rear, aiding stragglers."

"Then get word to him immediately, it is time to act. We shall hold council, the three of us."

The woodman sprung to my directive and within moments, disappeared into the throng swinging his axe over his lethargic shoulder.

In the incessant drone, my mind spun in ambivalence at the calling of my name and the noise was overpowering, so much so that I had to act in an effort to abate the din. I rose unsteadily, which fuelled their shouts to a pinnacle instead of quelling their excitement. While glancing at them I turned full circle in the cart with arms aloft, appealing for calmness and at this moment, Matlock returned with Fallan. I greeted the traveller warmly before instructing them both to re-board.

"We must get moving for night will soon be upon us."

On my warning, Matlock signalled to the populous and without any rebuff the exodus continued to move eastward again.

"Do you have a plan?" Fallan asked.

"No," I replied, making room for him on the cart, "well at least not quite yet. My primary concern is for the people and others who join. Somehow we have to get them to safety, and very soon, because if my theory is correct tonight maybe the last battle for most of them."

"If so is it not then pointless running?" Fallan pressed.

"Instinct I suppose."

"What is this 'theory' of yours Arton?" urged Matlock "Have you seen the outcome of tonight?"

"There are visions yet to transpire and all I can say is my survival is secured for the immediate future, but alas cannot give neither of you two the same assurance. Yet it is possible to survive if we can somehow avoid the Laddians."

"But how?" prompted the woodman.

"By putting ourselves in the same mind as the enemy. Attacking and chasing as a mass no longer holds their element of surprise. The Laddians know, word of their arrival will reach every corner of this land soon and they will adopt a very different strategy. I suspect they have divided into smaller groups with the purpose of stopping us from reaching Collington. They know I need to get to Ulcris."

"Impossible," Fallan contended.

"There is deceit among us, someone knows of my purpose."

"It is common understanding where we are going," remarked Matlock, "the Laddians could have heard it from anyone."

"True enough, but few know of my tryst with Ulcris."

"Are you suggesting…?"

"…No Fallan I am not suggesting anything. You and Matlock are noble friends and proven your loyalty to the Good Lord and me, but there is someone who needs finding and eradicating, someone I have overlooked. We must be vigilant in all we say and do from this moment and let no man, woman or child for that matter ever hear of our intent."

After a brief ill-fitting silence, Fallan proffered his candidate.

"It must have been Ebden, he knew of your plan as much as I."

"Yes, but to my awareness he never met up with any Laddian."

"Then it had to be the sheriff," he offered.

"He is unlikely too. He never had opportunity and until his collusion with Ebden, did not even acknowledge my existence. No, there has to be someone else. Somebody we have not yet considered."

"How are you so certain about this?" Matlock asked.

"Because woodman, I have seen fear in the eyes of our enemy. Until now, they were content to crush whatever lay in their path like ants marching unremittingly, devastating everyone and everything obstructing their way. God knows we have all been witness to it, yet now they detract from their original purpose and change their method by simply hunting us down. They intend to stop us and unless we plan an escape, they will succeed.

Come Fallan you are much travelled, where can we seek sanctuary?"

"Arton, there is no place I know in Aeria to hide such numbers."

I turned to Matlock who shook his head disapprovingly before having chance to repeat my asking to him.

"Then we are damned," I conceded.

"Lord?" said the boy popping his head over the back of the cart.

"Ablett!" I shouted incredulously, stopping the woodman from swinging his axe at the lad.

Not that I doubted his endurance but reaching me through the mass and sneaking up undetected, did surprise me.

"Lucky you are known to Arton or you'd be headless by now," said Matlock, dropping his weapon. "How long have you been listening?"

"All but a moment sire," he replied timidly, keeping pace with the cart. "Forgive me my lord for I meant not to eavesdrop but I know of such a place."

I grabbed the boy's arms and with assistance from Matlock pulled him aboard the cart.

"Do not hesitate lad, where is this place?" I asked.

"The Steps of Fellingfay," he said.

Fallan openly laughed at the boy's suggestion.

"There is no such place; it only exists in the minds of romanticists. Arton it is a place of invention and impetuous whim."

"Believe me," insisted the boy, "I know it is exists, I have seen it!"

"Nonsense!" Fallan reiterated with insurrection. "You would be advised to scorn at the lad's ego Arton."

"Let him have his say Fallen and I will make assessment. Now then Ablett tell me more of this place."

"Sir," he responded sheepishly after the traveller's rebuke and certainly with loss of enthusiasm. "I know not who believes or what the place signifies but it is real for sure. Some say it leads to the heavens."

"Where is this place?" Matlock asked.

"Not ten leagues from here. See that ridge?" the lad pointed over my shoulder. "Beyond it lays the haven you seek. A narrow cutting between rocks trails down into a small valley surrounded by steep cliffs and is easily defendable."

We looked westerly at the gentle rise but it offered nothing in evidence.

Ablett's brief description intrigued me as to what the place may imply but if it were a holy shrine, Treggedon would have incontestably told me of it. Of all the sites, monuments and tabernacles he mentioned, this one eluded me so perhaps it may have eluded him also. I envisaged an old settlement long discarded, perhaps partially sunken by the wind of change but Ablett put me wise.

"It is the lair of your dragon, Lord Arton."

"Oh this is preposterous!" Fallan upheld, shaking his head from side to side.

"On the contrary my friend the dragon is to come from somewhere and maybe the boy's speculation does proffer some validation," I smiled.

I had no need convincing myself, evoking the dragon was not a figment of imagination for in itself to believe in wizardry one accepts its consequence as reality, such beasts subsist within my macrocosm and therefore it is unnecessary to endorse it. Convincing others however, is, has and always will be a laborious challenge but I no longer cared for their thoughts, whether they believe or not. I had no doubt either, fear and misconception generated by my intense magic earned me respect among the realmsfolk, but alas compounded the hatred of me to the enemy.

"We shall go there and seek refuge. Woodman," I instructed, "call the councillors to a halt and let us see what lies beyond that hill. Steps or no steps, it will erase any future speculation between us."

Fallan took steer of the cart and led us off toward the ridge. The gradual rise laboured our movement enabling Matlock to rejoin us quickly. Halfway up the sharp incline we abandoned the vehicle and ventured to the summit on foot. I set pace with the aid of my pole, compelled to advance in eagerness, fuelled by my intensifying curiosity.

It was a strange place, proffering a setting illusory as any vision, whilst behind us in a green valley stood the mass of realmsfolk, afore lay a dusty barren waste surrounded by impenetrable rocks reaching to the sky; a sheer grey wall dulled the earth, setting the boundaries to condemnation, uninviting and eerily daunting. Even the sun shining high above failed to erase the cavernous and latticed shadows spread before us.

Ablett demonstrated no hesitation in descending the slope; we were forced to run because of the sudden steepness of the hill's opposing facet. Oblivious to any lurking danger or our apprehension, his sureness proved his words for he knew his aim and directed us to the descending steps. As we tentatively approached, our wariness increased when the wind suddenly whistled in sporadic gusts as if reproving our intrusion, perhaps warning us not to enter or testing our mettle to penetrate and goad us into defiance. I could show no diffidence despite my dread, for Matlock and Fallan undoubtedly looked upon me for nerve and resolve.

I followed the boy down the steep slabs, clinging to the grey walls with my free hand for steadiness. The decline, sharp and winding, cut into the sand-rock like an exhausted river bed leaving swathes of frayed projections smoothed by erosion and revealing empty chasms filled with the blackness of pitch, unconcerned of our being. Relentlessly we traversed deeper into the forbidding abyss and the dispirited taps emitting from my staff began ill comforting me. The blue sky submitted intermittently to the rock-face, finally surrendering to the hardness and as it did so, an invigorated light shone the way ahead. It opened into an enormous hollow filled with pleasantries of early autumn. Trees garnished with golden hues and stubborn fruits shimmered in the soft relenting wind, lofty grasses swayed gently like an ebbing sea, and our ears filled with the sweet melody of songbirds.

Ablett stopped and turned to me, reflecting his achievement with a broad smile.

"Here is your haven lord Arton," he said.

"Perfect," I affirmed, "and a fitting retreat for our needs."

"Lord," added Ablett, "if we dare to venture a little further I am sure we will find the Moonstairs, they lie here somewhere."

"Moonstairs?" I questioned.

"Why yes. It is reputed that within these rocks a mysterious passage leads to the Gods."

"Here we go again," scorned Matlock, stopping directly beside me.

I could see the disappointment depicted on the lad's face and quick to ease him.

"I believe you Ablett and if time availed then willingly I would seek them with you. For certainly if such a place does exist, how wondrous it would be."

"I am feeing very apprehensive," said Fallan. "We could get trapped in here."

"He's right," supported Matlock. "If the Laddians were to follow us down here we shall perish."

"Precisely…" I confirmed, "…if! Let us not forget they must tread these very same steps too."

"Meaning?" urged Matlock.

"Meaning they will have to descend one by one to filter through this narrow path and then it will be too late for them.

Come Ablett; lead our return while I consider more of my scheme."

I patted my two friends across the shoulders to re-inspire their confidence in me. It was not a matter of appearing vague for my plan was already being aspired, but a sense of distrust that one of them could be the informant to the enemy and holding such doubt prevented me elaborating more.

Our return from the gorge was swift and by dusk we were poised in readiness. I spared Fallan the ordeal of venturing back down the steps and set the woodman the task to take others and to position lighted torches in the gorge. I instructed carts, animals and unnecessary belongings be discarded before telling Nalos and Imesh to guide everyone beyond the hill and continue eastward. Once Matlock and his band returned, we sat and waited silently in hiding.

It would have been safe to reveal my strategy now and would have done so willingly but neither of them asked. I suspected their awareness of my earlier misgivings of them and judging by their attitude toward me, prepared for their rebuff and my repentance. Even if my plan were to succeed, it would not absolve my doubts of their integrity.

I sat discontentedly despite my wondering the feasibility of the Moonstairs' existence and wishing my informant would reveal himself, to alleviate my dear friends from condemnation. The uneasiness of guilt made my wait purgatory, suffering this long silence was far worse than the uncertain outcome of the impending battle. I could feel their frosty stares ripping into my flesh, tearing at my heart and perhaps deservedly so. I prayed inwardly.

I never conceived ever welcoming the enemy's approach but hearing their heavy tread, lifted my drear. It was the perfect night, with the moon's iridescence spotlighting them and their torch-less arrival gave no surprise, for it was God's very creation to shine the light for us. Oh, how they must have cursed.

Laddians in their hundreds spread across the valley and thrust up the hill toward us without fault. Immediately I recognised the warlord resolutely commanding his men at the front with enviable purpose. He noticed the distant glow beyond the rocks and darted for the stairs, leading his army with him. I feared the sudden surge of them would spill into our hide but the speed of their filtration quashed my temporary anxiety. We watched from the edge of the rock-fall, scaling higher to avoid them until the last Laddian sank into the chasm. From the height of our vantage point we broke cover, peering down to witness their confusion and anger of our absence.

I stood upon the summit flicking back my robe to free my arms from hindrance and aimed my staff skyward shouting to the heavens.

"Grant thee thy strength O' Lord and infuse thy power within me. Let me Arton, cast aside the venom tormenting your divinity, and give me the might to decimate our foe."

Although nothing apparent at first but lingering in the distant western sky, intermittent bolts of lightening began flashing and activated deafening trembles of approaching thunder. I continued summoning power as the intensity of the storm amplified, cold gusts lashed against me unsteadying my footing and transmuting into a continual gale, which forced me to recoil against the hail and sleet. My kinsmen cowered alongside rocks to avoid falling or being swept over and with my trusted staff lodged firmly in a fissure I endured to remain upright.

"Father of all heaven, unite me with your purity. Entrust me with your wisdom so I may thwart these transgressors and return the kingdom to the pureness of your creation."

There was neither gradual subsidence in the wind nor decrease in the torrent, a melancholy silence prevailed and the raging storm terminated promptly, then out from the heavens came a deafening explosion of light, so pure and resplendent I averted my gaze. It pierced the night sky like a bowman's arrow, speeding toward me in a precise and challenging arc. Hastily I turned, scrambling across the ridge calling for my men to follow, I ran frantically over the rough contours desperate to avoid the imminent collision with the bolt. Below, people watched the falling spectacle in awe, waiting eagerly as I for its effect. Another explosion broke the stillness and a crashing blast left ringing in our ears. Shards of rock splintered with the force of impact, erupting into the sky and showering onto the foe trapped in the abyss. Another bolt followed, equally as imposing as the first, pursuing the same arcing path across the sky. Still we kept running, risking our own safety by gaping aloft until the thunderbolt sent a mass of bursting boulders onto the Laddians below. I was unable to witness the devastation caused but in the suppression following the wake, contemptible groans of suffering proclaimed the severity. Cries of jubilation sang out from the lips of every realmsman, content and daresay relieved by the act of God upon our enemy before good reason had chance to defuse their merriment. Though far from satisfied every Laddian had been eradicated, it would have proven futile as well as pointless for me even to attempt abating their elation, so I resorted to walking among them with my friends, aiming for the anterior to regain initiative. I presented my rod aloft which sent a loud reverberating crack emanating from its tip.

"Tonight," I yelled, "we will journey on for soon we will reach Collington. There we will feast and rejoice the dragon."

A feast well deserved for it had been a long time and exalted roars greeted my thoughts.

We veered eastward again, treading blithely with the knowledge of the crushed foe behind us. The night could offer no ills, nor the arriving morn any doubts. We had been successful in our dogged plight and new hopes emerged within the hearts of everyone.

When we arrived at Chadwir-Gawl four days later, rumours were prolific; the exodus straggled into the town throughout the late afternoon and well into the night amid continual cheers and salutations.

"Hail Arton!
Hail Matlock!
Hail Fallan!
Hail the dragon!"

Intoxicating words indeed and stimulating to hear my name uttered from the mouths of my kinsmen: not for the glory but for recognition and final acceptance that the realmsfolk of Aeria had something to believe in, giving purpose with hope and

David Greely

dreams with aspirations - the necessary aspects for an enduring and prosperous kingdom.

Chapter Nineteen

Unfortunately, there was little time for me to wallow at Chadwir-Gawl, I stopped only to bathe, eat and change my clothing. Shaving off my scruffy beard and cutting my hair to reveal my full face again felt good.

Though some opted to stay, most were eager as I to get to the capital and continue through the borough without any diminutive respite. It was only a matter of a few more days before I would meet with Ulcris and this prospect overwhelmed any other thoughts. There were many issues to discuss, accounts to dwell upon and probe into the welfare of Hebren and Tolin, but above all these, plot Talteth's expiration and eradicate the confounded Laddians once and for always.

I gave no time of introduction to the lords and found myself apologising for my preoccupation but they understood. Appreciably Fallan acquired three horses and long after dark he and I, along with Matlock rode out onto the road leading to Collington. On our trek, woodland relinquished to open meadows and farmsteads where sheep, goat and cattle idly grazed. Furrowed fields clung to the hillsides, ploughed in readiness for the following spring's sow; a wonder, considering the recent turmoil but then again, being close to the city harboured a safer emphasis on the way of life, unlike that of Vledor Beacon where exposure and isolation was always more likely.

Caer Marweyn was a night's ride equidistant from Collington, once a fine fortress, now laid a forsaken vestige. A forgotten glory impetuously disowned and solitarily abandoned on the tor overlooking the newer city. This was the kingdom's heart and sanctuary of the east for hundreds of years past. Many battles had been won here, its grounds a sardonic grave for those that fought and died for the cause. A ruin is all that remained as representation of a formidable stronghold and hardly sturdy of withstanding another winter.

Sad, so sad are we, the people too dispassionate of our heritage, what would we have become if our ancestors had not built such a remarkable place? Its importance then to repel all threatening enemies so willingly yet now a desolate site, not even warranting a man's second glance. I felt humble and sad for it, so much so, I could not pass it by, however earnest my need to meet Ulcris.

"Where are you going?" Fallan called.

"To the Caer," I shouted back, spurring my horse into a full gallop and leaving my friends behind.

I rode like lightening, unconcerned if they chose to follow and dismounted when arriving at the base of the decrepit wall. I remained motionless for some while staring and imaging the fortress in all its distant splendour. The darkness of night failed to conceal its ambience and large banners rippling in the breeze heralded the king in attendance. Arbereth's army heavily engaged in duties they felt honoured to serve, their horses donned in refinery unequalled to others in the land, battlements alive with sentries willing to protect their king, their castle and their realm. Minstrels and bards full of voice, skilfully rendering their crafts to those assembled within the hall. Tables saturated in a plenitude of meats and fresh vegetables accompanying the best ale and wine in a gluttonous magnificence, and least of all, a hearty fire raging against the cold, forcing subjects to move away from its heated roar. Merriment that never waned, dancing that never stole the breaths of the participants and singing that echoed from the hall, out beyond the castle, stretching down the long hill.

I considered what kings resided and what lords and ladies had come to honour their ruler. Arbereth would be one candidate for such acclaim here too, with Treggedon seated at his side deeply engrossed in schemes, relaying in his mind their outcome before presenting them to his king and then smiling, if only privately, at the artfulness of his success. I sat beside him on a stool similar to the one at the apothecary, content on studying him to learn his traits and master his proficiency at the art of wizardry. No one will ever know how resourceful he was, no one except me.

My reflection adapted to the raging fire of my vision and out from the flames came those ghostly figures shrouded as before: pristine, vibrant and full of purpose, galloping toward me on saddle-less steeds with manes quivering in slow exaggerated animation, and behind them the exhausting furnace of a raging battle, engulfing the stricken castle with its blaze. Still the riders pressed at me, forcing me to evade from their course...

"...Is all well my lord?"

I cursed secretly at Fallan's intrusion.

"Everything is fine," I confirmed.

"Then perhaps we should get to Collington."

"Yes," I sighed weakly, "perhaps we should."

I returned the bones into their pouch, pondering how I managed unwittingly to clutch them.

Chapter Twenty

Our arrival at Collington the next afternoon was not aspiring as hoped although word preceded our coming sure enough and frenzied preparation for war was strongly in evidence. Detachments of horsemen galloped up and down the waysides taking little care and thought for other users, the bell constantly ringing from the wish tower ingested the shouts of command and the furore of the city folks' consternation. Obsequiously, commoners burdened themselves with their dearest possessions, striving for the shelter within the city's walls only to have them cast away by the vetting guards making space for others. Babies wailed and women openly sobbed for dread of the Laddian coming. Dogs barked, asses brayed and fowl flapped in a persistent tone of discontentment heightening the cacophony of disapproving treatment. Scuffles between folk broke out in the disquiet causing further anxiety among them. We rode in the midst of it eager to seek council with Ulcris, fending off the grasping hands prepared to steal our horses, fighting to remain upright and not be dragged to the ground and trampled on. The main gate echoed the madness and the swelling crowd refused to let us pass through. Fallan's demand for entry was denied as too the woodman's.

"Can you not do something Arton?" implored Matlock.

"Such as?" I reproached.

"Cast a spell or something and get us through."

Apart from feeling incapable, my agitation at this moment would not allow me to do such a thing.

"Come," I shouted to them, "this way."

I pulled hard on the reins directing my horse off the road, forcing a way through the throng, along the base of the perimeter wall and continued tracking it almost until encircling the whole periphery. On sighting a guard high in the battlement, I called out to him.

"We need too seek council with Ulcris. Let us in." I ordered.

"And who are you to demand such privilege?" he asked.

"Arton," I replied, "Arton of Wendatch."

"Denied!" countered the guard sharply. "Anyone can use his name, besides the lord is already in council."

"I demand you let us in," I shouted again.

"Take your turn along with the rest. Best you hurry now there is little room for many more of you," the guard laughed.

"I am in mind to put pay to your tone!" Matlock shouted in recalcitrance.

"You have to get to me first!" the guard goaded.

I had not seen the woodman so incensed and in his rage he drew the axe from behind his shoulder ready to throw it at the laughing sentry.

"Stop!" I instructed, seizing his arm. "That will not be necessary Matlock."

His fury turned on me.

"Let me be Arton, I will not be treated this way! Who is he to deny us the right we have earned?"

"We shall gain access," I assured the woodman, "put your axe away."

David Greely

I did not doubt Matlock's ability of killing the guard, even from this range, he was quick and keen and had it not been for my intervention the kingdom would have been one man less in the fight against our foe.

I pointed my stave's tip at the wall and instantly a chasm opened before us.

"Here is our entry," I said. "Well, stop gawping and let us get to Ulcris."

We rode through singly, me with the satisfaction of my instantaneous spell followed by Matlock and Fallan in state of apprehension. Once through, we dismounted, our horses were readily grabbed by the fortunate and we walked among the multitude toward the inner chambers. The heavy cordon of guards around the keep's entrance made ready their pikes at our approach.

"What do you want here?" demanded the first guard, curtailing our rapid steps.

"Council with lord Ulcris," I replied.

"He is occupied," he said curtly.

"Then can you get word to him?" I asked.

"Impossible, he is not to be interrupted."

"I must speak with him. I am Arton of Wendatch."

"You don't listen do you? Now be off before me and my men cut you down!"

The guard's agitation set his cohorts into uneasiness and in turn, pointed their weapons, primed to lunge. Matlock was still incensed and in preparation for dispute clasped his axe. I turned around as if making to walk away before spinning back on my heels and making a dash at them. Fallan, smart to accept up my ploy, darted beside me with sword raised and the woodman, though reacting somewhat slower, swung his axe aloft. I rammed my rod into the gut of the first guard and made him collapse against the door. The traveller deflected a swing from a pike and followed immediately with a swipe from his sword severing the defender's arm. Before the other guards could react, we gained entry into the keep and rushed up the steps daring not to look back. Shouts of contempt wailed out along the lengthy passage, reverberating against the walls behind us.

"Stop!" shouted a guard running from a doorway ahead.

"Too late!" Matlock chortled and barged him over with his axe.

We continued running, climbing more sapping steps still at the far end of the passageway and with tiring legs ascended them. Frantic cries of disdain trailed us and the clattering of weapons sent deafening peels of wanted attention, acknowledged by the arrival of additional guards. Having ventured through a set of double doors, we met our reward and Ulcris, with his back to us, stood gazing haplessly out of a narrow window, beside him was a tall willowy man scowling upon our incursion.

The spacious room felt welcoming enough and identifying the king's colours, be they sparse hanging on the far wall, assured me I was amidst loyalists. From the ceiling a dulled iron candelabra with nigh-spent wicks hung heavily, directly below it an assortment of caskets and coiled maps lay spread indolently on a huge table stretching the entire length of the room, and beside it, elaborate armed chairs with tasselled bolsters awaiting occupants of importance.

"What is the meaning of this outburst?" the thin man appealed, drawing a dagger from his belt.

Directly on voicing his enquiry the pursuing guards barged through the door and surrounded us. The Druid turned to face me.

"Lord Ulcris it is me, Arton!" I declared excitedly.

The Druid glared at me reprovingly as if doubting he had heard me announce my name.

"Arton?" he questioned sceptically, taking a few paces closer as if to inspect me.

The guards were swift to overwhelm us and their blades threatening to pierce our throats forced us to relinquish our weapons.

"Wait," he instructed, "let him speak."

"It is me Arton," I established once more.

"Come lad, let me look at you."

The Druid favourably nodded and my captor released his grip from me. I collected my stave and walked slowly toward him.

"It is good to see you lord Ulcris for it has been a very long time, longer than wished and regrettably not under better terms."

"I heard of your coming lad, is this really you before me?"

"Of course," I smiled, approaching him, and then we both readily embraced.

"But you have changed so and look here," he said, grasping the tip of my master's staff, "is this proof you are now a wizard?"

"Did you ever doubt I would be?"

He smirked, briefly breaking the deep scowl of apprehension upon his brow.

"No," he said promptly, "I did not mean…"

"…It has been a long time."

"Seven summers have passed," he sustained, turning his attention back through the window to look down at the court. "Seven years of continuing hardship, as each new season arrives so it gets worse and the lives of our folk tougher. I see dissension and distrust among them Arton. They are weary of hardship and discouraged by lack of progress. Talteth I fear, wins over their hearts with fickle pledges of better times and each day more give up the struggle to follow him. God, I have tried warning them but they will not listen to me, nor do they follow the Lord's way. Crop yields dwindle and worse still in the north with no heaving stocks of mutton or pig. He steals the crumbs from their very mouths with excessive taxation methods whilst advocating better times ahead. How can they be so foolish, don't they realise…?"

"…Such days are soon to be over now we are in allegiance again," I encouraged forthrightly. "I have won the heart of hundreds, why even at this very moment they make their journey here. They believe and are not discouraged."

"I note your optimism has not waned Arton thus it has to be you standing afore me."

Ulcris shifted around again with a beaming smile.

The stranger replaced his dagger and coughed, bidding for his acclaim.

"Oh yes," said Ulcris responding to the man's prompt. "This is my chamberlain Silas Inch. Silas, I give you Arton of Wendatch."

"An honour sire," bid the chamberlain, staring deep into my eyes.

'God in heaven was this him, the same sallow individual I had seen in my vision?' I kept restraint of my uneasiness giving time to assure myself it was indeed he. His gaudy tunic did little to conceal his wiry frame, nor mantle to hide his hitched lip and hooked nose. Now I was certain.

He spoke condescendingly and his mannerism made my flesh crawl, his self-assurance proved he had certainly achieved favour with the lord.

'Who is he and where does he fit within the plan of things?' I felt an urgent need to find out and peered across to Matlock and Fallan for some reassurance but neither could rescue me from apprehension.

I offered my greeting with a slight bow of my head, that he returned, and I introduced my friends.

"That will be all," said Ulcris signalling the guards to depart.

Both traveller and woodman stood uneasily, clasping their weapons.

"We have much to discuss Arton, though with little time to do so," said Ulcris.

"Indeed so," I confirmed.

"Then let us waste no time. Silas, please see to their needs."

The chamberlain dipped his head with what appeared an expression of reluctance and ushered us through the doors.

"Freshen yourselves," Ulcris called out, "but be hasty in your term, there is much we need to deliberate."

David Greely

The chamberlain escorted us along a series of short passages that brought us to our individual chambers and directly wine, bread and cheese was served along with a welcome change of clothing.

Whilst refreshing myself and eating little, I spent time mulling over the chamberlain, dubious of his values, intentions and the fresh gash to his forehead and contriving a thousand questions demanding answers. Deep in my gut, the feeling of considerable mistrust and abhorrence churned. 'Perhaps,' I considered, reflecting back to the vision at the shrine, 'he was confiding with Ulcris and if true,' I concluded, 'then my fears would soon be allayed.'

Matlock's rap at my door caught me by surprise and his entry caused my heart to race.

"It is you," I welcomed him with noticeable relief.

"Were you expecting someone else?"

"No," I replied listlessly.

"You do not sound very convincing Arton, what is wrong?"

"Nothing," I replied stubbornly.

"Come Arton, I know you better."

The woodman was not going to relent on my foreboding.

"Very well," I submitted reluctantly, "I am in fear of the lord's chamberlain. There is something telling me he is not what he portrays."

"Why should that be? He is Ulcris's confidant is he not and probably has been for some while. Perhaps after resting your mind will be refreshed and such fears of him will dispel."

"Perhaps so, but I know there is something," I sighed noisily.

Matlock was probably right, though truthfully, since the conspiracy back at Belthorpe I had lost my faith in everyone around me and even now found myself contemplating the worthiness of Ulcris, knowing I had no right to do so considering I murdered his brother. It was I who had deserted him to raise arm against Talteth alone and force him against shallow odds to wait indefinitely for my return. How was he to know how I had faired, speculating if or when I would ever return? God knows he trusted me and took me at my word when just a boy, incapable of a simple errand set by his master. Who was I to doubt him?

"Once we have spoken to Ulcris and his chamberlain you will have a change of heart for that I am sure."

The woodman's words left their mark of assurance upon me and with another sigh, discharging my stupidity I left for our council. Fallan joined us the moment I closed the chamber door and the three of us went to the lord's office. On entering, Ulcris and Silas Inch sat in deliberation.

"Ah gentlemen, please be seated," welcomed the chamberlain raising his head from a map, offering the chairs to the right of Ulcris. "Others are set to join us."

Just as he declared it so, the doors opened and in walked the final party to complete this council. When everyone eventually sat, the chamberlain rose.

"Now that we are all gathered please let our lord speak."

"This is indeed a day of good fortune my friends for here with us is an undisputed advocate of our faith. I give you Arton, Arton of Wendatch," announced Ulcris.

I lifted myself off the chair slightly and nodded to him.

"Thank you my lord. My only wish is that our meeting, again, could have been under better circumstances, nevertheless it is an honour to be here."

I acknowledged the newcomers in turn.

"Ectorus of Ipana," divulged one of the latter arrivals, standing to proffer his identity.

"My friend," I replied, scrutinising him, "this is Matlock of Scullycrag Fen," I continued, nodding to the woodman, "and to his left Fallan, Fallan of..." I paused, realising I did not know where he was from.

"...Forgive him my lords," interrupted the traveller, "Arton is right to flounder for I have never disclosed my origin. Alas I fear, I know not either," he smiled.

"Hexar of Galtuan," announced another gruffly, barely lifting his weighty carcass off his seat. "Are we to entrust ourselves upon a man who knows nothing of his own kin? Is he nothing but a bastard?"

I stood enraged at the bearded stranger, toppling my seat backwards with my knees.

"What transpires here? Who are you Hexar, to doubt the integrity of this man before you or indeed any other set around this table?"

"I think my opinion is the voice of the others present. We have learned to trust and confide in no one and names without origin certainly hold no worth here. How can it be so without first examining their credibility?" He leant back in his chair.

"Names and places mean nothing to me. Who are you Hexar? Your name means nothing to me either! And where is Galtuan, this birthplace of yours, Laddia?

Damn you man!" I contested furiously. "Fallan has done more for this kingdom than all of you put together!"

I said my words up righting my chair.

"Enough!" Ulcris shouted, quelling my rage. "Lord's please," he added promptly, moderating his tone, "let us conduct ourselves in a more congenial manner, after all are we not in this together? God knows how we have all suffered the misery of conflict and forced to endure the callousness of Talteth's rule, and let not us forget the threat of the Laddians. We all need to display our accord."

"Indeed so lord Ulcris," Inch acknowledged pathetically, and I cringed openly at his condescension.

"I think the lord's words are met with unanimous adoration chamberlain and needs little confirmation from you to say so," I said bluntly.

"Careful," whispered Matlock from the side of his mouth.

I recognised the woodman's distress but was not prepared to sit calmly and tolerate the sinewy man's slithering haughtiness and continued to speak.

"We three are here to put the kingdom to right and for what we have endured begs no man the right to question or be subject of unjust and tenuous scrutiny. I for one became fatherless, does this then make me a lesser man than any of you seated here? Perhaps you should give grace to the Good Lord that he chose to give you a place of upbringing and not allow the dread of uncertainty force you to fend alone. Either except us for what we are or fight this war alone!"

"Nebis of…" the plump man hesitantly spoke for the first time, "…well I suppose it is unimportant now but you have my support lord Arton."

"Thank you," I acknowledged, finally reseating myself.

"Well," smiled Ulcris, "now that some of us have introduced ourselves perhaps we can contend our strategy. Lord Ectorus what is your account?"

The chamberlain unrolled a large waxed map, setting weights on all corners.

Ectorus stood and began pointing out his verbal references on the chart.

"Talteth has split his forces into three main bodies; the largest company is pushing down from the north here, along the eastern coastline heading toward Illeken, his two smaller armies are encircling Ipana this very moment and will meet with little resistance. For what men I have available they now lead the common-folk south."

"Nebis?" Ulcris prompted.

"Sire," he acknowledged, "we have not as yet had any confrontation in the south. The islands prove a safe haven though sightings of Laddian ships become increasingly noted."

"Do you think this may lead to an attack from them?" Ulcris asked.

"I am doubtful sire. The Laddians are aware of our strength there, they skirt wide around the coast and head north, and perhaps they will combine in the attack on Illeken. I have sent several ships in pursuit of them but the Laddian craft are swifter and I doubt we can stop them joining forces."

"So are the Laddians in collaboration with Talteth?" I asked Nebis.

"It is my opinion, yes though my theory holds little substance."

"Like he said," Inch interjected, "it is but his opinion."

"An opinion equally met with mine," I emphasised.

Hexar needed no asking of his outlook and pounced directly on the open map with his thick hands.

"The north, as we know, is under Talteth's control from the mountains across to the eastern ocean perhaps as far south as Caer Tuan and east to Werthe. If his campaign is successful then by early spring he will reach Collington."

"Then we pray the oncoming winter is harsh and long," concluded Nebis.

"Arton?" Ulcris urged me.

I rose from my chair and deliberated the chart in depth, searching for the places of recognition and plotted my course, leading me to Collington. I met my conclusion in silence and with dread at the closeness of Talteth's armies.

"Matlock and I first saw the Laddians here at Vledor Beacon," my forefinger stubbed the canvas at the town, "and since that day they have moved steadily eastward across land. Despite our heavy stand at Belthorpe, they continued and we later trapped them at Fellingfay. We dwindled their might considerably there will not be an invasion from the west for some while," I smiled, turning to Matlock and Fallan confidently.

"Where precisely is Fellingfay?" quizzed Inch scowling.

Although I could find no reference of it on the map I pointed to its proximity.

"Impossible!" the chamberlain contended bending over the chart, "you must be mistaken, perhaps it was another place. Caer Emec maybe, that lays close to the rocky valley. I have ventured most corners of the kingdom and Fellingfay does not exist, other than in the mind of dreamers."

"Then my lord Inch, I am a dreamer," I retorted, looking directly at Hexar.

"What of Fleddon?" I asked him.

"Decimated by Talteth's men and nothing standing is fit to house a rat. The town was wiped out within two days."

"When?" I entreated, feeling the surge of concern for Hebren and the boy overwhelm me.

"Early summer last year."

It was ill news and my fears for them struck hard for if they had escaped surely they would be here with Ulcris now. I felt my insistence for them to wait for me at Fleddon now proved to be completely senseless and my delusion finally over, that they were dead because of me.

The woodman sensed my sorrow and consoled me in the moment of need.

Fallan with sensitivity spoke to excuse me.

"Arton had two dear friends at Fleddon, a man and a young boy."

"There is no time for sentiment lord Arton," endorsed Inch curtly. "We have all suffered loss of some degree and undoubtedly we will suffer more."

"What are you man?" Fallan raged. "So heartless, that not an ounce of emotion exists within you?"

"Precisely," the chamberlain confirmed unmoved. "I have no room for sentiment and nor can there afford to be. Compassion is for fools and fools will not win our battles."

Though I harkened his words I could not contrive a way of dealing with them and left the traveller to challenge.

"Then if compassion be your lacking lord Inch, where is your love for the kingdom? For their can be no love without compassion."

"There exists a difference between love and honour my friend. To love is to worship and to honour is to serve is it not? No man can have room for love."

"Then I take pity on your indifference," said Fallan raising his tone, "for a man without love in his heart possesses a desolate and lonely soul."

"This is leading nowhere," conceded Inch. "Let us just beg to differ, but I will say this to you lord, lord of nowhere, let us see who will be the survivors amongst us, eh?"

"Now I see why you wear a scar Inch!" shouted Fallan. "I speculate your attitude has led to it. Has someone thwarted your tongue of late? For if not I shall!"

"Enough!" Ulcris's demand brought their pathetic altercation to an immediate curtailment and in the subsequent silence I regained my composure.

I felt anger toward the chamberlain but pressing further conflict with him would not resolve the dilemma nor would it create better harmony between us. He was wiser with his words and an argument I would have to surrender to if it were to continue.

"Obviously we are failing to establish our feelings and thus think it wiser we conduct this another time. Arton and your two friends, I know you are tired and deserve rest…"

"…Lord," I interrupted Ulcris, "may I be bold as to seek a request?"

"Arton?" he doubted.

"I have promised my followers a feast this night; will you help me honour it?"

"What foolishness my lord!" blasted Inch.

"On the contrary Silas," contended Ulcris, "I think it warranted. It will also mark the return of Arton."

"And for me," I added, "it will reward the people for their show of fealty and courage. For without them Collington would now be engaged in battle."

"Then tonight it will be. Silas please arrange it," declared Ulcris.

"But sire there are far too many people."

"Do not trifle with excuses," maintained Ulcris, "let it be so. It will also be an opportunity for me to speak with them. The people are in need of guidance and I shall address them accordingly."

"Very well my lord," complied Inch resentfully.

All too soon, our meeting expired with no outcome established and we all rose save for Ulcris, vacating his room.

I chose to remain alone in my chamber excusing myself for the need of sleep. I closed the door and flopped heavily on the bed face down and though the urge for slumber pained my eyes, fought back and turned staring up at the ceiling. Daylight expelled itself succumbing to the inevitability of the night and with it, blackening shadows substituted the objects that in the light of day were innocuous, yet now filled me with nervous dread. I feared this night equally as any night isolated in the forest, vulnerable and ill at ease, festering in the sorrow of Hebren and Tolin, cursing my decision by allowing them return to the realm and sending them to their deaths. I tried recalling sweeter memories but the thoughts of them returned clawing at my stomach like waves of mordancy, begging for attention and forcing upon me the unrelenting vexation of guilt. For hours, the sensation continued remorselessly and condemned me to the torment in penance for my cruel misjudgement. My weariness eventually brought Silas Inch to mind; the odious man cared for nothing other than himself and what of his principles; was I mistaken prejudging him or had my scant vision swayed my logic? If he were a misrepresentation of the faith then surely Ulcris would have seen it and undermined his purpose accordingly.

I resolved to speak with Ulcris alone and without interference, an opportunity to recapture the acuteness of our plight and cast aside any undesirable speculation from others. I knew what needed accomplishing and had that purpose instilled within and be it alone or not, no one would prevent me.

I rose abruptly from the bed, slouched over the water basin and waited for an inner signal before dunking my head into the cold water. The refreshment diffused my feelings of confusion.

The woodman and traveller had already vacated their rooms and with enthusiasm to join them I dashed to Ulcris's chamber. He too was absent so I assumed he accompanied them to the hall. The two guards made way for my entry, on opening the doors I was greeted by a resplendence that up until this moment went unsurpassed.

Wendatch even in its days of majesty, held no comparison to this. Files of benches bordered the lengthy hall and amassed between them and the walls, ranks of trestles and more wondrous, a spectacle I thought I would not bear witnessing again, the Almighty's colours emblazoned on every pillar toward the pre-eminent table. The richness of crimson and the blackness

David Greely

of the eagle so bold and proud stood out like a guiding light, renewing my belief in Arbereth and his realm and more essentially reinstating my faith with the Lord.

Ulcris was quick to greet me and gestured for my presence beside him. To my left sat Matlock and Fallan, to the right of Ulcris, Inch and then in turn, Hexar, Nebis and Ectorus.

The hall filled with countless aromas including meat and boar, goose and mutton arranged in front of us, trimmed with a host of roasted vegetables. Exotic fruits the like I had never seen expelled their sweet scents and pitchers of ale and casks of wine filled every available space on the table, yet there was something else. Within these delectable wafts, mingled the heady and slightest fragrance I swear was woodsuckle.

Ulcris and I sat for best part of an hour giving our accounts of the lost years between us. He showed his surprise at my survival in Laddia, almost dispelling my tale impossible and my magic it seemed was the hardest attribute he failed to comprehend. Meeting up with Mullyfoddy and my pitiful addiction I preferred not to disclose to him, nor too my continuing vision of the riders galloping out of the flaming ruin. It was not so much a matter of privacy but if I was yet to understand its significance, there seemed little point in telling him. When giving my chronicle of my escape from Wendatch I changed the dialogue, stating I had stolen Elcris's animal and cart whilst he slept. Admitting I killed his brother was all too irksome and knew I would have to face some consequence from him. My falsehood he accepted without doubt.

Inwardly, I was astonished at the Druid's accomplishments for he reached far and beyond even my optimistic expectations. He strived to gain fealty from the lords in the south, this only came to fruition with the help of his chamberlain. It took him the best part of three years to gain residence as lord of Collington, and with the arrival of Silas Inch another three years to build the strong trust of his followers. The most difficult of tasks he explained, was winning the confidence of the common folk, justifying his actions and instilling in them the deviousness of Talteth. Though he could never substantiate his mandate, they gradually accepted his claims, all of which were proving true. He continually acknowledged his chamberlain's assistance in acquiring all his achievements.

I turned and gazed at my two friends, feeling overwhelming guilty and penitent for allowing the wave of mistrust to fall upon me and drown the worthiness of them. They both endangered their lives for my cause without force and neither of them displayed much scepticism of my actions. I wanted forgiveness for such irrational thoughts by embracing them and display my deep misconceptions. Matlock caught me staring at him.

"Everything well?" he asked.

"Indeed so my trusted woodman and in God give grace to you and Fallan's friendship for what would I have become without you?"

"Kind sentiments Arton but what brings this on, the ale perhaps?"

"Certainly not!" I contested smiling. "I just thought it a fitting moment to express my feelings. Take it willingly for I do not show adoration often."

"Indeed not and thank you kind wizard," Matlock grinned widely.

He turned his head to Fallan and I assumed he repeated our brief words because the traveller bent forward returning his smile.

Expressing my emotions gave me a warm glow and it defied the chamberlain's earlier tasteless words. Man does need love in his heart and it felt good to embrace it.

Ulcris's bard Astithium took all our attention and his harmonious music pulsated through the hall quelling the noise prattled by the revellers. He sung of days long past and praised Arbereth in his prose and to my amazement followed a song of the dragon, my dragon.

"Especially for you Arton," said Ulcris.

I sat and remained speechless until its end and upon conclusion stood giving the bard generous applause.

"Now is the time my lord," Inch urged.

David Greely

"Indeed so," confirmed Ulcris rising, draining his goblet of wine.

Ulcris walked across the hall and opened the window shutters overlooking the gallery. Instantly the drone from outside pitched like a raging storm and he raised his arms aloft beseeching calm.

"People of the realm hear my words and inspire others of my telling, for in the morrow we will raise arms together and fight our foes until Talteth and the Laddians are banished from our realm. This is God's kingdom, your kingdom and a land of peace and harmony. There is no room for greed nor must there dwell deprivation. Let us make our realm pure once more. Eat heartily this night and on the new day's dawning face the enemy with contented bellies and with the Lord God in our hearts."

A rapturous furore resounded about the city and no dusty corner or deafened ear could have escaped such elation.

Lord Ulcris returned to his seat and clapped his hands to signal the continuance of the entertainment.

"Now then," he said softly, "while others revel we must plan. Let us take leave from this celebration and discuss the matter in private."

We sat around the table in the lord's chamber with two additions, Deblin of Arrinfae and Oche from the eastern isles of Wesset.

I had not considered a plan of battle and feared Ulcris would force a view without my participation. Much as I intended to give assessment, my mind became preoccupied and incensed with Silas Inch.

After their short introduction, Ulcris asked the other two lords for their accounts.

"Sire," substantiated Oche, "we have sighted scores of Laddian vessels and despite regular engagement only succeeded in sinking two of them. They always out-manoeuvre us. What now transpires sets an element of confusion among us. First they sail north through the channel and without a week's lapse their boats return south again."

"Why would they come back?" I asked him.

"I cannot be certain, but perhaps they await their troop's return. It would be pointless for them to dwell at anchor where their armies land. They would have to relocate after the battle and I believe the ships lay far south, ready to rescue their army should it fail."

"Equally plausible is their continuance in ferrying their armies to the north," stated Inch. "Perhaps they will return ferrying more men."

"It is but speculation," said Oche.

"Arton?" the Druid requested.

"Well," I offered, "we have little option but to monitor their movements and cast a small but speedy vessel with the best crew to attain their objectives. We cannot possibly act on assumption my lord."

"That will take weeks if not months," the chamberlain argued, "and we cannot afford to wait. Let us head north and squash them before they are prepared."

"Aye!" supported Hexar.

"There has been no movement in the northwest domains," Deblin submitted, "thus it would seem they are going to strike directly from the north and east."

Inch rose from his chair.

"With your permission my lord, I shall ride out tonight to Caer Emec and see for myself this desolation of the Laddians that Arton claims. If we can establish they were wiped out then at least we can erase one doubt from our minds and make our strategy easier to compile."

"You still continue to doubt me chamberlain," I crossed him.

"I doubt your location Arton and because of that it gives rise for me to doubt the actuality of the enemy's destruction."

"You will never find them Inch, not at Caer Emec," I insisted.

"Oh?" he quizzed wryly.

"The steps of Fellingfay remember?" I smiled.

"Lord, give me three days and I will unearth the truth," enforced Inch.

"So be it Silas, we will not act until you return."

Ulcris confirmed his approval and the chamberlain immediately left the assembly.

"Do not mind him Arton," continued Ulcris. "Admittedly he is set in his ways but has proven himself a loyal and most worthy subject to me. Neither without his counsel would I have secured Collington nor for this long."

I chose to say nothing further. I did not agree with the chamberlain's ethics and nor did I liken to his manner.

"In the morrow we will all assess our strengths and weaknesses and make ready our departure. On the return of Silas, we will decide where our fortune and fate lie.

Now let us return to the feast. Come," said Ulcris finally.

The Druid led us back to the throng and we rejoined the festivities. A brief moment lapsed before we cast away our trepidations and me additionally, the ill thoughts of the contemptible Silas Inch and the coincidence that the redolence of woodsuckle had since vanished with his departure.

Chapter Twenty-One

I should have realised something was to occur in the depth of the night, God knows my senses forewarned me.

Despite my fatigue, it had taken me long enough to sleep and my restlessness continually disturbed me from any deep much needed slumber. Mulling over the intentions of the Laddians was paramount and found myself dithering hopelessly in a sea of speculation, considering every option springing to mind and repudiating it for yet another as it entered my thoughts. I took heart still having three days to seek answers, though at this precise moment invented a multitude of misgivings that perhaps, if I had drunk more ale then sleep could have erased such torment.

Meeting with Ulcris left me somewhat unsatisfied and in all the years apart, the time taken to grow from boy to man, I yearned for this day yet he was still very much a stranger to me and wanted to know him more, I had too. If I, the one possessing power to constitute his rule over the whole kingdom then it was crucial to find his weaknesses as well as his strengths.

"Remember," said a whisper, "man is but the dream of God."

I cared not to open my eyes. Too many situations led me to believe it the voice of my own perception, so why should this occasion be any different? Nor did I want to see the dense shadows within the room, harbouring distorting and writhing beasts desiring my very flesh.

"His eyes watch over you Arton. You must do what needs to be done."

I spoke out to the whispering voice with my eyes tightly closed.

"I need not reminding of my duty but covet for the strength of decision. Will you not honour me this?"

"Look to the west Arton and you will find the answer."

The voice diminished.

Hesitantly I opened my eyes, caring not to linger at anything too long, hoping the voice now gone, the sickening shadows of forbidding vanished with it. I groped around in the darkness and dressed eagerly. Though strongly tempted to awaken Fallan and Matlock, I deemed it necessary to myself. to prove trust in them by departing alone. If either instigated such a plot against me then it would soon unfold besides, I was compelled to follow Inch unaccompanied and only I to be a part of it. In my absence, they would confide in Ulcris and the lords and speculation as to where I ventured readily assumed.

Considering the mass of people cluttering the city streets, it remained relatively quiet save the hapless individual who chose to vomit loudly as I passed. Dying fires radiated enough light to guide me beyond the walls and out onto the westward road. I led the horse beyond the city fringe before mounting, giving it rein to a speed that would win the favour of any contest. Its hooves rattled a regular beat on the ground as I steered toward my objective, caring only to glance at the distant silhouette of Chadwir-Gawl when riding past.

Swiftly, dawn approached and I rested the steed briefly before continuing franticly on. Now daylight had arrived the realmsfolk began taking to the road again, funnelling toward the capital in an endless stream that eventually forced me to leave the easiness of the road onto the strain of open fields. With God's speed, I arrived at Fellingfay by late afternoon. I tethered the horse and traversed on foot, setting about finding the entrance to the steps. I scrambled over crumbled fissures, trod precariously along the summits and ascended great ravines, desperate to locate the dead Laddians before darkness fell. I took no respite and could not afford to, trying not to concern myself with any misgivings Ulcris believed about my disappearance, and remained forthright and confident in determination to find Silas Inch.

It is a wonder when all seems lost and futile an answer always offers a resolve. Just as faith in my endeavours all but diminished, God offered me his guidance. I slipped on loose boulders and fell tumbling into a steep ditch. I shook my head in an attempt to bring back my wits and before me were the steps. Hastily, I gave praise to the Lord for deliverance and without indecision ventured forward. The steps retained their sinister peculiarity, daring me to proffer into their depth and when descending I began questioning whether the chamberlain ever arrived, knowing his doubt in my words and the obscurity of its position but still needed confirmation for myself.

Signs of the aftermath gradually manifested, crushed bodies with deathly expressions on their faces stared up at me with gaping eyes as if judging me the guilty instigator of their horrific demise. I felt no pity for them and why should I after their atrocities upon my people and my land? Death was served upon them in recompense for their sins and by the Lord's vengeance, the method settled.

I continued my search with disbelief, finally absorbing the aftermath and trying to amass their number but there were countless hundreds and all very much dead. Thankfully, the crows had yet to discover their feast, exonerating me from a supplementary abhorrence for which would have indubitably tested me. The unrequited task of seeking the Laddian warlord was next.

The black of night hindered my chore but for light from the waning moon it would have become an unavailing task. Undaunted, I inspected the dead, apart for those all but buried by the fallen rocks, convinced no one, not even their formidable leader could have escaped the wrath of the Lord Almighty. After many hours of fruitless groping and searching, I was prepared to abandon my aim, inwardly content of the warlord's death and resigned to face Inch's cynicism back at Collington. On the first step that would return me up the steep incline, I heard whispered tones compelling me to halt and take check of its direction. Pensively, I sought the voice, daring not to breathe or tread heavily underfoot.

It was as my vision foretold, two men sitting round a small fire one with his back to me the other with the long hideous nose of Silas Inch. I knew this occasion not to be a divination and acted cautiously, dreading not to get too close though near enough to hear their devious scheme. Alas, I only heard their final words.

"Then all is set?"

"It is your excellence," confirmed the chamberlain.

They stood and gripped each other's arms before congratulating themselves with a pat on their shoulders. Inch pulled away from their embrace and turned, walking toward me, which urged me to dart off and run back up the steps in dire need to return swiftly to Ulcris ahead of him.

I rode like fury, forsaking the horse's welfare. Confused was my mind at the reason for their meeting and undeniably peeved the warlord had survived the might of God.

Daylight broke after several hours of hard galloping and at times when forced to change direction the sun shone its hot brilliance directly into my eyes. With the frantic pace, I failed to notice the abandoned cart on the road; neither did the horse and the steed let out a pitiful cry on impact, sending me crashing to the ground. I rose sluggishly, dubious as to how long I lay unconscious and gently rubbed my head, breaking my stare from the inert steed to salvage my thoughts. My contemplation of returning to Collington came immediately and though loathed to tread the distance on foot again, did not falter in restarting my tread.

The sun still shone though much higher in the pastel sky and the prevailing wind owned the bite of winter in its breath.

My aspiration of defeating Inch back to Ulcris burdened me. I was angry for the chamberlain's sedition and now prepared to kill him, the least his judgment deserved. My intuition was correct and from the onset should have condemned Ulcris's trust in him by following my conviction. The conspiracy was now unfolding in my mind and no longer a speculative accusation. My inner senses alleviated any nagging suspicions but what use now? Being wise after the event will not change what transpired.

Day drew to night and night back to day. I never took rest and forgoing fatigue and hunger, pressed on with a steady stride. The road still brimmed with commoners, most of whom were old or infirm and proceeding despairingly toward their fragile salvation. I tried to bargain with one woman for the use of her mule but grew tired of her petty negotiation and gave up. Even disclosing my name meant nothing in way of value and falling upon her unenlightened ears dispelled any such entitlement I felt due.

I was pleased to see the ruin again and dearly wished resampling the atmosphere upon its depleted battlements, and rekindle the divine resplendence if only for a brief moment, but had to press on.

The greeting when reaching Collington was equally cold as our first arrival, though on this occasion I was able to secure my rank with the minions. The walls almost heaved with expansion by the wretched citizens continuing to enter for sanctuary; these same folk eager for tidings of the enemy and selfishly wanting protection without regard for those chosen to confront and do battle with the foe.

Thankfully, Fallan and Matlock waited and were there to greet me when I entered the lord's chamber.

David Greely

"Well," I implored looking at them, dismissing their surprise at my appearance, "what has transpired in my absence?"

"Where have you been?" the woodman asked curtly.

"I will tell all but firstly, where is Silas Inch?"

"He has gone with Ulcris," replied Fallan.

"Gone where?"

"North," he continued. "Ulcris has taken up arms and gone to engage with Talteth and the Laddians."

"The fool, it is a trap!" I cursed. "How long ago?"

"Two nights," confirmed Matlock. "Inch rode in and said you gave instruction to wage battle, and that you were seeing to the last of the folk and would follow once they were in the haven of the city. Fallan and I chose to wait for you Arton, he sounded so convincing."

"My God, his treacherous tongue has no bounds. He may have long succeeded in winning favour over Ulcris, but certainly not over me!

We must despatch a rider and get word to the lord. No wait, better still, you my dear woodman, you have the speed of the falcon, you must go."

"But Arton...," contested Matlock.

"...Tell him though in solitude mind, his so-called loyal chamberlain is leading him directly into a trap. You must convince him, the realm is depending on your success."

"What if he chooses not to believe me?"

"That my friend bears no thought," I replied.

"Where did you go?" Fallan asked.

"Fellingfay to find Inch and I did, but it is grave information. He has been scheming with the Laddians and it is he who is our traitor."

"Laddians?" queried the woodman. "There were none left, well at least not at Fellingfay."

I explained the circumstance though did not reveal what little I overheard. They would have doubted my actions if I told them I heard nothing of consequence, but knew I was right and nobody was going to defy me. I just needed the answer to one question.

"Fallan, what exactly did you do to the last councillor at Belthorpe?"

"Nothing Arton, nothing other than gag him and knock him senseless. You seemed in favour of sparing him so I left him in the room on the assumption the Laddians would discover him wait, you don't think…?"

"…Yes, I have discovered the cause of our ills, it is the remaining councillor."

"Silas Inch!" gasped Matlock. "I should have known."

"We all should have done my friend and a lot sooner too," I cursed. "Why did you not recognise him?" I questioned the traveller.

"I never saw his face. I did not bother to pull back his hood. I just grabbed him by his garb, smashed his head against the wall and left him bound and unconscious. I should have killed him but it was your reluctance Arton that stopped me from doing so."

"Obviously my mistake and I was wrong ever to doubt you two. Will you ever forgive my mistrust?"

"There is nothing to forgive," reassured Fallan.

"I will make amends.

Now Matlock, you will get word to Ulcris and get him to return immediately. Fallan, gather what guards remain here and we will head south. If my assumption is correct we shall meet with the enemy very soon."

"How can you be so sure?" Matlock questioned.

I pondered briefly. In truth, I was uncertain but had to act oppositely of the chamberlain's scheme.

"Oche spoke of Laddian ships so think for a moment and listen to my interpretation. What if the vessels sail north empty but return south laden with Talteth's men?"

"So wherever they have taken port, join forces with the Laddians."

"Precisely woodman," I smiled.

"But why," he examined, "would Inch lead Ulcris and his army north if there is nobody there to engage them?"

"Simple. Collington retains only the meek and there is futile resistance here other than a few guards, old men, crones and babies hanging from their mother's breasts, hardly the enemies dread is it? They will overpower the city within a day and that my friends will give Talteth the anchorage in the south. With Wendatch in the north, he can sustain his armies, whereas Ulcris is destined to wander the kingdom searching for him. The men will lose heart and with the harshness of winter repress their loyalty, becoming unwilling to continue."

"Then we have lost," resigned Fallan.

"On the contrary," I said cheerfully, "we have the upper hand. Inch knows nothing of my witnessing his treachery and will assume we will follow his path north."

"But we don't possess an army," reminded the woodman, "and our resistance will be ineffectual."

"Have you forgotten my magic? Have you forgotten the Good Lord?"

Judging by the expressions of blankness on their faces, I suspected Fallan and Matlock gave rise to doubt.

"Collington will not be attacked for some while, at least not until Ulcris is far away. This gives us time in hand, time we shall put to good purpose. Now then my honourable friends show me some food and ale and let us steep ourselves in a deserved moment of serendipity."

Chapter Twenty-Two

In my night of turmoil, I reconsidered my plot though uncertain as to why, perhaps it was the ale or the influence of an earlier vision or even some inner intuition born from my power but whatever the reason, it was influential and compelling and would have been foolhardy to discount.

Impatient to execute my revised scheme, I rose long before dawn brushed the eastern skyline and sat in Ulcris's chamber. Setting out the chart I studied it relentlessly under the strain of a paltry flickering candle, lingering at Wendatch and Fleddon before retracing the journey from Collington back to Vledor Beacon, taking mental note of places meaning nothing and often sparing a little time romancing of their wonder. My finger trailed north, far beyond the mountains to Belscotia, which immediately brought Elberdor to mind and mused at my master's trick with my sandals back at the alehouse so many years whence. Further north still, my digit meandered idly crossing the whiteness of the linen, passing over the realm's bleakness the map interpreted and harboured on a region now very much lost and forgotten where ancestors once opposed their enemies, struggling in their countless generations to preserve their lands. I sensed a feeble wish to return if only to re-establish my roots and sample the wonderment of those antediluvian times I yearned.

Matlock and Fallan eventually entered the room, sitting silently opposite until I broke from my study and revealed to them my new strategy. Barring a small remonstration from the woodman, they accepted it.

"Fallan, I think it best you find Ulcris and under the guise of furtiveness, turn the lord's attention to Wendatch. Inch needs eradicating and I leave it to you to end his term in the kingdom. Talteth will realise our intent much too late and by then we will have secured Wendatch."

"Willingly Arton," replied the traveller.

"Matlock, you will ride out with the speed you possess and seek out the combined enemy. Find out not only their position but also their strength and purpose. Once established, make for Wendatch and rejoin Maddox and Ulcris to aid their defence. I shall take leave for Fleddon."

"But," the woodman objected, "Fleddon is decimated, you heard Hexar's account, nothing exists there any more."

"I am certain Tolin and Hebren are safe. So potent is this sense I must abide by its command and have to find them, least of all Tolin."

"With respect Arton, what purpose is it going to serve once you have found them, assuming you do of course?"

"You are right to feel apprehensive Matlock but without Tolin we will fail. He will aid us in the kingdom's future battles."

"He is but a child!" the woodman contended.

"No less than when I first set out," I argued. "He will soon become a man."

"Is this then the outcome of your vision?"

"Yes, it has been ordained so," I answered him.

Though it was not a vision, I preferred telling Matlock so. In truth, the monk gave Tolin to me and it was not just to get him into Aeria. It had to mean more, much more and I believed the lad was to play a very fundamental role, not only in my success but also in the realm's future. Find him I must.

"What of the people here?" Fallan asked with scowling brow. "We cannot possibly leave them to the whims of our enemies."

"Is there any other choice?"

"But Arton…?" Matlock supported.

"…I can only add this. Do not think for one moment I pass off my action unaffected, believe me it is painful but there is no other solution. We cannot drag them with us and it is pointless sending them away from here."

"Lambs to the slaughter," Matlock reconciled.

"It is not a sacrifice woodman; they will have God beside them."

"I wish I could share in your conviction Arton. They will be wiped out."

"It is through the Lord's guidance I have to act in this way. He will keep them safe and if what is to be will be."

My words did not convince him at all.

"Then I remain in doubt of the Good Lord," said Matlock, returning his gaze onto the map.

"Please," I implored him, "let us not fall into scepticism over this. You have always supported me and my reasons woodman, so why should this moment be any different?"

"They are defenceless and incapable."

"There is no other option for us. We cannot stay here and defend the city alone and nor can we lead them anywhere. Few will survive the winter outside of these walls and it is here they must remain. Trust in the Lord Matlock, he will provide. I will say no more on the matter, it is to be determined this way, now let us return to our preparations.

We have to assume winter will be harsh as others of late and trekking to Wendatch will be slow. There will be pockets of resistance, all of which I feel confident we can overcome.

David Greely

Do not allow yourselves to deviate from your course, not for anything. We will win through; if not for the sake of the kingdom then it has to be for the glory of the Lord. Come spring we will be reunited and prepared. I will be waiting for you my friends and should any of us falter let the reward awaiting us in heaven lift the sorrow from our failing."

"Amen," whispered Fallan softly.

"Amen," I repeated.

That was the way of it. We did not utter our intent beyond the room and later in the morning assembled provision, gained our horses and set off. As far as the populous of the city were aware, we sped to join Ulcris to do battle beside him in the north and ignorant of the ill fate looming with the approach of winter.

At good length from Collington upon the northern road, we parted company. Words were unnecessary and thus nothing said. Matlock, with an uncharacteristic air of disquiet galloped unceremoniously south, scything through the meadows that would eventually lead him to the enemy. Fallan with vigour, continued on the road to reach Ulcris, I veered west clutching my pouch of bones for reassurance, and though I waved farewell at them with my staff, neither responded. My spirits remained eminently unperturbed despite the gravity of our separate missions; I did not allow them to dampen with the feasibility of misfortune that may bestow upon any one of us.

The weather over the subsequent six days reminded me of the threat of the nearing winter and the sharp frosts at dawn left a white crust, portraying it so with shortening days of solitude and freezing nights filled with the ice of the devil's breath. It penetrated my clothes and stirred my rasping cough that for some while remained dormant. The gentleness of the even terrain conceded to forest with stubborn granite outcrops devoid of growth and exposed, as if in a morbid defiance to do battle with the elements. Travellers were a rarity the further north I drifted and though yearning for company I wanted to avoid harkening to their pitiful tribulations. They had the right to voice them of course but of what use would it have been to me?

The appearance of devastation and destruction become all too commonplace the further I rode. Wishing towers, hamlets and isolated homesteads cleaved out of woodland lay either flattened or burnt in the wake of Talteth's attacks. Mutilated carcasses of my once-proud realmsfolk lay discarded and spent, nameless and often featureless bodies left to decompose with the added willingness of the crows and their ripping maws. Strangely, my detestation of such regular sightings only motivated my urgency to curtail Talteth. I ate and rested little so intense became my obsession at reaching Fleddon.

Late in the morn of the eleventh day, I stopped at a brook, more as a priority in resting the horse than for my own need, I laid my staff on the ground beside me, stretching my aching arms in the air. It all seemed peaceful enough and a siskin's sweet melody confirmed my temporary sentiment. It had little care for me, content to flit from bough to bough discharging its catalogue of tuneful diversities.

"I appear to have caught you off guard wizard!"

On immediate recognition of the voice, dread punctured my heart. I wanted to grab my staff and swipe a mighty blow at him.

"Warlock!" I responded almost breathlessly, daring not to turn and display my fear of him. "Consequence assigns us to meet again."

I felt the earth tremor at his approach as if it too held equal trepidation of his forbidding presence.

"You travel alone. Such foolishness do you not think?" he said.

"On the contrary, do not placate yourself with what your eyes see for I am never alone," I replied, refraining from turning around.

"I see no other with you. You have lost your associates."

"State you purpose Laddian. I have no time for feeble divergence."

"Purpose?" he questioned. "I am suspicious of your intention, wizard of the realm. I have been tagging you for three days now and…"

"…You need not have isolated yourself from me, why, we could have travelled the same road together!"

"I see your effrontery has not waned."

I felt the keenness of his sword in my back.

"The time for words is over magician and so too is my search. You should have killed me at our last meeting; it has proven to be your downfall."

"Then," I said, "I will die suffused with regret."

"That you will," he confirmed, "but not yet, I have plans for you."

His words were of no comfort. If I were to perish, then let it be now with the sharpness of his thrusting blade. I did not want to become another victim of depraved suffering. I cursed inwardly at my uselessness, fearing now I had ultimately failed in my objective.

He kicked away my rod before grasping my shoulder, forcing me to turn and face him. He was ready for battle and his awesome headdress indicated so. A huge bear's skull covered his head for protection and in the confines of the open jaws, our eyes met with an unparalleled distaste. No longer respecting one another or our powers and abandoning all veneration once prevalent between us. Briefly, he turned skyward.

"I look but I do not see. Where is your dragon Arton and where is your God?"

He returned his gaze upon me, smiling in condescension.

"It seems your friends have forsaken you too."

"What of your fear of my death?" I invited. "Does it not still linger like the plague upon your mind?"

"I have studied you Arton and know your debilities. You do not possess such strength; nothing does, other than Sangal the true God, the only God! I no longer fear you."

"Then slay me now Laddian."

"All in good time wizard, I want to see you suffer first and let your people bear witness to your pretentiousness and worthlessness, to let them discover how feeble their miserable conceptions are. It will demonstrate you have no God and neither do they."

"They have seen my dragon," I contended.

"It was a dream Arton and nothing but fantasy."

I was disheartened at his transformed courage, uncertain if it was a bluff or whether he was actually untroubled by my potency, yet now I was unable to test him and there was nothing I could say or anything I could invoke to cause him uncertainty. His words were strong and full of conviction, and not persuadable. For the moment, I had to be appeased at the delay of my execution and opportunity would befall or at least I hoped it would.

Four Laddians appeared on his command and bound me tight before dragging me onto a barrow and thrown in as if an old carcass, left to dwell not just on my misfortune but also on the rankness of death harbouring within my fetid incarceration.

We trekked steadily south flanking rocky inclines, avoiding the denseness of trees that led back across the flat meadows and far beyond. I was spared nothing, neither water nor morsel for days on end. I became the subject of ridicule among the increasing mass of the enemy though tolerating such pathetic jibes, I could not withstand the punishment fast developing into their daily ritual. They thrust pointed sticks into my legs and just when I thought they tired of such abomination, drove splinters of wood through my palms, barbed needles jabbed into my fingers and left to fester. Oh, how they jeered and drank heartily at my suffering.

I could not sleep through the intense pain and discomfort. Cold pierced every part of my body adding to my sufferance, even the stinging from the nettles on my hands reinstated its fire but worst still, the feeling of overwhelming dejection, a sensation I thought I would never ever feel again. I lost control of my own fate and the sullen destiny of the realm by deserting Fallan and Matlock on the final quest of liberation. What was to be the fate of the kingdom? What was to befall my companions? What was to become of me?

David Greely

I prayed hard but never got the revocation sought. I was rankled in my inability to touch the bones and even more distraught witnessing my master's staff used like some child's toy by the warlord. I wished in all heaven the wrath of God would smite upon him but this aspiration went unanswered too. My cough gave further distress and at times, which became ever regular, blood substituted the vileness of phlegm. Unconsciousness was seizing me all too often, forcing me to weaken further and if this was the suffering the Laddian wanted me to endure, then indeed this was his moment and death, if it came now, would be the only comfort to me. Visions never came and even if they did manifest themselves, I was unable to offer any conviction to uphold them. No voices, no encouragement and no God, and left helplessly exposed without strength to witness the coming of my death that rapidly loomed.

Distant communications between the Laddians developed into a distorted drone, incoherent, superfluous and blindly meaningless. Whatever they plotted now, I had no further care for, my strength had expended and too weak even to open my eyes. I could think of nothing other than my imminent death and even the glory of meeting the Lord and my master waned. Everything fell silent.

The delicateness of the hierophant's touch stirred me, her weightless fingertips brushed my forehead so softly it felt as if silken thread lay upon me, I opened my eyes to witness her beauty. Nothing changed in her, no look of anguish or concern and no indignation of my failing, just the reflection of pure and flawless resplendence. Her glassy eyes concentrated on mine as if searching my very soul for my deeper inner self. My lightheadedness appended to my confusion of invention, unable to distinguish the occurrence. I wanted to believe in her and needed to but where was my strength and determination to aspire from as testimony? I felt her breath on my face, appealing, soft and warm as a midsummer's breeze. Her ample breast heaved delicately with each breath, un-laboured and in perfect unity. Her left hand brushed away the fallen locks from her face, revealing her satiny tinted cheek, adorned in milky flesh so chaste and bright. I wanted to respond and touch her but feared my movement would dissolve her image. I chose to remain motionless waiting for her words but she never conversed and in the prevailing silence, she persisted merely to touch my brow in a manner incongruous to anything I ever experienced. My subconscious begged for her utterance but again I grew anxious that my innermost demand would dispel her company. As if my astonishment had not already suffused, the fox approached and sat beside me with his long tongue lapping rhythmically in the air and his brush flicked once more before tucking in close to his body. His hazel eyes glanced knowingly at the gracious lady before settling with his ears twitching in vigilance for any unnerving sound. I blinked several times to allay the spectacle, trying to affirm in my mind if this was but a dream, just another inconsequent figment of imagination before my death. The fox did not bark nor did it speak and they both remained silent at my side, appeased simply to abide in vigil over me. I cared not to wonder the lapse of time, perhaps a fleeting moment, an hour or a day but whatever the term it was superfluous. It was of little importance but at this instant I wanted to relish in the splendour and evaluate their term with me. Then with all the grace of God, I saw him; at first indistinctly, just a shadowy figure drab and shabby in the hazy distance, yet I recognised him as he neared and his face reflected bewilderment as if, like me, he was unable to comprehend this phenomenon, then his knowing beaming smile greeted me. It was good to see my master again, a sight I did not contemplate witnessing until the day I reached heaven.

"Will you not speak with me master?" I whispered courageously. "I am in great need of solace."

"Rabbit," he returned softly, "dear Rabbit."

"Oh, master I have missed you so. In all the heavens I…"

"…You must fight and contest against your plight. You must win through Arton."

"I have not the strength. I am beaten and willing to concede. There is nothing left within me."

"Nonsense boy!" his words pronounced his agitation. "You have all the strength you need, just look about you."

I blinked my eyes forcing back the developing tears and examined them all in turn, first the fox then the beautiful hierophant and lastly Treggedon.

"Look deeper Arton, can you not see them?"

"Who master? Who?"

Then I saw them; Maddox, Fallan and Ulcris.

"This has to be a dream!" I cried out.

"If that is what you believe it to be then it is so but do not forget Arton, magic has influence and the strength of creation and can turn any dream into a reality. You have done it, so and I can attest your dragon. 'Arton's dragon' the people call it, resplendent and precise and something far and above any of my creations."

"What use is it now?" I questioned.

"The dragon, nothing, though perhaps in the future, it has served its purpose by saving you but there are better, more powerful enchantments needed and you can generate them. Do not forsake the kingdom Arton it needs you. You must resist and fight on. We will be at your side when the moment warrants it."

"I doubt your words master. You have not always been there in my time of need."

"Preposterous lad, have you not survived?"

"Yes, but…"

"…then you did not need me did you? Take your strength from your own potency. You have the tenacity and now I give you my assurance. You can and will succeed Arton."

The vision disseminated at the calling of my name.

"Arton? My lord?"

My eyes gradually opened fully in astonishment.

"Woodman," I sighed softly.

"Thank God, I thought for one moment there I had lost you."

"Lost?" I quizzed.

"Yes, you have been lifeless for days and as good as dead. You certainly had me fretting. It is good to see you and alive too."

"You too my friend. But...?"

"...First drink this and then I will tell all."

Matlock propped my head, holding the hot broth to my lips. It was difficult to swallow and but for his insistence I would have promptly refused it.

"Well?" I encouraged feebly, ingesting the hot gruel.

He sat beside me and poked at the small fire sending sparks into the darkening sky.

"This is the way of it," he began explaining.

"I sped south as you instructed, passing abandoned hamlets and towns. The Laddians spared some places but the further south I journeyed, evidence of their destruction became very apparent. It was dreadful Arton. Bodies lay everywhere, disfigured and maimed beyond such belief. I doubted my own eyes at such horrors and thought I had seen the worst of it but as God is my witness, nothing like that."

Matlock's account did nothing to shock me, for I too had seen it for myself.

"I reached the coast after eleven days and spent the next three searching for them..."

The woodman paused to tend the fire again.

"...You are not going to like this Arton."

"Let me be the judge," I told him feebly.

He raised his head and looked sternly across to me.

"I saw them at the mouth of the river Goule at Tane. Hundreds, thousands oh, I did not count. You were right in your presumption; Talteth's armies were there too, disembarking from Laddian vessels. I got as close as I dare without being discovered and killed a Laddian for his clothes, I managed to infiltrate among them but there was little knowledge to glean. They knew as much as I about their plans and only the coming of Talec was on their lips. Although there are others, he is their ultimate warlord and protagonist. His arrival was due and word embellished his coming with tales of his capture of the Dragon

David Greely

Wizard. I knew it had to be you Arton so fled like the devil to find you."

"So you know nothing of their plans?"

"No, nothing but I had to seek you as it was far more important."

"Where is this Talec now?" I asked with intensifying distress.

"Over there," replied the woodman, tenuously raising his arm and pointing to the tethered Laddian against a tree.

It was all I could do to raise my head and glance.

"What of his four aides?"

"Dead of course," smiled Matlock, looking at his blooded axe. "I have tried to get information out of him but he is very stubborn," he added.

Now you must rest. I shall tend your wounds again in the morrow."

I sighed heavily out of exoneration of my death and gave a short prayer to the Lord before slinking back into oblivion.

It was two days before I was able to move and in that time, Matlock tended me compassionately by changing my dressings and feeding me with his foul broth. I felt the way Ulcris must have done when first rescued from Wendatch, fully dependent and vulnerable though I did have the advantage knowing my aide.

I became increasingly vindictive toward the Laddian warlord and nothing at this specific moment was going to reward me greater pleasure than to exterminate him. No longer could I tolerate his piercing gazes, stares personifying the odium he possessed for me. No doubt, he was rueful at not slaying me sooner and the pleasure he had sought from my torture was probably too inadequate to fulfil his lust for debasement, I survived thanks to the woodman, Talec's disapproval of my emancipation displayed openly on his face.

Winter was at our heels now and even under autumn's late tread the journey would be tiresomely long, I became anxious to head north to assign with Fallan. I trusted the traveller had fulfilled my wishes by eradicating Silas Inch and had hopefully persuaded Ulcris to aim for Wendatch.

My bandaged hands restricted me no end, though stronger and able to walk I still felt relatively useless. I was complete again when Matlock handed me back my staff for it somehow regenerated me, I clutched it loosely, and with my free hand felt the pouch of bones secured around my neck with an air of humility.

"What of him?" asked Matlock, gathering his diminutive belongings.

"He is of no use to us now. If he were to escape then we would be causing ourselves further concern. There is to be no alternative," I said finally on the matter.

The woodman strolled over to the bent Laddian drawing his massive axe and with might capable of felling a mighty oak, swept his blade across the warlock's neck. The dull crack forced me to avert my gaze as his axe sank true. No sound emitted from the victim just a softened thump as Talec's head toppled to the ground.

"It is done Arton," confirmed Matlock, though it needed no testimony.

"Then let us move on," I spurred.

Chapter Twenty-Three

We rode off swiftly on our acquired Laddian horses leaving the dead warlock to the crows, heading north yet again in another attempt to reach Fleddon. The weather, in spite of being dry was exceptionally cold and the wind penetrated our chests with its cruel and scathing bitterness. We trekked most of the first night, stopping only briefly to redress my bandages which had worked loose from my hands. The woodman's pace as always, was much too keen for me and at times thought I may lose sight of him. It needed someone of his exigency of course to influence the stride, but at this moment I would not admit it.

With little time for talk between us, I succumbed to my own contemplations and muses, which invoked my recent capture, but dismissed them forthrightly now the Laddian warlord was dead and thankfully surviving my ordeal in the enemy's clutches. Issues more important needed consideration because the time of judgment neared and I was ill prepared. I recalled for a transitory moment the last vision, if indeed it was one, for even with afterthought, I still believed it reality. I sensed the hierophant with her tender fingers stroking my brow and sampling her sweet breath. I could also smell the fox and experience my master's power, something that had not occurred before. Most times I had to break away from my divinations but not this time, it was unique. My focus wandered to Fleddon and with reckless imagination, willingly invited a composition of what it had become. I spurned the chamberlain's theory of its decimation sensing it untrue, the town with its inhabitants seemed to be supportive of Talteth's regime in my term there and with this in mind, suspected it had since become another fortress, a stronghold to gather his armies and doubtlessly too, Laddian's combining in readiness to overpower the realm. My compulsion to reach there was fervent, not that I had a liking for Fleddon, why even now, I can taste the acridity of death upon my tongue, it was purely to locate Tolin and Hebren and once found, drive onto Wendatch.

After countless days, we reached the western road and I thought it wise to pass under the drape of night. The road was eerily hushed with no more realmsfolk staggering into Collington, nor Laddian scout scurrying for a victim. Perhaps there were no more people left to journey, probably all killed by Talteth's men or too fearful even to contemplate wandering in the dead of night.

We continued until dawn and took rest. The weather shifted against our favour and persisting on the northerly gusts the initial snows of winter with minor flurries turning to heavy with prolonged falls. Our fire did little to fend off the icy flakes but saving us from the chill, we slept in turn during the day attempting to strengthen our declining resolve.

Matlock's heart seemed heavy and ponderous and I did all I could to warm his spirits. I told him my chronicles from Wendatch in the summer days with Treggedon, his spells and trifling habits all of which seemed to amuse him. In a brief moment of good humour, we ate till our bellies were full of the unusually luscious stock the woodman concocted.

It was time to venture onward and return to the drudge of travelling. The density of snow drained the horses, often as deep as their flanks but we had to continue. My pains had all but diminished, only fatigue and a rattling cough gave my body concern.

I gave my wishbones renewed thought and in a brief moment of consternation gripped them firmly through my clothing, relieved to feel them safe. My attention had me theorising yet again and as with all previous speculation I could not submit an ounce of their intent. I even caught myself searching for the fox knowing he would be able to guide us but alas preferred not to present himself.

A loud clap of thunder drew my interest and I forced my head skyward to glance at God's wrath. I hoped his intention was aimed to retard our enemy and gave the sign of the cross in acknowledgement of his act.

Eventually the howling wind eased as did the snow. I yelled out to Matlock.

"We must rest the horses."

"A little further Arton. We can take refuge in the valley."

The vale of his reference was another league to the west, at least an hour's traverse but there was no point in opposing his suggestion as it would have fallen on deafened ears. I resigned myself to his objective, adjusted my tunic and sank my head deeper into its folds to stave off the cold.

The snow lay much thicker in the dell, so deep it forced us to wade by leading the horses until finding shelter in an upturned cart lodged between some trees. Matlock was quick to find fuel for a fire by breaking off the splintered spars from the wheels. Though hungry, we sat appeased, staring at the flames and estimating our distance from Fleddon.

"Another day perhaps two will lead us to Sterin," he offered.

'Good news,' I thought, 'and sanctuary from this confounded iciness.'

"And how long before reaching Fleddon?" I asked him.

"At our rate about another month," he replied despondently.

"Be cheery my good friend we have until spring and time is on our side," I told him.

"What will become of us Arton, should we fail?"

"We shall not fail," I replied, although my stubbornness did nothing to quell his distress.

"I fear for us both. With the Laddians behind and Talteth ahead, we will soon be joining the dead."

"Do not fret so Matlock. Talteth may not even be at Wendatch."

"Then why are we going there?"

"To meet with Fallan."

"But you said…"

"…I think you assumed," I said interrupting him. "There are two possibilities open to us."

"There are?" questioned the woodman.

"If Talteth is in the south then he will most certainly attack Collington to gain strength in the south. Once he has established himself he will seek to destroy us, when we ignite rumour of our hiding at Wendatch he will come and by that time we will be ready for him."

"But what if he is already there?"

"Then my dear woodman, we shall simply defeat him long before any Laddian can come to his aid."

"You make it sound so simple."

"Why complicate matters? Providing we employ the correct tactics there can be no scepticism."

"I wish I could share your conviction Arton."

"It is your cynicism that encourages me woodman," I smiled. "What would I be without you?

…No, do not tell me, dead!"

We both laughed, something lacking on our escapade of late and it felt heartening. I saw nothing wrong with a morsel of frippery within the severity of what awaited us. Our conversation died swiftly, we seemed mutually content to sit and stare at the spitting flames of the fire, deep in our own conceptions. I hoped my appraisal of Talteth's whereabouts at Collington was correct and we would win back Wendatch with some relative ease, but if the tyrant was there with his forces then perish my thoughts.

    Daylight was ending and the icy canopy of night would yet again grip our bones. Matlock saw to my dressings for the final time before setting off again. I kicked snow over the fire, it emitted an irritated hiss and subsequently a discontented ball of vapour spat into my face. As always, the woodman led but fortunately his pace was much slower, hindered by the deep snow and comforting as the rate was, I was prepared to forsake it if only to accelerate our arrival at Sterin. The horses seemed more reluctant to travel and whether the cold gripped them or fatigue, it was beyond speculation. Selfish maybe, but all I wanted was warmth, hearty food and a decent night's sleep without dream or uneasiness, just a night of uninterrupted respite.

    The long bitter night passed with drudge and without event. Cloud hindered the glow of the moon, but for the momentary break in the greyness at early dawn, it would have proved difficult to ascertain the new day from the night. So dark and daunting was the morning, both the woodman and I passed comment upon it, it seemed there appeared a new emergence and enlivened dread about it, something far stronger than either of us had attested. The hostile wind eased and the threatening snow remained aloft. Underfoot was soft and giving, and again we were forced to lead the animals. We continued in silence, preserving what little energy we possessed and concentrated on our path. Raging conflicts were beginning to confuse my sanity as hunger fought with the bitterness for attention.

    The day deteriorated and the howling gale re-emerged, whipping up the fallen snow like a dessert storm, blasting into our faces and impairing our sight. Siding up against the horse for protection proved inadequate against the frigid blasts. Then the heavens opened and snow fell in a continuous blizzard for hours; not the subtle and complex pattern of a light individual flake but a flood of grey, fused clumps falling heavy as stones.

How we managed to venture through such fury was a wonder in itself.

We secured ourselves together with a length of rein for fear of separating, although hindering our progress somewhat; it did give us the security we sought. I lost all sense of duration and could not recount how time passed before Matlock first sighted the distant light flickering high on a peak ahead of us. He smiled, cracking the snow congealed on his frozen beard.

"It is too soon to be Sterin perhaps it's an isolated homestead," he wailed against the howling wind.

It gave heart to my depleting spirit that a place of refuge somehow escaped the rampage of the war, too far north for the like of the Laddians with their destructive manner, but it meant if such a place survived within these terms of enmity then surely to God there had to be others. 'Perhaps,' I considered, 'the kingdom was not as dire as I imagined, but for how long,' was indeed, a repressive thought. My anxiety was not going to quell my excitement nor was it going to stifle my aspirations of food, warmth and good company. Though frivolous, particularly at this ill-favoured time, it was very trying to allay such ambitions and indeed these motions spurred me, though nothing was noticeable in my pace but most certainly was in my heartiness.

We advanced thigh deep through the snow, often falling in our haste and in the duration of locating the light that shimmered brighter as we neared. The sudden steepness of the rocky tor was upon us, and but for the engrave cleaving a convenient pathway it would have been an ineffectual effort to ascend under the present circumstance. Matlock felt loathed to abandon the horses and if it were not for my insistence, he would have willingly carried them up the hill on his shoulders. The driving snow continued to lash at my face, forcing me to blink repeatedly and daring me to wipe away its coldness with my free hand. My nose dripped at my exertion, adding to the mounting discomfort of the climb. The summit finally came into view and hidden by three giant monoliths stood the bleakest of buildings, cold, stark and remote. Its footings seemed to

David Greely

ooze out from the ground blending with the darkened confines of the rocks supporting it. A single tower stretched tenuously toward heaven in a forlorn effort to lure the needs of God, it was here that the light beamed from one of the narrow slits cut haphazardly from the stones, flickering at the adverse draughts whistling at such height. There were no devil's birds that surely would have enraptured themselves in such a commendatory site as this. Encompassing the spire was a wall, deteriorating by both age and constant pounding of the elements and just beyond to the northwest, the tor rose further still in an easing slope. The place was quiet and eerie, if it were not for the weather's inclemency I would not have dared to encroach any further.

"What is this place Matlock?" I asked, halting at the bank of snow.

"I am not sure that I am in a care to know. Perhaps we would be wise to overlook this sorrowful place and continue to Sterin as planned, for certain it looks scorned."

The woodman's tone was grim and of disregard.

"Let us speculate to its door before we decide."

"That maybe too late," Matlock warned, "I am all for departing now. There is something sacrosanct about it and it frightens me."

"Nonsense, it is only the foulness of this weather that brings about your concern. It will give us shelter at least. Come, a little further," I encouraged.

I untied the binding leash letting it sink into the snow.

To be forthright, I held the same opinion as the woodman, the place seemed swathed in something inviolable, and I felt an uncertainty as to whether it was malevolent. Perhaps hidden and lurking in its darkest gloom were beasts both repugnant and detestable, like mutants of the antichrist, trolls or even the devil. Within the confines of its tower, I could almost imagine rancid wafts of rotting flesh stifling the already stale air with its pungency, haunting wails of dying innocents ensnared by the same warming glow now beckoning us, and fleshless bones of the long dead, gnawed to all but powder by the jaws of the despicable creatures skulking in its cavities.

We followed the cutting through the rock, slowly and alert, ready to flee at the slightest hint of uncertainty. I was feeling vulnerable and a disheartening unwillingness to proceed, hemmed between the rocks and the steep retreat behind.

I admired Matlock's courage, though always had, but this occasion was different and regardless of his fear reflecting openly on his face, he advanced boldly with his gruesome axe, prepared to protect me before himself. I smiled, taking encouragement at his resolute fealty and how humble I was, who could boast such a friend of a parallel equal to Maddox.

The steep gully relented gently to an open tract with moderate pleats and ripples of snow; mounds for sure though barely rising from the whiteness, but visible by their uniformity and lining the way to the gloomy tower. The light had since disappeared and the spire's visible dark silhouette made it even more testing and forbidding.

If the woodman requested to take leave of this place now, I would have promptly conceded and doubtlessly run ahead of him in eagerness. He seized and squeezed my shoulder reassuringly with his massive hand, obviously aware of the apprehension I failed to hide. I sighed deeply, gripped the bones through my garment and knocked the tip of my staff against the crusty wooden door sending a strong and un-diminishing reverberation through my entire body. A strange sensation agitated me, though not daunting but a sense of warmth and opulence, which began filling my veins with a surge of rejuvenation I could do nothing to repel. Footsteps resounded from within, slow and deliberate, almost contemptibly heavy by our intrusion and my heart suddenly raced with expectancy, waiting for the solid door to open and reveal my mind's concoction of some hideous degenerate or simpleton with no regard for dignitary or manners. At length, the jingling of keys unlocked the door before it finally creaked slowly open revealing a small man shrouded in dark grey. His draping hood and the lamp's candescence hid his features. Striking though was the strong

David Greely

waft of poppy oil discharging from his lantern, which on my intake of breath immediately filled my lungs and forced me to cough.

"With forgiveness my friend we are seeking shelter from the winter's rage. We saw your light…" I released my grip from my bones and gesticulated feebly at the blizzard, "…for indeed it is dire."

The robed man pulled on the door latch opening it fully and bowed his head in welcome. He was quick to observe Matlock's axe.

"You would be wise to leave your weapon outside. my lord," he said timidly, "and perhaps your rod too sire. This is a place of worship. There is no need of them here."

Without diffidence the woodman heaved his axe off his shoulder and leant it against the doorframe, I followed placing my staff by the wall. We entered secondary to the influx of snow and almost as if in the same motion. the man eased the door shut to a shuddering thud that reverberated through the dim passageway.

There was little time to study the man for strange he was – by this, I mean by his dress. A long mantle tied at his midriff with a thick plaited cord danced about his sandal-clad ankles. and hanging loosely around his neck on a tessellated silken sash the sign of our Lord, a large cross of dulled pewter pocked with age.

"This way my lords," he ushered. clipping the keys onto his cord and walking undeniably faster than when he came to greet us.

We followed in his gait without utterance.

At first appearance, there seemed nothing glorious about the place. just a high passage leading to a lobby comprising of six doors. Nothing adorned the walls. not even tapestries that after all, were much the trait of the realm's faith and nor too, any banners to signify the Almighty's colours. I would not even have objected if Talteth's blaze been prominent. but seeing bareness and no colours of any fealty fomented my uneasiness.

The custodian gently rapped the nearest door and entered, motioning us to ensue.

The small dim chamber was equally depressing as the vestibule, devoid of colour and sparse of paraphernalia other than a few seasoned ledgers discarded apathetically on a dusty shelf and a large wooden cross set upon the wall beside it. Seated behind a high robust desk was a veteran, perhaps four score or more and partially obscured by a thick candlestick. His eyes, a cold and glassy grey, met mine the instant he raised his head from the manuscript he was evaluating. His skin was ragged and leathery with a furrowed scowl pronouncing a permanent crease blending into the thinness of his wispy white hair. His eyebrows scant and wiry matched the hair obtruding from his large drooping ears.

"Venerable zenith," poured the custodian voluntary, "we have visitors. They say they saw a light…"

"…Thank you brother Demius," interrupted the old man curtly.

They both gave each other a cursory nod before the first man departed from the room.

"Gentlemen, I am Obediah, holy master of Caermudden and bid you welcome."

He placed his clenched hands firmly on the table and rose feebly on his knuckles that turned white from supporting his rising weight. He struggled in his frailty to offer an open hand of amity and Matlock saw to it in his precipitated riposte.

His declaration of the place prized at my memory in a hope to recall Treggedon giving it mention yet there was nothing I could associate with it, just another place unknown to me within the vast kingdom of Aeria.

"I am Matlock of Scullycrag Fen." The woodman shook the man's hand delicately, breaking my preoccupation.

"Welcome lord Matlock," the zenith returned.

"I am no lord master Obediah, just Matlock."

"Then Matlock it is," smiled the old man. "And you…" he continued hesitantly, "…you must be lord Arton."

David Greely

"Indeed so," I confirmed, somewhat startled, "Arton of Wendatch. We saw your light, a welcoming sight on such an abysmal night."

"I know of no light you refer but nevertheless you are here now and most welcome my friend…"

He took my hand with eagerness and held it loosely.

"…My house is open to you and your companion," he continued.

"Gracious you are Obediah to shelter strangers in these present climes."

Tentatively I retracted my grip from his hand.

It should have come as no surprise the master knew of me, for I had become as much travelled as the woodman, particularly in the light of what occurred since my arrival back into the kingdom; the battle at Belthorpe, my dragon, the exodus and the massacre of the Laddians at Fellingfay, nevertheless I humoured the old man.

"You are perceptive, master Obediah."

"A trait that needs to be upheld," he said.

"Then you are remarkable sire," I added obligingly.

"Please Arton you may dispense with the compliments, you are not on trial here. I know all there is to know of you and your friend, it is but common knowledge."

"Then may I enquire of your good self for humbly know nothing of you or this sanctuary?"

"Sanctuary this is Arton," the zenith confirmed, "a shrine for the good Lord and for those possessing the want to worship. Do you worship?"

"Not as often as I should perhaps but yes, I do. I am impassioned with God and his faith," I replied.

"Then you will be comfortable here, and what of you Matlock, are you an advocate too?"

The old man shuffled his feeble frame toward the woodman.

"Conceivably not as potent as Arton," admitted the woodman, "however, I am a believer in the denomination."

"It is inspiring even at my age to hear sweet words of vassalage. These torrid times and the people suffering through it have for too long shut their eyes to the Lord and his ways. Too many blasphemers and desecrators lost and without purpose, but they will repent and God shall see to it!"

"Amen Obediah, amen," I added.

"Amen," concluded the woodman, staring blankly at the ceiling.

"You must excuse my ranting gentlemen but it grieves me at the wretchedness of this kingdom's people…"

"…Your passion for our Lord is commendable master. People of the realm have taken for granted what the Lord has provided them, unless they atone, there will be no future for them in his kingdom."

Did I hear correctly, Matlock actually speaking such words? Praise the good Lord, there is hope for everyone! Never did I envisage such utterance would proffer from his lips.

I smiled at him and he must have realised my sentiment for he turned his head sharply from my gaze with a reddened face.

"Pray for my ignorance Obediah but where exactly is this place?"

I fully expected some rebuff from him for not knowing, for if indeed I was a man of God then I should have made this tabernacle and its workings familiar to me.

"Caermudden," the zenith began explaining, "is undisputedly the most sacred place in all Aeria. It is here we edify the ways of our Lord and by having this honour bestowed upon us, attend those souls who have sought his divinity. For over three centuries, the brotherhood of the Kindren have sermonised and tended the graves of their forbearers. Nothing dampens their belief or spirit for ultimately this path will lead them to the Lord and his domain."

Much as I wanted to converse with the zenith and preach the Lord's way, time as ever, was pressing. I was cold, hungry and tired, and wanting a short term to rest before proceeding onward and break from his rambling without causing any insult to him. Perceptively Matlock sensed my deadlock.

David Greely

"Excuse what must seem my ignorance lord Arton but we must return to our purpose."

"Indeed so Matlock. Please accept my apology grand master…"

"…No, it is I should beg forgiveness. I can see your predicament and shall see to your needs immediately."

The old man tottered to the door, opened it fully and wailed for assistance as loud as his decrepit lungs allowed.

The diminutive custodian returned forthrightly.

"Brother Demius, arrange fare for our honoured guests, see to hot water and a change of clothing."

"Yes your holiness," Demius complied willingly, bowing his head before leading out through the door.

"I am afraid you may find the food is basic, as is the clothing but we are in need of no luxuries here."

"We are eternally grateful Obediah," I said.

"Then enjoy your stay. Mass will be held in the chanting room on the eve'n bell."

"Then we shall attend," I confirmed.

The zenith focused his attention back to his scripture and Matlock and I left his chamber, succeeding Demius across the lobby and through another door opposite.

"This," he said, tugging at the door's latch, "leads to the chanting room and this," he added, pointing unenthusiastically to a narrow hollow in the far wall, "takes you to the dining quarter. You will find the sleeping chamber halfway up those steps."

"Excellent," said Matlock.

Again, the brother responded subserviently with a minimal bow of his head.

"If you care to retire, I shall fetch fresh clothing."

"We are grateful Demius," I thanked him.

"Bless you Lord Arton," he acknowledged with another bow, before taking leave through a secondary door.

The woodman and I climbed wearily up the steep steps eager to reach our chamber. Inside was cold, scant and very gloomy and nothing other than the sultry flickering taper giving suggestion of habitability. The narrow window on the eastern wall fuelled the hostile wind blasting its icy breath across the room. The bedding was simple but praise the Lord, welcome comfort enough for us and we both fell simultaneously onto our berth, laying in a momentary silence before the woodman eventually spoke.

"Must we suffer mass this night?"

"Come Matlock, have you forgotten your commitment to the Lord?"

"Of course not but surely just our own private prayer will suffice, besides we have little time for…"

"…Time enough for prayer and time enough for slumber my dear Matlock."

My smile at him did nothing to repress his anxiety. Something was preoccupying him and I probed him further.

"So what troubles you?"

"To be perfectly honest Arton, Obediah unnerves me, in fact this whole place does. The light we saw he has denied and his explanation of the brotherhood seemed all too simplistic. Surely no one tends the dead just to serve in honour of being here, there has to be something more to it."

"Indeed my friend there is. This sect is very much a way of life…"

"…I am acutely aware of that," Matlock interrupted. "You forget Arton, Christianity has become a part of my life too."

Of course, I had not forgotten nor overlooked how I suffered for the sake of the Lord and perhaps it was time for me to remind him so.

"I think your concept has overshadowed your logic. Whatever your perceptions of the good Lord may be, consider this my dear woodman. It is a man's entitlement, however humble he conceives himself to be, to protect that faith to the Lord and thus will he not welcome any soul into his divine kingdom?"

"Yes of course I understand that," admitted Matlock.

"Then will he not also greet benediction with equal salutation?"

"You are missing my point Arton. I do not doubt the Lord nor his ways, it is simply this brotherhood has a diverse and questionable distaste."

"Just visualise it as another practice, why, they would probably scowl at Druidism or even at our own methods of prayer. I think perhaps after the mass your fears will be allayed."

"Then we shall see," yawned Matlock, stretching his arms wide.

Sleep fell upon us instantly. I did not dream nor stir until one of the brothers roused the both of us and hurriedly we bathed and dressed before proceeding to the dining quarters. Surmising the abandoned dirty bowls most had already eaten and departed from the long trestle, and of what food remained, Obediah was correct for it was very rudimentary fare; bread left to fester in some damp pantry and salted mutton rendered from a carcass suffering with some form of malnutrition. Delectable the wine was not, but it was highly intoxicating and readily made my head spin. I gave prayer though somewhat motivated by the fact two of the fraternity sojourned at the table with us.

Without questioning directly into their habitual lives our nonchalant method of approach proved difficult and stubbornness apart, they were wise and saw through our probing, discovering little of the brotherhood and nothing of the illusive light. Liffery and Ganos chose only to disclose their routine, rather than their perceptions of the Order and offered trivial insight into mundane tasks of farming, irrigation and weaving.

Curiously as it came to be, there were more disciples than first envisaged, and some forty or so brothers was a large host, considering the time of struggle and upheaval. We were enlightened that other than us, there had been neither infiltration from the enemy, nor even a limited visitation from Talteth's regime and yet more strikingly, no other realmsman sought refuge here in avoidance of the war. The brothers went about their menial tasks oblivious to the strife constricting the realm, endorsed and content to trade in nearby towns, untroubled and impervious. They never challenged Matlock nor me of our intent or belief and nor for the fair of the kingdom. It appeared they were in a realm of their own, untouched and painfully ignorant of the harsh realities coming to an apogee. All in all they were an apathetic and unemotional congregate.

The indolent peal from the bell sounded eve'n mass; the signal the woodman dreaded, yet in contrast, for me it was somewhat of an opportunity to honour the Lord in a righteous place such as here. We trailed the assembling brothers up the spiral steps through an arched opening, choosing to position ourselves at the chancel. Most gathered to one side of the room and opposite stood the esteemed zenith adorned in fine blue regalia with an ornate gold trimmed chasuble. His aide Demius was similarly dressed though less the vestment and gently swung an orb of burning incense. Without prompt, the wail commenced, softly at first, almost as if testing the pitch and seeking approval from the master before intensifying to a vehement tone echoing about the spire. The dirge lingered for several minutes, time enough for me to glance along the line of cowered heads reflecting the epitome of subservience and unquestioning, yet seemingly content with their subjugation. I cast up and down the files several times before the chanting subsided to allow Obediah to say prayer. He orated in an ancient tongue far and beyond my comprehension. I could only offer 'amen' when the brotherhood mumbled some passage at the end of their master's supplication.

Inwardly, I presented my own prayer to the Lord with more conviction; I felt my words were of greater worth and sincerity than that of the zenith. Not that I was in mind to, nor intending to invoke comparison but it did not go unnoticed by me, and spare such thoughts if the revered master heard my silent words of prayer instead.

Matlock was correct in his earlier apprehension for there was an element of uneasiness at the sacrament, caused by our intrusion, because no such fellowship would entertain strangers no matter how Christian they were.

David Greely

No sooner had mass curtailed we ambled back into our chamber. I for one was exhausted and much too fatigued to ruminate on the near future. I was tiring of Matlock's speculative conjectures and became willingly exempt when sleep finally swaddled me.

We would do well to remain unassuming in our short stay so before retiring, I bade the woodman not to go wandering off. It was just as well he did not heed my words and that his curiosity went unspent.

Deep in the night, Matlock stirred me. The pathetic flicker from his candle took me awhile to recognise him and at first gave me a petrified start. He placed a single finger against his lips motioning silence and gestured me to rise with his hand and follow him. We clung to the wall, carefully descending the steps passing the dining area and along the hallway. We ventured further, daring not to lose our footing, stifling our breath to avoid any noise; the woodman's intension immersed us deeper into the entrails of the tor. Malodorous drafts of stale air whistled about us blowing the flame of Matlock's infinitesimal candle, corroborating with the freezing squalls cutting our ankles. Block-work surrendered to jagged rock and the musty atmosphere submitted further to a vileness cleaving at my stomach, a stench so thick the woodman's axe would have trouble penetrating. His shimmering taper danced amid the craggy surfaces, materialising contorted skulls of intangible dread and terror; intaglio carvings disintegrating with the fading light into the pitch then re-emerging with expressions of horror. I wondered how Matlock could have dared venture here alone for it was an execration. I have never judged such looks of fear, even on those unfortunates shackled in the gibbets in Laddia displaying the suffering upon their faces, offered little in comparison to these contorted nefarious creations.

The rock-face transformed into uniformed hollows on either side of the narrowing passage; dark and sinister chasms carved intricately and accommodating long-departed predecessors. Each recess engaged a mummified progeny and as much likely an immediate descendant of their neighbour sorrowful and detestable, fusty and rotten. For as long as I dared to stare at any one effigy, my conclusion considered them all as victims of antipathy, with an unwillingness to surrender themselves as if prematurely, to God. That each sufferer undergoing hardship or abomination to prove their own honour in their faith to the Good Lord.

We had challenged this far and reached the catacomb. I gave the sign of the cross and clutched the bones to admonish myself from our intrusion though it offered nothing to repress my consternation. If my imprudent conclusion was appropriate then their sacrifice was hypocrisy in the belief and with no regard to the faith of God. No true God nor advocate of such teaching would allow any immoral sacrifices such as these wretched souls, and underestimated the intensity of sermon and the words spoken from the lips of eminent preachers or heralded masters from the past. This Kindren was an impassioned sect that did not have to justify itself to anyone, a distortion of the truth that lay behind the Lord and his way - or was it?

Though even as I considered it was my preaching that was, in truth, perhaps further removed from the reality of God than the brotherhood. I had preached far too long alone and not having neither a master nor elder to guide my benediction; it could have affected me and inclined me to deviate. If this were the result and the very essence to serve my God then I would no longer yearn to be part of it, and immediately renounce my claim to the faith yet in my heart I knew the way of the Lord and more importantly, knew how I prayed and preached was the right practice, the only practice.

I wanted to disavow the Kindren's observance now, curse Obediah's methods and convert the brothers back onto the path of righteousness. Where did the fault lay and with whose tainted tongue did the piteous words of self-sacrifice originate?

My internal fury quelled despite never reaching any conclusion. The grasp upon my shoulder sent a keen wave of fright deadening my senses, I wanted to cry out at the unexpected touch now gripping me in apprehension, yet no sound expelled from my open mouth. I fully expected a prompt inquest as to my reason for venturing here, yet pleasantly, to my astonishment it was a warm and familiar greeting and an affectionate salutation that filled my heart with elation.

"Respects Arton," he whispered.

I knew I was right. It had to be him and without doubt I called out his name in the dimness, with total disregard for noise.

"Hebren!" I yelled, turning urgently to seek testimony with my own eyes.

"Arton," he whispered again.

We both examined each other in the forlorn obscurity, desperately seeking confirmation of our long-forgotten faces, in the confounded flickers of the woodman's taper. Hopefully, the blackness of the catacomb hid my disappointment of his aging, for his face looked gnarled and profoundly furrowed by the undulating process of time. If he had changed so much in the lapse then what did he think of me? It had been many years now and my beard and long matted hair would have frustrated his recognition.

"Arton," he continued to whisper, "I cannot believe it is really you. I took you for dead. If it were not for brother Demius's announcement then truly I could have forsaken this moment and our ever meeting again."

"Do not concern yourself with ponderings Hebren, it is me and in the flesh."

"Arton, it has been such a long time."

"Consider my distress. Until this moment, I did not know if you survived the crossing from Laddia. Tolin, what happened to Tolin?" I asked eagerly.

"Abate your fears Arton he is safe and resides here with me."

"I could not wish it better. Oh, Hebren my true friend, if only you knew what this means to me. I feared the worst, not that I doubted your capability to return to the realm, but so much unrest has transpired since the day of our parting. I am sure you…"

Legacy of Bones

The woodman's soft but exaggerated cough halted our whispered conversation.

"...Rightly so Matlock, please excuse my ignorance. Hebren this is Matlock, the woodman from Scullycrag Fen. Matlock, I give you Hebren of Fleddon."

"An honour Hebren," smiled the woodman.

"The homage is mine," insisted my old friend, squeezing Matlock's free hand.

"What of Fleddon? Did you ever make it back there?" I asked Hebren.

"We did eventually but left and never returned. We had difficulty in remaining hidden and lost our way, then winter set in yet again and well...

...What are you doing down here?" he asked, cutting his explanation short.

"I do not know, perhaps Matlock can answer that. Matlock?"

"There was this unearthly cry some while back that stirred me and I rose quickly to investigate. After it sounded again, I tried tracing it and eventually found my way down here. Seeing all these cadavers put the fear of Christ in me and that is when I came to fetch you Arton."

"Obediah will be displeased if he learns you have come here, this is a very consecrated shrine and no one, other than those entrusted with the keys is permitted here. We really must leave at once. Come," Hebren gestured, "quietly now I will take you to Tolin."

Hebren shuffled past and led us hastily along the widening passage, dashing through openings, clambering up strength-sapping steps cruelly winding in a dizzy and endless helix. I lost sense of direction and felt sure we had risen far too high even for the apex of the tower. We came to a halt at the end of a short passage lined with narrow shafts of light and beams of varying sizes penetrated through purpose-built gaps within the stonework illuminating the solid door afore us. Hebren tapped his code gently and entered then swiftly closed it immediately after Matlock and me.

David Greely

"Tolin is this you? What I mean…"

"…What he means is," interrupted the woodman in my stupefaction, "greetings and praise the Lord. It is good to see you after all these years!"

Matlock smiled and sped past me to shake Tolin's hand vigorously.

"I am Matlock," he introduced himself, "friend of Arton and defender of the realm."

"With a mighty grip like yours my friend it is well lord Matlock I am not your enemy," laughed Tolin.

I was content just to stand and observe. Encountering two trusted friends after so long was reward in itself and though I had much to say and an abundance to hearken to, I preferred to savour the brief moment for now and all time. Only Ulcris and Fallan were missing from my fellowship and that could not be a too long a wait for me, then I will test the mettle of the pretender once and for always.

"Please, I am no lord," corrected Matlock in his usual manner, "merely a humble woodman."

"Then forgive me Matlock," said Tolin, "for what stories reach our ears, a woodman must be of higher ranking than any lord."

Tolin's words embarrassed Matlock further.

It was necessary to interject, even if only for the woodman's sake.

"Thank you Matlock, you have saved us from the drudge of introduction. Perhaps now we have dispensed with the formalities we can restore the intentions of the realm."

"You have not changed Arton," Hebren said smiling. "You still manage little time for emotion."

"Until my work is done I cannot afford to. There is very much at stake but nevertheless my friends, under the circumstances I think a wizard can afford a dash of friendship and a pinch of love in return."

I could not refrain a moment longer and dashed to Tolin, embracing him for several minutes, patting and squeezing like brothers and then only pulling away from our hold after Matlock's nervous cough.

"You must enlighten me on all that has transpired. There are many years to catch up on, doubtless too, you want to hear our tales of courage and misfortune eh, Hebren?

It is gratifying to among friends again, I can hardly believe this moment."

"Arton," Tolin insisted, "much as this moment is treasured by us all, something far more pressing than reflection prevails."

"Come," I urged, "what exists that can transcend our need to dwell on our heroics?"

"The evil existing here," said Tolin sullenly. "Here at this caer."

"There I told you…"

"…Shh Matlock," I insisted to him.

"Tell them Hebren," appealed Tolin.

I sensed dread in Tolin's voice and not too soon conceded to his wish and remained silent.

Hebren strolled closer to him beckoning the woodman and me nearer.

"We must rid ourselves from this place. The profanity within these walls is unfitting even for the devil. Men have been subject to debasement that takes little explanation."

"Nothing can be as vile as the traits of the Laddians. Tell them Matlock," I urged.

"It is true Arton and I…"

"…Hear me out damn you!" Hebren's contention was very abrupt and stopped the woodman's talk instantly.

"I do not refer to simple persecution to feed the want of a man's desire, which is to be expected, particularly in war. Here I talk of irreverence that is far and beyond a Laddian's craving, contemptible and depraved beyond the imagination of anyone. I had best explain."

"From the beginning Hebren," Tolin encouraged him.

"Very well," he submitted, turning to each of us in turn, "from the onset but please, no questions, there is no time for doubt or challenge."

David Greely

I stared at the grimness on his face, which twitched nervously.

"We left Fleddon after gathering news of a Laddian invasion, rumours stated Ulcris was surrounded at Collington and that Talteth's armies were driving down from the north. Aimlessly, we drifted south, avoiding any confrontation by trekking at night, not that we could offer much resistance but reckoned after so many years, you would have found us. You said you would come for us Arton but you never did."

"I can explain that," I offered ineffectually.

"It is of little consequence now Arton."

"Hold on Hebren!" stormed Matlock. "Here your lord out. He has his reasons for not reaching you. Have you any idea what he has endured? He almost died ..."

"...We have all suffered Matlock. Look at me, a withered and powerless man, not even capable of fighting a lamb. There is nothing left within me, no more defiance, no more passion and no more love for the Lord God. For what I have given him he has taken from me. There is nothing left for me, nothing!"

I saw it wise to let Hebren continue, expelling his misgivings and gripped the woodman's sleeve to refrain him from pressing his view further.

Hebren persevered after a lengthy pause.

"For too long we waited and in the meantime the kingdom was falling and Talteth was gaining strength. Only the south and the extreme west were escaping his grip. No longer could we sit and be patient, nor could you have expected us to Arton. Ulcris needed us and we had to go. The foul winter had long set in and we were lost and hungry. You would have no doubt seen the light, the same light that beckoned Tolin and me, equally as friendly then as it was for you this bleak night. We inched nearer the infernal light but it just disappeared from view and we found ourselves welcomed here by the brotherhood. At first, it was stimulating to preach and pray to God once more without having to look over ones shoulder, considering such practices abolished or emasculated by the ruination of our wishing towers. Though we could not tarry for Ulcris's sake, we agreed to see the winter through, taking regular mass and performing lesser duties to earn our keep. Then, as nights unfolded, peculiar things began happening, at first I thought the screams and whimpers in the dead of night were my imagination. The wind is apt to whistle deathly tones about this tower and I believed it thus, that is until one night I witnessed the light, the same light always denied as a folly of radiance perhaps. 'St. Elmo's fire' or 'aurora borealis' submitted Obediah at the time. Tolin saw it too and not long after the light's demise, a pitiful scream intoned our chamber. We rose to investigate as you did and entered the catacomb, up until then we did not know it existed. The grill was left open and we entered, again as you did. The screaming ceased, yielding to a new and equally strange tone, an eager panting at first rhythmically but transforming into frenzied gasps and groans. Forgoing being sordid, a brother was locked into necrophilia. A corpse abused by certain members of the Kindren lay cold and rigid across a slab, drooling onlookers waited excitedly for their turn of service. God in heaven, it was despicable."

I felt sickened by Hebren's account and turned to Matlock for words of opinion or question but he stood silently as stupefied as I.

"We slipped back into the darkness and ran to our chamber," Hebren continued.

"What of the screams?" I asked, having taken a long swallow.

"We are still uncertain. Perhaps they were the muffled cries of the victims, for always they are strangled to avoid damage to the body you understand?"

"Perfectly!" the woodman concurred, emitting a shiver.

"Then again," added Hebren, "they may have been the moans of pleasure from the wretched sinners."

"A combination of both perhaps," said Matlock finally on the iniquitous matter.

"So the light...?" I asked, though having contrived my answer.

"...Fresh victims," interrupted Tolin.

David Greely

"That does it!" Matlock blasted. "I'm getting out of this hellhole."

"We said the same my friend, if it were that simple do you not consider we would have long left this God-forsaken place?"

"There is nothing to stop us leaving Hebren," insisted Matlock.

"Probably not, now there are four of us."

"Why did you not escape when you discovered what transpired?" I asked.

"Well," resigned Hebren, "the following day Obediah insisted Tolin tend the light and brought up here and shackled, along with others for most of the day. T hey interrogated me after a report suggested someone had run from the catacomb the previous night, but it was a pathetic ruse and my alibi proved worthless because, you see, everyone was and still is, involved in the abhorrent practice. No one else had reason to flee and subsequently, Tolin has been chained here ever since. And I…"

"…Please," implored Tolin, "spare him the unnecessary distress. It needs no other imagination."

"I want to say this," resolved Hebren. "Nearly every damned night I have been subjected to sexual deprivation. You see Arton, I had to appease Obediah or he would have killed Tolin. The only nights they spared me was when a new victim care to rap upon the caer's door. Can you imagine, I was actually pleased every time someone arrived, despite knowing what fate awaited them, how Godly is that, eh? I could not refuse, how could I? Doing so would have brought about Tolin's death. By now you must understand how low and insignificant I feel."

I spoke in an attempt to ease his burden.

"No words I say will right the wrongs put upon you Hebren and no vision warned me of the impiety you have endured. They will pay for this, every God-fearing one of them, I swear!"

"Revenge is no longer sweet tasting to me Arton. Nothing said or done by you or your God will alter the opinion of myself. So worthless do I feel I might just as well be dead."

"Nonsense Hebren, I need you now more than ever before. If you were to concede now, then we all just as well might. You were prepared to suffer for Tolin so ask yourself why you did so. Well, I will give you your answer, you did it for love. Love for a boy just like your own son Pecos and a reflection of what you personify, an image no less than yourself. You did not need me to tell you to protect and care for him all those years ago. You have become his father; you bestowed it upon yourself to be so and admirably too. Despite his age, Tolin still needs you and I will defy any man regardless of years to say he has no need of his father. I need you Hebren, we all do and more importantly so does the kingdom. There, I have said my piece."

And I had. I could not find any other words of comfort nor could I offer him any constructive anecdote to how he felt. It would have been pointless, least of all to forward God's patronage upon him at this moment.

Tolin shuffled forward dragging the heavy chain behind him.

"I must rekindle the flame," he said. "Obediah will..."

"...Stop!" Matlock commanded. "Stop this charade and let the damned flame die."

"If I fail to tend the beacon they will come for us. We will all die!" Tolin insisted.

"Then let them come," I said in defiance, turning myself toward the door. "We will stand firm against these sinners and I swear here and now that I Arton, will cleave each and every one of them down."

"I admire your courage Arton but if we are to make a stand might I suggest we prepare ourselves in a little more readiness." Tolin shook his chains. "And some weapons may prove useful too!"

Tolin's words were worthy. We could offer no defence other than our fists. It was time to ponder and in the brief lapse proffered ideas between us that would see to our flight.

The woodman's plan to swipe his axe at everyone on the next eve'n mass was encouraging, if he could get access to his weapon. My strategy was too complex and relied upon the habits of the brotherhood that in retrospect was far too contestable. Hebren offered nothing thus, we adopted Tolin's scheme.

Brother Demius always served Tolin food at breakfast and agreed after much reluctance, that Hebren would entice him down to the catacomb for sexual deviation. Once there, the woodman and I were to seize the custodian the moment the grill opened. Hebren and Matlock would then make their escape through the underground network while I returned for Tolin. It went perfectly but for one calamity.

As soon as the tempted brother twisted the key in the grill lock, Matlock set upon him and gripped his mighty hands around his neck. I wrenched the keys from his waning grasp, yanking them from his sash and speedily ran up the spire to release Tolin. Nothing stirred until Tolin and I passed by the dining quarter and if I had not been so clumsy, we could have gained departure without confrontation but as we crept down the steps I rattled the keys accidentally.

"Demius?" a brother called out.

"Come Demius, you are late for breakfast," said another.

We could offer no response to their calling and immediately their suspicions emerged. We darted along the hall amid anxious shouts of defiance from the gathering brothers.

"Tolin is escaping!" shouted Ganos.

"Stop them!" another one wailed.

I cursed when noticing Obediah blocking the outer door, poised like a cat ready to pounce on its prey. We could not turn to face the ensuing mass behind us and had to lunge forward to confront him. Much as I was loathed slaying the old and feeble man, it had to be done.

"Let me take him," urged Tolin.

"Willingly," I said.

I halted, waiting for Tolin to set upon him, inwardly admitting relief at Tolin's timely offer yet he hesitated.

"Go on!" I urged him. "What are you waiting for, in God's name, kill him!"

"There is no need, look," he insisted.

I turned from facing the closing horde and watched Obediah's eyes distend and his mouth ooze blood. He let out a pathetic whimper before his head flopped heavily into his chest. In the split moment when I was trying to acknowledge the zenith's demise the door slowly creaked open with him pinned to it, and beyond, the woodman struggling to prise his axe from out of the door as well as his victim's back.

"Saints be praised," I heralded. "Freedom!"

Hebren hurled my stave and I snatched it out of the air. Readily I turned about to face the charging Brotherhood and aimed the pole directly at them, ordering them to stop.

"Come no further or be smitten!" I yelled.

Much as I wanted to turn and run, my gaze remained transfixed on the Kindren. I was anxious and hoped by this time Matlock would have come to my aid.

"Matlock?" I called.

There was no reply.

"Matlock?" I yelled again.

It would seem your friends have deserted you Arton," announced one brother, inching forward confidently.

"Matlock! In God's name!"

Again, my plea went unrewarded.

My whole body shook with terror and my eyes closed in dread as the mob set upon me. I feared the worst, of becoming another object for their sexual atrocities that had already defiled Hebren and carried off to the catacomb, locked away in deprivation forever, joining the many dead and deserted not only from my companions but also from God. My prayers dissolving within the belly of this forsaken place and then to witness the cadavers with their once expressionless and hideous faces, laugh in awakened rejoinder at my plight. Dragging the very soul from me, forcing me under desolate protest to close my eyes and surrender myself willingly to their depraved covetousness.

I clung to my staff in resignation, knowing if I were to let go now my life would ebb and with it, everything I had strived.

"In God's name help me! Someone help me!"

"Lord Arton?"

My eyes opened torpidly and uncertainly, fearing what vile consequence awaited me. Expecting the gathering of the Kindren gasping and panting, fighting over me as to who shall have me first.

"Tolin!" I gasped in relief.

"What a feat!" he said excitedly. "Never have I seen such ability. You killed every one of them. Your skills have much improved since Nopi."

I cast my examination along the length of the hall where bodies of the butchered brothers lay strewn, inert and all very much dead. Blood soaked robes clung to their forms in a superfluous attempt to mask the gaping wounds administered with my pole. Again, I had sunk to the debasing necessity of murder. My fear had transcended into the actuality of my vision and I swept along with it unwittingly. I could not immediately recall my fight or the damages inflicted and stared at my hands which were still tightly gripping my staff, dripping with the blood of my prey. Truly I was sickened, though in retrospect I should not have been, for did I not wish it? I promised Hebren their deaths and I had complied.

"Let us take leave from this place," I said, barging past Tolin coarsely.

"Where were you Matlock?" I questioned him as we met outside the door.

"Behind you. You made the stand alone; it was enough for me to avoid your swathing stick! If I had lingered I would have joined that lot in there."

I resigned myself to pursue the matter no further and what occurred was nothing unique. I had battled alone before, with equal comparison and grimness, and it was time I came to terms with it.

I hoped the woodman took my aimed smile as a way of an apology to him for my unnecessary curtness.

Tolin slammed the door shut, turned the lock and hurled the keys far into the engulfing snow. We left the annihilation perhaps instigating to any later discoverer, the deplorable capabilities of Talteth upon the sorrowful victims within.

Chapter Twenty-Four

    Thankfully, Hebren employed some forethought and after snatching another key from the zenith's room, assembled a team of mules and a little food, not that I was ungrateful but the hoard he acquired was hardly noteworthy.
    I was troubled for him and although physically able to traverse, his mind could prove to be an incumbency. I certainly did not want to tell him thus and he did not deserve so either, who am I to say if a mortal has outlived his purpose. I had no such right, as quickly as I admonished myself I made a humble and inward apology to the Good Lord.
    'God! What am I thinking? Here is a man that befriended me, saving me from uncertainty though more probably death, who cared for Tolin when ultimately it was my sole duty to do so.'
    I am sure the Lord must have harkened to my thoughts for he repaid me the remaining two hours of daylight, by not once relinquishing me from the burden of guilt or ill thoughts and it

ended with me promising to the Lord and myself I would make it up with Hebren.

With an element of invigoration inspired back in our hearts, the woodman led us away from the tor. His eager manner and selfish pace northward reflected his loathing for the Caer and its abhorrent brotherhood. If he could have sped any quicker, then surely would have done so.

Although snow ceased falling, it was still treacherous underfoot and we spent more time out of the saddle than in, guiding the animals through the dense pleats of snow. Scarcely had night fallen before we began moaning to each other about the bitterness.

Tolin was anxious to hear my account leading to our reunion and became excited when I mentioned the dragon. Hebren however showed far less enthusiasm.

"I'm too old for all this," he remarked, "much too old. Perhaps it would have been wiser to leave me back at the Caer. I could have seen my final years out there."

"Don't be so absurd!" denounced Tolin. "What of your suffering? They had different morals to us, in fact I go so far as to say they did not have any! Each day you remarked you wanted to leave; well now you have, and be thankful for it."

"But I am a hindrance to you all," said Hebren.

"Nonsense, you will be needed in the test of time as anyone of us," insisted Tolin.

"Listen to Tolin," I added, "he is right. We have all, as individuals, achieved wonders but let us not allow it to cease here. We are at the pinnacle now and in a few more months, if that, will have finally accomplished our dreams and aspirations. Then we can sit back and reap our just reward, then watch the realm redevelop into the reality we once promised ourselves. Giving up now would destroy the toil and hardship we have endured."

"Think of Pecos," said Tolin, "would he want you to abandon everything now and surrender? Are you not doing this for him? His death would have been inconsequential if you were to give up. Avenge him, as he so richly deserves. Talteth and his murderous men need retribution."

'Strong words,' I thought, from a young man I hardly knew and a far cry from the faerie rings of Laddia. Words that were not the way of the Lord and I had to tell him so, maybe this was his teachings instilled by the Kindren for they certainly were not mine, or were they?

I remember swearing revenge to many. Talteth and his cohorts were only but a few. Had I also neglected the sheriff and his jailor Perdy at Fleddon, and the not-so blind man Beladon that tricked me into all this strife, Mullyfoddy and the horseman who murdered the king? My inventory was endless.

Tolin was right about revenge but I found it difficult to accept his anger toward Hebren, for he done little to cause offence, certainly not in the days we were together. Perhaps over the years and with the infestation of his creeping age it must have changed his ways. He had it cruel, what with his subjection at the sect but then again we had all suffered in some variable way. Grief, loss, adversity and forced to make many sacrifices, surely this was the essence of our purpose, to rid the realm of it all and avoid further and needless suffering. Not just for us but also for others too, for the children and their children's children, let them know of no need nor want and be able to live in harmonious times and let them be thankful to God for it.

I turned to Hebren.

"Come my friend let us travel our final leagues in oneness and of good heart."

"This is my last league Arton," he announced, "my very last."

"And so shall it be my friend, hopefully mine too," I smiled.

Even after speaking, I conceded to doubt my own words, wishing if only I could foresee whether they would be true.

Having pacified Hebren though be it probably temporary, we saved any further inclinations to ourselves in the sparse cosiness of our scant clothing.

The night of the half moon was chill but thankfully remained calm and dry. We pressed forthrightly in the cavernous snowdrifts and as always, the woodman's pace was punishing but nothing troublesome emerged and we kept our lonely vigils until dawn.

Hebren called out for a brief halt, passing bread among us and just when feeling content with the respite, Matlock gestured we move again. This was the account for the numerous days and nights that followed, stopping only to pass miserable scraps of stale food to each other. Nothing crossed our path. No hare or pheasant, not even a distant howling from the wolves in the mountains and this uncertainty made me feel ambivalent; just a distinct void with a curious calm and yet it felt as if the eyes of everything living in the kingdom gazed upon us. The further north we ventured the worse this feeling of vulnerability grew. Each open pasture or narrow tract bestowed the sense of our exposure and if attacked, cut down instantly. Any stray band of Laddians or supporters of Talteth could seize us with doleful ease. We had little defence and our fatigue probably our prevalent weakness. The only consolation in the disquiet was assurance that the Kindren brotherhood could not pursue us.

I wanted to enliven my companions and indeed myself but we scarcely conversed. There was little to say; besides they only wanted to listen to the tales of triumph, but such chronicles needed expansion under the canopy of contentment with full bellies, heads swimming in ale aside the warmth of a raging hearth, not in the wilderness, abandoned to the harshness of the elements or in consternation of attack.

Although I contemplated a myriad of battle strategies, I knew each one of them was just an ineffectual objective. There were too many uncertainties in all of them and besides I could not predict the response of the enemy; this I learned a long time ago and even as an enchanter I could not perceive to withhold such ability. Talteth with his calculating mentality was apt to anything and I had to make ready to stake my astuteness against his. Thus, I instilled in my mind when the circumstance emanated itself, I would be alert and prepared to make an immediate appraisal and execute a thorough design of combat.

Wearily the leagues wore on and days gradually shortened and with the monotony of the winter's clime it seemed night draped permanently over us. The sun no longer shone and though the severity of the recent snows quelled, the bitterness of night frosts continued to gnaw. My hands stung with pain, an ache far and beyond the sting of the nettles and my confounded cough rasped and gripped my chest with renewed reprisal. My only encouragement was Hebren's stubbornness to continue, if he could survive this ordeal then I could too.

I cannot recall how many weeks elapsed since fleeing Caermudden but can only reminisce days beginning to lengthen once more. I calculated the day of Christ's Mass and duly held a brief service to mark his honour. The following day a strange sight beset my eyes and if my fellow voyagers had not witnessed it too, then I would quite readily dismiss it as a revelation and certainly one exceeding all others. For only such wild imaginings could manifest a spectacle far and beyond any vision, surpassing any welcoming sunrise yet transcending upon the kingdom.

We all drew a willing halt at the brow of a tor relishing the new day before us. A day created by God, for the gods. The sun pierced the pastel orange skyline like a resplendent yellow orb, which with a stretch of an open arm and a molecule of imagination, could have touched with our fingertips. Not that I wanted to, I dared not to even consider it further, for fearing the splendour would dilute if I were even to move. It was an incredulous sight and the very moment met the silence still haunting us. Delicate wisps of white clouds laced with the purest transparency drifted on the gentle breeze, creating curious and chimerical configurations needing no imagination. We were content to rest in our saddles and wonder at the spectacle, grinning perhaps nervously at the changing formations. The pictorial display seemed endless and yet seemingly depleted no sooner it had begun. All had melted but for the final image that haunted me for the rest of that day and one I see as vividly now as if it were that same morn.

First, an image of a horse's head with nostrils emitting additional wispy clouds that in turn, contorted into fresh configurations. A ship with sails billowing in the fullness of the friendly wind that carried across the sky, and a castle with towers stretching beyond the eye to heaven, promptly followed by a hawk whose wings spanned the entire vista in delicate cadence. More animals appeared contorting from one to another in a spectacular creation before reaching conclusion, as if suddenly aware we were watching and concluding with an image of my master.

Though my friends saw it only as a wizened old man bent over his stick, I knew it to be Treggedon. A likeness so perfect that with colour created, he would have materialised. I watched, impassioned by his gentle movements, his tread full of purpose and as if not content enough, he stopped and smiled at me, setting my heart into rapid throbs. His free arm slowly rose and pointed to the west and in the flux, his effigy melted into a picturesque mackerel sky.

I wiped away the tears welling in my eyes and smiled at the calm sky, pondering if I should have given it more attention. Nevertheless, his image left me in good tone and my mood never altered for the rest of that day.

We persevered through the thawing snow and our progress, fully intent and certainly more eager, aided by Matlock's obdurate pace.

Hebren's appraisal to our location was far more welcoming than that of the woodman and even I calculated our position closer to Wendatch than his. Saxby indeed! If we listened to him, he would have had us marching throughout the whole spring! We took his miscalculation light-heartedly and it added to the good cheer of the day.

We achieved everything we assigned ourselves. Matlock set himself a hunting task and snared a fine brace of hare, Hebren gathered enough tinder for a grand fire with ample wood for his own pyre and Tolin found enough feed for the mules.

David Greely

Meagre though the accomplishments may have seemed, but when times are exacting, one is grateful and I praised the Lord thus so. As for me it came late in the day, in fact it was not until dusk before achieving something that would curtail the enigma blighting me since the day I left Wendatch.

We had long since eaten and warmed ourselves thoroughly by the roaring fire, no longer caring of our openness. Brief tales of heroism and impartiality exchanged fervently between us, drifting into the early hours until eventually the three of them fell into deep slumber. I stayed close to the fire and reflected upon the magnificence of the morning's cloud formation in its flames. The sudden redolence of woodsuckle emitting from the blaze provoked deliberation of Silas Inch, the same smell contemptible as he, so I tried to dispel my thoughts from him. He did not deserve rumination any longer, particularly now he was dead, eradicated by Fallan or if not by him, then certainly Ulcris, who would have asserted to the task after learning of his treason, yet the image of his face stubbornly remained suffused in the headiness of the burning wood. Nothing I invented swept away his vision and in my moment of superfluous uneasiness, Inch continually haunted me. I persistently sniffed the air, testing for the sickly fragrance and whenever the suggestion of woodsuckle tainted my nostrils, the chamberlain lingered. If in realising this association earlier, I would not have left the satisfying chore of killing him to another, I would willingly have slain the man myself with the finest of pleasure. I was angry with myself for not comprehending this sooner, plenty of matters could have been resolved and lives spared, too late however for compunction, as the deed had now been done. How witless was I at Collington to allow him countless opportunities to kill me.

Hebren's gentle prodding wakened me. The heat from the fire had all but dwindled and the coldness of the day set me into an immediate shiver. We mounted our animals and set off into the grey morning in good spirits though I suspected trepidation began to unnerve them.

Wendatch was not too distant now and seeing the outlying mountains later in the day confirmed our position. Although unintended, I formulated plans of varying contingency and despite the countless uncertainties I knew most would not be necessary. Regardless of Ulcris's position, we were to head to the western edge and follow the coastline. Unless word got to Talteth, his army would not be expecting any attack, least of all from seaward.

Night fell by the time we reached the shoreline and Tolin after a lengthy debate, unwillingly released the mules before guiding us somewhat apprehensively along the cliffs under the guise of a smuggler's moon. If it were not for the sound of the crashing waves, we could have been trekking in the mountains, for steep and rapine they were and one unsure footing would be death for any one of us. The wind added to the severity of our traverse, blasting indiscriminately up the cliff edges and strapping our ankles like gripping hands, trying to unsteady us and pull us over. Cries from restless kittiwakes screeched hauntingly overhead contesting their pitch against the whistling gusts. I was thankful for my master's rod and used it for dependence in assisting Hebren. We previously agreed to approach Wendatch in darkness, therefore enabling us to travel the rest of this night and the following day with ease of pace, because as sure as an ass brays, I knew we were getting close.

It was difficult to resist my excitement though in truth, there was little to be joyous about, knowing Talteth and his men were at Wendatch; undoubtedly waiting for the realm to disintegrate at the valour of the Laddians, wallowing in richness ill fitting and unworthy. Drinking the blood of the countless victims of this gory war and feasting on the food snatched from the very mouths of the few managing to subsist, and of course there was the battle, our battle; the one awaiting settlement and soon enough its outcome would be made absolute.

As in all confrontations, there are many deaths and unfortunately victims indiscriminately selected. The good die along with transgressors and the young lay beside old. Everyone is equal in bloody conflict, death strikes readily at a king as it

David Greely

does a pauper, alas they are all, in effect, superfluous sacrifices for one man's greed. I perceived this a fight for justice, good against evil and God opposing the devil, and if it were not for Talteth's avarice none of this would have ever transpired.

I possessed foreboding for my cherished friends knowing the odds of their surviving were as bleak as midwinter. It was going to be impossible to fend for them and I loathed contemplating the arising necessity to save one in preference for another. Yet curiously, I was not fretful for my own welfare and accepted my accomplishment was now good as met, and confident the battle would be won despite overwhelming odds. God was with me and if the outcome different, then I knew I would need to survive to face another day until duty concluded and if death were to strike at me then let the execution be by God's own hand.

The arrival of dawn confirmed our position. I stood on the very edge of the cliff to sample the keenness of the ocean air, never believing I would welcome the sight of northern mountains with their snowy caps, nor enjoy the density of the forbidding forest laid before them, yet there they were, beset intrepidly in their own comparable veneration. I looked out across the swelling sea, subconsciously expecting perhaps to catch glimpse of a Laddian vessel, feasible of course, considering the current turmoil and if any were evident I would have renewed my approach. My gaze slowly traced the horizon until the ocean touched the distant shoreline west of the mountains. I yearned to see Wendatch beyond the rise of the vale with its tower standing proud.

With scarcely few hours travel we bided time under cover until darkness, this being the ideal moment to rest and prepare ourselves. If my scheme were to succeed then certain events would need accomplishing. My primary concern was the location of Ulcris, there would be little point attacking what armies were there without his backing and though brimming with confidence at having God as an aide, I could never conquer Wendatch without the Druid's force.

Having descended a crag, we sat hugging the under-cliff, activating my plan and what little I schemed, this was the way of it.

At low tide, I would infiltrate Wendatch through the hollows with hope of establishing Ulcris's situation before sending a signal for the others to approach and if, though I did not wish to contemplate if, Ulcris failed to arrive, I would immediately return. It would be far too perilous for all of us to scramble through the pitch of the tidal hollows, and if any of them were to lose sight of me then I would dread the outcome. Although I knew the place well, it had been an age since braving through them, one erroneous step would send me falling into the bottomless abyss to oblivion and much as it loathed me to venture through, I had no other option.

We waited with saintly patience for the outgoing tide and I tried to remain content by studying the exposing stones of the receding flux, stones that have turned and shattered more times than breaths taken. Shells surviving wholeness, ultimately for the next flood tide to splinter them into incalculable mites of sand.

Sleep came to us all at some point and it had turned late afternoon before we were awake together. We imbibed in shallow conversation but it needed little perception to sense the dread within us. It was time. The ingress to the hollows was about to be exposed and I had to be swift. I dare not miss the moment for did not relish drowning as a chosen method of death. I rose smartly and cast an upward glance at the top of the cliff to clarify no eyes peered at my movement.

"Until tonight my friends," I said.

"What will be your signal?" Tolin invited.

I had not given it the slightest consideration.

"I am uncertain yet," I smiled, hiding my culpability, "but you will notice it sure enough. Now I must go."

"Good fortune Arton," bade the woodman.

I appreciated his sentiment and it accompanied me across the strand.

David Greely

Too quickly, I was breathless but could afford no faltering for the tide would expose the hollow only for an epigrammatic moment before consuming the opening again, I ran like fury, forsaking want to look back to my friends. I leant against the side of the craggy opening with heart palpitating, more out of apprehension than the dash across the sand. Much as I wanted to check my senses, I had to enter. I stooped to avoid jagged protrusions of barnacles and my frame penetrated the gloom. Pointing my staff ahead, I invoked a shaft of pure light, its brilliance astounding and as bright as a shard of sunlight. Adjusting to its keenness took awhile and in that lapse, the light revealed the daunting cavern. A volvox of insipid green weed clung to the walls and dripped incessantly down, saturating me. The cavern floor a sodden carpet, squelched its slimy sediment under the weight of my tread. I aimed the light into its deep crevices searching for the fracture to direct me back to dry land, aware that any one of the numerous fissures could harbour death for me. After a little pondering I squeezed through one of the openings and prayed to God my recollection, after all this time, was true. My height made progress testing and no longer could I run through as I did when a child, I was forced to bow and bend continually to avoid the hazardous rocks hanging like the teeth of the giant cockatrice. I was enormously unnerved, more so now than when first venturing here, this time aware of the danger and loathing to touch the slimy algae, nor daring to breathe in the rancorous effluvium of its deadliness. I weaved hesitantly in advance, attentive of the tenebrous abyss laying in wait open-mouthed, ready to devour me and the faltering pressed me into making mistakes. Often I lost footing and slipped over, cracking my head on the unseen stalactites materialising directly in front of me. The taste of the blood from the wounds trickled down the back of my throat and it tasted disgusting. Inevitably, I began dreading the surge of the tide, failure to get through soon would result in the sea flooding the channels and eddying into the chasms taking me with it. I tried to inject a speedier pace but the hazardous tract denied me, I cared not to look back praying the next surge would not envelop me. The incoming roar was intense and already water lapped around my ankles. The next swell took me down and I helplessly grappled to stop myself sinking. Somehow, I battled against the torrent and tripped on the steps but despite the wrench to my body, I smiled at my fortitude. Sharply they rose, hooking round a colossal pilaster gripping the footings of the citadel. The rocks altered hue some tread further, from the banal green to the blue-grey stone of Wendatch's very foundations. A stark ring levelled itself around the shaft to mark the boundary of the seawater, defying the ocean to rise higher. I shook my head and gasped for breath while watching with immense relief the final surge of water well underneath me. I turned, squeezing through an opening long overgrown with bramble and the end of my staff fizzled to an acquiescent phut leaving a thin plume of grey smoke trailing into the still night air. The walls of Wendatch lay a short distance ahead, encircling the great tower that still looked capable of touching the clouds.

Oh, how my heart was singing, at last I was here and no matter how dire the situation, I could only but rejoice.

Narrow glints of light from the castle's high slits pierced the night, suddenly reminding me of the hostile denizens dwelling within. On my first study under the restriction of darkness, Wendatch appeared grand as the day I had left but my heart began sinking at the impoverishment before me. Everything was silent as if expecting, as if a lull in the wind prior to a thunderstorm; it would be fitting, because immediately I gleaned information on Ulcris I was going to release my fury upon it.

The moat contained all but a trickle of stagnating water unfit to house the larvae of the caddis and discharged rankness as foul as a vagabond's undergarment. Its walls stained heavy with oil, led me to believe battle had already served here and large chunks of grey stone from the tops of the south and eastern battlements lay strewn at the base, partially submerged in the surrounding mud. The half-raised portcullis and lengthy chains that drew the heavy bridge fused in rust and neglect.

I turned away sharply, dispelling any thoughts that may have intensified. The state of my master's apothecary, the alehouse and indeed the great hall, was not given any consideration from me, least not at this moment. I felt bitter enough and fuelling torment to my rage would affect my judgment.

It struck me, the onerous smell far and above more acute than any stench ever encompassed at Wendatch. Woodsuckle! The detestable and sickening odour could only mean one thing but it could not be Silas Inch, he was dead. Fallan would have seen to it and not failed me.

'Oh God, surely not?'

My dismay of Fallan's dissolution manufactured an explosion of scepticism that meant only one of two logical resolutions, either Fallan failed to get to Inch or my dedicated countryman was dead. I did not want this, not now with the battle planned. I could not face news of his death now; I did not want it ever! Yes, I was selfish with my thoughts but felt entitled. The dependency of the realm rested on this battle and upon my shoulders. What was to become of it or me should I falter? Will my opinions be heard and judged fairly in what I achieved for the kingdom, no of course not, I will get appraised purely on the outcome of this gruesome war and if that inference were to hang over me like the sword of Damocles, then I had to react sharply and decide an immediate course of action.

Foolishly, I thought the heady aroma of the repulsive woodsuckle grew nearby yet knew it could not grow in winter; this realisation was enough to convince me, not only did Silas Inch still live but also he was inordinately close.

I stooped low, creeping in with the shadows of the surrounding shrubs and prayed no feeble twig would snap under my tread to reveal my presence. It felt an eternity waiting for the waft to dissipate and even when it finally did, I was still apprehensive that the chamberlain skulked nearby. Somewhere he haunted these grounds like some feral cat of the night with claws drawn ready to ambush. I could no longer wait as Ulcris needed seeking. I crept out from cover on my hands and knees and scurried across the road into the redundant field opposite, carefully controlling my breathing to avoid vaporising zephyrs announcing my arrival.

I could take no fortitude in the prevailing quietness for surely the enemy was ready for me. They would be off guard and confidently arrogant if Inch was dead because no word would have reached Talteth of my objective, yet I sniffed woodsuckle and it was no freak. It had to be Inch and the enduring silence a trap. Furthermore, what of Ulcris, had he too befallen the wiry man's plot and lay inanimate with heart gouged, next to Fallan? The ongoing questions in my mind were equally speculative as the unanswered probabilities making me irresolute. I felt like running back inside the hollows and await the turn of tide. I could not fight the forces of Wendatch's present army, not just me with Tolin, Hebren and the woodman, but somehow had to invoke a method to deploy, as if we were a hundred strong. If Ulcris and Fallan were to show now then let the realm cheer for their salvation and let my heart sing out to God for their safety. If they should fail, may they rest in the bosom of the Good Lord eternal.

Chapter Twenty-Five

Unyielding hands gripped around my shoulders forcing me to shrink under their administering potency and my courage submitted swiftly to the sudden fright conquering me.

"At last my young spellbinder, where in heaven have you been all this time?"

I fully turned, expecting the voice to be but a trick of the night and the gripping pain in my shoulders nothing other than cramp.

"Owell, it cannot be!"

"If not, then am I but one of your conjured spells," he laughed.

"But," I dispelled, "you were killed in Laddia. I saw Pennypot..."

"...It takes more than a bunch of Laddians to kill me Arton. Let me look at you. I would hardly have recognised you, what with all this..."

Owell released his grip from me and tugged hard at my long hair.

"…And of you," I said poking him gently in his ample paunch with my rod, "I see you have not gone without."

"You know how much I like a full belly," Owell maintained.

"I still cannot believe it is really you. How did you get back into the kingdom?"

"I escaped the Laddians that fateful night and immediately set out to look for you. I lost your trail whilst dodging those confounded vagabonds. They were mean and full of reprisal. I stayed at Nopi until the spring and made track to a port before stowing in the hold of a Laddian trading boat. Each day I looked hoping you were behind me but saw no one, no Maddox, Hebren or the lad. I was so lonely and desperate. Then I got to thinkin' perhaps you'd already sought the hierophant and returned to the realm. I got my passage and shored at Glas-y-Fwar. It took me all summer to reach Fleddon and still I looked for yer but…" He suddenly broke off with a deepening scowl.

"…What has happened to the kingdom Arton?"

"Talteth, he is the cause of all this," I cursed.

"There is so much suffering. I was witness at the battle for Fleddon. By land, Talteth's army attacked and the Laddians invaded from the sea. God, the atrocities, I hang my 'ead in shame to think my fellow man is capable of such things. What must God think Arton?"

"I have seen it too and it is time to put an end to it once and forever more. Come let us move from here before we are discovered."

He put his arm back around my shoulders and we set off to seek cover a little distance from the outer walls. We both puffed breathlessly as we sat on our respective rocks.

"And of you my friend," Owell continued, "how did you return and what's this I hear of yer dragon?"

I explained everything briefly, forsaking detail though it was still all a bit too lengthy. I insisted we cease our respite and disclosed to him my anxiety for the others to join us. I also expressed my fears for Ulcris and Fallan.

"Have you news of them?" I asked.

"Ulcris?" he repeated the Druid's name with question.

"Yes Ulcris, have you information?"

"It is grave my friend. Ulcris and his legion were decimated and I could only watch helplessly."

"In God's name no!"

I sank my heavy head into my hands and openly sobbed. Waves of emotion poured from me, confusing the feelings I was supposed to endure. For one flighty moment, I thought there was a degree of chance that Owell's words were inaccurate, knowing how facts distort with travelling tongues but he stated that he was there and bore witness to it. He gave me his account.

"Ulcris set camp before winter in a valley south of Caer Marwyen. It was strategic enough, with a fast and wide river to the north and thick forest to the west. He dug a deep ditch on the eastern side to make it secure but what he didn't foresee was the danger from within. His army was discontent and struggled on empty stomachs, neglecting everything for his cause. They heard of Talteth's men wallowing in opulence and gradually his men defected until it left him all but a handful. That is when Talteth struck. They had no chance; I could do nothin' to help other than watch his decimation in hiding.

There are no more legions Arton and there is no more Ulcris. It is just us."

"There are others still prepared to fight Talteth. Allies in the south like Ectorus…," I encouraged.

"…Only Nebis remains loyal though 'e has not been seen of late. What now, Arton?"

"I do not know," I sighed.

Everything needed reconsideration. Five of us left to win the war, how pathetic and three of them waiting for my signal to storm the castle, fully expecting to join ranks with Ulcris and his army. Much as I revered their fealty I could not let them fight against Talteth now. I was without option and had to enter

Wendatch alone. It only needs the blade from one man to kill him and that man was going to be me.

"I shall penetrate Wendatch alone, kill Talteth and return before dawn."

"Huh," scoffed Owell, "you make it sound so simple. This place is swarming with his men; you'll be cut down the moment you set foot inside the walls. Have you not even considered whether Talteth is actually here?"

"Oh, be sure of it Owell, if I know Talteth, he will be far away from any battle and least of all south aside the Laddians bloodying his hands. He will let others do his dirty deeds while sitting contentedly and waiting reward."

"Let me come with you and help you get to him. Should you fail…" he paused.

"… Sorry, I am not suggesting that you will."

"I know what you mean Owell but no, I must do this alone. The others await my signal and I leave it to you to tell them of my ploy. Wait with them until my return."

Owell seemed pre-occupied and it was making me nervous.

"Owell," I yelled at him. "What transpires here?"

Out from the pitch sprang a group of Talteth's men and two of them pounced on me before I had a chance to stand.

"I'm sorry laddie but you know how things are," said Owell, edging away from the melee.

"God damn you Owell!" I shouted. "Why?"

"Well if you must know it was that night back in Laddia," he said, breaking out into a pitiful smirk, "the night the others met their deaths. I bargained with the Laddians and told them everything about the kingdom, your purposes and your magic Arton. I had to save myself, surely you can understand that?"

"Not if it meant forsaking Aeria as payment, no!"

"Everything has its price remember?"

"How poignant, traitor!" I yelled.

"I'll take that," he said claiming my staff.

"Your words," he continued, "are quite useless now and so too is your God. Everything you've set out to achieve has failed Arton. But…," he paused considering his words, "…if it be any consolation, my intension was to get to Ulcris for you. I had only bartered for my immediate freedom but my good friend Silas Inch made me see sense. He and I are much the same."

"That deviant? He does not deserve to be a realmsman!" I contested.

"Oh, he is no realmsman Arton. Inch is a Laddian and of very high regard too."

"You leave me baffled Owell for I know not whom the kingdom's worst enemy is, you, Inch or Talteth!"

"You've said your piece wizard."

"You will be stricken Owell, I swear it so and before I gasp my last breath I shall see to your undoing!"

"Your idle threat does nothing to unnerve me," he responded complacently.

"By the break of day, I swear!"

His swipe across my jaw ceased any further conversation between us.

"Take him to the king!" he ordered. "I will find the others."

Owell disappeared into the night with four of the men, undoubtedly finding some means of the downfall of my associates.

How could he do this and deceive me so? I was far more resourceful than he yet I let him lead me to this. I should have stuck to my original opinion of the man and admonished him. I knew he was untrustworthy but in defence, needed him then when I had no other to help me. I wished he had been killed with the others, damn him!

I got my entry into Wendatch sure enough but not under my terms and knew were I was being taken. I tried to get a glimpse of my master's apothecary before entering the hall but it was still too dark. There was little sign of any change in my absence except perhaps for the great hall itself, now displaying the bland colouration honouring Talteth as king.

I felt useless and very vulnerable without my staff; apart from the bones around my neck I had no means of magic.

The renewed waft of woodsuckle filled my nostrils and sent an inner signal racing to my heart. Sure enough within moments, I was face to face with the odious character, standing beside a window.

"God in heaven, if only I had a sword!" I hissed through gritted teeth.

"Lord Arton," he said derisively "we finally meet again. Ah, and how satisfying it is on my terms this time."

His conspiring pitch sickened me and his wiry fingers fumbled continually with some amulet dangling on a thick golden chain. I likened to think he was nervous at my nearness but doubtful, he seemed too confident and assertive to display any type of debility, least of all to me being cognizant of my attributes.

"Inch," I sighed as if confirming to myself it was he.

There was no point pretending to be surprised, he was astute enough to realise I was aware of his deep involvement, words would be futile now no matter what I uttered but he chose to continue.

"All through your campaign I have monitored your progress Arton and loathed as I am in admitting so, full of admiration for your guile and tenacity but even a wizard meets his match and unfortunately for you, this is the very moment. You have eluded me too many times; I should have killed you the day you fled from here."

What was he admitting to? Preposterous! No Laddian could have infiltrated Wendatch under Arbereth's rule.

"Nonsense!" I repudiated.

Or was it? Admittedly, I did not see his face then, but would have recognised his voice. Then I recalled, 'woodsuckle!' The essence sampled the day I fled, apparent then as it is now, delicate, sweet and nauseating.

"So you are the king's murderer," I concluded.

"Take heart Arton because if my aim had been true, you would have been killed by my sword, not the king. Arbereth's death was not pressing and he would have followed you soon after, once you were eradicated, nevertheless, it saved Talteth the irritating deed."

The Laddian laughed aloud cocking his head back in his delirium.

"You have always managed to stand in my way Arton but not any longer, this night will be your last!" the chamberlain's words turned to anger.

"Do it Inch!" I urged him. "I cannot abide your presence or your words of complacency and condescension. Just kill me!"

"Oh, no my friend, if it were that simple I would willingly comply, but I am under instruction to spare your contemptible life. The king insists upon seeing you."

"Talteth is no king, he is not worthy!" I remonstrated.

"Your objective has failed and so too has your God and it is time you realised there is no other king than Talteth and no other god than Sangal!"

"Blasphemer! Traitor! Laddian!" I yelled.

"Please Arton no more compliments," he laughed sarcastically, before walking behind me.

If I had an ounce of might left to release the constraint of the guards, I would have turned and spat directly into his eyes. God, how I loathed him!

"I swear Inch; you will be castigated for all you have done. By the power of the Lord…"

Then I suffered his blow on the back of my head.

"…Ah, our wizard has arrived," Talteth's abrasive voice rang in my ears.

I shook my head to alleviate the pain administered from Inch's stern swipe and simultaneously came to terms with the reckoning of addressing my lifetime adversary. Words willing a thousand curses could have burst from my lips the moment I set eyes on him. He had not altered, he still epitomised an air of indecency of equal abhorrence as Silas Inch. His smug sallow face donned a broad smile, knowing he finally won me over.

"Unhand him," he insisted to his men. "He cannot elude me now."

Immediately they released their grip.

"Well I must confess Arton I was beginning to doubt this moment would ever arrive."

"Damn you Talteth!"

"Come, come," he said softly, "don't be so testing I just want a few answers," he paused briefly. "Tell me, what did you do with Elcris?" I assumed your paths crossed seeing as you had his cart."

"You are right to assume and he is where he belongs," I said sternly.

"That does not answer my question."

"He is within these very walls of Wendatch, in the crevice of the holy room."

"Impossible!" he doubted. "I had it blocked up the day I first arrived here."

"Magic, remember?" I smiled broadly.

"Curse you and your sorcery! You have caused me a lot of unrest and superfluous misery Arton, your master would have been very proud of you. Sadly, however would your efforts were never quite enough were they? You have been very foolish perhaps Druidism would have got you further."

"Curse the Druid faith and curse you too!" I raged. "Burning roots of woodsuckle is as useless as its aroma; there is no power in it, or anything else they meddle in."

That is not true of course. Too many objects have power and the Druids know how to extract and use them well, but I knew Talteth and he was no Druid. He proved that by needing Ulcris and because he refused to teach him, sent for his brother but fortunately for the realm, I stepped in unwittingly before Talteth had chance of meeting Elcris to learn of the ways. Perhaps Inch possessed some knowledge of the art but then again, anyone can stink of woodsuckle should they stand close to its burning.

"Where are your armies Arton for I cannot see them?" Talteth asked.

"Where are yours?" I returned glibly.

"Where they belong, at Collington and soon the capital will fall and become mine. There is no more resistance, none of your allies and disciples nor is there any of your magic. How miserable you look."

"God will win over you Talteth, I swear!"

The king laughed falsely.

"Swear? You are in no position to swear to anything. Everybody and everything has forsaken you, why even the bones have no significance do they?" he smirked.

His awareness of the wishbones startled me; if I were to relinquish them now then indeed they'd be deemed worthless.

"Don't look so surprised," he added, "I know of the bones. They are powerless because you know not how to use them."

Talteth held out his open hand.

I reached inside my tunic, grasped the pouch and tore it from my neck. I opened it and rested the five bones in my palm. They chinked delicately as they had done a hundred times over, like ethereal shards of lustred crystal that burned at my skin. I feared Talteth's intension and the consequences if they got under his control, so before he seized them from me, I threw them out the window.

"No!" he screeched. "You will rot in hell for that!"

He punched me hard and I winced with the pain searing across my face. By now, I had resigned myself that death was but a moment away. He wanted nothing else from me now and would not take pity nor spare me.

An agonised wail came from beyond the tower halting the interrogation. The second scream immediately following set the hall into confusion. One guard restrained me whilst others dispersed on Talteth's order to investigate. Talteth and Inch peered through the window, searching for the source of yet another deathly screech breaking the night's silence. Then came fused shouts of disbelief, the battering of shields and the clashing of weapons.

I was bewildered as my captors and could only surmise the woodman was running amok with his axe, making a last stand for my cause.

"Impossible," Inch shouted, "I killed him with my own hands! Witchcraft is at work here my king."

"You incompetent fool I should have seen to it myself!" Talteth raged. "Summon everyone to battle!"

Inch sped off like a kicked hound and ran down the length of the hall. This was my last chance to escape from the clutches of Talteth and without dithering, elbowed the guard in the stomach and dashed off behind Inch. The Laddian was oblivious of me for he would have turned and squared up to me in readiness with his blade. I succeeded him through the door, down the spiralling steps and out into courtyard, slipping into the shadows of the keep, away from the disturbance. Though intrigued by what may have caused the stir, I remained concealed, fretting over my companions and it left me undecided as to which exploit to undertake, knowing Owell's devious proficiency, he would attack my friends. I crept my way around the wall amid the running groups of Talteth's men, it was only Arbereth's calling that halted me from running out through the portcullis.

"Stop!" he commanded.

I spun on my heels to witness his spiritual form. His vestal image was mounted upright and proud upon a dappled stallion, beside Ulcris and my master and just behind them trotted the steeds of Fallan and Maddox, dressed in white silken gowns untarnished by the dust stifling the air. Maddox held the king's deep crimson standard aloft, animating the eagle in the rippling breeze. It was an incredulous spectacle and surpassing all reason as an apparition. My emotions radiated inside me and not too soon, tears of joy flooded down my cheeks. This had to be real, for I could taste the dust the horses created, hear their erratic snorts and smell their sweat. The enemy reacted too, firing arrows and throwing spears and pikes at them.

The almighty beckoned me to him and not fearing the enemy or their strike, went directly to him. Arrows continued to whistle accurately in incessant arcs yet not one penetrated, though their aims were faultless and their points deadly, they deflected off me. Spears cut through the night like bolts of lightening yet they too glanced away from me as if striking a holy shield of protection. Talteth's army gathered in their hundreds joined by the townsfolk willing to fight with the pretender. It was a daunting prospect, merely staving off my final downfall, but encouraged by my allies' presence I knew this conflict was going to be appeased with copious deaths.

A fireball exploded at the tower and burst into flames expelling thick, choking smoke that clung to the grey walls and cascading like the breath of my dragon, consuming anything daring to remain in defiance. Men screamed in piteous inflections at their suffering. Some jumped screaming into the stagnant moat to dowse their flaming bodies; others did not succeed and hit the ground with dull life-sapping thuds. The five sacred images moved forward, scything through the advancing army with incredible ease and casting them aside like spent wheat stalks. Precise and deadly they thrust toward the steps of the keep, pinning back the enemy on their tireless horses and killing everyone affronting them. From the uproar, I could hear Talteth's ineffectual orders sending his hapless accomplices to their deaths. Boiling oil spilled from the ramparts creating a river of molten destruction for those inadvertently wandering into its course. Men crawled blindly with limbs ablaze, beseeching mercy from their suffering but despite their frantic cries, they went unheard and unaided.

I caught my stave which Matlock tossed at me. Seeing him with Hebren and Tolin gave me inspiration and swiftly I advanced with them, falling behind my holy army's swathe. I had no time to consider the occurrence of our reunion other than Owell had obviously failed in his quest to stop them.

The woodman slashed his axe from side to side in adroit keenness and Hebren fought with broadsword to fend off any attack on the lad, yet Tolin needed no protection for his deftness was remarkable and every swipe or thrust of his blade was fast and true, dispensing the advance of the enemy. I continually swiped my staff at them, knocking aside any man escaping the celestial force. We scattered amidst the forlorn town, and no narrow street, blind alley nor could dismal courtyard hide Talteth's faction, even those seeking refuge in dwellings from our assault, faced ultimate death. Everywhere we searched, our deadly surge met yells for clemency but our blades failed to heed to their pitiable screams and they fell dying.

In the confrontation, I came face to face with Silas Inch. His features were bitterly contorted and his arms rose aloft in dread of me. No more, did I want to neither bear witness to his sullen appearance, with crooked nose and hooked lip nor suffer his sickly stench and in fulfilling that yearning, the Laddian tensed his arms in protection as I raised my staff aloft in readiness.

"For the kingdom Inch!" I yelled, gallantly bringing down my rod with the ferocity of a warlord, severing straight through his forearms.

He fell exhaling a doleful whimper, but discontented at his agony I struck once more, this time directly across his head with a might that split his skull. Now he was dead and I cuffed away his blood that splattered into my face.

The doors of the keep burst wide open and what little remained of Talteth's defenders sped off into the great hall. We pursued them unchallenged until all of his men were unceremoniously expended. I heard the rush of footsteps behind me and revolved to see Talteth bolting. I gave chase through the tower and out beyond the courtyard, catching up with him alongside the outer walls. I threw my rod at his legs bringing him crashing down to the ground. The others joined me standing over him.

"You have nowhere to run Talteth," I told him breathlessly.

"Curse you a thousand times Arton!"

"You have lost Talteth. Did you honestly expect you could win over me and my God?"

"That to you!" he cursed, spitting phlegm at me in contempt.

Arbereth's hand snatched the staff that I held in eagerness to administer my fatal blow. He never spoke but gently pushed me aside and took my position.

His son's eyes must have witnessed his father's image, for they were stark and wide open and though his mouth gaped, could afford no shriek of dread. The almighty seized Talteth's

David Greely

throat with his left hand, forcing him to stand and continued to lift him until his feet dangled off the ground. Progressively, the constriction around the pretender's face drained him of colour and amid restricted splutters and suppressed moans, forced his eyes to shoot up inside their lids dissolving his life. His flapping legs surrendered their final twitch as he hung torpidly until Arbereth released his grip. His son fell motionless into the mud.

For a while, no words were exchanged, it was not until the woodman let out a wail of triumph did we begin celebration. We had won the day and we had won the battle, finally conquering our foes.

I wandered back to the foot of the keep, passing what I can best describe as a sorrowful paradox. Sat against the wall in utter dejection was Owell and beside him a face, for a fleeting moment I failed to recollect.

"Beladon"? I tested the stranger. "Is it you?"

"Boy?" he verified, gazing vacuously at me with equivalent doubt. "Please spare me. Is my blindness not payment enough for the ills I have served upon you?"

"More than enough," I appeased with pity.

I turned and looked at Owell.

"Now what of you?" I considered briefly.

"Will yer not show mercy on me too laddie?"

"Why should I? You betrayed your friends and me and more significantly, you betrayed God, the very God that lifted your encumbrance. You were wrong ever to doubt my power Owell and foolish even to consider I would never find you out. There will be no negotiation Owell. What the Lord giveth so shall the Lord taketh away."

The beleaguered tinker struggled sluggishly to his feet cradling his gnarled arm and awkwardly, his head hung in despondence upon his deformed shoulders. He took a concluding and ignominious glance at me before his hunched form undoubtedly filled with renunciation; he hobbled slowly away into the choking smoke.

Legacy of Bones

I sat exhausted upon the steps amid the dead and dying. I did not want to listen to their cries any longer, I had heard enough. My reflective phase was ruptured and indeed surprised, to sense the sacred images approaching me, their horses now abandoned and dissolved. They were no longer a figment of invention or any magical deed but incredibly real and not just for me. Other mortals witnessed them too and had fought along with them. Fallan came close with Maddox behind him.

"Did Inch...?"

Fallan knew my asking before my words were complete.

"...Yes, I tried to save lord Ulcris as God is my witness."

"I am so sorry. I did not know the outcome would lead to this."

"Why such grief, I am with God now. Say nothing Arton," he continued, "I know your sentiment and it is met with mutuality."

The traveller continued to walk up the steps and his effigy passed straight through me before evaporating.

"You have served me great honour Arton and very much a credit to your master. Here," said the king handing back my staff, "I hope there is never a need to use this again."

I could only but afford him a smile as his image transformed into the fox and with a swish of his full brush came next to me. Briefly, he stopped and licked my outstretched hand before fading.

"My lord Ulcris," I announced humbly at his approach. "I believe I owe you a confession."

He looked at me impassively.

"Your brother...," I began.

"...Say nothing for I already know. Do not forget the strength of Druidism my friend. What you did was none too soon enough. He was responsible for my incarceration in the keep and my suffering. From the outset he plotted with Talteth, acting as intermediary with the Laddians."

"There is something I fail to understand," I said on my master's nearing, staring at him for some clarification.

"The bones were very powerful Rabbit, if only you had used them wisely."

"But you did not instruct me," I objected gently.

"That would have proved pointless. If you were to become wizard then it had to be up to you to discover things for yourself," he added, easing his lean frame closer.

"But there were times when I almost met my death," I opposed.

"Ah, but you did not, did you?"

"Meaning?" I scowled.

"That I was always there to offer you guidance. You have done exceptionally well Arton, but then I knew you would, now, I must take leave for my work is done here."

"Please master answer me this, my last question. The day you sent me out on my own, did you know the outcome?"

"More or less, yes I did. There were two alternatives Rabbit, this one and another I dread not to contemplate; if you had lost all faith or changed your decision then the consequences would have been very different. Your term in Laddia did concern me somewhat, with you lying in your hovel full of self-pity, but I got through to you in the end," he scoffed openly. "And you thought it was your senses alerting you, eh boy?"

Treggedon smiled before his vision faded for the ultimate time.

"Good bye Rabbit and god bless you," his whisper melted into the swelling smoke.

"What of the bones? Whose were they?" I shouted to him, but my probing was too late and there was no purpose in calling him back.

Other than the mystery of the bones, all other doubts were acknowledged and fitting now to let them rest. I became aware of a sudden emptiness around me and quickly returned to reality. The noise of the bloody battle had suddenly ended and there were no screams of death, no flying arrows and no clash of sword. Only the wind carrying the asphyxiating smoke billowing from the keep proved testament of such wrath.

Legacy of Bones

My three associates lingered, respecting my brief moment of solitude.

Friends and kin alike slain for the cause; morose thoughts at this time perhaps but I deserved the right to consider them and feel a little pity for myself. They have abandoned me and gone forever. Now I have to suffer without them and finish my term in the realm whilst they remain in the bosom of our Gracious Father.

"How did you...?" my question to Matlock went incomplete by his immediate interruption.

"...We heard Owell faintly whistling on the cliff top, when we saw him clutching your staff we realised something was amiss."

"The guards did not struggle and reclaimed it easily," continued Tolin. "Owell soon enlighten us as to what was emerging, with the help of Matlock's axe of course," he jested.

"We heard the skirmish and came as swiftly as we could," Hebren enthused breathlessly, concluding his very brief synopsis.

"Soon was good enough my dear friends," I smiled, walking away from them.

"Arton, let's take leave of this place and head south," appealed the woodman, wrapping his massive arm about my shoulders. "We still have plenty of Laddians to expel."

"All in good time Matlock, they will not be able to hide from us," I told him, "but firstly the realm needs a new king and it is decreed Tolin shall rule Aeria."

"But I thought he was to be your lad?" surmised the woodman. "Was he not presented to you as his mentor?

"You assume wrongly my friend, much as I loathe letting him go, his fate is already destined."

Retaining my smile, I turned toward Tolin, noticing the glinting half-crescent amulet around his neck.

'Faeries...,' I contemplated disdainfully, '...faeries indeed!'

Printed in the United Kingdom by
Lightning Source UK Ltd., Milton Keynes
141613UK00001B/153/P